Eternity

Michael A. Brooks

There's no shortage of supportive people in my life. I have great parents who still to this day help me navigate the complications of living in the modern world. I'm friends with many people from diverse walks of life that have filled more than a few moments of my life with laughter and great stories to tell. However, I believe the ones most deserving of this dedication are my wife and my daughter. The two since arriving into my life have seen every up and down I've encountered on my adult journey. Whether or not their sanity's are intact is beyond my ability to discern, but I am thoroughly grateful for the enrichment and fulfillment I receive from sharing my life with them.

Prologue

Seneca Mason, stands as a registered independent captain, affectionately referred to as an "IC." Among the pioneers of galactic travel, he's among the first souls in the galaxy's history who boldly severed ties with the shelters of planetary life, their governments, and organizations to embrace true freedom to explore unfettered— or perhaps to escape from something within himself. The boundary between the two is sometimes less than clear.

He captains *the Phantom*, a ship feared by adversaries and revered by allies. This imposing craft, comparable in size to a mid-size corporate jet on Earth, boasts a matte black paint engineered to enhance its stealth capabilities. Armed with lasers on its forward swept wings, two 21-millimeter Gatling guns flanking its longitudinal axis, and three missile hardpoints capable of housing four missiles each, *the Phantom*'s hawk-like shape is a formidable presence in any confrontation. However, its true strength lies in the skill of its pilot.

A former ace fighter in the US Air Force turned outlaw legend, Seneca is one of just three surviving captains in the galaxy to hold the prestigious rating of 'Apex Pilot', a prestigious distinction reserved for those demonstrating remarkable skill and record. Seneca stands chief among Apex pilots as the reigning king—Seneca's unintended heroics have earned him the highest kill tally in the galaxy, cementing him and his ship as a force to be reckoned with among the stars.

Chapter 1: Press Start to Begin

The Phantom sits parked, at rest, in one of the many space colonies scattered across the galaxy. The station in question revolves around a planet locally renowned for tourism and vibrant nightlife. In the hazy wake of recent activities, Seneca can't pretend to remember the name of the city-sized colony since they're all the same after a while. Right now, his head feels like it was struck with a heavy tool. He runs his hands through his short brown hair in a feeble attempt to relieve the pain.

Recently he'd accepted a contract mercenary role, aiding the military of this system to repel Imperial invaders seeking to annex them unwillingly to exploit their resources and citizens. He doesn't recall how long he's been in the area. Despite the lack of attention to the length of the campaign, it's another victory under his belt. The successful endeavor in question has incited riotous celebration among the grateful people in the system. Though he's seldom inclined to celebrate alongside anyone, he's more than willing to accept liquor laced tokens of gratitude and there is plenty of gratitude to go around.

Now that the recent stereotypical adventure is drawing to an anti-climactic close, the last few days have seen the celebration die down. Within his mind, wanderlust is calling upon him to leave in search of a fresh adventure like many times before. Not all that dissimilar to his usual habit since the last century or so has been exceptionally mundane for Seneca. His life has fallen to the chokehold of a cycle; Word comes to him that somebody doing something somewhere could use help. He answers the call to adventure; fights the fight, wins the battles, helps the people, saves the day, celebrates for brief moments before he moves on; Rinse and repeat. Repetitive as it may be, this serves Seneca's agenda perfectly.

Loose ends, however, need to be addressed before the next adventure comes knocking. The latest envoy ended with a substantial Imperial bounty on his head, requiring him to temporarily mend relations with the Empire in order to discourage overconfident imperial headhunters from wandering hopelessly into his gunsights. Seneca does not find them threatening, rather an inconvenience and unwanted reason to take human life. Furthermore, it is significantly easier to move around with the occasional illegal munition when there is no bounty levied against you. Thus, setting him wandering the pedestrian paths of the station looking for a bounty kiosk.

Despite having access to the online galactic bounty compendium on his own UniCom, he doesn't want to employ it and betray his future destination, giving time for Imperials or other overly ambitious ICs to intercept him while he clears his name. He can use local public kiosks anonymously to procure a quick bounty contract apprehending a rebel leader or the like, which will win him some forgiveness from Imperial Security.

An IC Bar—an establishment reminiscent of an Earthly biker bar along a back country highway catches his gaze as he ambles with his hands stowed in the pockets of his jet-black flight suit. Passing ICs, usually in search of work or trouble, typically fill watering holes like this that have a kiosk that will suit Seneca's needs. The bar itself is dimly lit on the inside and filled with smoke snaking from the mouths of other ICs that chatter amidst the sounds of vibrations of music that waft through the ambiance. Flashing signs line the walls advertising various drink and smoke-able products. Never being one to care for the aroma, he waves his hands to divert the musky scent of burning tobacco intermingling with smells of stagnant cheap booze as he strolls to the counter to ask the bartender for something to drink and query the location of a bounty kiosk.

Seneca motions for attention with his hand. "Hey."

The bartender grumbles at him, obviously unaware of the celebrity in his presence "You new here or somethin'?"

The barkeep's reaction (or lack thereof) to his presence is surprising. Seneca's face is well recognized within the cosmos. He grooms his brown hair at a functional length and style, similar to haircuts worn by those in military service, to ensure manageability beneath a helmet during combat flight operations. He deliberately chooses to consistently wear a light stubble on his countenance, which gives him an air of maturity since he looks barely over twenty-five, with his toned athletic appearance. Though he lacks a foreboding presence, his ability to draw glances from women suggests his average height and build does not degrade his attractiveness.

In a monotone voice, Seneca replies, "Not exactly. Let me get whatever doesn't taste like sanitizer or warm piss and point me to your kiosk if you have one."

He pours what appears to be beer into a thick glass vessel and slides it down as he points, "Down the hall to the left."

"Cliche..." Seneca mumbles to himself, subtly shaking his head as he pays for his drink.

He washes down a painkiller for his head while sipping on his drink, a semi-cold light ale—not a preferred beverage. Painkillers and alcohol aren't the brightest of choices, but it doesn't matter. It's not like it will kill him. His eyes scan the grimy ceiling momentarily as he careens down the hall, passing a glance to examine the faded brown artificial wood walls looking for the kiosk.

The disheveled kiosk awaiting him has seen better days. Its plastic colors have faded from black to gray over the years. Cracks litter the screen's corners, and a sticky film coats the obsolete plastic buttons. The device is outdated and looks akin to an ATM in a run-down gas station on the rough side of town. Touching it is a displeasing sensory input and would make anyone with texture aversions cringe as they interact with the screen.

He finishes the drink and rubs his face as he opens the bounty compendium and wades through an ocean of bounties posted by the Empire, the vast majority for souls involved in the current galactic conflict; the very one his current location would have found itself involved with had Seneca and other brave ICs not intervened. The affectionately named "Whisper Rebellion" started some years ago, Seneca has neglected to keep an absolute date in his head, in response to the Empire's latest imperialistic habit of annexing independently governed stellar systems against the will of their citizens. These societies are either recently settled, were previously isolated, or are otherwise not already under the protection or jurisdiction of one of the three major galactic governments: the United Federation of Democratic Space, the Empire of Socialist Governments, and the Confederacy of Systems.

The oldest government in the galaxy is the United Federation of Democratic Space. The "UF" as it's called, was formed shortly after mankind established widespread, permanent settlements throughout the original solar system, now affectionately called "Sol". During the first fifty years of humanity's expansion into Sol, mass confusion invoked Earthly conflicts regarding what nations held sovereign control over early space colonies. Logistical nightmares bred tension that eventually caused Earthly superpowers of the time, and their accompanying alliances to spiral into World-War Three. NATO emerged victorious from a ten-year bloodbath and established the first planet-wide government that eventually united the rest of the solar system, utilizing a modified version of the United States Government that eventually became the UF known today.

During the three decades following the war, the United Federation dedicated itself to unifying the solar system. However, on the distant outskirts of Sol, a lone space colony found itself embroiled in a heated dispute over its perceived forced inclusion within the Federation—a situation that makes the Empires' current behavior rather ironic. At that time, the appointed leader—someone Seneca himself had once worked closely with during the establishment of the first Mars colony—Byron McClaine, garnered support for his socialist ideals of mutual prosperity and dispersed burden among citizens. These convictions were pivotal in the establishment of numerous early colonies under Byron's authority. When he and citizens of the colony, Vista, faced threats of treason for refusing to recognize the UF's governance, Byron McClaine took a gamble by launching the colony further into space using early warp technology. Many believed that the novelty of the technology had destroyed the colony in the attempt to flee. However, they were successful. Byron strategically positioned the colony over one-thousand light-years from Sol and out of the Empire beyond the UF's reach. They remained uncontacted, orbiting and eventually settling on the current capital of the Empire, bearing the namesake of the original colony. The Empire as a people remained hidden until the mastery of faster-than-light travel unveiled its existence. However, the history during their isolation is known only to the royal family and imperial historians.

The UF and Empire stand as colossal superpowers, casting a stark contrast to the Confederacy of Systems, the youngest and smallest among the three major galactic governments. The COS emerged from private colonization initiatives aimed at expanding and exploring the Milky Way, dispersing libertarian-minded individuals across the galaxy. Almost all societies within the COS fled the perceived oppressive reach of the UF and Empire, seeking autonomy and freedom from centralized large government. With a shared history of defiance in the face of government oversight, the people of the COS harbored a collective aversion to external control. Over time, these systems realized the necessity of collective defense against the growing threats posed by the UF and Empire. Thus, they formed a loose confederation with the primary goal of mutual protection against external influences. While the unified government exerts minimal authority over member systems, it relies on contributions from each state to maintain a modest standing military and accompanying council.

Seneca, a legacy Earth resident and veteran, technically holds citizenship within the UF. Despite this, he maintains a hereditary disdain for government and holds no allegiances. Rather than viewing governments as protective entities, he sees them as tools to advance his own agendas, exploiting loopholes and flaws in their laws and rules for personal gain—much like his current endeavor to exploit the Empire's bounty rewards to once more cleanse his name.

After what feels like an endless dredge through Imperial bounties, Seneca finally strikes gold when a contract of notoriety catches his attention. While reading through the details, the bounty is against an imperial spy who betrayed critical information to the rebellion and is currently wanted for desertion and espionage. The contract provides several pictures of the spy, along with a textual, physical description and last known location. Authorities want the individual returned alive, presumably for interrogation. Despite the target's low combat experience, the payout is lucrative. The Empire is offering a reward of five hundred thousand for capturing him, and also declares that any existing transgressions against the Empire will be forgiven—perfectly tailored Seneca's needs. It's a distasteful affair to do business with the Empire because of their particular incursions against his personal ethics, but he needs a clean slate.

He accepts the contract and transfers the commission sheet to his UniCom. Subsequently, he stands up from the ragged and heavily used kiosk and proceeds back to the station's port. On the way, it's imperative to become familiar with all available information regarding the target, so continued reading engages much of his focus as he walks through the bustling station, still roaring with celebration. The target was last seen in an abandoned shipyard on Rossi 451. Flushing fugitives from localities like Rossi 451 can be infuriating and tedious, but it's also reported that the target's ship is in critical condition from fleeing the Empire and there's a chance he'll be easy to nab.

That is… if it weren't for the fact that the bounty is already a week old… His target has most likely evaded several other headhunters by this point; it isn't outside the realm of possibility that he's out of the system completely or in a new ship. In the worst-case scenario, he'll have to spend weeks tracking him, giving him time to hunker down on a high gravity moon with a proper stealth outfit—an agitating amount of time to have a price on his own head. Either way, Rossi 451 is still his best starting point.

After a night of rest in the crew suite aboard *the Phantom*, Seneca wastes no extra time entering the cockpit and performing appropriate pre-flight procedures. In fluid succession, he completes preflight checklists and sets his navigation computer to Rossi 451. Once he configures and prepares the ship, Seneca starts the engines, and *the Phantom* roars to life, lifting off from the station to hunt.

Chapter 2: Chasing a Shadow

A day or so of travel brings *the Phantom* to Rossi 451 where it drops from warp—the form of faster-than-light travel achieved through moving a ship through dark matter surrounding it (think of it like moving space around the ship instead of the ship through space). Seneca initiates his search with a swift succession of pulse scans using a "squawk scanner," a device akin to Earth's air traffic control radars. Radio waves traverse the vacuum, probing for a distinct echo that pinpoints a ship by its unique radio identifier. He conducts the search methodically, zigzagging back and forth along the orbit path of the system's planets for several hours until he finally identifies his target. The ship's onboard AI pinpoints the target's location—stationary in space, orbiting a dwarf planet that circles one of the system's several colorful gas giants.

A grateful sigh escapes Seneca's lips. He was starting to worry the target had moved on. Readying himself for anything, he applies throttle and accelerates towards the fugitive to begin a process he's done hundreds of times before. He also increases his ship's stealth by lowering its heat signature, disabling the non-combat systems onboard. In moments like this, remaining unnoticed provides a desirable advantage and lowers the amount of time he spends chasing a target as well. Unfortunately, on this particular encounter his efforts to render himself unnoticed are in vain, and the target notices his approach and quickly flees from the dwarf planet's weak gravity back out into space with impressive speed creating distance between the two of them at a rapid rate.

The fugitive's attempt to flee is baffling considering the observed state of his vessel —a small, lightly armed commuter craft, no larger than a twin-engine airplane. Its rounded hull, mounted on a single engine with a vertical fin on the empennage, is peppered with scars from its escape out of imperial jurisdiction. The speed of the ship surprises Seneca and explains how his target has avoided capture the past week.

* * *

"Oooh, fast one, aren't you?" Seneca scoffs as the fugitive accelerates away. "I take it. I won't need these." He mutters, disabling his shields to divert more power to his engines, allowing *the Phantom* to close the gap. Typically, fleeing targets seldom fight back, so the shields are an unnecessary power expenditure at this point.

"Come on, buddy," Seneca broadcasts to the fugitive's ship. "Just come quietly. Don't make me come get you. We both know who I am…"

While closing in on the fugitive using a boost charge, he receives a response, albeit an unwise one, on the fugitive's part. A smarter person might have accepted their fate, but a volley of small weapon fire and tracers emanates from the battered ship and flies toward *the Phantom*. Metallic thuds from bullets contacting the hull echo around the ship like rain on a tin roof.

The Phantom sustains no damage of substantial impact since its armor is far too thick for the other vessel's small armaments to penetrate. The action is more of an annoyance than a threat, prompting Seneca to exclaim over the radio in frustration, "God-damn it! I just had this paint touched up."

The fugitive continues firing volleys in a hapless attempt to intimidate Seneca, but only frustrates him further. Seneca broadcasts again, "Stop! Damn it, I'd like my ship to look nice for more than a couple of days at a time."

Again, the target reacts from either questionable intellect or sheer despair and fires another volley as he tries to outmaneuver Seneca, to no avail. With a simple sequence of stick movements and calculated use of the throttle, Seneca effortlessly positions the Phantom behind the fugitive once more while rolling his eyes and shaking his head. Continuous small corrections and basic-level fighter maneuvers keep him in the optimal weapons envelope as he opens fire, setting *the Phantom*'s targeting computer to aim the guns at his opponent's engine.

The fugitive finally breaks radio silence. "I thought you were against the Empire! Asshole!"

Seneca replies, "On most days, but not right now."

"Go to hell!" the fugitive curses.

"If only," Seneca mumbles as he fires two missiles at the helpless vessel's engine since guns were taking more time than his patience is willing to impart.

The missiles make contact in spectacular fashion, the first one nullifying the protection of the fugitive's protective shields, the second eliminating the fugitive's engine. Though the opposing craft, now disabled, spirals uncontrolled into space, indicating the craft's inertial dampeners are not active.

"Ugh, that's annoying. Why does this have to be a live capture?" Seneca asks himself as he watches the dilapidated ship elope away.

Capturing people on moving ships in space presents unique and time-consuming challenges—it doesn't stop moving once disabled (thanks to Newton's second law). As such, many bounty targets will intentionally disable inertial dampeners, systems that automatically manage directional thrusters in a desperate attempt to avoid capture. In this agitating complication, a bounty hunter's next task is more difficult than combat: matching one's own ship to the escape vector and axial rotations of the disabled ship as it spirals into the void. This must be done while remaining close enough to establish an airtight connection between craft for boarding. The task is aggravating even for someone of Seneca's skill, but after a few attempts and some aid from AI, he matches his ship's motion and rotation to the enemy vessel. Once alongside, he eases his ship and achieves a seal between the belly of his ship and the hull of the fugitive. Tailor-made laser cutters make quick work of the thin metal and breach the hull.

Stepping into the narrow fuselage of the fugitive's ship with his plasma pistol drawn, Seneca moves cautiously. This is the only dangerous part of a live capture. While he is as formidable as it gets behind the controls of a fighter, his expertise in the realm of close-quarters firearm combat does not exceed the average trained individual. Skillfully maneuvering through the cramped ship, he silently approaches the cockpit, where the target conveniently has already surrendered with his hands up.

"Well, at least you made that part easy," Seneca says, quickly securing cuffs on the fugitive's wrists. "Why didn't you just start with this?".

"Fuck you," the fugitive spits.

"Gross," Seneca remarks at the disrespect.

He pulls out the fugitive's ID and takes a moment to compare the man before him to the photo on the bounty contract. The guy appears weathered and worn, a stark contrast to the clean-shaven, middle-aged man with short-styled red hair depicted. The current version of the target seems like a shaggy, fading reflection of his former self. It seemed strange he looks so disheveled despite the contract being only a week old, but Seneca figures conditions might have been difficult for him long before he crossed the imps.

He extends a helping hand to the beleaguered soul and guides him into custody, securing him in the jump seat behind him on *the Phantom*. The guy might as well have a decent view, plus it's up in the jumpseat or in Seneca's sleeping quarters, and the last time he left a fugitive in there he found turds inside his pillowcase... With no further hesitation, he flips a switch on a panel above his head, which uncouples the seal between the ships, allowing the fugitive's vessel to continue its elopement through space.

Now he has to analyze the matter of delivering the new cargo. Seneca looks at the galaxy maps for nearby ports with minimal Imperial influence. A confederacy port would be the best choice, though none in the vicinity have an Imperial Security embassy. After considering various options, he chooses Oberon, a planet located in Neutral Space, an area of star systems that are deemed neutral territory under galactic law. Oberon, with its breathable atmosphere, is only half the size of Earth. As such, only certain regions are suitable for human life, as it orbits two small orange stars. Oberon's capital station, simply named "Oberon Station" is home to embassies of all the galactic governments. Since it's only a day's journey, it's the fastest option available option to reach what should be a low-traffic Imperial embassy.

The ship's autopilot and navigation computer has them underway in no time towards Oberon. Seneca glances at the man sitting behind him, feeling a twinge of guilt about taking him in. However, he's determined to reset his bounty with the Empire. He values his time and freedom too much to have droves of bounty hunters setting traps for him. It's easier to move about Imperial space without a wanted ship ID. It isn't uncommon for him to traverse the area to smuggle alcoholic beverages or other prohibited substances—many systems under Imperial control have strict prohibitions on "productivity-limiting substances" he transports (illegally) from time to time. In an attempt to ignore his guilt, he tries to ensure the rebel that the action isn't personal.

"Look," Seneca exhales, "take it from me. It takes balls to steel from the Empire and get involved in the rebel—."
    "I wasn't involved!" the fugitive interrupts. "I just sold them some information on systems the Empire is targeting for future expansion to fuck over the lords. They can't pay me enough to put up with their shit anymore."
    Frowning, Seneca offers him a drink. "Either way, it's not personal, selfish, but not personal. My life is just easier when I'm looking out for myself, and this is my way of keeping the imps off my back."
    "Hmph. Sounds lonely."
    "Call it a side effect of living too long."

Seneca's cynicism, deeply rooted in a lifetime of evading attachments, finds its origin amidst Earth's pioneering days of space exploration. As humanity propelled itself into the cosmos, Seneca, a high achiever from the outset, soared alongside these aspirations. Graduating at the top of his class from the Air Force Academy, he swiftly ascended to become a distinguished fighter pilot, patrolling Earth's skies with precision. But it was his selection for NASA's Mars colonization initiative that marked a pivotal moment in his journey.

In accordance with the needs for long-term colonizers to man the Mars mission, NASA initiated a series of medical experiments to improve the longevity of humans in space. Undergoing experimental procedures with others as part of what was dubbed the "Human Life Extension Program" (HLEP), Seneca received many genetic treatments and augmentations that boosted his immune system, prevented aging, and enhanced brain function astronomically. Like many other HLEP participants, he's since far outlived the programs initial estimates, and it's very likely he and death will remain estranged unless introduced by outside influence of space combat or nefarious malice. Despite the program's remarkable success for Seneca and the other survivors, the toll it exacted was steep, with a mere fraction of its participants surviving. As such it was never repeated—though rumors float about every now and then.

Yet, as the years stretched endlessly before him, Seneca found himself grappling with a profound sense of loneliness. With faster-than-light travel still beyond reach, his timeless existence stood in stark contrast to the fleeting lives of those he held dear. Each return to Earth was a poignant reminder of the relentless passage of time, as loved ones slipped away, leaving behind an ever-widening chasm of lost friends and family.

Haunted by the weight of his past and the specter of inevitable isolation, Seneca made a solemn vow to shield himself from further heartache. Determined to avoid forming new attachments, he fortified his resolve, bracing himself against the loneliness that stretched out before him. The conversation continues when Seneca admits, "I need the freedom to keep moving when I need to. Staying put is not my style."

The disheveled man scowls. "Cry me a fucking river. Some hero you are then,"

"You know, you kinda suck. I'd have more sympathy for you if you were a rebel. Could probably return you to them if I got more—"

"I'm not a fucking rebel." He slouches in his seat. "...Doomed fucking idea going against the strongest military in the galaxy like this."

Chapter 3: Invitation to Adventure

The flight passes peacefully and without a notable occurrence. His ship exits warp and Seneca stretches, squeezing out a yawn in the process. He's prepared for a peaceful landing at Oberon Station's starport. However, his expectations shatter upon seeing the unexpected heavy Imperial presence on the ground. The sight upon touchdown is more than enough to inspire caution. Numerous Imperial executive transport vessels, adorned in pearlescent cyan paint, dominate the landing pads, overshadowing even *the Phantom* in size. Among them, the Princess's ship stands out, its elegant ivory-colored paint and crimson accents signaling its high-profile status. Seneca wonders why the Princess is present at Oberon Station amidst the chaotic Imperial traffic, realizing that any plans for bribery will have to wait amidst the bustling activity.

He mutters, "The fucking princess is here? Why here? Oberon's in the middle of fucking nowhere."

His captive laughs and looks at him and says, "Why wouldn't she be here?"

Seneca turns to him. "What do you mean?"

"Hasn't been uncommon for her to visit places like this lately," his captive explains with a condescending chuckle. "If you knew anything about her, you'd know she's desperately trying to hold the Empire together. Her and the other Imps are likely here convening with the other two governments regarding their unwanted expansions."

Seneca huffs and asks, "Think the Emperor's with her?"

The fugitive shrugs. "How the hell would I know?"

The princess, 160 years younger than Seneca, is in the ballpark of 140 years old. Seneca isn't sure of his own age, let alone hers. In the grand scheme of things, age has become a rather unnecessary concept. For Seneca and any HLEP survivor, or apparently their descendants, age is just a superfluous number after reaching normal adulthood. Sometimes, he wonders about her experiences, as she shares his extended lifespan. Does time feel lonely for her like it does for him?

* * *

An approaching group of Imperial security beckons Seneca to exit his ship. With little desire to increase the bounty levied against him by lifting back off and opening fire, he reluctantly complies, wishing he hadn't forgotten to ensure the ship's AI's landing preferences didn't land him on a pad near so much Imperial traffic. The belly mounted door opens, and he clambers down *the Phantom*'s access ladder and lowers the captive via the ship's harness and cables.

The Imperial agent addresses him as Seneca offloads the fugitive, "For someone with such a hefty bounty on their head, you'd better have a good reason for stopping in here, Captain Mason."

"Oh shut up," Seneca says, dragging his get-out-of-jail-free-card to his feet and shoving the fugitive into the hands of the agent. "I've got cargo. Here you go, one high-value ex-Imperial spy."

The security agents pause as they look the fugitive over and verify the identity of the sullen soul Seneca delivered. All the while, they shake Seneca down as well, checking for banned substances and illegal weapons or hoping for some other reason to arrest him, considering the bounty reward is about to free him from their persecution once more.

"It all checks out," the agent says begrudgingly, "Wipe his record. One of these day's Seneca, you'll find yourself in a situation you can't weasel out of."

"Not likely," He Seneca replies tauntingly, saluting the agent as Imperial security takes the fugitive. After which he wastes no time directing his attention to the sound of music drifting through the early evening air.

"Don't you want the rest of the payment?" the agent sarcastically yells, as Seneca is almost out of earshot.

Turning around and walking backward, Seneca shouts, "Why don't you keep it?" He already got what he wanted out of the bounty contract. "Maybe buy yourself out of your commitment and move somewhere outside the Empire… like Florida."

New aged music spills into the street out the multitude of clubs and fills the air of Oberon station like water fills a glass. The second of Oberon's two suns has started its slow journey down below the horizon, and the rest of the Milky Way is seeping into view. He's officially reset and ready for the next adventure, but he's in a rare social mood and wants to check out the nightlife first. Neon-colored signs hover over establishment entrances. Windows vibrate with bass tones of the unfamiliar music while he strolls past several clubs until finally settling on a club called "Yzinny's". There's little need to be picky, since each of the clubs are equally loud with quality booze available. He's unsure of what exactly he's looking to experience, but he's open to anything from a bar fight to a heart to borrow for an evening.

He pays the cover charge and enters the club. Inside, a vibrant crowd packs the dance floor, moving their bodies in sync to the pulsating beat. He watches as their heads, arms, and wristbands sway in perfect rhythm to the music. By incorporating lights that vary in color and movement, the club intensifies the experience of getting lost in a moment, captivating his senses and transporting him to another world. Combinations of scents, including the familiar odor of rubber floors, faint aromas of sweat, a medley of perfumes, and subtle hints of alcohol, mingle in the air. Accompanying this sensory experience is the loud music, which reverberates through the room, causing a rumbling sensation in his ears.

Seneca, with his age and experience, favors his outdated playlists that include country, rock, and folk songs from various time periods, mostly before 2020. Nevertheless, he can't deny the energy and joy the music brings to the younger generation. The sight reignites memories of various parties he'd attended in his own youth. He catches himself from wandering too far down memory lanes and sets his sights on an empty seat at the bar beckoning him, where he parks himself to place a drink order—an Old Fashioned with just a trace amount of club soda. The barkeep concocts Seneca's order in a flashy manner with little haste as he spectates. He finds it intriguing how far people will go just to impress complete strangers by flipping a bottle in a fancy manner to pour a cocktail.

Hoping for the night to present him with a path to follow, he downs a few more effervescent "old fashioned's" before paying his tab with a generous tip. Relinquishing the bar seat, he stands up to stroll to the next establishment in hopes that something greets him there. However, as he's about to leave, a voice catches his attention amidst the music. "Isn't that Seneca Mason? That dude's one of the highest-rated combat pilots in the galaxy."

Curiosity piqued, he turns his head to pinpoint where the voice was coming from. The culprit, a young woman, had asked another who showed no interest as they nonchalantly walk away without acknowledging the question. His confident gaze meets hers, and he takes advantage of the moment to start a conversation, proudly declaring, "I am the most skilled combat IC in the entire galaxy." Upon activating his UniCom, a projection showcasing his impressive kill record instantly captures her attention.

His action catches her off guard, causing her to jump. She whirls around to him and greets him, "Well met, stranger. Do you often project death tolls in people's faces?"

"Stranger? Don't pretend you didn't already say my name," Seneca chuckles, "and you mentioned combat records. I figured you'd enjoy hard evidence."

"Maybe not so close next time," she says, swaying from side to side to the tune of the music.

Judging by his estimates, the woman's likely twenty-six or younger. Her straight blonde hair is configured in a short asymmetrical cut that only extends past her ears on the right side. A delightful sight to behold, her large hazel eyes highlight her soft face, adorned with a tasteful application of makeup. A maroon and silver dress drapes over her slender, athletic frame, the longer hemline on the right side echoing her hair. Although she isn't his usual type, her seemingly vibrant personality captivates his attention.

* * *

"What are you up to in Oberon, Seneca?" she asks, sounding somewhere between flirtatious and serious.

He tries to come up with a cool response to make him sound more appealing, "Hopefully getting into something I haven't done before."

She laughs and says, "I may have something in mind then. Have plans tomorrow?"

"No ma'am," Seneca replies. He pauses for a second to calculate a proper response. "How about yourself?"

"I'll be in town," she says. "I work for the princess."

He laughs at the sentiment before questioning her, "Yeah, right. In what capacity?"

Smirking, she replies, "I'm a close friend of hers and a trusted political advisor."

"Outstanding..." Seneca throws in another calculated pause. He doesn't quite believe her. "Why don't you prove it?"

"Hmmmm," she hums, pantomiming thinking by tapping her chin with a finger. "I'll think about it."

They both sit in the club, listening to the music rattle the walls and watch the mass of partygoers enjoying themselves. "So why the club? Shouldn't you be with the princess... That is, if you work for her?"

"I'm usually with her," she explains. "But she's finishing up a meeting regarding things far beyond what could be considered your business, and she sent me out early to mingle with folks to spare me from the meetings."

Seneca playfully mimics barfing as he mutters, "Gross politics."

"Yeah, it is, but my family is Imperial nobility, so I was destined for a job in the arena. I've been the princess' friend for forever, and she offered me the job and spared me from doing something much less interesting." She goes on, "It's still boring, but the perks are great."

Seneca remains skeptical but doesn't question the logic further, chalking it up to an attempt to impress him. "I didn't catch your name.", he says, changing the subject.

"Serena Shields," she replies.
"Cool...Pretty."

They chat and engage in casual, flirtatious banter for a while longer as they spectate the other club occupants continue the debauchery upon the dance floor until the conversation seems to have run out of steam or a viable direction. He entertains the momentary thought of bidding her a goodnight and excusing himself in the event the encounter is a dead end but doesn't want to risk missing out on the opportunity for good company. Company is an asset that can be rare to find given his chosen lifestyle. He's contemplating silently until a funky tune coming from her own UniCom device pulls him out of his reverie and draws him back into the club.

* * *

"One second." Serena holds up a finger. "Getting an important call. Don't go anywhere."

With a nod, Seneca stretches his limbs, and then casually runs his fingers through his hair. The circumstances suggest he has found a potential companion who is willing to accompany him back to his ship (although, tonight's maiden is harder to read than most). With plenty of night left, he waits for her to come back to invite her over to *the Phantom* to continue their interactions. He waits patiently as he observes her attempt to communicate over her device.

She ends her call and extends an invitation, saying, "Alright buddy, come with me." It happens before he has the chance to invite her to his ship.

It's not very often for a girl to extend an invitation somewhere. They're seldom local to the area, since spaceports and their surrounding spaces are full of people coming and going. Even when the odd local citizen is involved, hotel "rooms" in many locales are simply a bed in a tube, more for sleeping than anything else. He isn't sure where she'd take him, and he still isn't ready to buy her work-for-the-princess claim yet. Still, he follows her, oozing with curiosity and a sly attitude.

"Yes, ma'am." He responds.

Following her lead, he walks down the music filled, neon-lit streets back toward the main area of the port. He is taken aback when he realizes that instead of leading him to one of the nearby luxury hotels with proper rooms. Instead, she gradually steers him towards the restricted area where Imperial ships are docked. "No way," he thinks silently to himself, spectating curiously as she flashes an Imperial government ID at the agents.

A short, heated conversation quietly ensues between Serena and an Imperial security agent that he can't quite comprehend. "Yes, I know who he is... not your concern... contacted her... thank you!"

The agent yields, and she leads him through the checkpoint, striding among the Imperial transports parked nearby. They continue forward and Seneca can't shake the disbelief creeping into his mind. There's absolutely no way this is happening, he thinks to himself. His skepticism lingers but weakens with each step they take towards a beautiful ivory yacht-shaped cutter with vivid crimson paints accenting its contours. She continues onward, guiding him until they reach the entrance of the Princess's cutter at the far end of the port, bearing a name appropriate to the beauty of the ship: "*Solace.*"

She beckons him to accompany her up the boarding stairs and opens the cabin door to the ship, and ushers him inside. The interior is just as grand and impressive as the outside. As soon as he steps inside, he's prompted to remove his boots and allow his feet to sink into the luxurious, rose-colored carpet, its velvety texture providing a comforting sensation. The vessel showcases curved ivory walls that mirror the exterior's color palate. Every few feet on the ceiling, the space features beautiful crystal light fixtures, which add an elegant touch. It's a flying piece of artwork meticulously crafted with no expense spared. Serena guides him to the lounge area across from the entrance and casually opens a bottle of champagne that looks extremely expensive. She pours him a glass and smugly places it into his hand as he stands mouth agape and lost for words. He never imagined in a month of Mondays that he would stand in the lounge of the princess's personal cutter.

"Toooolllld yooooou sooooo," Serena flirtatiously taunts him, taking a seat on the cream-colored lounge seat on the right side of the ship.

Following an invitation to sit, Seneca obliges while tilting his head to the side. "I guess you did. I honestly thought you were bullshitting me so you could get me out of my flight suit."

The ship is marvelous, even if somewhat pretentious for his taste. Nevertheless, the seat is comfortable, and the drinks are cold.

She laughs with a hint of sarcasm in reply but says nothing, prompting Seneca to continue talking. "Never imagined I'd be in the Princess's cutter. Doesn't security get bent out of shape when you bring random folks aboard?" he asks.

"The Princess has an open-door policy for folks like you, plus the odds of you injuring her are low. You'd be dead before you could draw a weapon," Serena says, nodding toward a couple of security guards posted throughout the room.

"Badass, but I make it a point to avoid upsetting governments too much, so I'm not keen on threatening royalty," Seneca says. "I'm high profile and too easy to identify. It isn't always easy to get rid of a price on your head..."

"*Hiiiigh* profile?" she says sarcastically, "Don't get too excited."

"Oh please, you knew me by my face alone, and you've never seen me before. You can bet all the major governments keep tabs on me."

"Celebrity aren't you," she snickers, becoming increasingly disinterested in Seneca.

Seneca raises three fingers, leaning forward with his elbow on his knee, displaying a hint of arrogance. "Sort of. I'm the highest rated combat pilot in the galaxy, one of only three rated as an Apex."

She shrugs, "Whatever you say. Save the celebrity flex for later. Princess Ilana loves to meet celebrities, but I couldn't care less."

"Aren't you a shrewd one," Seneca chuckles, realizing she will not be the temporary romantic flame he thought she'd be, "Also, don't lie about meeting princess; you'll break my heart twice in one night."

Her tone shifts to serious. "Break your heart twice? What? Shut up. No, I told her you were here on Oberon, and she wants to meet you."

Seneca laughs, full of doubt. Serena, however, looks dead serious, so he calms down a bit. Returning to a composed state, he reminds himself that he is on the princess' cutter. He looks around, trying to evade the awkward moment he just manufactured with his cackling.

"Ugh," she moans, "Just make sure you return the favor one day and introduce me to one of your more *modest* friends."

A false smile adorns Seneca's face as he utters, "Sure would. If I had any, I don't meet too many people nowadays, so you'll be waiting a bit."

Serena seems aware that she touches a nerve, but Seneca isn't sure. "Please, a celebrity like you must have friends all over the galaxy."

He raises his guard a little. Personal conversations with strangers aren't particularly enjoyable. He diligently avoids opening himself up or relying on anyone other than himself, and for the longest time, he's been successful. As such, he genuinely has no trusted friends. Trust leads to attachment. Attachment leads to grief. He will outlive everyone he meets by a considerable margin. Companions are only a setup for heartache.

"Is the princess actually coming or...?" Seneca asks, finishing his glass of champagne whilst realigning the conversation down a more desirable path.

She replies, "It's her ship, so wait around long enough you'll see her, but she didn't mention what time she'd be back."

Seneca shrugs and asks, "So should I leave before she gets back or—"

She cuts him off, saying, "No, it's fine, open-door policy and stuff. Plus, I promise she wants to meet you" and finishes with a wink.

Seneca waits and carries on chatting with Serena for a while longer. The topics they cover are entirely random, and the flirting has ceased at this point. Although, he still learns more about Serena. It turns out she has a deep passion for flowers and plants. She animatedly rambles for about fifteen minutes about her extensive collection of rose varieties at her home on Vista, expressing a keen interest in the unique flowers that can only be found on Earth.

Chapter 4: Royal Encounters of the Fourth Kind

Abrupt sounds of latches and hinges shatter the silence, causing Seneca to snap to attention at the realization that someone is opening the pressurized doors of the cutter. True to Serena's prediction, the door opens, granting passage to several security guards who were accompanying Princess Ilana. While exchanging a few glances with Serena, he widens his eyes in an unsuccessful effort to be acknowledged, displaying a complete lack of awareness regarding the expected traditions and courtesies that follow when meeting royalty. Outside of standing up, he's lost for actions. Does he bow? Does he offer a handshake? What? Serena's deliberate lack of assistance, combined with her mischievous body language and the way she turns red from chuckling, leaves him in total confusion, worsening the situation.

While he is familiar with her image, the stunning presence of the princess in real life is incomparable. Although her height does not differ significantly from Seneca's, she still has to tilt her head back slightly in order to meet his eyes. With the grace of a waterfall, her long wavy hair flows over her shoulders, showcasing a stunning shade of blue that resembles the deep ocean—a remarkable characteristic that she inherited from enhanced genetics. Her hourglass silhouette gracefully embraces healthy curves in alluring places. The makeup decorating her face is tasteful; however, unnecessary since her warm complexion is already pleasing upon appraisal. Her dress mirrors the elegance of her ship, adorned with sparkling ivory and crimson accents, and revealing just the right amount of bare skin. Seneca tries to conceal his wandering gaze, but he can't help but notice that she is assessing him with her green eyes similarly.

After leaving him in limbo a few moments more, Serena stands up and walks over to where the princess is standing awkwardly, awaiting some action on Seneca's part. "Okay, I found the pilot guy you keep talking about."

With a mix of nerves and excitement, Seneca steps forward and extends his hand for a handshake, his smile betraying his slight unease. She obliges and offers her own hand, which feels as soft as expected based on their appearance.

"Hello, I'm Princess Ilana," she says with a pleasant voice. "Nice to meet you in person, Seneca."

"Likewise," he exhales nervously.

Serena hugs Ilana, bidding her farewell. "Alright, you two talk; I'm going back to the club."

Before Serena completely departs from their embrace, they take a moment to exchange a couple of other whispers and giggles. Seneca watches the two swap glances and smiles at him before Serena exits the ship and latches the door behind her.

Giving a small wave, the princess gestures to the guards, who promptly motion for Seneca to surrender his pistol. He glances over at the princess as he complies with her security. She makes her way past him. As she walks to the lounge area, a delicate fragrance of sweet vanilla and citrus trails behind her, lingering in the air as security finishes patting Seneca down.

"Full disclosure. I didn't plan this at all. Your friend Serena told me to follow her here to prove a point; I didn't believe that she knew you," he rambles.

She chuckles in response. "It's quite alright. Once she told me she saw you at Yzinny's I told her to bring you here. I've been hoping I'd run into you candidly like this for a long time. Full disclosure on my part, I've been a huge fan of yours for years. Even my father recognizes your name."

"I used to work with him and your mom, actually."

Most don't believe him when he tells them, but Seneca does, in fact, know the emperor and empress. They were both HLEP survivors, like himself. When the experiment took place, they were married and known as Byron and Winter McClaine. They were selected for their executive leadership and organizational skills and assigned them the role of establishing functional sub-governments in some of the early colonies within Sol. They both survived and worked together, establishing many of the early colonies in Sol. Their daughter, Princess Ilana, was born on the planet Vista shortly after the founding of the Empire and is currently the only known offspring of two surviving members of the HLEP. As it turns out, she inherited the genetic augmentations her parents received and shares the longevity of the rest.

"So they tell me. Something about medical procedures and early space colonization," she says.

Seneca nods. "I haven't seen them since I dropped them off at the original colony of Vista when it orbited Neptune. Shit, back then, ships and colonies didn't even have artificial gravity. Colonies still had to use rotational forces to keep folks from floating around."

She shrugs. "Dad doesn't talk much else about you; our most recent news about you was an Imperial colonel informing us you helped prevent an expansion effort... the lords were quite irate, they'd been eying Delici for quite some time."

Seneca gets nervous at the recognition of his previous activities. A troubling thought sneaks into his mind, hinting that perhaps he had stumbled into a dangerous situation, lured by a combination of alcohol and a pretty face. He stealthily scans the room and quickly rehearses an escape in his mind, should the need arise. In a dire situation, the princess herself could be used as collateral for negotiation.

"Oh, you can relax," she assures, noting evident anxiety on his part. "Besides, your criminal activities or lack thereof aren't my area of concern, and the Imperial bounty registry says you're currently clean anyway." She smiles and gestures for him to take a seat.

It would have been better to remain standing near a door rather than venturing away from the only means of escape. However, he opts for compliance and apprehensively seats himself on the lounge chair across from her.

She continues, "So you're from Earth like my parents. That's interesting."

"I am, specifically I was from the US, born at Northside Hospital in Atlanta, Georgia."

"How'd you wind up on Mars with my parents?"

"I flew fighter jets in the military and just got lucky enough to fly spaceships, I guess," Seneca says, sneering at the word lucky. He pauses. "Your parents ever bring you to Earth?"

She says, "Not yet, no."

They make more small talk until a moment of silence descends, leaving Seneca to ponder whether the princess has lost interest in the conversation or maybe in him. Her intentions remain unclear, and he hasn't been able to decipher her mood. There are no obvious signs of a trap, and her level of enjoyment in the conversation remains a mystery. Silence that hangs between them awkwardly, akin to the pauses high school students use before cracking a crude attempt at humor. Then, with a wave of her hand, the security entourage exits into other nearby rooms.

"Fuck it!" Suddenly, the princess jumps to her feet and bounces up and down in excitement. "You're Seneca Mason! Sorry, I can't pretend to be calm about it anymore. I have wanted to meet you for at least like twenty years, but you know I have to be a 'princess'." Mocking her own title with finger quotations.

Seneca is caught off guard by the sudden outburst. It's not unusual for women to feel a childlike excitement when they come across him, similar to meeting a rat in a Florida theme park. However, he wasn't expecting this level of exuberance from the Imperial princess known for her straightforward and calm approach to politics. Despite the charming change in the room's ambiance, he finds himself unable to shake the suspicion that it could be a clever deception.

"It's alright. I'd be a liar if I said I wasn't hoping for an opportunity to meet you as well," Seneca replies, pretending to relax.

Excitedly, she says, "I've heard all about you from so many people! You're a legend!"

"What kind of things do people chat about? I wouldn't exactly consider myself a legend, good definitely, but you generally need to be dead to be a legend."

"Please. I've followed all the societies you've helped, your work with the early space colonies, and… oh! You saved an entire fleet in the Orinian War by charging ahead into their formation."

The war she's talking about unfolded one hundred and fifteen years ago. It was a brutal awakening, a sudden reveille that humanity was anything but alone in the vast galaxy. At the fringes of inhabited space, a humanoid alien race hailing from the vicinity of Orion's belt launched a surprise attack. These beings, known as "Orinians" by humans (Seneca can't understand their language, so their true name eludes his understanding), had a mission in mind: to push humanity out of space and confine them to terrestrial planets.

Despite their possession of advanced and lethal technology, the Orinians failed to realize the strength and adaptability of humanity, which proved to be a critical mistake. Due to their over-reliance on their perceived technological superiority, they did not anticipate the exceptional skills of pilots like Seneca, resulting in a stalemate.

Over the course of three grueling years, as the war raged on, Seneca's combat prowess was on full display to both friend and foe in battle after battle. Through his remarkable feats during those turbulent times, he accumulated a kill count that far surpassed the requirements for earning the notorious title of "Apex," achieving this prestigious honor. Since then, humanity and the Orinians have maintained a fragile and uneasy peace.

The particular incident the princess is referring to occurred when a fleet of Orinians intercepted a retreating convoy of vessels transporting wounded souls' home to the safety of human controlled territory. The fleet found themselves outnumbered, and Seneca, driven by his own personal reasons, charged ahead and broke through their attack formation directly towards their command vessels. He was able to single-handedly eliminate two of the Orinian destroyer class ships by baiting their AI enhanced targeting systems to engage in friendly fire. Leaving the attacking fighters without suitable leadership for the remainder of the confrontation.

"I wasn't trying to be a hero back then, that fight wasn't really about protecting a fleet…" Seneca replies, scratching his head, trying to appear modest, hoping she would not question his rationale further.

"That doesn't mean you weren't a hero," she replies. "You saved thousands."

The princess continues bombarding him with a variety of questions about other places he's been. Her overt curiosity appears genuine, and Seneca slowly relaxes his guarded stance. However, certain conversation topics, such as his enterprises regarding previous affiliations, incite him to return to a guarded mindset before easing once topics shift. Despite the fluctuations in their conversation, he slowly appreciates her genuine interest in his experiences and gradually opens up more than they exchange dialogue regarding their respective journeys and adventures.

* * *

As other questions pour out of her mind, her inquisition returns to the present, "So what brought you to Oberon?"

"I was dropping off a wanted ex-spy to wipe my record. Dude sold some information to the Whispers." Seneca answers.

"Ah, yeah, the whole rebellion thing," she says. "This is neutral space, so you're free to tell me who you supp—"

"Nope, no stake in it," Seneca quickly interjects before she can finish her question. "I don't live anywhere in Imperial or rebel space, so until a bidder comes along, it's not my fight."

"Where do you live?" She asks.

"That's personal."

Her smile fades away as her tone lowers. "Oh, sorry."

Her joyful demeanor fading in response to his efforts to conceal personal details briefly stirs a sense of commiseration within him. Currently, the chances of him being captured or facing any immediate danger are highly unlikely. Therefore, he embraces the opportunity to engage in a pleasant conversation with a beautiful woman for the night. Seneca attempts to loosen up by stretching, hoping to release the tension.

"It's fine," he says. "As far as where I sleep most nights—that'd be my ship."

Her smile returns. "By yourself?"

"Most of the time," he winks.

Her cheeks momentarily flush with a hint of red before returning to their normal color. "I technically live in the royal palace in Vista Capital, as you can imagine, but lately I've been doing the same."

"This ship looks cozy, so I'm sure it's not too bad," Seneca says, gesturing at the lavish interior.

"I guess... Although neither the palace nor this ship are really my favorite places to be," she says. "I've spent so much time surrounded by fancy chattels; at this point, sleeping outside is a bucket list item."

"Like on the ground?" Seneca says with a tone of surprise. "Trust me, I've done that. It isn't very comfortable. Tents and air beds make it better, but camping is an acquired taste."

"I'm open minded."

Seneca and the princess continue their conversation and an intriguing transformation occurs. The longer they talk, the more amiable and open he becomes. He ponders whether the influence of the alcohol he consumed at the bar earlier, as well as with Serena aboard the Solace, is playing a role in his newfound affability. Conversely, he cannot resist pondering the potentially hazardous scenario in which he sincerely relishes this opportunity for connection.

Even before he shut himself off from the world, Seneca has never been the type to share easily with others. His career took over his entire life, especially when he was on Earth. He never settled down, never had the chance to start a family before the HLEP. Only after which did he eventually start a family, but he never gave up his wings; life was always career centric. With unwavering dedication, he pursued his love for flight, aiming to one day travel to the stars in rockets. Eventually, this dream became a reality for him. Unfortunately, the pursuit of his dream came at a significant cost, as his parents and extended family were deprived of the chance to witness his long-awaited return from Mars. The cruel reality of time dilation prevented him from sharing those precious moments with them.

"You okay there?" She notices him lost in thought.

"Yeah. I'm just not good at getting to know people," Seneca says before he catches himself. "Well, rather, I'm not good at letting people get to know me."

A brief spurt of anger sparks within him. Why did he say that? It's not a sentiment he'd readily share, and he blames the allure of a pretty face.

"I'll be right back then!" she exclaims, leaping out of her seat once more. Swiftly, she darts down the hallway, leaving Seneca momentarily stunned. Her voice echoes faintly as she chats to herself, and Seneca can't help but speculate that she is on a quest for something. Seneca's suspicions are confirmed when she reappears after a brief interval, triumphantly clutching another bottle of inhibition-lowering elixir. It is becoming increasingly evident that he is indeed caught in a trap, just not the typical category one would expect.

"Oh, boy..." Seneca ponders silently, a sense of trepidation creeping over him. The bottle she's holding in her hand was none other than Kepler fire whiskey, a formidable libation renowned for its fiery flavor and high alcohol content. A creation from a family of whiskey distillers who lived on Kepler 452-b, where they meticulously crossbred augmented cinnamon trees to produce the most incendiary flavor possible, infusing it into their high-proof whiskey to craft the potent spirit.

"Want to play a game?" she asks, putting the bottle on her hip and leaning.

"You have my attention." Eyeing the bottle of fire whiskey and not wanting to betray his prideful reputation. "What kind of game?"

"Ever played never have I ever?" She grins.

"What is this, high school?" Seneca chuckles, rolling his eyes. "I used to play that at academy parties back when I knew how to have fun."

She says, "Okay then, you know the rules. If you've done it, you drink."

Seneca loosens up, giving an agreeable nod to her challenge as they dive headfirst into the lively game.

Despite both of them brandishing vast lifetimes of experiences, Ilana held a dear advantage. His additional century of life with experiences exclusive to those born and raised on Earth, leads to him drinking more than his competitor, a fact that became increasingly dear as the game progressed. He couldn't help but notice that she wielded her extensive knowledge of his achievements with ruthless precision, while he remained in the dark about the details of her own life, symptomatic of his lack of desire to care about others.

With each passing moment, it becomes increasingly evident that Seneca is losing ground in the battle for his liver. The searing sting of the Kepler fire whiskey lingers on his palate and throat, overpowering any other flavors that he might have experienced. The game carries on until the room spins around him, creating a dizzying atmosphere. They continue to down shots of whiskey, which not only fuels a competitive spirit but also sparks a brief candle-flame of camaraderie. All of this takes place in a dimly lit space until, finally, they realize that they have consumed enough, and the bottle is nearly empty.

"Okay." He cringes, finishing another gulp. "I yield."

"Victory!" she yells, jumping up and dancing around, her hair and dress dancing around her as a slow-motion blur. It's the last thing he sees as darkness fills his peripherals and falls into a drunken slumber.

Chapter 5: Breaking the Mold

The next, morning Seneca is greeted by a massive, throbbing headache pounding relentlessly and reverberating shockwaves of pain through his skull. The room still spins as he slowly sits up, and he swears to himself that he'll never touch alcohol again. Struggling to adjust his eyes to the darkness, he blinks repeatedly while scanning the room for any clues that can offer a hint as to where he might be. It takes a few disorienting moments, but he eventually manages to regain his bearings amidst the headache and nausea.

His fingers fumble about as he pats his chest, and the familiar touch of his flight suit provides a small anchor of reassurance. Yet, the memory of the previous night remains shrouded in haze as he gingerly pushes the covers off and stands up from a bed he can't recall getting into. He struggles to discern any clue to his location, a heavy metal door creaks open, and blinding light floods into the room, momentarily blinding him and intensifying the pounding behind his temples.

A woman's laugh radiates from the other side of the blinding light. "Look at him, I told you, you were both plastered last night, but he was waaaaaaaay worse. You'd think a space badass could handle some whiskey."

He rubs his face and massages his throbbing head, struggling to make sense of the voice that had disrupted his uneasy slumber. It may be a woman's voice certainly isn't an angel. If this were heaven, the pain wouldn't be so excruciating, and she'd be saying kinder words. Gradually, his eyes begin to cooperate, and the world around him slowly comes into focus. Ivory walls and a rich crimson carpet materialize before him, sparking vague recollections of the previous night.

"Am I still..." he groans as he stumbles out of the bedroom into the light, "on the princess' ship?"

"Oooh yeah," Serena says, cackling maniacally. "You helped the princess drain a bottle of fire whiskey playing some teenagers' game. When I got back from the bar, you were both passed out in the lounge, naked and tangled up."

"How'd I get into the bed?" Seneca asks, rubbing his face, her words taking time to process, "and can I get some of the... fucking... shit? No, I fucking wasn't."

"Like you'd know even if you were. But yeah, you weren't that lucky." She remarks, ignoring his question as a sharp pain hits his arm.

"Shit!" Seneca exclaims, gripping his arm.

Shortly afterwards, his head stops hurting, and he no longer feels congruent with a water balloon ready to expel its contents.

"All better, big baby?" Serena taunts, holding an empty syringe of what is referred to as "hangover-be-gone" throughout the galaxy.

He doesn't bother trying to pronounce the true complex drug name. It's a convenient medication to keep on hand if one expects drinking heavily since it absolves hangovers within seconds. The only undesirable side effect from the drug is an annoying prolonged sensation of dry mouth; it also does little to assist recovering memory from blackouts.

"Thanks," he says, looking around the posh ship which is still docked in Oberon.

"No problem," Serena says. "Sit down, don't go anywhere; the princess wants to chat some more. Business this time."

"Oh?" Seneca says inquisitively.

"You told me last night you were looking to do something you haven't done before," she says. "You'll be offered a chance. She's just getting dressed right now."

He said that. Seneca distinctly remembers his attempt to impress Serena with smooth talk last night at Yzinniy's. It's also the truth. For a while now, putting distance between himself and his previous adventures has been his modus operandi. His constant movement serves as a clear message to others: he won't be staying long. Some endeavors may be more extended than others, but they all conclude with his departure.

"Don't worry, Ilana will explain," Serena says, handing him a glass of water.

"Was last night a job interview or something?" Seneca asks as he downs the water to quench the parched mouth feel induced by medication.

"No. She just wanted to meet you and talk," Serena says, "and she said you just wouldn't loosen up."

"I went too loose if you ask me," Seneca frowns, adjusting his short hair and clothing to a more appealing configuration.

The princess emerges from the hallway, looking fully recovered from her own severe overindulgence of fire whiskey. The room fills with a pleasant aroma as she enters, her hair still damp from a shower and carrying the sweet scent of her chosen soap. Even without makeup, she remains immensely alluring. This morning, she captures Seneca's attention in a maroon and gold halter dress. As he appreciates her well-rested and freshly groomed appearance, a soft snicker from Serena distracts him from his visual assessment.

* * *

An energetic greeting escapes the princess. "Good morning!"

Seneca politely waves but refrains from saying anything. He's reluctant to admit embarrassment, choosing instead to pretend that he didn't black out in the presence of royalty. Beneath the surface, curiosity tugs at his mind, recognizing the potential for a powerful alliance with the princess to advance his personal interests and shape a different sort of adventure than he typically undertakes. There's also no fallacy in his silent admission. He's also looking forward to the prospect of spending more time with her.

"Let's talk business," she says, sitting down, crossing her legs, and situating her dress. "I'm doing a great deal of traveling in the coming future, and I am a high-value target for the Whispers among other ill-intentioned individuals."

With a subtle gesture, she calls one of her agents to her side, and they promptly arrive with a portable kiosk that bears a striking resemblance to a personal electronic tablet. The kiosk displays a page that details a job offer. "So," she continues, "I need a new head of security, not only for taking point on travel convoys but also to help me create a reliable security team if future ventures require it. The ones here with me now don't travel with me and the traditional escorts don't perform to the standards I need to make me feel comfortable and protected."

Seneca flashes a look of uncertainty. "This isn't my usual gig; normally, things I do are more short-term..."

"I know but let me tempt you..." she says as she continues to another page on the tablet. The application details the job description, among the perks and pay. The job is straightforward: escort *the Solace* and her occupants through space, sit with the princess in meetings, and accompany her at her request when needed. Pay is beyond lucrative, and perks eerily reflect the demands he would place for a job like this. He would get to pilot *the Phantom*, wear his own uniform in place of the Imperial uniforms, carry weapons of his choice when and where he sees fit, receive free fuel and repair services at Imperial ports, and diplomatic immunity among many other desirable benefits.

Carefully absorbing all the information in front of him, Seneca sighs. "That's quite a deal. What's the catch?"

Serena jumps into the conversation with a snarky voice, "You get shot at. Nothing new for you, mister Apex."

Ilana gently slaps Serena on her shoulder. "Yeah, that, but I was going to say it nicer."

Seneca turns his head and shrugs. "Can't argue with that; where do I sign?"

"Awesome!" Ilana squeaks, as Serena smiles and shakes her head.

She rises quickly from her seats and returns with his pistol and a stack of papers. Physical paper is an exceedingly rare sight in modern times. Although most documents are now digital, people usually synthetically create them through chemical means when they print them. In fact, museums now exhibit authentic paper documents, such as W-2's, I-9's, and military enlistment contracts, similar to how ancient Egyptian parchment is showcased on Earth.

* * *

He points at the pages of paperwork lying before him. "Is that *paper?*"

"You don't like it?" The princess frowns.

"No, it's not like that. I just haven't filled out anything on paper in well over a hundred and fifty years, give or take a decade," he responds.

The fact that the princess went to the trouble to print out the job contract on physical paper in a funny way fills him with an immeasurable amount of nostalgia. In an ironic sense, it's one of those things that went away silently that he never believed he'd miss in the slightest. The rise of the digital age quietly removed physical paper from business and legal transactions, rendering such proceedings to the disposal of digital platforms.

"Cool," the princess bounces. "Let's go through... this..." It becomes evident that the princess went through the trouble to have the job put onto paper but has no idea how to manage paper contracts. "I forgot the inky thing," she says, looking around.

Seneca reaches into his front jacket pocket, grabbing the ancient writing utensil that lives within. "What you are looking for is a pen, and as it so happens, I have one. I never use it anymore, but old habits die hard, and it's been in that pocket forever. Chances are it doesn't work but try it out anyway."

"Cool." the princess replies as she guides him through the paperwork, and Seneca winces as he puts pen to paper. Miraculously, he scribes his initials in ink after a few attempts, though his penmanship is rusty since he has underutilized the muscles for writing for a lifetime. Page by page, he scrawls his initials under the princess's direction until they reach the last page, where a line awaits his signature and print. He cringes as he signs; the task feels as antiquated as the instrument he's using. It is strange how, after more than a century, seeing his name haphazardly inscribed on paper fills him with subtle emotions. Thanks to the memory enhancements of his curse, he can vividly recall the first time he wrote his name in kindergarten and the handwriting is reminiscent of the occasion.

Seneca sighs and looks up after completing the paperwork. The princess regards him with a mixture of concern and curiosity, her eyes searching his face. "That was fun," he says, snapping back to his usual attitude.

"Cool, you'll start immediately," the princess responds with a smile as she collects the contract. Once again, she seems unsure of what to do with them and hands them to Serena, who looks equally perplexed at the stack of forms.

"Fun fact," the princess admits, "You and my dad are the only ones I know who can write. I don't even know how."

"I'm not as good at it as I used to be. My hand hurts," Seneca grumbles while massaging his right palm, "those muscles haven't been used in a long time."

She smiles at him and makes the eager squeaking sound once more, "Glad to have you aboard, Seneca! Serena will brief you on what we are doing for the remainder of our stay in Oberon."

The princess stands up and takes the papers from Serena to a room in the back, presumably to have them copied and converted to digital format, though Seneca appreciates the sentiment. He looks across at Serena, who has since seated herself opposite him. "I was told there would be a briefing," he says.

Serena lounges back and adjusts her skirt as she stretches. "Yeah, she just said that, but truth be told, we are here for fun for the next few days. You're just gonna hang out with us until we move on. Just keep us alive and you're doing your job."

Seneca nods. "Sounds like a good plan."

Serena returns the nod and walks away, but then she spins around. "Oh, yeah. Almost forgot, we already went over this, but you've got a special commission as a major within the Imperial Space Fleet. Uhhh, what else? Oh, get the ISF decal thrown on your ship while we are still docked."

She tosses him an Imperial Space Fleet Major lapel pin, and it sails gracefully through the air, landing perfectly in his outstretched hand. With a deft motion, he secures it next to the IC lapel pin he already wore. A sigh of relief escapes his lips; he is grateful that this was the only modification to his trusty jacket. His flight suits are the only clothing he has in space, and it'd leave a sour feeling to hate the sight of them.

Rubbing his face, he gets up from his seat, a newfound sense of purpose settling over him like a warm breeze. It is as if this new job marked not just a new rank but a welcomed shift into the unknown. With purposeful steps, he makes his way to his ship, a gleam of curiosity in his eyes as he wonders where this new adventure will lead. He couldn't help but feel the urge to freshen up with a shower before rejoining the princess afterwards; after all, he was now in the service of royalty.

Chapter 6: Dinnertime Interruptions

Throughout the remainder of the week, Seneca accompanies the princess and Serena as they move from one venue to another. It seems like the princess is celebrating something, but he hasn't bothered to find out what it is. He discovers the princess is a music lover who prefers dancing and listening to various types of music, rather than drinking excessively in public. However, she's not immune to the allure of a few drinks or the excitement of her favorite songs. Every now and then, she playfully invites Seneca to join her on the dance floor, but he politely declines. There is a conflicting part within him, one that feels the need to dedicate himself to his job and the other that wants to refrain from forming bonds with others.

The final evening descends upon the group as they depart from the day's last music venue. Seneca and the duo, growing hungry, opt to embark on a quest for dinner. An endeavor which evolves into a playful bickering match between Serena and the princess over their culinary preferences. Serena contests that Oberon's seafood is exceptional due to their use of selectively bred fish from clean water sources on the planet. On the other hand, the princess has a strong longing for pizza, a mouthwatering delicacy that has withstood humanity's journey into space. Serena contends that pizza in the locale is lacking in quality. Nevertheless, the princess is determined to satisfy her pizza craving, despite Serena's objections. The mental image of the princess staining her expensive clothes with pizza sauce makes Seneca chuckle, which unintentionally escapes his throat. The sound catches their attention, and the princess turns to him.

"Okay, tiebreaker: seafood or pizza?" she says, projecting a digital map of the port.

Their intense staring makes Seneca feel like he's deciding between two pills of different colors and unknown effects. He exchanges glances with each of them and leans away from Serena, as he suspects she might be crazy. "I'm gonna side with the one who signs my paychecks," he chuckles.

"Pizza *sucks* here!" Serena exclaims, her shout echoing. "Ilana, please!"

Seneca and the princess share in a brief chuckle while Serena groans. "She'll be okay," the princess reassures, patting Seneca's shoulder as they resume.

The three casually walk along the paved sidewalks next to the road, and then a magnetic-levitating ground transport, known as a "MagLev," effortlessly lifts them up and swiftly transports them through the bustling harbor town to a charming locally owned pizzeria.

The restaurant, covering a cozy seven hundred square feet, stands amidst the city of Oberon Station as a charming brick building adorned with a round, mustachioed man proudly clutching a pizza box on its signboard. Stepping inside, one is transported to a quintessential pizza eatery, almost as if it were designed through an AI's rendition. Classic black-and-white checkered tiles grace the floor, simple yet inviting steel trimmed wooden tables run along the walls, and bright red upholstered seats beckon diners to take a load off. The princess selects a table positioned by the expansive front window overlooking the concrete sidewalk and MagLev stops where they arrived from, where a tabletop kiosk awaits their order. After a brief discussion, they opt for a pizza loaded with all the potential toppings it can hold with a side of garlic bread.

In a surprising twist, this pizzeria still employs human staff to prepare and serve the food, an uncommon sight in a world dominated by robotic food preparation and delivery. Mind-boggling machines in many space born locales operate like a 3D printer to synthetically print food at your table—though the taste can leave much to be desired depending on the quality of the synthetic ingredients. Human-operated establishments are a rare treat now, especially near a bustling spaceport like Oberon Station.

As if no time has passed at all, handcrafted and personally delivered pizza arrives at their table, its aroma of tomato sauce, melted cheese, and seared crust wafting through the air. The waitress places the steaming discs of culinary artistry on the familiar box-shaped "pizza stands." The sight of the pie alone is enough to excite neurons responsible for decoding taste leaving Seneca unable to resist commenting, "It's been a while since I've been attended by human waitstaff in a restaurant and decades since I've seen pizza that looked that good."

"Oh, yeah," the waitress responds with a hint of the nearly extinct New England accent, handing out hand wipes to everyone. "My great-grandfather was actually the first person to open a pizza restaurant in space. It was on..." She pauses, trying to recall. "Phoebe Colony!"

"Oh, cool!" he exclaims as scooping up a slice of pizza onto a plate, watching as the cheese stretches into fine strings as it pulls from its brethren "I uh... used to live there... shit I probably flew him there all those years ago."

"Goodness, you're Seneca Mason!" she says excitedly, realizing who she's serving. "Small galaxy. We still try to do things the same way he did. Of course, some ingredients and spices are harder to find out here," she explains, nodding as she continues sharing details about the challenges of procuring certain ingredients. According to her explanation, the cooks substitute some vegetables and meats with high quality synthetic versions or omitted them altogether.

* * *

The waitress departs and Seneca redirects his attention to the princess and Serena, who are halfway through their first slices of pizza. While it may not evoke the same nostalgic feeling as the local pizza restaurant he used to frequent after Friday night football games in Duluth Town Green, this meal more than makes up for it with its delectable flavors that far surpass the average "pizza" he encounters during his travels. The cheese is undeniably authentic and reputedly crafted by hand, boasting an almost flawless texture. Made with real ingredients, the sauce is delicious, and its only artificial component is olive oil. Olives don't fare well during space shipments, a problem that few have cared to address. With each bite of the fantastic pizza, Seneca's face subtly reflects joy… quality pizza is indeed hard to find.

Seneca nods along with their dinner-side conversation. The princess teases Serena about her choice of cuisine, adopting a rather haughty demeanor since they indeed found a worthwhile pizzeria. Serena playfully responds with sarcasm, relishing the meal. Amidst the comings and goings of other customers, the trio find themselves engrossed in light conversation, thoroughly enjoying their delicious food.

Upon finishing the last helpless slices of the meal, Seneca notices a couple of unscrupulous individuals approaching the store. Their heads are bowed and their hands firmly gripping something concealed in their back pockets. One could interpret their actions as a sign of readiness to draw a weapon. Nervously, they fidget and shuffle towards the restaurant's entrance in the fading light of twilight. Sensing trouble, he orders the princess and Serena to take cover beneath the table, and they obey, dearly bewildered. Seneca swiftly rises and positions themselves in the corner near the entrance, anticipating the suspicious pair.

The duo makes their entrance, banging fists on the counter, demanding attention. With a worn plasma pistol in hand, one individual with bald hair points it directly at the waitress, who appears both startled and confused. It's evident that she has never laid eyes on a plasma weapon before. It wouldn't be a far-fetched possibility if she hadn't; the cost of the technology is still rather expensive for the average person.

Plasma weaponry has evolved significantly over the past century. Initially resembling tasers that fired pins with sacrificial wiring that would burn as the plasma moved forward, it now consists of sleek firearms with polarized rods in the barrel that ionize photons to propel plasma to the intended target. These advanced weapons offer various power settings, from low-powered "blanks" to high-powered shots capable of causing fatal injuries. Seneca's plasma pistol, for instance, features an eighteen-volt, seventy-amp battery, enabling it to discharge approximately two hundred lethal rounds.

The other criminal, a short stocky man with black hair and sunglasses, brandishes a more recognizable firearm that still uses 9mm bullets as he directs his attention toward the dining area, shouting for everyone to get down. The waitress freezes, and the armed individual insists she transfer two-thousand credits to him using the kiosk, projecting an ID bar-code onto the counter for her to use in the transaction.

Seneca rolls his eyes, finding the situation rather cliché. He raises his plasma pistol; a distinct hum of its charging mechanism fills the air. Using his thumb, he clicks the safety switch to the non-lethal setting. A resounding metallic buzz fills the air when he fires three rounds into the back of the armed individual, capturing the attention of the room. Sharp cries of pain escape the man's lips as he collapses onto the ground, writhing in torment. In the same instant, the other criminal spins around, only to be met with Seneca's gun positioned firmly between his eyes on the bridge of his nose.

"Drop the gun, buddy," Seneca commands, "Mine is currently set to non-lethal, but at this range, between your eyes, you're gonna wish it killed you."

The man wisely complies, nervously relinquishing his weapon. Seneca directs him to kick the other weapon away from his companion into the opposite corner of the room. "Take your buddy," Seneca grunts. "I'm not going to arrest you, but I've put a bounty on each of you. Let's see how you guys like people targeting you for a quick paycheck. Get the hell out."

Swiftly scooping his injured companion away from the store and around the corner, the two thwarted criminals disappear from sight, likely to seek shelter. They won't get far since the injured man will remain in agony for several hours after being hit square on his spine. Seneca smirks at the thought as everyone else stands up. The waitress expresses her gratitude, catching her breath and recovering mentally from the ordeal.

The princess and Serena emerge from under the table and approach Seneca. Serena asks with a puzzled expression, "How did you know?"

"I saw the way they were dressed and approaching the door, and it didn't seem right. They had their hands in their back pockets before they got to the curb," Seneca explains, gesturing toward the window.

"Why'd you let them go?" They both inquire, equally puzzled.

Seneca raises an eyebrow. "Too much work to arrest someone." He pauses. "Leave it to rookie bounty hunters to get some practice. Besides, I like cruel irony sometimes."

"Nice," Serena smirks. "Should have shot the other guy, though."

The princess, Serena, and other patrons ask Seneca more questions about his experiences, prompting him to delve into the intricacies of his military training. He speaks about the lessons learned of situational awareness, recounting stories of his rigorous small arms training, and how he had honed these fundamental skills over years of service. People around them show a keen interest, their eyes lighting up with fascination as they absorb the details of his experiences. Many cannot resist joining the conversation, sharing stories of their ancestors who had served in various military branches back on Earth. The restaurant buzzes with animated discussions, each person adding their own perspective and anecdotes to the mix. As the evening wears on, conversations continue, creating a warm atmosphere of friendly dialogue as customers slowly and reluctantly trickle out.

Chapter 7: Questions and Answers

Despite the establishment's spirited attempts to offer the meal on the house, Seneca pays the bill for their meal and, to show his appreciation for handmade food, adds a generous tip. They catch the MagLev trolley back to the dock, and he escorts the girls back to *the Solace*. Looking up into the evening sky, the second of Oberon's suns is setting. The star squeezes a purple twilight from the horizon and calls upon the stars of the Milky Way to emerge and cast a shimmering glow over the night sky that blankets their journey. Once they had safely returned to the steps leading up to *the Solace*, the princess and Serena leisurely make their way up the stairs towards the cutter. Work for the day is over and it's time he heads back to his own ship, but not before the princess intervenes.

"Where you goin'?" the princess calls out.
"Just back to *the Phantom,*" he replies, turning around to respond.
"Come on, don't be a stranger, come earn some overtime!"

With a casual shrug, he accepts the invitation and changes his course to join them aboard *the Solace*. He has no other obligations that would take up his time. Later, night hours settle in, and the second sun has long since set, he finds himself seated with Serena and the princess in the lounge area of the luxurious craft. They engage in a wide range of conversations, from reminiscing about past memories to delving into less exciting topics like politics and work-related matters. The discussion takes a turn towards romantic experiences and relationships. Seneca prefers maintaining his status as a passive observer, but Serena has other ideas and involves him.

"So, stick jockey," she says with a notable flare of sarcasm as she looks over at him. "I'd imagine from our run-in at Yzziny's that you're not involved with anyone."
"I'd rather talk about anything else," he responds, flashing a frown at the idea of revealing too much personal information. "My situation isn't exactly catered to bringing others into it."

"Sounds like you need a therapist," Serena interjects.

With no words exchanged, he communicates his distaste through a swift, disapproving glance. The statement doesn't hurt his feelings or anger him, but it stirs up uncomfortable emotions he'd rather keep buried. The conversation stagnates into an uncomfortable lack of dialogue before the princess finally returns to work-related matters, a much more palatable subject for him to entertain, "So, tomorrow afternoon, we're scheduled to depart Oberon and head to Idalia-15c to meet the governor of Idalia at Myanmar Hall in the city of Myanmar," she says. "Apparently, they have concerns that the rebellion is a threat to their sovereignty."

Idalia and its capital, Myanmar, is a familiar destination that boasts a singular inhabited planet with a diverse economy. In recent weeks, Idalia has been a talking point in Imperial news circuits. For the past month or so, Moniear, a previously independent nation recently annexed by the Empire, has witnessed a massive evacuation sponsored by Whisper rebels. Being populated by individuals who come from different earthly backgrounds, they have a notable reputation for producing some of the finest jewelry in the galaxy. Moniear's inhabitants also excel in various other artistic domains, such as music, fashion, and the visual arts. Their extraordinary talents garner them considerable fame and the great financial success, which ultimately drew the attention of the Imperial authorities.

Consequently, the Empire forcefully took over their home against their wishes and brutally suppressed any protests against this annexation, leaving no room for open dissent. Whisper rebels arrived shortly after but were unsuccessful in their attempt to remove the Empire by force. Currently, their primary focus is on evacuating the system of those seeking asylum from further persecution. Idalia is a nearby member of the COS that is playing a crucial role in resettling the refugees.

The situation for the displaced refugees is dire. They are forced to rebuild their lives in new lands with next to nothing to their names. At present, the Confederate governments are allowing refugees, but the heightening levels of poverty, crime, and homelessness are causing turmoil in the border territories of the Confederacy like Idalia. As a result, the member governments are becoming increasingly uneasy.

The princess continues, "We are meeting with the governor of Idalia as a means to appease his worries and set a standard for other COS territories that are in a similar situation. The Empire has no interest in invading COS lands, but also cannot prevent the rebels from entering Idalia or any other COS territory. It's going to be a fun conversation for Serena and myself."

She turns to Seneca, "You aren't here for the politics, but in order to make our meeting in time to get to Idalia, we have to move through an eleven-hour stint in Malachi's Arm."

"Oh fun, the Pirate's Playground," Seneca nods. He's all too familiar with the area since he's done a fair bit of pirate hunting as well as dabbling in piracy himself. "Has your pilot ever traversed the arm before?"

"No. He's actually relatively new as well." She says, shaking her head.

"Cool, so I need to talk to him specifically."

* * *

Seneca quickly assumes a commanding role in the conversation as soon as the pilot of *the Solace* enters the lounge. He sets guidelines on handling a pirates attempt to "pull" them from warp—a tactic where pirates use a sophisticated electromagnetic pulse weapon to momentarily shut down a victim ship's warp-propulsion and dragging out from warp—*The Solace* should come to a stop and follow the pirates' negotiation attempts until Seneca can drop from warp at their location and fight them off. However, should a second pirate pull *the Phantom* before Seneca arrives to protect *the Solace,* they should attempt to run or otherwise stall for time. If running is not an option, they must do everything to prevent the pirates from disabling *the Solace*'s engines and shield and subsequently boarding the craft. If the ship's identity and distinct markings do not disclose that the princess is aboard, a manifest scanner will. She'll be the target cargo since pirates could expect hefty ransom fees for her safe return.

Seneca finishes briefing the pilot by saying, "And for the love of God, do not shoot first." He waves his finger. "You aren't the main character in a sci-fi novel. It won't end well for you."

Everyone nods, and Serena retreats to her quarters to sleep. *The Solace*'s pilot returns to his quarters as well. Seneca stretches and yawns before collecting his personal belongings, preparing to make his way back to *the Phantom*. The sounds of his jacket zipper catch Ilana's attention after she finishes bidding goodnight to Serena.

"Are you leaving?" she asks, looking up from her seat as Serena retreats to the rear hallway.

Seneca responds, checking the time on his UniCom, "I was planning on it. Did you need something?"

Like Seneca, the princess also displays symptoms of drowsiness and imitates his stretching. She yawns as she mutters, "I was hoping you wouldn't mind showing me your ship before I head to bed."

"Sure," Seneca says with a shrug. "I don't imagine that'll hurt."

Evening air has set in outside as they both make the stroll over to *the Phantom*. The princess and Seneca walk silently, the rhythmic sound of their shoes on the pavement echoing through the station. It is not an uncommon occurrence to be on other planets and have nights devoid of sound. Most planets don't have insects since they disrupt agriculture, and governments implement very strict measures to prevent bugs from establishing populations anywhere other than Earth, where they belong. Sometimes Earthlike planets contain biological life that takes up a similar niche in that planet's ecosystem, but not all of them make noise at night. As such, the nocturnal silence is profound across the galaxy.

Seneca makes a swift glance over at the princess. Goosebumps prickle her delicate skin, decorating her crossed her arms her skin in response to a cool breeze sweeping the surface of the port. The high-tech two-piece black and red pilot outfit Seneca wears keeps him comfortable in most weather and prevents untimely death in the event of pressure seal failure aboard spacecraft, so temperature and its associated discomforts often evade his notice. The princess is wearing the same silver silk dress he saw her in this morning and is not likely to offer her the same level of protection from the elements. Seneca unzips the coat of his suit, and the brisk night air creeps over his arms immediately.

"Here," Seneca says, handing her the coat.
    The princess attempts to refuse politely, saying, "Oh, you don't—"
    Asserting again, Seneca says, "Just take it. I'm not cold."
    "Thanks."
    "No problem, princess," Seneca says as they approach the halfway point of the walk.
    Just then, she stops abruptly, and her face contorts into a look of disapproval. "Gross. Do not call me princess." Her face transitions to a smile as he looks back at her. "Ilana is fine."

Seneca expresses agreement by nodding. It's not typical of him to engage in arguments about titles. If she were to call him "Major Mason," he would react with the same disgust.

When they reach his ship, he uses a device similar in appearance to remote car keys to open the access port in the middle of its underbelly and deploying a ladder for boarding. Since it is a formidable fighter craft, there is no passenger-friendly door to facilitate comfortable entry. The princess eyes the ladder and access port nervously from underneath the ship. It's only about a six-foot climb in comparison to a large playground ladder, but she appears uncertain all the same. Seneca presses another button on his "keys," to lower a cable with a harness.

"Okay, that's much better heels and ladders don't mix," she sighs in relief. "You can go first, since it's your ship and all."

Once again, Seneca nods silently. He ensures Ilana equips the harness correctly before he makes the quick climb up the ladder into a narrow corridor between the living quarters and the cockpit. Once inside, he presses a button on the wall, lifting her and the ladder up simultaneously. On board the ship, the lights flick on with a switch, and Ilana looks around.

"Definitely a lot bigger outside than inside," she remarks, squeezing by Seneca to explore. "I want to see the cockpit!"
    "This way, then," Seneca says, escorting her to the forward end of the ship.

The cockpit is beyond a thick armored door and opens at the swipe of an ID barcode. The cockpit of his ship is small and cramped, making it difficult to stretch or move around comfortably. It has tandem pilot and copilot seats wedged between switch panels, displays, power distribution modules, and of course, the actual ship controls that are surrounded by the oval-shaped canopy that is composed of a thick, specialized material that protects the occupants while permitting them to see. The angular cockpit widens toward the back wall, where there are two jump seats on either side of the door.

Ilana walks in and looks around and places her hands on the rear pilot seat.

"Fun place to sit for long trips." Seneca says as he watches her look outside the cockpit, "Usually, if I know I'll be in arduous combat, I sit in the front pilot seat. But if I'm doing a lot of traveling, I sit in the rear copilot seat since it swivels and slides," Seneca explains, demonstrating the sliding motion. "This makes it significantly easier to get up to go to sleep or use the bathroom."

Ilana sits down in the seat, swivels, and ushers it forward. "Wow..."

Seneca remains vigilant, ensuring Ilana refrains from inadvertently tampering with any controls that might put them in harm's way. She cautiously reaches for the control stick, but a hydraulic locking mechanism, designed to prevent any unintended adjustments when the thrusters and engines are at rest, thwarts her efforts to move the controls. Driven by her inquisitiveness, she sporadically inquires about the purpose of various switches and buttons scattered across the control panel. Eventually, the line of questioning turns to the weaponry that the arm the ship.

"You'd think with as formidable the ship is you'd have fancier weapon technology on the ship," she says, gesturing to the gatling gun.

"Eh, there are a couple of reasons my ship and so many others don't have fancier modern weaponry..."

Seneca elaborates on the intricate world of combat ship armament, where a myriad of factors dictate weapon selection. Across the galaxy, a multitude of high-tech weapon systems exist. Lasers, plasma cannons, railguns, and particle accelerators are among the most modern available, but each demands substantial energy resources. However, not all vessels possess power plants capable of sustaining these weapons in prolonged combat engagements. Galactic regulations further complicate matters, with certain weapons banned, steering both law-abiding and rogue entities towards more permissible armaments to avoid unwanted attention. Diminishing returns from modern systems regarding their cost-effectiveness also play a significant role in shaping a captain's armament choices. Ultimately, the defining factor in determining a ship's armament lies in its mission profile, with every weapon selection tailored to optimize performance and achieve mission objectives.

In the realm of medium-class endurance fighters like *the Phantom* (a Raytheon SF-33 to be specific), captains like Seneca strive to strike a delicate balance between durability and agility to ensure versatility across a range of combat scenarios. Engineered for extended combat, medium-class fighters boast heavier armor and stronger shields compared to its lighter counterparts, without sacrificing speed and maneuverability that the heavy-class makes. Its armament configuration reflects this balance, with gatling guns selected for their efficiency in damaging enemy hulls over prolonged engagements. Paired with lasers designed to pressure shields, *the Phantom*'s arsenal creates strategic opportunities in battle. The inclusion of missile hardpoints further enhances its adaptability, allowing for the customization of armaments tailored to specific engagement scenarios.

* * *

The princess nods in understanding of the logic and afterwards, her curiosity takes a different turn. She swivels in her seat, her eyes now brimming with newfound interest, and expresses her desire to explore the rest of the ship. Seneca readily grants her request. They exit through the heavy, armored door and continue to the aft end of the hall, where they encounter yet another door that bears a striking resemblance to the oval entryway of a submarine. Inside is the crew suite, a space that's compact yet functional. Soft, dimmed lighting bathes the room, casting a cozy ambiance.

To the left, there's a small galley area with a compact countertop, a microwave-sized synthetic food assimilator (Seneca refers to it as a printer), and a sofa with plush cushions. It's a quaint albeit cramped spot for eating a quick meal or just lounging while taking in the views of the cosmos through a small, rounded window.

Another window on the opposite wall overlooks a single double bed occupying most of the remaining space. Seneca maintains a neatly configured bed, and a soft navy-blue blanket rests atop it. Other models of the ship present a bunk bed in this area, but since Seneca is typically the sole occupant of the ship, he has opted for a more spacious arrangement. A compact but efficient combination toilet and shower unit is tucked into the wall forward from the bed. It's a marvel of space-saving design, allowing for basic hygiene needs in the confines of interstellar travel. Above the toilet, there's a wall-mounted steam cleaner, a high-tech solution to keep Seneca's limited wardrobe fresh and clean during his journeys through space. The soft hum of the ship's environmental systems provides a soothing background sound, and a faint scent of recycled air mingles with the sterile, metallic undertone of the ship's interior.

"Cozy," she says, parking herself on the sofa. "Is this it?"

Seneca chuckles. "Yeah, it's cramped living, but she does the trick. Fighter craft are small inside to make room for larger power distribution units among a bunch of other combat-oriented systems. Light fighters don't even have much of this since they usually travel aboard larger ships."

She nods. "Yeah, the Solace only has some self-defense turrets and countermeasures."

"Makes sense. It's meant to be fast and comfortable for important people to travel in," Seneca says, sitting on the bed. "Whenever you're ready, I can walk you back, but you can look around more, too."

She nods, remaining seated as her eyes explore every corner of the small room. The interior of Seneca's ship is not lavish. The room's drab, military gray paint gives it an austere and unwelcoming feel to those unaccustomed to the color palate. The presence of bulkheads every four feet further emphasizes the strict and regimented nature of the space. Overhead and along the sides, there are cabling, plumbing, and air tubes running through the space. The space resembles the interior of a military cargo aircraft rather than a cozy living area.

"Sorry about Serena earlier," she says, catching Seneca off guard with the sudden shift in conversation.

"Oh, it's no problem," Seneca replies, sitting up on his bed.

"She can be kind of snarky and direct with people," Ilana explains, "but she means well."

The statement from Ilana causes him to let out an audible chuckle. "I've noticed."

She then sighs. "But I am curious to know..."

"Uh-oh," Seneca thinks.

"We are both like my parents. They tell me we all may never die of natural causes." She pauses and cocks her head to the side, shifting her blue hair in the process. "Why are you alone? You have so much freedom. You've had all this time."

Seneca sighs heavily and looks down before pausing. "That's a loaded question."

She nods. "I guess so."

Seneca, not wanting to upset her, pushes himself through his desire to close off as he sighs, "Before I got selected to fly for Operation Rejuvenation and space colonization efforts that followed, I was a career fighter pilot on Earth with the Air Force..."

Sharing his experiences with her, he highlights the commanding role that flying played in his life on Earth. It was this dedication that allowed him to continuously advance his distinguished career, always pushing the boundaries and reaching for greater achievements. When the opportunity to fly in space became available, he immediately jumped at the chance with no hesitation. Ilana remains quiet as Seneca moves through the details of the early part of his career.

He tells her how he received news about friends and family passing away with every return to Earth. In fact, his parents did not live to see his initial return from Mars. He persevered on missions amidst the sorrow until he'd returned from his final mission to Vista colony. He shares memories of his life with Sophie, his first wife, a woman of gentle demeanor and flowing auburn hair, and their son Oliver, whose bright brown eyes mirrored Sophie's. Their love story began in the aftermath of a medical examination post-mission, where flirtations blossomed into a lifelong commitment. Together, they ventured into the picturesque South Carolina mountains, dreaming of a tourism venture, finding solace in each other's arms. Oliver, a spitting image of his mother with Seneca's tousled brown locks and infectious smile, brought joy amidst life's uncertainties.

However, tragedy struck with cruel force when Sophie and Oliver met their untimely demise in a car accident while Seneca was away, testing faster-than-light technology. The news shattered Seneca's world, drowning him in a torrent of grief and regret. Overwhelmed by emotions he couldn't bear to face; he began his streak of running.

"After that, I left Earth. It took a decade or so, but I eventually met my second wife, Kelsea, in Phoebe Colony." He says as he continues.

There, fate introduced him to Kelsea, his second wife. She was a woman of resilience and grace, with piercing blue eyes and sun kissed skin, became his anchor in a sea of sorrow. Their love endured Kelsea's battles, from infertility to a harrowing bout with cancer in her final years. As Seneca watched her fight with unwavering strength, he found nothing but pain in her presence since his ageless existence might never let them reunite, a fading light leading to his darkest days. After her passing, he found himself adrift in an unforgiving sea of memories and loss. With a heavy heart and a lost sense of purpose, he cast himself into the cosmos.

"After so much loss in my life between friends, family, wives, and my son, I didn't want it again," Seneca says. "The Orinian war broke out two days after Kelsea's funeral, and I sold our estate on Phoebe Colony and used the money to buy *the Phantom*, and I left to fight in the war."

Ilana reaches up and gently wipes away the tears trickling down her cheeks. "I —" she stutters, struggling to get her words out. "I didn't know."

The recount of his past leaves Seneca choking back a swell of anger. He doesn't even like dwelling on his skeletons of his own accord. It's not in his nature to be so kind to another and open up. He wants to yell at her for asking him to re-live his pain, but something about Ilana drew him to speak. It doesn't change the swirl of emotion.

"I barely know you...." he says, pulling himself together with a deep breath to avoid directing anger at his new, curious employer. "I can walk you back if you want, but I want to be alone right now."

She nods silently, and Seneca walks her back to her ship. The well of feelings in his mind churns, tearing at him as he tries to force the past back into proverbial holding tanks in the depths of his mind. He escorts her silently into *the Solace* and makes his journey alone back to his ship.

Chapter 8: Loud Gun Diplomacy

Oberon's second sun rises, heralding the morning of the group's departure for Ilana's business in Myanmar. Most of the other Imperial officials have already gone their separate ways after their conferences with COS and UF leaderships. After a hasty meal and an abbreviated re-briefing via video conference, the port traffic control tower grants clearance for *the Solace*'s departure as a flight of two with the Phantom serving as an escort. The vessels gracefully take to the sky, burning the atmosphere of Oberon with their thrusters and beginning a formation flight with Seneca positioned at an elevated six o'clock position to *the Solace*.

They exit Oberon's atmosphere and different traffic control centers take control of directing their departure. The pilot of *the Solace* gives the go-ahead, and both ships engage their warp propulsion systems to begin the journey. Since *the Phantom* travels slower at warp than *the Solace*, Seneca sets the pace. At his maximum warp pace, they will reach Idalia in about two days, including an eleven-hour stretch through Malachi's Arm.

The first eight hours of the trip will take them through various Imperial systems with high levels of security. Seneca seizes this opportunity to retreat to his quarters, where he lounges on the couch and indulges in his private collection of old movies from his younger years. Periodically, *the Solace*'s pilot interrupts Seneca's movie binge with requests for correspondence. Eventually, it's time to return to the cockpit for the more dangerous portion of the trip.

Seneca occupies the forward pilot seat, combat gear ready. Inhaling deeply, he readies himself, setting the emergency survival system on standby for the long, eleven-hour trek through Malachi's Arm. Hours drag on, and Seneca remains focused on his task, fingers hovering over the "drop" switch, poised to reroute or drop from warp at the first sign of trouble. While he is confident in his combat abilities, *the Solace* has limited defense systems, and a pirate encounter could be perilous if he cannot respond swiftly. Hour by hour, time inches forward until they finally exit

45

Malachi's Arm.

The remaining twenty-nine hours of the trip take them through numerous independent systems, each with varying levels of security. Seneca spends most of this time in the cockpit prepared for any other threats that may arise, briefly stepping away for a four-hour rest. With Idalia now just two hours away, Seneca reflects on his conversation with Ilana from the evening she felt inclined to visit his ship. Inexplicably, he feels a sense of catharsis. It doesn't quite make sense to him. Revealing his pain had not been enjoyable, but Ilana's curiosity had left him contemplative. Her intentions were clearly well-meaning, perhaps warranting an apology and the possibility of continuing their conversation in the future. He isn't sure, though.

They soon arrive in Idalia, and the formation between *the Phantom* and *the Solace* disengage from warp travel. A red star at the center of the system bathes the cockpit in its light as they begin their approach to Idalia-15c. Comparable to Earth in size and gravity, this planet has undergone significant terraforming in the past sixty years. If someone were to fall asleep on Earth and wake up here, they would likely feel almost no difference, except for a slight drop in their weight. What they would see is a different story. Vast stretches of barren gray land dominate the planet's landscape, interrupted only by a handful of craters that have been converted into shimmering oceans and lakes, many with underwater cities to shield from the high levels of surface radiation. Data on the planet reveals a liquid iron core and an abundance of precious metal deposits scattered across its surface that composes the backbone of the system's economy.

The underwater city of Myanmar, their final destination, is nestled within a vast expanse of sea that was once a crater. On their approach to Idalia-15c, the system's traffic controllers guide them to Myanmar's spaceport, vectoring their formation to a safe landing. Seneca touches down first with *the Solace* close behind. Bathed in the crimson light of the summer sun in Idalia, the ship stands out with its radiant ivory pearlescent coating, exuding a robust beauty that demands the attention of all who pass by. Port workers scurry to position boarding stairs, while the faint hum of *the Solace*'s underbelly-mounted engines gradually fades away.

To ensure the safety of *the Solace* and its occupants, Seneca assumes control of a small team of port security agents to create a secure boundary. He efficiently delegates assignments, acknowledging the initial awkwardness of inexperience conducting the task—though leading is not a foreign concept. In no time, he has the landing pad secured, and Seneca signals *the Solace*'s pilot that Ilana is clear to exit.

"How was the trip?" Seneca asks Ilana and Serena as they trek down the stairs, offering friendly smiles and waves.

Ilana smiles in return and replies, "Good. Probably more cozy for us than you."

Seneca nods in agreement and assumes a six o'clock position to follow behind them. A common form of transportation, a rail-guided shuttle system is standing by to take the three of them down to the city. The shuttle's design is like most, resembling a sleek, transparent tube. It's reminiscent of an old bank's pneumatic system used to exchange deposits and withdrawals from a car to the teller, except on a much larger scale that transports twelve people at a time in place of mere currency. A single row of seats lines the interior of the tube in a horizontal arrangement, affixed securely to the floor.

Seneca and his fellow passengers sit in these seats, facing the transparent walls. As the shuttle door seals them inside the glass tube, it moves and gradually lowers into the crystal-clear sea. The vibrant glow from the city beneath dances through the water, painting mesmerizing patterns and hues across the transparent walls. Despite its wealth, the area, like many cities in the Idalia system, is experiencing an influx of refugees from Moniear that are posing a challenge for the local government. Myanmar has a very high cost-of-living index, and the people there are often seen as affluent, arrogant, and lacking empathy towards those who are financially disadvantaged (especially outsiders.)

The rail shuttle comes to a halt at the central shuttle station, revealing a sprawling underground chamber, skillfully hewn from the planet's own bedrock. The walls and floors of the space were smooth and polished, reflecting a rich, earthy color that showcased the exceptional craftsmanship involved in its creation. Embedded into the ceiling, the fluorescent lighting casts a gentle, blue glow that bathes the station in a comforting ambiance. The area serves as the bustling transportation hub for the capital, with a constant buzz of people coming and going filling the air. However, at this moment, their destination is just above them. A mere staircase separates the group from Myanmar Hall's entrance.

Ascending the stairs, they're met with the sight of Myanmar hall. The building itself is a grand structure. Like the bustling urban landscape surrounding it, the hall is constructed from meticulously polished red granite and embellished with intricate decorative stones. Serving as the epicenter of governmental power, it holds sway not only over the city but also over the entire star system of Idalia.

Following in the wake of Ilana and Serena, Seneca finds himself at the building's imposing entrance. The landing beside the street becomes a hub of activity above them, with paparazzi, news crews and Confederacy officials, setting the stage for an atmosphere charged with anticipation and formality. Amidst the chaos of camera flashes and a curious crowd, they finally reach their destination—the large wooden doorways where tranquility awaits. Stepping inside the building, ushers escort them down a series of hallways to a circular conference room that immediately captivates their attention. Sleek granite adorned with blue tinted glass composes the walls, giving the room a modern yet elegant feel. Several Confederacy officials are present, including the governor of Idalia. The governor, who had a rather unpleasant complexion, is a plump man with straw-colored hair and glazed blue eyes.

"This should be fun," Serena whispers as everyone takes their seats.

Seneca sits beside Ilana and takes a moment to admire the woodworking of the table—a long dark wood with a pretentious gold coral centerpiece bespeckled with sapphires.

"Let's get this started," the Governor says, addressing Ilana. "First and foremost, welcome to Idalia and Myanmar, Princess Ilana."

"Thank you, Governor," Ilana responds professionally.

The Governor's voice loses its warmth, becoming stern and condescending as he captures the attention of everyone in the room. He delves straight into the urgent matter of the Empire's rebellion and its wide-ranging consequences. While in the pretentious conference room, Seneca finds himself growing disinterested and drifting off during the discussion. He daydreams about the many star systems he has explored in his lifetime, finding fantasy more captivating than the realm of political discussions.

However, as the Governor and Ilana exchange dialogue, Seneca's attention immediately redirects when the governor rudely interjects and interrupts Ilana. He watches intently; It is increasingly clear that the Governor is less than willing to listen. The Governor's deep-seated anxiety resonates through his words as he details the strain the inundation of refugees is imposing on resources, infrastructure, and the local economy.

"I couldn't care less why refugees are coming here and I regrettably cannot overturn the asylum the Confederacy is granting, but these refugees are not my people and are here because of the Empire's failure to maintain control over their own." The governor shouts.

Amidst the charged atmosphere, Princess Ilana recaptures her moment to speak. Her voice, though gentle, carries a firm resolve as she steps into the spotlight of this high-stakes discussion. She acknowledges the Governor's concerns with a respectful nod, "Governor, I understand the strain that our citizens are placing on your society and assure this is no ploy to weaken your sovereignty, but there is nothing within my power to divert military resources to pursue non-combatant refugees out of Moniear, and you know as well as I do that the Imperial lords will certainly not divert military units from fighting the rebellion…"

She continues with a grace that commands attention, articulating the complexities faced by the Empire. Ilana draws attention to the harrowing tales of families torn apart, innocent civilians caught in the crossfire, and the overwhelming challenges of providing humanitarian aid to millions displaced by the conflict.

Seneca finds himself watching curiously with a hint of admiration, exchanging impressed glances with Serena. He's seldom interested in the realm of politics, but Ilana's ability to remain calm as she navigates the intricacies of diplomacy and conveys genuine empathy has him actually listening to pass the time. Amidst escalating tensions, she confidently employs an empathetic yet unwavering rhetoric, her body language speaking volumes about her unwavering position.

Sadly, the confederacy officials do not reciprocate his admiration for Ilana's words and remain unwilling to grasp the logic she endeavors to convey. The meeting draws to a close as Confederacy officials trickle out. Ilana and Serena finally stand up. Following their lead, Seneca rises from his seat to escort them when a hand taps his shoulder. Seneca turns to find the Governor standing behind him.

"You're Seneca Mason, aren't you?" the Governor inquires.

"Who's asking?" he inquires, annoyance on his breath as Ilana and Serena stand outside the door waiting for him.

The Governor shakes his head. "How'd you wind up on the Empire's payroll? I thought you were on our side!"

A puzzled expression flows over Seneca's face. With a side-to-side headshake, he responds, "Unless you follow American football or bear some relevant roots to the Blue Ridge Mountains on Earth, we share no common allegiance. Out here I go to the highest bidder."

"Hmph," the Governor snickers. "How noble."

Seneca dismisses the scowl of the Governor with little extra thought and walks out with Ilana and Serena. Myanmarian security guide them to a crowded exit of the building and they walk outside. The moment the news crews spot them, they waste no time in rushing the trio, their footsteps echoing urgently. The Governor's conversation had a negative impact on Seneca, leaving him with a distasteful feeling and no desire to shout at the paparazzi. He firmly grips his pistol, raising it with a deliberate motion, ensuring that it is set to fire blanks. Before anyone gets any closer, he fires three loud pulses into the air, startling everyone. The thunderous pulses reverberate through the air, making everyone nearby instinctively cower as the deafening shockwave leaves their ears ringing. Paparazzi scatter like chickens fleeing a fox in fear of further escalation.

Serena and Ilana look at Seneca in shock, rubbing their own ears. "Why though?!" Ilana says. "You're going to get us arrested!"

"Not likely. While y'all were chatting, I was reading through local news. Apparently, open carry and non-lethal fire were just legalized here to allow store owners to force refugees off their storefronts," Seneca smiles.

"This guy is growing on me," Serena says, patting Seneca's shoulder.

A look of unmistakable pride illuminates Seneca's face as he walks, a subtle swagger in his step. In contrast, Ilana seems completely defeated following the discourse of the political envoy, a stark contrast to her typically lively and energetic personality. This shift in her mood leaves Seneca wondering if maybe her demeanor on Oberon was actually the outlier, and this is the status quo. Delicate waves of curiosity pass through his thoughts, pondering if he should speak to her briefly.

The three of them head back to the station, with the girls going back to *the Solace* to wrap up their eventful first day in the city, while Seneca spends the evening alone on *the Phantom*. He finds himself deep in thought while his mind wrestles with conflicting desires. A part of him prefers the safety of maintaining elevated emotional defenses, maintaining a safe distance without getting involved. However, he's facing the sight of Ilana's somber state...

* * *

Her sullen expression reflected his previous wives on days they'd faced hardship. For instance, he recalls how Kelsea, with her unyielding resolve to cultivate plants in the challenging environment of space, would occasionally come back home feeling discouraged due to losing months of exhausting labor when plants would unexpectedly succumb to an unforeseen illness. A simple hug could instantly uplift her spirits on those occasions. He also reminisces about the emotional toll that Sophie endured when patients under her care would pass away. On those nights, Sophie would toil with guilt for hours and he would just hold her until she fell asleep. He cannot say why his mind is drawing those parallels, but it does, nonetheless. However, Ilana is a stranger to him, and it's a startling revelation that she echoes images of past lovers.

The second day of negotiations unfolds much like its predecessor, following the same ritual as before. They ascend the stairs to the conference room, and relentless news agencies and their eager crews unleash a barrage of camera flashes, accusations, and a relentless stream of questions. Ilana and the Governor exchange political jargon in the charged atmosphere of the familiar conference room, leaving Seneca somewhere between bored and bewildered for several hours, and evening casts its approaching shadow over the proceedings. Unlike the previous day, the evening shift of paparazzi maintains a wary distance today, refraining from attempts to get closer. It's not just the imposing presence of Seneca, but his pistol unholstered at the ready in a non-lethal mode, that keeps them at bay. Ilana looks completely and utterly defeated again, once more reigniting his memories. It makes it difficult for Seneca to ignore her plight.

Before she re-enters *the Solace* for the evening, Seneca calls out to Ilana. "Hey!"

She turns back, and Seneca tells her, "Cheer up. Tomorrow will be better. I promise."

She flashes Seneca a weak smile and says, "Thanks. I hope you're right."

The next morning marks their final day in Myanmar. An unmistakable air of tension hangs heavy in the atmosphere. Ilana, usually composed, appears visibly nervous as they ascend the imposing steps leading to Myanmar Hall from the shuttle station. Upon reaching the summit of the steps, the clamorous swarm of reporters and photographers immediately engulf them, hungry for any morsel of information or a scandalous snapshot. It's at this critical moment in time that Seneca takes control over the crowd, swiftly retrieving his pistol. Without hesitation, he discharges a series of blanks into the air. The sudden metallic ringing of plasma blanks startles not only the paparazzi but also the Myanmar security personnel, causing them to flinch momentarily. In the ensuing chaos, the once-bold reporters scatter like startled birds, their pursuit momentarily disrupted by the unexpected display of force.

"Sir," one of the security personnel begins, "I'm going to need—"
   "Kiss my ass," Seneca interrupts as he walks past the guard and holsters the pistol.

* * *

He glances back at Ilana, who tries to hide a smile, showing signs of increased confidence as a result of Seneca's dismissal of nosey onlookers. Seneca hopes to maintain this positive change. They exchange a swift glance, and he gives her a quick nod of encouragement. The Governor enters the scene as they walk into the conference room once more, pointing a finger at Seneca. "I should have you arrested."

Seneca squares his shoulders to address the Governor. "I didn't break any laws, so give it your best shot."

"Rules can be changed, Captain."

Seneca closes the gap between himself and the governor. He can see every pore on the governor's nose, filled with sebum, and in a hushed tone, he whispers. "I'm not sure you wanna make threats like that if you want to keep your military budget and infrastructure intact."

The Governor falls silent, bowing his head like a scolded pup.

"That's right, tubby." Seneca whispers angrily in the Governor's ear. "As far as I'm concerned, this whole situation is bullshit. Either change your amnesty policies, pay the funds to relocate the refugees, or better yet, help out by providing food, shelter, and stability to the less fortunate." Seneca motions to the Governor's seat. "However, I'm not a money hungry politician with an expiration date, so I'll let that be between you and Ilana, so sit your fat ass down and listen to the princess."

Seneca backs away and takes his seat as Ilana stands up, and the meeting begins. "Gentlemen, please excuse Major Mason," she flashes a quick smirk towards Seneca. "He's not a politician, nor is he expected to behave like one, and nobody in Imperial diplomatic endeavors takes kindly to threats. Now, in order to validate your concerns and take a degree of responsibility for the Empire's citizens, I am willing to negotiate, if you will listen."

During this round of deliberation and negotiations, a noticeable shift in demeanor sweeps over the COS government officials and the Governor. The once-frequent confrontations and contentious exchanges dwindle into sporadic mutterings, hardly audible above the otherwise smooth proceedings. The heated arguments that once punctuated the discussions are now conspicuously absent, replaced by a more cooperative atmosphere.

Seneca, despite his characteristic disinterest in politics, maintains a vigilant presence. He occasionally reserves his piercing glares for the Governor, who appears to be gradually transforming towards compliance. The summit concludes an hour earlier than the previous day, marking a pivotal moment in the negotiations. Under Princess Ilana's astute leadership, the COS has conceded their attempt to prevent war-stricken refugees entering their territories. The Empire's commitment not to allocate financial resources for the repatriation of refugees to Imperial-controlled territories remains steadfast. Likewise, the Empire will continue to refrain from pursuing rebel vessels beyond the boundaries of uncontrolled space, specifically within the domain of Malachi's arm.

* * *

However, in the spirit of cooperation, individual COS states will receive concession payments proportional to the number of refugees residing within their respective territories. This measure aims to alleviate the burden on host states and foster stability in the rebellion's wake. These outcomes reflect a small step toward resolving the ongoing crisis and reaffirm Ilana's commitment to a resolution suitable for the people she cares for. With an agreement signed and the diplomacy mission complete, Seneca, Serena, and Ilana exit the building, finding no paparazzi in sight.

Chapter 9: Comfort Food

With the trip ending, Princess Ilana is regaining her positive outlook, though there is still a hint of concern in her expression—which Serena acknowledges with a tight embrace. Seneca, too, feels drained from the toll of political negotiations, though from sheer boredom opposed to anything else. The shared exhaustion amongst the trio is unlikely to end here, considering the concessions Ilana has secured don't constitute a resounding victory for the effort expended. The entire purpose of the journey was for Ilana to assert the Empire's stance on refugees and the rebellion. Seneca doesn't know much about the Empire's political landscape, but he doesn't imagine they'll be pleased regarding the emphasis Ilana placed on the refugees. To defend her efforts and stance, she is now faced with the delicate task of explaining the concession payments to Imperial underwriters.

Seneca's stomach rumbles and gives him an idea. Believing to have a solution to the group's political fatigue, he pulls up a city guide containing details of noteworthy hotspots for visitation. He generates directions to a favored eatery of his and projects the menu in front of the two women, momentarily diverting their attention from their chatter. The holographic screen shows a delectable array of food served at a restaurant on the city's edge, with breathtaking views of the ocean as a picturesque backdrop.

"Let's grab a meal before heading back to the ships," he suggests, hoping a filling meal will lift their spirits.

Both Ilana and Serena sigh and relax at the sight of food, shedding some of the day's weight off their shoulders as a result of the invitation to embrace normality and step away from political dealings. They nod and follow Seneca through the rail-shuttle hub and board a different rail shuttle, heading for the northern end of the city. The restaurant, known as "Sammy's," is a creation of a fellow HLEP survivor who had served as a cook on the Mars colony and has never stopped honing his culinary skills.

* * *

However, Mars was not where Seneca and Sammy's paths crossed. Instead, they eventually met here at Myanmar station whilst Seneca was picking up a shipment of Myanmirian wine, enroute to smuggle it into the Empire. Sammy, upon meeting a fellow Earthling with roots from the Southern United States, immediately invited him to his restaurant and, as such, Seneca visits the establishment every time he finds himself in Myanmar.

"Sammy's" is an eatery that showcases exquisite craftsmanship, with its intricately carved features blending seamlessly into the city's aesthetic tapestry. Upon entering, an atmosphere of elegance and refinement immediately greets diners with round granite tables adorned with immaculate white linens and intricately crafted mahogany chairs that beckon patrons to sit and savor. But what truly captivates the senses is the dining area's pièce de résistance—a colossal fish tank that reigns as the room's majestic centerpiece. Within the transparent aquatic piece of art, an enchanting ballet unfolds as a diverse array of majestic sharks and graceful rays glide gracefully through the crystalline waters among thousands of colored fish. Their movements appear almost choreographed, a captivating dance set to the backdrop of soft strains of jazz music that gently caress the senses.

"This seems a bit high profile for you," Serena says to Seneca, examining the atmosphere.

Seneca gives an acknowledging nod as he says, "Sammy's an artist adapting to the tastes of the folks here, but he's also a fellow southerner, so he also knows how to cook *food* as well."

Seneca selects a table using a sleek tabletop kiosk at the entrance, and they make their way to an outdoor table where they sink into sumptuous chairs, hungry from the length of the day. Serena and Ilana both still boast confused faces regarding the level of establishment Seneca chose. The menu is a high-class array of steakhouse selections, with all dishes consisting of real, not synthetic, ingredients. However, Seneca is interested in something…less conventional…for the reach of the galaxy they're currently occupying while he scrolls down the menu and chooses the custom order button.

"Hey, let me handle the ordering. I have a special order here," Seneca says, typing out "Seneca's favorites." On the menu kiosk before the girls get too invested in the main menu selections.

"Sounds good," the two women reply in unison, curious to see what Seneca is talking about.

Sammy is absent; otherwise, his unmistakable southern hospitality would've surely welcomed Seneca and company upon receiving the order through the AI maître-d. It's rather unfortunate that Seneca hadn't had the pleasure of engaging in conversations with Sammy during previous missions to Mars. He would have enjoyed the distinct cadence of his southern heritage that rings dear in his speech, along with a culinary prowess that allows him to skillfully recreate the comforting flavors of the southern dishes Seneca grew up with. Homesickness was (and still is) rampant in Seneca's mind in those days and the friendship of another akin to him would have taken the proverbial edge off.

The AI maître-d acknowledges their order and sends them a notification, informing them that the food will be on its way shortly. Time passes smoothly while Seneca sits quietly among the chatting women as they wait. They don't have to wait in anticipation for much time. Soon an enticing array of custom-made dishes grace their table, presented family-style as if it were Thanksgiving. The ensemble of flavors is a heartfelt homage to Sammy's southern Alabama roots: crispy southern fried chicken, golden cornbread, the comforting scent of collard greens cooked in fatback with bacon and beans, flaky and buttery biscuits, a velvety white gravy speckled with sausage, hearty black-eyed peas, and the savory richness of salt pork. It's a feast that transcends mere sustenance with the smell alone enough to incite nostalgic memories of Seneca's grandparents, inviting the diners to partake in the cherished traditions of the American south.

"What's all this?!" Ilana and Serena exclaim, their eyes wide with delight. "It smells amazing."

"Just a taste of where I come from," Seneca replies, piling his plate high with food and using a biscuit to scoop up gravy. He quickly pours a glass of sweet tea to wash everything down. "I cannot describe how hard food like *this* is to find these days."

The three of them savor the meal while conversations about Seneca's hometown, Duluth, and visits to family in the smoky mountains flow freely, unhindered by Seneca's normal tendency to avoid such topics. He catches himself in the conversation and ponders his sudden lapse in character and blames the food for inducing nostalgia and coaxing him to be hospitable. Ilana asks questions, and Serena adds her characteristic sass. Shortly, Seneca realizes that he's *bonding* with others for a change…a dangerous notion.

Moonlight soon descends into the water's depths, refracting slivers of moonlight dancing onto the scene as they finish their dessert—a staple in southern cuisine, banana pudding with wafer cookies. The girls work carefully to conceal their full bellies with adjustments to their dresses, but eventually stand up, abandoning the hopeless task.

"I'm going to head back to the ship," Serena suddenly announces with a stretch. "Thanks for the food stick jockey. Earth folks know how to cook! Although the beans with black spots have a funny texture."

"Are you going to be alright? We won't be far behind," Seneca calls after her as she nearly exits the restaurant.

"Nobody wants to assassinate a political advisor!" Serena hollers back with a hint of well-intended sarcasm evident in her tone.

Seneca turns to find Ilana leaning on a railing of one of the restaurant's balconies, her gaze fixed on the moonlight dancing on the water's surface several hundred feet above them.

"If the Empire weren't... the way it is," Ilana says, her voice heavy with contemplation, "maybe people wouldn't need to flee. This rebellion wouldn't—I hate it..."

She lowers her gaze and lets out a sigh, as if holding back tears. Seneca inquires, "Is something on your mind?"

"Everything," Ilana replies. "There's just so much happening with the Whispers and the Empire. I want peace for the people, but I also... empathize with the change that the Whispers are fighting for." She pauses and her facial expressions morph as she thinks, as if she is choosing her next words carefully. "I'm not really supposed to speak out against the Empire, but I don't support the annexations, and I believe the Whispers are a natural consequence of our actions."

He doesn't know what to say, as he isn't well versed in this realm of politics. He still has no stake in the rebellion. However, he isn't enjoying seeing Ilana fighting against her own convictions. It's his firm belief that people should not hold back from supporting such things, but also, he's not a royal individual, so his ethos likely would not help her. Her face, laden with a sullen expression, continues to induce echoes of long-lost sentiments he'd felt toward his late wives. In an effort to shift the trajectory of her mood, he takes a deep breath, preparing to discuss the events of Ilana's recent visit to his ship. "Do you recall that night on my ship?"

Ilana looks up, still staring out into the ocean, and nods, prompting him to continue. "Talking to you about my past felt like a release. I'm sorry I pushed you away." He says softly, "and if your personality is enough to get through my thick skull, it's not unlikely you'll find the change you're looking for."

"Thanks," she mutters.

The two of them turn to face one another, their eyes locking together in a profound moment. In that intense locked gaze, everything else fades into the background, leaving only the two of them isolated in the moment. Ilana's captivating dark green eyes shimmer with a mesmerizing sparkle as the moonlight gently dances within them. Seneca's heart quickens as he feels a spark, subtly longing for a connection that's been missing from his life for far too long. It's as if their souls have found each other on the balcony, and during that brief moment, time stands still. Their gaze lingers for a short moment more, mystified, before reality pulls them apart. With a slight sense of hesitation, they both turn their heads and complete the moment. Ilana shifts her attention back to the boundless sea with a tinge of red on her cheeks, her thoughts hidden beneath the surface. Seneca follows suit, trying to reel in new intrusive thoughts surfacing within his mind.

Adjusting his train of thought, Seneca asks, "So, what's next on the agenda?" after realizing that he hasn't been informed of their upcoming travel plans.

Ilana's head shakes slightly. "Oh. Yeah. Shit. There's a 'peace' summit on Vista where I need to deliver a speech, and afterward, I'll be spending a few days at my family's mountain estate. You and Serena are invited and encouraged to join me."

"Seems like it's time for us to head back to the ships, then. I need to review our route and put together a security plan. Another eleven hours through Malachi's arm means I'll have to dig into the piracy reports to get an idea of recent activities."

Ilana nods, and the two of them stroll along the marble-lined avenue toward the rail shuttle stop, engaging in small talk as they traverse the town on the way back to the ships. Back at the port, Serena waves to them upon their arrival, and Seneca bids them goodnight. Without another word, they close the door to *the Solace*, and Seneca makes his way alone back to his own Vessel where he needs to prepare himself for another long journey through Malachi's Arm... and try to make sense of what just happened on the balcony.

Chapter 10: Minor Inconveniences

The next afternoon, another departure in a flight of two formation ensues. After approximately twenty-nine hours of travel, they find themselves entering Malachi's arm once again, where Seneca once more is taking great care to prepare for the difficult passage. He's well rested, well fed from leftovers from Sammy's, and ready. With his helmet on, he sits in the forward seat in the cockpit, ready for combat if necessary—a strong possibility. Reports from other escorts tell of heightened activity on the border of the arm and Imperial territories (likely due to the Imperial military focused on the rebellion as opposed to the border).

His ship's engine's hum softly, providing a familiar lullaby that has accompanied him on countless journeys through the vastness of space. Soft bluish light shimmering outside his canopy bathes the cockpit, creating a calm ambiance. His finger hovers over the "drop" switch on his stick just like before, a precautionary measure in case those with nefarious intent snatch *the Solace* out of warp. Hours pass as they delve into the pirate's playground. Time seems to stretch, causing minutes to drag on and feel like never-ending hours. Two passes through the arm and no activity? The Princess' ship should have attracted some attention.

Just as he thought the last two hours would pass uneventfully, without warning, *the Phantom* lurches and shudders. The ship's metal skeleton creaks under stress and the cloudy dark blue void that had enveloped the ship slowly gives way to the twinkle of distant stars returning into view. It's a disorienting sensation, the sudden transition from the warp's eerie tranquility to a harsh reality of normal speed, and the ship's inertial dampeners engage to bring him to a gradual stop. He's been pulled, but there's no time to dwell on the abrupt change of circumstances. He knows what happened, but a few seconds of "shock factor" set in the telltale sign of enemy fire against his shields readjusts his focus. Flashes of light and sparks shoot out as Seneca's shields deflect solid matter, while the ship's AI chimes in urgently, confirming that they are under fire.

Seneca's frustration boils over as he curses aloud, slamming the throttle to full power in an attempt to escape the predicament. *The Solace* is about to be attacked. Urgently, he broadcasts a message to the princess' ship, his voice tinged with urgency, "Full warp, full warp! I've been pulled!"

The response from the Solace's pilot comes swiftly, and it's equally grim, "Unable, we've been pulled as well, eight light-years from your coordinates. Taking fire."

"Shit!" Seneca curses as he turns his attention back to the adversary who seems intent on either distracting him or dying in the process of robbing him.

He relays another message to *the Solace*, "Make a jump if you can! Otherwise, it's scenario B, don't comply, keep all power in your shields and don't give him a shot at your engines!"

A disheartening silence follows his transmission from the other pilot. Seneca won't be able to assist them until he deals with the pirate who initiated this confrontation, since it's likely he will get pulled again if he tries to escape. With calculated efforts, he activates a booster charge that thrusts his ship forward, then cuts the throttle entirely while applying full back pressure on the control stick. The maneuver results in a rapid gain in distance and a swift turnabout, bringing him face to face with the opponent. He initiates a quick scan of the adversary's vessel, seeking any advantage he can find.

The attacker operates a sleek, small-class fighter that must have perched on a nearby asteroid like a predator ready to pounce with a warp disruptor that detected their convoy. Its glossy, green, and yellow hull gleams from the light of a nearby star. This ship is purpose-built for intercepting escorts like Seneca's, designed to render the actual target, *the Solace* in this case, defenseless to a more formidable craft. Seneca groans at the inconvenience while he sizes up his foe, acknowledging the superior speed and agility of the enemy craft. However, his confidence remains unmoved. His own vessel boasts greater firepower and sturdier armor, accompanied by Seneca's vastly superior skills. The enemy is not a threat.

Seneca broadcasts to the adversary in a confident bravado, "This is a warning. You're better off wiping your ass with sandpaper than pull me from warp again."

No reply comes from the enemy pilot, prompting Seneca to lock onto *the Solace*'s location and initiate a jump to warp. But just as his ship enters warp and accelerates, he feels the familiar shuddering reaction of *the Phantom* being pulled. Evidently, his warning fell upon deaf ears. This time, as his ship is returning to normal speed, Seneca quickly disables the inertial dampeners before the drop, allowing the laws of physics to send his ship spiraling in chaotic circles. He waits patiently for the target ship to come into view, and only when *the Phantom* has the target at its twelve o'clock position does he reactivate the dampeners and accelerate with full throttle toward the adversary.

He knew the foe would try to lure him into a chase, but the adversary wasn't anticipating Seneca's maneuver that closed the gap between them enough to facilitate missiles to lock on and negating a chance to evade. He fires two missiles without remorse or further warning: a thermal pulse round from his center-mounted missile hardpoint and a Penetrative Delayed Detonation missile (PDD) from the left side wing structure. The latter is designed to pierce armor and detonate inside the target, a weapon banned in most systems due to the bias to kill occupants of a spacecraft before they can eject an escape pod. It's a perfect armament in the lawless expanse of Malachi's arm.

The missiles race toward the enemy ship without prejudice. The thermal pulse round overloads his shields, bringing them down, and the second missile performs as designed. Seneca makes a broadcast to the pirate just before the ship is reduced to nothing more than bits of metal and debris.

"Wrong choice." Seneca remarks, remorseless.

Now that the distraction neutralized, it's time to tend to *the Solace*. Thankfully, its navigation beacon is still active and indicates the ship is still alive and well. Although the ordeal has only lasted fifteen minutes so far, for the pilot in the minimally armed executive travel vessel, facing a fully equipped pirate, it likely feels like an eternity.

With no delay, Seneca swiftly locks onto *the Solace*'s navigation beacon and jumps to warp. The jaunt passes swiftly, and he arrives on scene in less than a minute. *The Solace*'s pilot has done an impressive job maneuvering the ship. Though his tactic prevents him from fleeing, he's keeping the ship's target profile low by keeping the nose portion of the ship facing the main pirate vessel. It's an admirable performance for a pilot with no combat experience, but Seneca needs to take control and do it fast. *The Solace*'s still has its shields up, but the usual shimmering glow that accompanies the deflection of enemy fire is fading...

The assailant is typical of what one would expect from a pirate vessel, stolen and heavily modified to disable victims and relieve them of cargo. This large-class multipurpose ship dwarfs its victim with a bullet shaped silhouette that's roughly comparable in size to a small ocean cargo vessel. Its scarred paint speaks volumes about the countless battles it has endured. The ship is bristling with electromagnetic and thermal weapons designed to drain shields and piercing flak meant to damage engines and breach the pressure seal inside the ship.

"Shit, this sucks," Seneca mutters under his breath.

His ship's stealth features have allowed him to remain undetected thus far, with no weapons being directed towards him, but now he needs to attract enemy fire. Seneca locks onto the bridge of the large craft and launches two thermal pulse missiles directly at it. He broadcasts to both *the Solace* and the pirate, injecting a touch of humor into the tense situation, "Howdy folks, hope everyone has had their fun. I'll take over the laser and fireworks show from here." He pauses before addressing the pirate specifically. "I'm going to give you a chance to run before I embarrass you."

A reply echoes through his com radio from the pirates, "Ha! You won't be doing much in that bug-smasher."

"Are you aware of who you're talking to?" Seneca asks the pirate curiously.

"Should I be?" the pirate asks in reply, "Don't matter who you are. You don't have the firepower."

Seneca frowns and finds himself slightly disappointed. This individual obviously is a lone operator and must be rather new. Pirates aligned with factions like The Revenge of Teach or Brethren of The Cosmos would certainly recognize his ship on sight.

"Let's test your theory, shall we?" Seneca says with a chuckle.

Larger ships, such as his opponent, have difficulty turning because of their mass, and upgrading thrusters isn't worth the loss of cargo space for many pirates. Due to its limited mobility and arrangement of weapons on the forward end of the ship, it has a blind spot where its flak cannons and lasers won't be able to hit him. Seeing the weakness, Seneca charges full throttle toward the ship to exploit its weakness. He waits a few moments to see if the pirate was going to acknowledge him, but the pirate remains focused on *the Solace*. He quickly radios his ally with a specific instruction, "Full throttle forward. Keep him moving straight for me."

The Solace's pilot doesn't answer, but he complies with Seneca's instruction, turning the nose of the ship away and steadily increasing speed. Looking at the data he received from a previous scan of the princess' ship, Seneca believes its shields will hold long enough to bring the pirate's shields down. It's common knowledge that larger ships like the one Seneca is pursuing require multiple shield generators, often divided into segments. The pirates ahead will have to allocate power among propulsion, shields, and thermal weapons. With the Solace distancing itself, they'll need to divert power to their thrusters, weakening their shields in kind. If he positions himself at the rear of the pirate ship, they'll channel most of the remaining power to the rear shields, leaving the forward shields most vulnerable. His plan is to exploit this weakness by firing at the forward shields and force the pirate to abandon the chase or lose shield power and be a sitting duck for his PDDs.

Swiftly, Seneca maneuvers into the pirate's blind spot on the left side, adjusting his ship's orientation accordingly. He matches the enemy's speed without maxing out his throttle. Then, thanks to *the Phantom*'s thrust vectoring capabilities, he angles the nose of his ship toward the forward section of the pirate vessel and opens fire. The attempt to dismantle the forward shields presses on for ten minutes while Seneca keeps his beam lasers and guns firing non-stop. He monitors the pirates' shield integrity closely, thankful that the captain lacks situational awareness and hasn't noticed Seneca is not firing at the rear shields.

"You've got to bring down his shields soon!" The pilot of *the Solace* shouts over the comms. "We're at twenty percent with no charge banks left."

There's probably too much power left on the pirate's shields for his missiles to completely deactivate them, but the urgency of the situation gets the best of him, and he tries anyway, firing the last three of his thermal pulse missiles. He bows his head in frustration when the forward shields flicker but do not collapse entirely. Another scan reveals the pirate ship has finally redirected power forward, but with just enough power to keep the rearward shields limping, weakening both the front and rear shields. Unfortunately, he's run out of pulse missiles, and he'll have to get creative and do it quickly.

"Come on…" he whispers to himself, thinking.

Seneca then recalls the concept of parasitic draw. If energy fields of two ships overlap at differing power levels, the resulting effect is the smaller ship losing its own shields, but drawing power from the larger ship as the shield generator cannot distinguish between the two vessels at such a close distance. If he vents power (think of it like siphoning water into a drain) while the other ship's generator desperately tries to maintain power, its shields will drop extremely fast; a risky maneuver that necessitates only inches between him and the larger ship. However, Seneca flew closer to more unpredictable craft when he did formation flights in the Air Force, so he's more than comfortable to attempt it.

Closing the remaining distance carefully, his ship's shields immediately drop as the larger vessels' shields attempt to adopt the parasite, and he initiates the shield reboot to charge them off the larger ship's energy field whilst simultaneously venting incoming charge. He keeps up a steady barrage of laser fire to accelerate the energy drain from the pirate's remaining shields. He scans the pirate once more to find his plan is bearing fruit and the shields are steadily faltering.

"Okay, those shields should be down soon… give me a count of five and try a jump." Seneca instructs *the Solace*'s pilot over the comms. Then, he switches his radio to broadcast to the pirates, adopting a more persuasive tone. "I'll give you one last chance to walk away. If you pull *the Solace* from warp when they try, I'll ensure you reunite with your buddy so the two of you can talk about how you both died making the same dumb decision."

Mocking Seneca, laughter emanates from the pirate's radio as *the Solace* attempts to jump to warp, and the arrogant criminal promptly pulls it back.

Seneca sighs, "Alrighty then."

Seneca continues to vent power from his shields while leeching off the energy of the larger vessel, and within thirty seconds, he completely depletes the pirate's shields. He falls back and ascends above the pirate vessel, targeting the aft end of the pirate ship's bridge with his PDDs. He fires all five, starting at from the bridge at the rear to the forward section of the ship, before the enemy's lasers can retaliate. Seneca relays a final message as the deadly missiles home in on their target. "Wrong choice, assholes."

A spectacular series of explosions that tear the pirate ship apart abruptly silence a response on the radio, sending debris scattering into the void of space.

* * *

Cheers echo in the background of the radio when he hears *the Solace*'s pilot shout "Nice job, saved our asses in here!"

It's another victory for Seneca and a unique opportunity to show his skills off to his employer. However, Seneca is not the type to bask in victory for very long, especially since the Solace's navigation beacon could draw attention from pirates up to thirty light-years away...

"Let's get going," Seneca says, returning to formation and jumping back to warp alongside *the Solace*.

The remainder of their journey out of Malachi's arm unfolds without further incident, and they find safety once again within Imperial-controlled space. Seneca takes the opportunity to rest, sleeping through most of the trip until the final hour when he awakens to exit warp and guides his ship into Vista. Imperial traffic controllers coordinate their descent, leading both ships to a safe landing at Capital Space Port not far from Vista Capital, the bustling heart of Vista and the Empire.

As *the Solace*'s doors open, Ilana and Serena rush down to greet Seneca, who awaits them at the bottom of the secured landing area. Serena maintains her trademark composure, offering genuine praise sarcastically for Seneca's impressive kill. Ilana, though dearly thrilled, restrains her excitement in the presence of Imperial onlookers. She engages Seneca in a discussion of recent events, expressing gratitude and admiration for his expert piloting skills. The pilot of *the Solace*, who also performed admirably, also steps forward to extend a sincere handshake to Seneca, commending him on their victorious endeavor. Seneca is slowly earning a place in the group, and he can't help but feel a sense of accomplishment amidst the nervousness of his slow growing attachment.

Chapter 11: Free lesson In Politics

Ships come and go filling the air of Capital Spaceport with the roaring sound of rockets and the smell of burning hydrogen. Seneca's arrival in his rogue vessel perplexes concerned security personnel, especially considering his non-standard uniform displaying an Imperial rank. However, they promptly take notice of Princess Ilana. She confidently steps forward, her demeanor commanding respect as she produces the necessary credentials to alleviate their...concerns regarding Seneca's presence. A bustling scene of organized chaos surrounds the docked ships as Imperial workers conduct thorough inspections, refuel the vessels, and restock supplies in preparation for future expeditions.

At the west end of the expansive landing pad, bathed in the warm glow of the planet's white sun, a sleek cyan limousine with exquisite golden accents sits ready to transport the group. Sensory evidence of fast-paced city life around them fills the air while they walk across the port. Skyscrapers pierce the horizon. The general hum of urban ambiance dominates the soundscape between the arrival and departure of various ships and monorails.

  Inside the limo, crimson leather seats with gold stitching create a lavish atmosphere as the group enters the vehicle. Two bench-style seats line the walls, with Ilana and Serena taking the left side, while Seneca opts for the right. The limo embarks on its journey through the city of Vista Capital to the Imperial palace, where Ilana is scheduled to speak the following day. The road meanders through the suburbs outside Vista Capital, bordered by meticulously maintained golf courses and bermudagrass lawns groomed with crisscrossing cut patterns before giving way to the urban landscape of downtown Vista Capital. Exotic birds, including parrots and gouldian finches, take flight from the variety of carefully selected hardwood trees that decorate the city streets as the limo passes beneath them. Vista (the namesake of the founding Imperial colony) lacks its own native flora and fauna, despite its Earthlike capacity to support terrestrial life. Consequently, the introduction of a multitude of exotic and brilliantly colored creatures adds to the picturesque beauty of the planet—even in urban backdrops that Seneca doesn't care for.

When Seneca and company arrive at the Imperial palace, sitting in the city's epicenter, Seneca is immediately struck by its pretentious architectural design. The palace soars to an impressive sixteen stories, with gracefully curving sides that converge into a triangular roof. The palace's exterior, crafted from pristine ivory-white stones, radiates a cloud-like sheen. Intricate carvings and sinuous patterns adorn every inch of its surface, gracefully winding around the towering entrance columns. Standing before this ornate structure, a realization of his many imaginings about what an Imperial palace would look like rests before him.

Upon stepping out of a limo, the familiar sight of paparazzi swarming around greets them with cameras flashing and a barrage of unintelligible questions. Seneca wastes no time and signals another Imperial security agent to help him create a protective barrier, "look sarge, you see this, make this better. I want at least 10 feet between Ilana and the nearest camera." He says.

The sergeant sneers, "Listen Major, you're new here—",

"Quiet," he flashes a sly grin toward Ilana "I'm her private security and I don't like the risk that large crowds present,"

The sergeant makes another face at him. Obviously taking commands from an outsider, especially one known for his efficiency at disrupting Imperial interests, doesn't sit well with the sergeant and his subordinate Imperial security agents, leading to a heated argument amongst the group and testing Seneca's waning patience.

"We couldn't keep these folks back, anyway; they're all media overseen by Imperial lor—"

He's cut short by unmistakable loud buzzing thunder reverberating out of the firearm gripped in Seneca's hands. The action of weapon fire garners a similar response as it did in Myanmar; The paparazzi scatter in fear, creating a path, and the guards react with surprise.

He holsters his plasma weapon with a noticeable eye roll before he shouts, "No more!" in a manner reminiscent of an army drill sergeant or Air Force MTI. "If anyone wants an audience with the princess, they can make an appointment! No more of this swarming bullshit!" He points at the sergeant once again. "I want a ten-foot escort around us. Now! Let's go! Hurry up!"

The security agents are confused at first but have the intelligence to respect the sight of a weapon in an outlaw's possession. They begrudgingly comply and help Seneca establish and maintain a ten-foot radius around the entourage as they make their way from the palace steps. Ilana taps Seneca's shoulder and smiles, saying, "I really don't mind them all that much."

Seneca whispers back to her as they approach the opening palace doors, "Yeah, but I do."

She nods while trying to conceal a flood of red into her cheeks, and Serena pats Seneca on the shoulder, saying, "Good boy, I'd give you a treat if I had one."

They enter the palace into the atrium of its grand hallway. The massive corridor of the palace stretches expansively, its high cathedral ceilings soar above them, adorned with intricate silver accents. Seneca walks along emerald-colored tiles that pave the floor of the palace, each step resonating with a soft echo. The walls display a cacophony of artwork, hosting various painted masterpieces and portraits that chronicled the history of the Empire along with AI rendered pieces that Seneca hardly considers art. Their journey leads them to a spacious circular room with a domed ceiling, also adorned with pastel colored artwork, where Ilana releases a relieved sigh. "I need to meet with the lords to discuss the Myanmar negotiations for a while," she explains and turns her attention to Seneca. "Serena can give you a tour of the palace—show you whatever you'd like to see."

Before Seneca can utter a word or offer a wave, a group of dignitaries dressed in impeccably tailored business suits meet and escort Ilana. Their attire gleams with hints of cyan and gold, echoing the traditional colors of the Empire. Judging by their demeanor and lack of formalities extended to the party, they must be Imperial lords. Seneca can't help but frown, a quizzical expression forming on his face as he watches the procession. He mutters to Serena in a low voice to avoid being overheard, "Shouldn't the lords answer to her? Why should she have to explain anything?"

"Ha!" Serena chuckles. "Cute idea. Anyway, looks like it'll be you and me for a bit. Wanna go make out?"

Her suggestion takes Seneca by surprise. "What?!"

Serena laughs at Seneca's reaction, saying, "Please. You can fly fancy, but trust me, you aren't my type. Anyway, I'll show you around a bit. This place is enormous, and since you can't fly through it, you're likely to get lost."

Seneca's heart rate steadies, and Serena takes the lead in guiding him through the lavish palace. Their tour traverses through the palace's notable locations, each branching off from the grand central hall. Serena begins with the awe-inspiring dining room, adorned with exquisite teak and mahogany furnishings crafted by Earth's Amish craftsmen. Breathtaking crystal chandeliers that cast an enticing luminous glow illuminate the room.

Next on the tour is the palace library, a bibliophile's theme park. Towering shelves stretch across at least three stories, housing an impressive collection of mint-condition, collectible books- none of which are intended for reading since oils from the hands could stain the ancient pages. The aroma of aged parchment and leather bindings fills the air, adding to the library's unique ambiance.

Serena's tour takes him through other rooms such as the study, kitchen, and other such areas, each as extravagant and pretentious as the one before. As their exploration ends, Serena leads Seneca to the guest quarters wing. With a blasé gesture, she points out his room and extends an invitation to join her in her own quarters, trying to burn some time. Seneca attempts to refuse, but Serena insists.

"Come on, I promise I'll behave," she says.

* * *

He obliges without further resistance, if only for conversation after a long duration of time confined inside *the Phantom* alone. They enter her room and Serena wastes no time making herself comfortable. She flops down onto her invitingly cozy bed, a well-kept nest of plush pillows and fuzzy purple blankets and stretches her arms out. Seneca takes rest on a recliner positioned strategically by the window, where the warm sunlight gently spills into the room from the cyan stained glass. Her space is a chaotic blend of personal effects, a multitude of flowers mingling with carefully chosen designer furniture and tasteful decorations that add character and warmth to the ambiance.

"Do you live here?" Seneca inquires, looking around the room.

"Ugh, basically," Serena responds, tossing a stress ball into the air and catching it. "Lately I'm always here or on the stupid yacht. However, I actually live with my family on the other side of the mountains. I have my own cottage on our estate and such. My father is a real-estate baron, and we live on an eight-hundred-acre polo horse ranch. Despite being rich, they're pretty grounded, and I miss them quite a bit when I'm on the road."

Seneca asks, "So how'd you wind up in politics?"

"I've been Ilana's advisor for eight years now, but I've known her since I was in school. She and I went to the Imperial Leadership Academy together. At the time, I had just turned nineteen, and she was like a bazillion years old… Apparently, her parents don't really push her to do things. She just kinda does whatever. WHY she chooses to do this political stuff is beyond me…" Serena says before she continues to ramble. "Not like they're going to die anytime soon and need her to take over…"

Seneca nods in agreement as Serena delves deeper into the princess' political involvement. She reveals the princess ventured into Imperial politics to compensate for her parents' largely ceremonial roles, much like the crown was for England and other extinct Earthly nations. While her parents held prestigious titles, the actual governance within the Empire rests with the lords who act as territorial managers. These lords follow standardized procedures for managing their territories. This includes appointing governing bodies and ensuring the allocation of resources and funds for vital services such as security, healthcare, and employment, all operating under a socialist system. In cases where a territory turns a profit, the lords claim any monetary surplus beyond the necessary capital required to sustain the territory, paying a flat thirty percent tax on those profits to the central Imperial government. Meanwhile, the royal family concentrates on diplomatic negotiations, international relations, and other non-ruling tasks.

"The entire freakin' galaxy loves Ilana, so she goes all over the place running diplomacy errands for the lords. But shit really kicked up when the rebellion started. Now we are constantly traveling or are stuck in the palace," Serena concludes, looking a bit exasperated. "I'd give a year's salary at this point to just have a week *home*."

Seneca offers a disapproving grunt.

* * *

"That's it?" Serena retorts, glancing at him and sitting up from her nest of pillows. "You don't have anything to say? I spend all that time explaining Imperial politics, and you just grunt? Fucking rude."

"Sorry, I told you both before. I don't play political games," Seneca chuckles.

"Your behavior on Myanmar communicates a different message. Plus, if you keep being a heroic badass, they'll probably give you fucking lordship," Serena scoffs, flopping back down. "That'd help Ilana a shit ton having at least one lord on her side…"

"Lordship? Elaborate," Seneca urges in a confused tone.

"Holy shit, dude," Serena groans as she once again provides Seneca with the necessary exposition. It's no secret that he is a well-renowned and feared pilot in the galaxy, known to anyone who follows the news. His career is littered with transgressions against galactic law levied by the three superpowers (and even the Orinians). He is yet to be seen throwing direct support in favor of any government, let alone the Empire. If Seneca stays in his role, lords will come to believe that Ilana has won him over to their side, as opposed to the rebels.

"Clearly, they still don't understand who I am then." He says pulling out his pen from his pocket and clicking it nervously, "I don't do politics. I don't take sides. I'll do something for a bit and move on."

"You say that now, but." She tweets.

"But what?"

"You're dense, just at least pretend to play a part of the game and it'd help Ilana out."

"How would it help—"

"Buddy, you said yes to this job and you're already playing the game like it or not. Take the ride until it ends or hop off sooner as opposed to later, but don't make waves. Ilana has enough to deal with taking care of this stupid rebellion and she's doing—never mind," she groans once more, dropping the stress ball.

Her outburst confuses him and is once more veering in a direction that necessitates personal commentary, so Seneca decides it best to change the subject and discuss other matters in the meantime. Hours pass by, and eventually, he makes his way to his quarters. The king-sized bed in the room is adorned with soft, cyan-colored velvet sheets, and a large window offers a view of the forest on the eastern side of the palace. Distant squawking of macaws intermingles with the urban soundscape as Vista's sun begins its descent below the eastern horizon. It makes for a suitable backdrop for the sea of questions in his mind. Is he in too deep? Is this the type of adventure he needs to be involved in? Is he over his head.? These questions pester him as the night descends upon him.

Chapter 12: A Royal Retreat

The following day, the palace courtyard is bustling with people and news crews as they gather to listen to Ilana's upcoming address regarding the rebellion. Incoming recent news about the rebellion has everyone riled up. Yesterday, there was another failed attempt by the Whispers to liberate another newly annexed system. The Empire maintained control over the system, but it suffered heavy military losses, including many young men recently drafted. The lords want to ease the concerns of the citizens regarding what they call madness and want Ilana to incorporate a response to these events into her speech right before going on stage. Their demands for last-minute alterations for the peace summit are causing Ilana some stress.

She's tucked in the palace. Meanwhile, Seneca closely collaborates with security to vet everyone attending the event and clear the area of any potential dangers. Snipers positioned in various locations carefully monitor the area, prepared to intervene if someone attempts to harm Ilana. Once the scene is locked down, Seneca stays by Ilana's side as she prepares to take the stage. Her face betrays her annoyance regarding the last-minute revisions to her script but begins her speech with eloquence and charisma.

"My fellow citizens, today we gather to reaffirm our allegiance to the Empire, founded as a bastion of stability and beacon of hope in a galaxy plagued by chaos. Yet, as we stand united in our devotion, let us not forget those who have strayed from the path. The Whispers, misguided though they may be, are not our enemies but our lost brethren, yearning for purpose and direction that can be provided by our glory. It is in their struggle that we find the seeds of change, the whispers of a new dawn. For in their defiance lies the spark of revolution, a silent plea for justice and equity. Let us, therefore, extend not just our hands, but our hearts, since we as a nation will need to aid those who walk the shadowed path, for in their quest for truth, they may yet illuminate the way forward for us all."

* * *

Her words captivate the crowd, and they cheer along when she pauses. She wastes little time moving seamlessly through an hour of speaking until her speech concludes "Together, with unwavering resolve, we shall guide our lost Empire in its entirety back to the light of peace, and in doing so, pave the way for a brighter future for all. As we stand on the precipice of change, let us not forget the sacrifices made by the brave souls in the recent battle for righteousness, both Imperial patriots and brave opponents alike. Their valor shall be forever etched in our hearts as we march forward, hand in hand, towards a swift and lasting peace."

The crowd erupts in applause as she thanks everyone for attending and exits the stage.

"Not bad," Seneca says to her, leaning in to offer a hand to assist her descent down the steps.

"I suppose," she responds, walking back into the palace with him and Serena, "now I have to put my money where my mouth is…"

He'd like to tell her he understands, but he knows all too well that he doesn't. Especially considering what Serena explained, he doesn't truly comprehend the options available to the princess. She can't deploy Imperial combat units; only the lords can. She can't sign a peace treaty; only the lords possess that authority. There doesn't seem to be any alternative for her but to speak positively, and he can observe the frustration on her face as she acknowledges these limitations.

"I've got to make some calls, and we'll have some time to relax on my family's mountain estate."

Ilana heads back to her quarters in the wing of the palace where the royal family resides, the sound of her high heels tapping the tiles echoes through the grand corridor. Serena approaches Seneca as his gaze examines Ilana's…departure whilst the soft glow of the chandeliers above casts warm pools of light on the hall.

Serena leans on him, applying weight onto his shoulder and causing his left side to dip. "Whatcha starin' at?" she asks, her voice a low, sardonic whisper that contrasts with the formality of the surroundings.

Mild embarrassment creeps and Seneca pivots his head back and forth, replying, "Nothing. Why?"

Serena bursts into laughter and says, "Figured you were enjoying the view."

Seneca isn't sure if Serena is joking or if she genuinely caught him in the act of examining Ilana's backside as she walked away. "Lighten up," she says, standing upright and playfully shoving him. "I don't blame you; her tush is a ten, anyway go do security guard shit. The limo should be arriving in a few minutes."

Indeed, only a short time passes when once again Seneca finds himself in the girl's company in the limo; on this occasion, traveling to the royal family's mountain estate. The picturesque countryside that occupies the view outside the window slowly gives way to rolling hills and thick hardwood forests. The road winds more and more. Rolling hills melt into mountain slopes and turnpikes, causing the occupants to list from the sharp turns. It's hard not to enjoy the view while Serena and Ilana talk about rebellion politics and potential diplomacy targets for coming endeavors.

The limo comes to a halt on the driveway paved with white pea gravel, the soft crunch of the gravel signaling their arrival. Before them stands a large wooden home, a plantation-style cabin painted in an elegant ivory hue—a color that the entire royal family evidently favors. The front of the house showcases a symmetrical design, framed by meticulously arranged rectangular decorative bushes, enhancing the property's aesthetics.

They step out of the limo, and the expansive covered area where it has parked provides shade and a sense of welcome. Trees and forest surround the entire area's front yard that slopes gently, offering a graceful approach to the impressive cabin. In contrast, the backyard has a sheer drop off that gives way to an impressive sight through the trees below. Beyond the cabin, a sprawling landscape unfurls, revealing an expansive view of an untouched mountain range with blue sky outstretched. Unspoiled peaks and valleys stretch as far as the eye can see, a breathtaking scene of nature. It is a place of serene magnificence, where time seems to slow, and nature's grandeur is on full display. Fresh scents of hardwoods and pines float along the breeze carrying a sensory reminder of his Earthly home. Unable to resist the lure of the clean mountain air, he audibly draws in a deep breath before he sighs, "This place is beautiful."

Ilana footsteps crunch in the gravel as she walks behind him and replies in her bubbly voice. "Yes, it is. This is literally my favorite place in the galaxy. I love the clean, fresh air. The peace, and the—"

"Mountains," Seneca says, finishing her sentence, a hint of shared appreciation in his voice.

"Yeah," Ilana sighs in response.

Once the limo driver unloads their bags and drives off, something unexpected happens. Ilana stumbles into Seneca as if someone pushed her. It isn't difficult to discern who the culprit is since she is currently running away from them.

Attempting to regain her balance, Ilana calls out, "Serena!"

Serena, laughing mischievously, darts into the house. Seneca helps Ilana regain her balance as she shouts at Serena, "I can't run in these stupid heels, Serena! Get back here!"

With Ilana back on her feet and chasing after Serena, Seneca walks into the cabin's foyer. The sound of rushing footsteps and friendly yelling between the girls echoes down the staircase from the floor above. Seneca examines the antiquated interior. He can't help but think, *"Byron is really showing his Wilmington roots..."*

By modern standards, the interior of the cabin possesses an ancient charm that contrasts with the high-tech environments most are accustomed to in the galaxy. Aged, dark stained wooden floors complement the pristine white shiplap walls perfectly. Pictures adorn the walls, seemingly placed there personally rather than by a professional decorator. Many of these photos, featuring Ilana as a blue-haired child engaged in various childhood activities with her parents, have gracefully aged over time. Brass antique frames hold these old pictures behind aged glass, giving the room a nostalgic ambiance. A faint scent of wood and well-preserved memories lingers in the air, and the occasional creak of the wooden floorboards adds to the rustic atmosphere.

The living room is spacious, featuring a grand stone fireplace against one wall. It makes for a rustic presence awaiting the chance to endear the room with firelight and the smells associated with clean burning logs. The large rectangular windows, adorned with southern themed curtains, frame breathtaking mountain views, seamlessly integrating the natural beauty into the room's aesthetic. A plaid sofa with hand-knit blankets sits opposite the fireplace. Next to it, a matching love seat offers an equally comfortable spot to relax.

On the left, an arched doorway leads to a cozy dining room, complete with an antique dining set. The table, made of rich mahogany, bears the marks of time and tradition, while the high-backed antique chairs have cushions loosely tied to them, adding to the "down-home" aesthetic of the dining experience. Above, a brass chandelier dangles, casting a soft, golden glow over the room.

Amidst the girls' continued playful shouts from the floor above, Seneca proceeds with his exploration of the cabin. The kitchen, humble for a vacation home designed for Imperial royalty, exudes warmth and simplicity. Wooden counters outline the room, and feature a traditional dual basin sink by a window looking into the backyard. An old-fashioned fridge, its enamel surface gently worn, stands next to a blackened wood-burning stove. The space resonates with a rare and authentic, down-to-earth feeling that Seneca wouldn't have expected to see so far from Earth.

 Ilana appears at his side quietly. He turns to her and comments, "Your dad hasn't completely lost his touch with his roots. This place reminds me of my grandparents' place in the smokies."
    She nods, a thoughtful expression on her face. "He tries to stay grounded... I remember stories he'd tell me about playing outside when he was a child. I can't believe it's the same universe," she gives a momentary pause. "The things that the Empire is doing... I think..." She pauses again, choosing her words carefully. "Let's just say some stories he used to tell about his hometown and the way people treated each other where he grew up convey different values than the actions of Imperial lords."

Seneca remains silent, taking in the surroundings. Ilana continues, "We used to come here a lot, but about twenty years ago, we stopped, or at least mom and dad did. I'm not sure what happened, but I know dad had a huge argument with the Imperial lords. Since then, he's just been angry and frustrated all the time. Mom won't tell me why... she's never been very forward and seems to want to protect me from something. I hardly see her anymore, and I hate it."

Pausing for another moment, she takes another deep breath. "I come here when things get to be more than I can handle."

Seneca empathizes with her and says, "Can't say I blame you."

Serena finds them and interrupts their conversation, shouting "Ilaaaanaaa" as she descends the stairs.

Ilana responds in kind, "Sereeenaaaa."

Serena explains that her family is in town, a couple of hours away, and she wants to spend a few days with them before returning to her duties. Ilana agrees, and the three spend time in the living room before Serena's ground transportation arrives. After she's loaded up and ready to leave, the group exchanges temporary goodbyes. During this farewell, Seneca and Serena share a brief...communicative glance. Serena playfully raises her eyebrows and gestures toward Ilana with her pupils, making kissing faces and winking exaggeratedly. Seneca, in response, furrows his brow and shakes his head slightly, silently communicating that he doesn't approve of the teasing.

He finds Ilana to be warm company. She's beautiful, kind, and very intelligent. Tactful, yet bubbly in her interactions, Seneca can see himself slowly making friends with someone like this. However, friendships are dangerous and romantic actions perpetuated by Serena's playful attitude are even more so... Does she do this to Ilana as well? This might turn out to be an awkward weekend.

Their exchange of glances evolves into a silent conversation as they share amused expressions and mouthed words. Serena's embrace with Ilana seems to extend longer than expected, giving them more time for their non-verbal exchange. Finally, when it's Seneca's turn to say goodbye to Serena, he offers a friendly and professional farewell. Serena steps into the car sending more mouthed sentiments, met with playful hand waves from Seneca, as if he were swatting away her teasing.

Chapter 13: Fire Hazard

Seneca finds himself alone with Ilana in the living room, their voices filling the empty space left by Serena's absence. They've been chatting for a while and there's been a subtle, yet noticeable shift in Ilana's behavior. She holds eye contact longer than usual. Sometimes she'll stumble over her words and get flustered to the point of blushing—unusual for someone known for her ability to articulate. She almost seems nervous to talk about herself and childhood without Serena around. As such, he can't help but wonder about the mysteries of Ilana's thoughts and what may be occupying her mind.

The longer they talk, the more out-of-the-ordinary her behavior becomes. Her usual animated demeanor shines through as she enthusiastically recounts stories from her past. However, conversational focus shifts to the present day, her energy noticeably wanes. Now, he cannot help but feel she is holding some detail back, especially when the topic of the rebellion comes up. He's curious.

"So, what's your role in handling the rebellion specifically?" Seneca asks her, "You get sent by the lords to negotiate, but you can't technically promise anything?"

"It's—complicated, well, I mean it is, but it isn't..." she replies, making the same face Seneca makes when he's trying to avoid a question. "Everything I do is for the people. All the citizens, which includes the Whisp—well, not them, but the citizens in the territories they're trying to protect."

"You're the only Imperial I've met who sees it that way," Seneca remarks. "Most regard them as traitors."

"Laws they didn't vote to follow make them traitors, and I don't think that's fair. They deserve a voice."

"I suppose..." He replies.

Throughout this part of their dialogue, Ilana hasn't made eye contact, but she's also listening intently for Seneca's perspective. Almost as if evaluating him. "What about you? You said you had no stake in the rebellion. Now you seem to care about mine?" She asks.

***

"Well, I was on an Imperial ship, surrounded by Imperial security guards, without my pistol. I thought I was being trapped." He chuckles. "Truth be told, I empathize with the rebels. I'm not big on government. Somebody I don't know gets to tell me how to live my life? For the Whispers, it's worse. They have their government that works for them and then the Imps—"

"Imps?" she inquires.

"It's what us ICs and pirates call the Empire."

"I know. I just never heard you talk like a rebel before," she says, smiling.

"Officially no, but I've done a lot of pro bono work helping the Whispers in the past few years. It's a matter of principle, I guess."

"So, you just pretend not to care?"

He doesn't have a reply and prompts him to think—it's a true statement, but it's only half true. He cares on principle, but he doesn't have a compelling reason to take a stand. At least not yet. His silent reaction prompts Ilana to adorn a curious smile on her face, and his gaze affixes to it. She notices and blushes, bites her lips and looks down. "*Fuck... she likes me...*" He says to himself, and nagging intrusions encourage his thoughts to return to Myanmar... Was that moment something significant? Or a singular occurrence? Did Ilana experience it too? What exactly is he getting into?

Ilana chuckles and claims she just remembered a story about a time when she and Serena got lost on a horseback riding excursion on Serena's ranch, a story that changes the subject and occupies the remainder of the evening. A check of his UniCom reveals how late it is and Ilana shows him to his room.

He lays down but he can't sleep. Questions bid him to toss and turn as he lays down, and all he can think about is Ilana's face. This woman... has him asking dangerous questions to himself. There's something enthralling about her, and he wants to know more. Is it time to let go of his past and embrace the future? Are his attempts to be solitary just lies he tells himself? Can he really keep walls around his heart forever? These questions... have answers. He could ponder them all night, but he's too stubborn or too prideful to embrace them... After several hours of tossing and turning, the sun rises, filling the quaint room with light.

He didn't get a good look at it the night before on account of it being dark, but there doesn't seem to be much to look at in the small room. The tall four post bed frame occupies most of the room's surface area. Pictures hang on all four walls, and a small dresser sits under a window across from the foot of the bed. It gives him the same feeling he had when his family would stay at a distant relative's house, so he doesn't waste much time trying to sleep longer and he heads downstairs.

The smell of bacon and cooking eggs floats up from the bottom floor. He follows the scent to the kitchen to find Ilana struggling through an attempt at cooking—scraping stuck eggs off a stainless-steel pan while hot bacon grease shoots at her. She's still dressed in pajamas, her hair isn't done, and she's got a pair of house slippers on her feet. It's the most adorable thing he's seen in over one hundred years. She squeaks as molten oil hits her hand, causing her to drop the pan and litter the floor with both raw and burned eggs. She catches him in her peripherals as she stoops to clean up the mess.

"Oh shit, good morning," she says, slightly embarrassed. "I figured I'd uh try cooking breakfast."

Seneca chuckles. "Want some help?"

"Sure." She says.

He grabs a broom from the nearby closet and helps sweep the eggs while Ilana focuses on the precarious task of handling the (slightly burned) bacon. After he finishes cleaning, he helps her start over with making eggs, making use of the extra bacon grease to keep them from sticking. Cooking is not a familiar task to most in the galaxy. Modern food processors make the time-consuming task irrelevant for most families. Those who do still cook do it as a profession to serve people who will pay for the novelty of a handmade meal. It's unsurprising that Ilana has had little practice in the realm. Seneca isn't great at it either, but he can manage his way around bacon and eggs. Once the meal is ready, they sit down to enjoy the fruits of their labor.

"Don't worry. Cooking gets better with practice. Daddy said Mama used to burn everything their first year of marriage." Seneca says, trying to encourage Ilana. "My mom grew up with a single dad who didn't really cook."

"I've cooked a couple times with my parents, but it's been so long," Ilana replies and takes a sip of coffee.

"I remember your mom used to make burgers for everyone when I worked with them on Mars… She jokingly denied me one once when the Panthers and Falcons played."

"I can't even imagine that."

"What her cooking burgers?" Seneca asks.

"No." She answers. "Being a normal person. Not royalty."

She makes another face like she had the previous evening when their conversation had shifted to the rebellion. It's an interesting experience to see royalty stripped down to a normal person. Something that he used to be before he became a renegade pilot. They finish breakfast with other small talk before Ilana takes Seneca around the estate for a tour. The property spans over two thousand acres, offering captivating views and scents of fresh water drifting through the breeze. One point of interest on her tour is a group of caves at the base of a roaring waterfall, surrounded by the silent woods. It's been several hours of walking the scenic property and he's taken notice that her behavior from the previous night has persisted into the present afternoon.

Nothing changes either as the day winds down… later that day, in the living room, the approaching twilight bathes Seneca and Ilana in the soft glow of the rising moon. Awkward silences have become common, their conversation dwindling as they sip vintage wine. Seneca's internal conflict is deepening in Ilana's presence. Either from lack of sleep or alcohol, he can't help but ponder. This woman…

What is it about her that makes her so inexplicably alluring? Is it her kindness stirring a mix of emotions within him? Is it a reawakened desire to connect with someone? Or… Is it their shared longevity that makes the prospect of… her… so tempting?

Through all these questions, as well as the ones that kept him awake last night, Seneca tries to remain steadfast in his attempt to avoid the intrusion of his commitment to solitude. Instead of seeking answers, he tries reminding himself of the complexities that would arise from their differing backgrounds and duties. She's a princess for a government he hates. He's a broken soul trying to avoid facing grief in his past. Like oil and water, such things don't mix. Just because they're both destined to live ageless lives does not mean it's meant to be.

Ilana catches him lost in thought. "You alright there?"

Seneca tries to recover, "Yeah, just thinking," he quickly tries to justify his moment of thought, but none comes to mind before Ilana speaks again.

"About what?" she smiles. "What thoughts entrance the minds of Seneca Mason?"

Thinking quickly, he responds, "I was trying to think of a good story to tell."

However, Ilana must see through his act with her piercing gaze, "Soooooo?"

"So what?" Seneca asks nervously.

She just laughs. "What story did you come up with?"

"I don't know. I'm running out of good ones I guess…"

"Oh, bullshit Seneca." She laughs.

They lock glances before momentarily laughing together before silence overtakes them, the uncomfortable variant that's hard to ignore. Finally, Seneca, seeking any excuse to break it, hones his attention to the fireplace and asks, "Does that fireplace work?"

Ilana nods, and Seneca tries his hand at lighting a fire. Long ago, he was a master at creating campfires. Carefully arranging the logs, he tries multiple times to light them with matches, but when all else fails, he angrily shoots a round from his plasma pistol into the kindling. It's not the intended purpose of the pistol but it works, starting the fire but vaporizing a portion of the wood in the process. The fire roars with life, filling the room with the nostalgic scent of burning wood.

Turning to look at Ilana with a proud grin on his face, Seneca realizes his mistake. Lighting a fire was a temporary escape from his mind but has made quite the atmosphere to make further stirrings worse. The soft orange glow from the fire dances on Ilana's delicate face, highlighting her amusement at his outburst and unorthodox fire-starting method. The dancing glow moves chaotically across her hair and the light shines in her eyes. And unintentionally, Seneca and Ilana lock gazes with each other once more, finding it difficult to break free.

Her facial expression changes suddenly, without a semblance of a segway, as if she had an idea. She runs toward another closet, and she asks. "What kind of music do you like? My dad has so much vintage music. Vinyls, 8 tracks, CDs, and even this weird dog thing that lights up when you plug music into it."

Seneca chuckles at the sudden change in conversation. "I like a bit of everything—If it's old enough, just show me what you got."

She bounces and her unmistakable infectious excitement fills the room as she downs her glass of wine and disappears into the basement. Soon enough, she returns with an impressive array of music in different forms—CDs, vinyls, 8-track tapes, and more. She also brings with her a rather complicated piece of technology. The orange and gray box in her arms has the remarkable ability to produce exceptional audio from any media that's placed inside. It's some type of data scanner that can even map out metallic music boxes.

Together, they listen to music whilst the moon moves high enough in the sky to flood the room with the moonlight. The light of the moon and glow of the fire wrestle for control as the two drink wine with accompanying dialogue regarding music tastes. The last song of a George Jones album fades out before Ilana swaps it for a CD album from the early two-thousands era, letting the late Spanish singer's music take control over the sound in the room.

"Oh, I love this song!" Ilana enthusiastically shouts and jumps around when she hears the opening chords of a new track.

The song is familiar, and Seneca appreciates Ilana's taste in vintage music that predates the digital era but shudders at the song. Unfortunately for him, it's a rather romantic hit that frequently could be heard surfing the radio during the early two-thousands. The song "Hero" by Enrique Iglesias is a powerful, heartfelt ballad that would invoke people to play it in tribute to their significant others.

"Dance with me!" she says in a hurried voice.
"Huh? No, I—"
Ilana interrupts him as she continues to bop up and down energetically, tossing her shoes aside and grabbing Seneca's arm. "Come on, dance with me, please, please, pleaaaase."

Caught between the melody of the music, the effects of wine softening his temporarily waning defenses around his heart, and the teasing foreplay of moonlight and firelight intermingling, Seneca sighs while making another feeble attempt to refuse. "I don't really—"

Before he can finish innovating his declination, Ilana pulls him to his feet, a playful tone in her voice. "If you could help me cook food, I can help you dance. Plus, I'm your boss," she says quietly to avoid overpowering the lyrics with chatter.

She clasps Seneca's right hand with her left and perches his left hand on her soft waist. Ilana's movements are graceful and fluid as she leads Seneca across the living room floor. At first, his lack of dancing experience is on full display as he stumbles over himself, but her patient guidance soon synchronized their motion with the song's rhythm as the first chorus begins. They sway together to the slow walking tune. She gradually closes the gap between their bodies until their chests meet.

Seneca can feel the warmth of her breath against his neck, and his heart pounds violently, unsure of what to make of the moment that organically manifested before him. At the onset of the final verse, Ilana rests her head on his shoulder and closes her eyes. Seneca can't help but feel captivated by her presence and remember what it's like to hold another—to feel something.

It's overwhelming and he's absent of a readable expression, displaying a complex misunderstanding of his own psyche. The sensation of closeness with another hasn't invaded his presence in a lifetime—a fact he dwells on deeply as he struggles to divert the desire to chase the brewing storm in the distance. Thoughts from hundreds of voices scream in his head but are all drowned out by the music and the moment.

Once the song finally finishes, they let go of each other, his pulses race and their breaths irregular. Ilana's cheeks show a vivid red blush, and she smiles shyly upon seeing Seneca's blank expression. "Sorry if I got carried away," she says softly and sincerely. "I saw that in a movie, and I've never really danced with someone like that before."

Seneca takes a deep breath, fighting to regain his composure. His mind is blank. He's absent of internal direction. Should he be angry? Joyful? Sad? Years of loneliness and an avoiding attachment have left him unsure of how to trust his emotions. He's no fool. There is substance to whatever is calling him and part of him wants to open up about his emotions. Other voices spout enraged rhetoric and call on him to hit the road and tell him he's in too deep. Whatever emotion he felt the last time he danced like that feels foreign now; his mind and heart are screaming incoherently over one another.

His monotone voice reflecting uncertain feelings, he says, "It's getting late..."

Ilana nods. Her smile fades as if she had more to say. "Oh... Yeah... we should get to bed then..."

Chapter 14: Pirates' Code

Ilana's voice, spouting a helladous number of curses and swears, pierces the atmosphere of the cabin the following morning. Apparently, while they slept, a major conflict erupted in Moniear. From what Seneca gathers by reading Imperial news, the presiding ruler of Moniear, Lord Marc Antony, is experimenting with means to evade concession fees owed to Idalia and other COS states. His stubbornness led to imposing martial law in Moniear. He's since sealed off all travel to and from the system, except for Imperial security personnel. His heavy-handed approach resulted in a costly skirmish between Imperial security and a contingent of Whispers that ultimately led to the capture of a high-ranking leader within the Whispers.

The article initially deemed the skirmish a victory for the Empire. However, the situation in Moniear took a turn for the worse. Opportunistic pirates in the nearby Malachi's Arm took note of the weakened system security. They descended upon the system, drawn by the prospect of salvaging valuable materials from the debris left by the skirmish. Amidst a fierce battle against these pirates, the pirates boarded an Imperial ship carrying the captive rebel leader and now have control of it and its occupants, comprising a rebel leader and a high-ranking Imperial general who did not manage to evacuate in an escape pod. Ilana, with her diplomatic expertise, is being dispatched by the lords to negotiate the release of seized ship occupants. This includes not only the safety of a valuable Imperial officer but also the potential bargaining chip of the rebel leader.

"I swear," Ilana continues her stomping, "This shit right here is why the Whispers exist in the first place. These greedy assholes won't change, and it makes bad situations worse every time they do something, but they are too stupid counting money to see it!"

Seneca walks into the living room to witness her place her face into her hands and bend forward. Her hair drapes forward to hide her face as she takes frustrated breaths. When she notices him, she looks up and says, "Sorry. The lords are just out of control…"

While engaged in packing, Ilana informs Seneca of the flaws in the Imperial system's method of appointing lords. According to her, it's corrupt and unbalanced, lacking a merit-based or leadership qualification. More often than not, individuals with influential connections and deep pockets secure positions of power within the Empire. These newly appointed lords, driven by impatience and profit motives, place unrealistic demands on their holdings. Oftentimes wanting to expand their territories rapidly. Instead of gradual and costly colonization efforts to populate uninhabited systems, lords push for invasions and annexations of already established societies. Ultimately, this habit led to the discontent that triggered the rebellion.

It certainly paints a lopsided picture. Throughout her explanation, Seneca wonders how Imperial politics devolved to its status quo. His recollections of Byron's style of authority would have never allowed corruption to sink its talons into the government. Perhaps it was such a slow action that he didn't notice… Like a frog in water with rising temperature, the frog doesn't notice the water is boiling until it's too late.

Ilana's passionate rant comes to an end right as the limo pulls up, prompting a swift departure from the mountain estate. They quickly descend the mountains and reach Capital Spaceport, where Serena is already waiting for them. Once back aboard the Solace, Seneca delineates a last-minute safety briefing for the upcoming journey, diving into the intricacies of the code of ethics employed by a notorious pirate group known as "The Revenge of Teach".

Only such a faction could be blamed for capturing an Imperial vessel of that size, since only skilled pirates with a knack for securing hefty booty gain admission into the group. Like all pirates, they kill, rape, and steal, but for whatever reason, they *do* have a code of ethics. Because you'd need vast experience with The Revenge to understand their code, his briefing is more of a crash-course. Foremost, the pirates are open to negotiating for ransom and will keep the captives alive as long as everyone adheres to certain ground rules. Any attempt to engage them aggressively will put the captives in peril. Furthermore, the pirates will respond with dire consequences for everyone involved if they encounter any deception or trickery. Seneca addresses both speaking etiquette and behaviorisms to ensure no one is "rude".

Seneca concludes the briefing and returns to the Phantom to once more escort The Solace on their diplomatic mission. Their convoy arrives at the coordinates they'd received from the pirates, an uncharted single star just inside Malachi's arm. A tense exchange takes place over the radios soon after their arrival. The pirates expected an escort fighter to accompany *the Solace*, but didn't know it would be *the Phantom*, a testament to Seneca's notoriety. In order to parley and recover the hostages, they agreed Seneca would remain out of his ship until the pirates received payment. As such, *the Solace* deploys a small AI-piloted shuttle to transport him from his ship.

* * *

A tense argument between Ilana and Serena greets him as he steps into the lounge. "They won't negotiate over the coms, Serena. I have to go on board *the Lassiter* and negotiate there."

In terms of size, *the Lassiter* is on the smaller side for an Imperial destroyer-class ship, the size of a US Navy Submarine. With its graceful curves and powerful capabilities, the ship *was* the perfect balance between aesthetics and functionality, a characteristic shared by many Imperial ships. Now debris float about the vicinity of its crumpled silhouette. The prospect that pirates were able to move it baffles Seneca.

Serena shakes her head. "And what if this is just a whole bit to get you?!"

Ilana grabs Seneca's arm and pulls him into the center of the conversation. "That's what he's for!"

"He's a great pilot, Ilana, but in a gunfight, he's not any more qualified than any other Imperial security. They aren't scared of him if he isn't on his ship!" Serena shouts. "That's why they don't want him in it!"

Seneca takes mild offense to the statement. It isn't because she's mistaken, but because of his sense of pride. He's well-versed in dealing with pirates and even has some business connections with them. He cannot resist interjecting, "That may be true, but I speak their 'language'. I can help negotiate and deescalate. I told you I had experience with pirates. Let me prove it."

"Shh. You're no help," Serena throws her hands up in frustration. "Ilana, just please tell me you know what you are doing?"

Ilana sighs, frustrated, before speaking in a cryptic voice, "You know my hands are tied. Besides, if we can rescue the rebel leader as well, maybe we can turn this rebellion around."

Serena sulks but slowly comes around, and it's decided that Seneca and another onboard security agent will take the shuttle craft over to *the Lassiter*. Ilana will do the bulk of the talking, but Seneca will coach Ilana and, more importantly, spot any lurking traps. With enough seats to fit six, they cram into the shuttle. Seneca turns to Ilana and asks, "Remember our briefing, right?"

"Yes but go ahead and remind me."

"Remember, you aren't a pilot, nor do you captain a vessel. Let the pirates speak first. Use as few words as possible while being specific. They are famous for twisting the context." He takes another breath and continues as the shuttle gets closer to the boarding point on *the Lassiter*. "We are at their mercy. They will kill everyone, us included, if we don't play this right."

Ilana swallows and asks, "Anything else?"

Seneca replies, "Yeah. If they demand any amount of money, that's it. You can't go lower; take the deal or get everyone killed. If they don't give you a figure, don't low-ball them; if you think it's enough, it's not and they kill everyone. If you think it's too much, you're probably in the ballpark and they'll negotiate. If it seems like an extremely unreasonable cost, that's perfect."

She looks at him nervously. "Okay... I think I get the point."

The shuttle links up at the boarding point, and their party exits onto the battle-worn ship to make their way to the cargo area where the pirate captain awaits them. An ominous ambiance within the decrepit corridors of The Lassiter sends unsettling chills down Seneca's spine, enveloping him in an eerie, nightmarish scenario. He's not accustomed to seeing the carnage of defeated vessels, only causing it. The flickering, dim lights cast sinister, shifting shadows that seemed to dance malevolently at the periphery of his vision as the group makes their way through the forbidden jungle of contorted metal. These once functional walls and floors bore the brutal scars of the relentless confrontation, with twisted, mangled bulkheads standing as grim witnesses.

Air hangs heavy with pungent odors of scorched metal, and in certain sections, torrents of water spew wildly from ruptured pipes, rendering the floor a treacherous, slippery surface. Sounds of air whistling out of holes in the walls from compromised pressure seals assault their ears. Lifeless forms of crew members, now akin to discarded ragdolls, lay strewn haphazardly across the macabre scene, a haunting reminder of the vessel's grim destiny. Navigating this nightmarish labyrinth proves an arduous feat, especially for Ilana, who, in her heels, battles to maintain her footing. Seneca can tell this marked her maiden encounter with the grim aftermath of warfare as she constantly covers her mouth and gags at the gore that lays out before them. Their tortuous journey leads them to the entrance of their destination.

The captives come into view as they enter the remarkably intact cargo hold. The pirate captain stands with his prisoners, commanding attention with his imposing height, rough demeanor, robust physique, and polished appearance. Covered in a red leather trench coat and a black single-piece flight suit, the tired and bored gentleman holding the valuable hostages is instantly recognizable to Seneca as they approach in the dim light of the cargo bay. Seneca never imagined he'd run into the gentleman candidly again.

Chapter 15: Friends in Low Places

They make their way across the cargo hold. In violation of the instructions he gave Ilana, Seneca shouts a greeting to the pirate captain like an old friend. "Clemson McAlister, in the flesh. How long has it been?"

"Too long, Seneca," Clemson replies in his gruff voice as he approaches to offer Seneca a friendly handshake.

Ilana looks at Seneca in utter confusion as he makes conversation with Clemson. "I take it you've been getting a lot of 'business' in these skirmishes?"

Seneca's familiarity with Clemson stems from a previous buccaneering contract he undertook years ago, during a quasi-war between the Confederacy and the United Federation. The UF was engaging in unfair trade agreements with member systems, and the COS military council took notice and silently contracted pirates and ICs to pillage UF vessels. During this time, Seneca and Clemson originally met as adversaries vying for the same loot. They were both impressed with each other's piloting skills, leading them to form a temporary alliance. Clemson kept all the plunder in exchange for not killing anyone, and Seneca sold the UF back their captured pilots and ships. By helping their cause, he earned brownie points with the COS and successfully sold back all the ships to the UF, ensuring a clean record by returning their pilots as well.

"Aye, you could say that," Clemson chuckles. "So, you're with the Empire now, are you? Colored me mighty worried seein' the ol' *Phantom* drop in with the Imps."

"I'm working for the Princess specifically, if that's what you mean,"

Clemson winks at him after examining Ilana's physical appearance. "Damn fine job, then."

"So, we'll, uh, let you get us started," Seneca says, stepping back to Ilana.

Clemson runs his hands through his beard. "I'll cut you a bit of slack since you reel in a fat catch a while back. Take a look at the merchandise, and I'll give you a number."

While Seneca maintains a friendly conversation with Clemson, Ilana and the other security agent thoroughly inspect the captives to assess their condition. In a battered and bruised state, the Whisper rebel bears the marks of harsh treatment; blood trickling from his nose, eyes, and a jagged scar marking his face. His blood-stained blonde hair and suit make it nearly impossible to look at him without cringing. The Imperial general is in comparatively better shape, able to talk and chat with Ilana without significant bruising or scars. He is still in his decorated Imperial "blues," a cyan-colored suit coat with a gold accent line down his sleeve matched with black pants and a white shirt; A matching "bus driver" cap displays his rank while it covers his short black hair.

"Satisfied?" Clemson asks after a moment.

Ilana nods nervously.

"So, here's what I'm thinking. On account of my good friend Seneca here. I'm thinking two mil a head, and I get to plunder this here ship for the remainder of the cost."

Ilana looks to Seneca for some guidance, and he nods. With a nervous voice, she asks, "Anything else?"

"*Shit...*" Seneca thinks silently. She should not have reopened a closed negotiation. He grits his teeth, hoping for the best.

"Since you see fit to open up the option," Clemson pauses and smirks. "I'd like a friendly sparrin' match with Seneca. See if he can drop the shields on my ship '*the Rot*' before I drop his."

A muted sigh of relief escapes between his teeth. Sparring matches are commonalities among Revenge members to improve their skills and identify their weak points. It's a way of keeping themselves strong. He nods to Ilana to accept as an idea enters his mind.

"Deal," Ilana says and shakes hands with Clemson.

Seneca smiles and presents a counteroffer of his own. "I'll up the stakes on the sparring match."

"State your terms," Clemson says, a devilish grin appearing on his face.

"Winner owes the other a favor?"

In the pirate world, favors are a broad concept. Outlined by their code, the terms of a favor are unconditional and set by the person owed the favor. As such, pirates highly value favors and trade them like regular currency. Seneca doesn't know if he'll ever need it while he's flying on Ilana's payroll. However, anytime he can earn a favor from a pirate, he likes to take it. To Clemson, the prospect of earning a favor from Seneca is equally irresistible.

"I'll shake to that," Clemson says, shaking Seneca's hand.

The group completes the official ransom exchange, and the shuttle takes them back from *the Lassiter* to *the Solace*. Seneca makes his way over to *the Phantom*, where he situates himself within his trusty craft and ventures to meet Clemson and begin their sparring match.

* * *

The Rot, which was originally a UF heavy-class fighter, has since undergone extensive modifications for piracy since Clemson acquired it. The sleek dark ship, with its sharp, angular shape reminiscent of a four-hundred-and-fifty-foot-long arrowhead, emanates an ominous energy that sends chills down the spines of those who encounter it. Four gatling guns, similar to the ones on *the Phantom*, are part of *the Rot*'s arsenal. However, these guns have been altered to shoot EMP pulse rounds, making them highly effective in both shield depletion and metal destruction. Its true centerpiece, though, is a devastating 180mm railgun. Capable of firing incendiary artillery, it can swiftly eliminate the engines or power supplies of smaller ships, particularly when their shields are down. Despite being well-armed, the ship falls short when it comes to speed and maneuverability, unlike *the Phantom*.

The Rot perches one kilometer away from Seneca. Sparring matches begin much like old western duels, with the ships facing each other at a distance. While there isn't a clock counting down to high noon, both Seneca and Clemson have timers that can be easily synchronized. Seneca smiles, waiting for the timer to strike zero. Clemson is a formidable pilot, potentially the only one in the galaxy to match Seneca's skill. His abilities are enough to make Seneca think twice about crossing him on less friendly terms… Their match promises to be an exciting engagement.

A timer counts to zero, a tone chimes, and the duel began. Seneca immediately burns one of his four boost charges to fly under *the Rot* as it immediately opens fire. Volleys of shield-ravaging bullets graze the aft end of the field and begin eating through the first ten percent of Seneca's shields as he maneuvers to get under and behind Clemson. Clemson cannot outmaneuver Seneca, so he utilizes reverse thrust to increase the amount of distance Seneca will need to cover to get behind him. It is an excellent strategy that keeps *the Phantom* in his crosshairs as long as possible. Seneca burns a second boost charge but vectors a portion up instead of traveling downwards.

This juke maneuver places Seneca momentarily behind Clemson and applies pressure to *the Rot*'s shields using his own weaponry. Since *the Rot* possesses very powerful shields, Seneca is unable to inflict much damage before Clemson aims its nose at him once more. Seneca, under fire from Clemson, employs a shield charge to restore his shields to eighty percent, enduring the continuous barrage.

The match continues. Seneca repeatedly gets behind *the Rot*, his ship's thrusters humming as he closes the distance each time to unleash a flurry of weapon fire. He continuously maneuvers to allow his guns to damage *the Rot*'s shields—five to eight percent at a time while doing his best to minimize the amount of fire he sustains. Rushes of adrenaline tempt Seneca away from careful management of his shield and boost charges, but deep breathing and impeccable composure allow him to save the last of each for a calculated maneuver known as a "joust."

In the heat of the moment, Seneca cracks his knuckles, a nervous habit that had become second nature over years of intense combat. He is aware of the risks of a joust: a head-on collision of firepower between both ships that could prove disastrous in this skirmish if he miscalculates it. His own shields are wearing thin, hovering at forty percent—once he consumes the final shield charge, and he will only have one shot at making this maneuver work.

Seneca boosts whilst burning his final shield charge as well, closing the gap between him and Clemson rapidly. It's a high-stakes game of chicken, and both pilots understand the consequences of hesitation. Clemson can't afford to let Seneca escape his gatling guns' range by getting behind him once more if he were to avoid the joust, but he also couldn't risk facing a barrage of missiles at close range where his countermeasures would be unable to defend him, though the closing speed should not permit that.

As the distance between them shrinks rapidly, Seneca takes one last calculated risk of his own. In a daring move, although it subjects him to extra fire from Clemson's *Rot*, he momentarily reverses his thrust, slowing his ship's acceleration momentarily and granting himself an extra second to unleash all six of his EMP burst missiles. He grits his teeth from the heavy tension as the projectiles streak toward *the Rot*, and the unexpected maneuver leaves Clemson no time to respond.

Seneca's gamble pays off as all six EMP pulse munitions detonate on target and reduce Clemson's shields to zero, while he retains a meager two percent from the onslaught of fire his shields sustained in the joust. A close and challenging match ends, leaving Seneca with a rush and mile-wide grin of satisfaction. He's won another dogfight against Clemson, but he can't ignore how much better Clemson gets each time.

"I'll get you one of these days, Seneca," Clemson says to him over the radio. "The winds will blow you to my shores when you call for that favor. Fly well, my friend."

"Thanks for the match. It's seldom someone gets as close as you did. I'll be in touch. Good fortunes to you, Clemson." ("Good fortunes," is a customary goodbye between pirates.)

Seneca hears Serena come over to the radio. "Friends in low places, stick jockey?" she taunts as applause is audible in the background.

"Sort of," Seneca answers as he collects his composure from the dogfight. "Let's get going. Ilana's probably got negotiations to take care of now."

He pockets his victory and returns to formation with *the Solace*, making their way back to Vista. The convoy arrives back in Vista Capital with the rescued Imperial general and the rebel captive in tow. Ilana appears stressed, lost in thought, as the entourage makes their way into the conference halls of the palace. Small hand gestures and lip movement subvert her usual bubbliness, symptomatic of talking to oneself. As they walk, Seneca ponders what is running through her mind. He watches her closely, noticing the furrow in her brow and the distant look in her eyes. Clearly the lords rattle her and make her nervous, and Seneca cannot avoid the allure of curiosity and concern.

* * *

"You good?" he asks her.

"Yeah, just planning what I'm going to say..." she replies.

She initiates discussion with Seneca as they stroll, her tone tinged with a sense of urgency and apprehension. Her speech elucidates the standard procedure employed by the Imperial government when dealing with prominent figures affiliated with the Whispers of Freedom, a grim habit of public executions used as a deterrent for potential recruits to the rebellion.

Ilana's gaze, however, reveals a firm determination beneath the apprehension. She voices her noble aspiration to thwart any impending execution, guided by an idealistic glimmer. Her words, holding a small touch of optimism, reflect her hope to leverage the rebel official as for negotiations with the Whispers. It is undoubtedly a difficult gambit for her limited power, a fact she acknowledges to great disdain, but she won't abide by another life needlessly extinguished by the realm of politics.

"Sounds like you've got your work cut out for you then," Seneca says.

"Yeah, gee thanks," Serena scoffs as she inserts herself into the conversation. "Ever tried to sway angry imperial lords?"

Serena puts a hand up before Seneca could reply. "Didn't think so. The lord of Moniear is the absolute worst too. He holds allot of voting power too."

"Chill, Serena, Seneca doesn't do politics." She nudges Seneca's side with her elbow. "If it doesn't fly, this ain't your guy."

Seneca laughs. "Well, regardless, I can help if you need." He then gestures jokingly toward his holstered pistol. "This puppy is pretty helpful when it needs to be."

The joke landed, and both Ilana and Serena cracked a smile.

Chapter 16: Hearts and Minds

The days after their return holds sway to an intense whirlwind of activity unfolds, marked by extensive debates in the conference hall with the Imperial lords. Just as Ilana had predicted, their demands for retribution are without empathy or compassion. Many of the recently appointed lords, tasked with overseeing annexed systems, are seething with anger that Ilana paid Imperial dollars to safeguard the rebel leader. Consequently, Ilana has spent lengthy durations appeasing the lords and pleading with them to see reason. It takes more than a week for Ilana to convince the lords to stay any action against the rebel leader, promising them the potential for a lucrative agreement with the Whispers for the return of the unnamed rebel official.

Ilana meets Seneca in the palace courtyard, a picturesque garden with a large koi pond and a variety of willows. Their eyes meet as a heavy sigh escapes her lips in an attempt to shed the weight upon her shoulders. "As of now, they won't execute him. He's going to serve a minimum of six months in an Imperial work camp. It won't surprise me if they try to work him to death, but I'll do what I can to make sure he's treated humanely."

Seneca nods and asks, "What are we doing in the meantime?"

Ilana's face takes on another expression, a mix between a frown and a smirk. "The Imperial security council believes that someone within the government is aiding the rebellion. So, we are going on a tour around newly annexed systems with conflicted loyalties and make sure the Empire maintains its influence, and to 'persuade' citizens to stop assisting the rebellion, since it's not clear who is helping the Whispers."

"Why send us?" Seneca inquires.

"Us?" Ilana responds sarcastically, shooting him a glance. "Pal, they're sending me. you travel *with* me."

Seneca can't help but appreciate the confidence in her tone. "I like the confidence," he says, playfully flashing her a quick wink. It's a dangerous action considering his mild infatuation, but he's still riding high from his recent win against Clemson.

* * *

A tinge of red flushes her face as she ducks her head. "Go get ready 'hot shot'. The 'loyalty tour' starts tomorrow."

They part ways for the evening, returning to their designated quarters after Ilana gives him their travel itinerary. And the next morning, they begin their six-month excursion through the marginalized communities swallowed by the Empire...

Three months pass quickly. The tour has taken them through various star systems that are now on the verge of joining the rebellion. At first, the people in these previously autonomous systems reacted with anger and resentment towards the Empire's recent takeover. However, everything changes when Ilana uses her extraordinary abilities to soothe the heated tension.

It's intriguing and slightly puzzling the way Ilana wins over the inhabitants. Time after time, system after system, initial hostility gradually dissipates, replaced by a more welcoming attitude once Ilana arrives. It's unclear whether it's her persuasive diplomacy, empathy with the strife of the citizens, liberal use of incentives that she sometimes promises, or a blend of all that accomplishes this remarkable shift. However, her trust and strength of character is on full display as she even agrees to meet leaders occasionally unprotected (despite Seneca and Serena's cautions).

Whatever she's doing, Ilana has an incredible ability to forge connections with the locals and infuse them with a glimmer of hope amidst their frustration that leaves Seneca among her constituents in awe. Even those staunchly opposed to Imperial influence mellow as they listen to her impassioned speeches, where she expounds upon ideals of peace, harmony, and mutual prosperity.

Currently, the tour brings the group to a particularly troubled system, Pyre Mining Colony. This system is rich in resources and should, in theory, be thriving. Three gas giants with metal-rich asteroid composed rings orbit a class-g star, accompanied by a rocky planet nestled comfortably in the goldilocks zone. Though the rocky world is not yet life-sustaining since it lacks an atmosphere. With such a vast amount of profitable resources, it makes no sense that the 300,000 inhabitants live on a ring-shaped colony orbiting the unnamed planet.

The Solace and *Phantom* touch down in the spaceport of the mining colony. Seneca ensures the safe exit of the passengers aboard *the Solace*, a process now as efficient as a well-oiled machine. Just as he'd done many times before, Seneca expertly coordinates with system security to ensure Ilana exits into a safe environment. Pyre's quieter than usual reception has not presented a particularly hazardous environment thus far, but there have been instances on the tour where Seneca had to employ non-lethal force to maintain security, so he's taking no chances.

Approaching the colony's shuttle system with Ilana and Serena by his side, a man named Marco greets them. Marco is an older gentleman, possessing a robust, barrel-shaped physique, complete with a noticeable beer belly. His wide neck supports a head adorned with an aging visage, along with a well-kept blackened-gray beard and mustache. Despite his rugged appearance, Marco welcomes them with a friendly disposition.

"Welcome Princess and company," Marco says with a slight hint of an endangered Spanish accent, shaking hands with Ilana, Serena, and Seneca. "And you must be Seneca Mason. We have heard much of your exploits."

Seneca smiles and gives a muted nod.

Marco motions for them to follow him. "Please, this way, my friends."

Marco promptly takes on the role of guiding the trio towards the awaiting shuttle. The system is similar to the one in Myanmar, but with a noticeable distinction. Pyre's shuttle system operates in circuits as opposed to lines, providing transportation between various stations using three interconnected circular shuttle lines that encircle the colony. One line operates on the colony's center most ring, another through the middle ring, and a third one runs along the outer ring. Additionally, there is a shuttle line that travels back and forth along the colony's diameter. Marco chats casually with fellow passengers during the shuttle ride to the initial destination, a compound of apartments and lodging facilities.

"These are the barracks, the main living quarters for our citizens," Marco says as they step out of the shuttle. "They aren't lavish by any means, but most people are happy. However, we desperately need more of them, as there are several families per unit. Before the Empire came in, we were procuring funds to expand them..."

Pyre's population calls the sprawling compound of the barracks home. The colony's domed ceiling safeguards the breathable air within while numerous eight-story complexes span three city blocks in width. Dimly shining lights adorn some windows of the bare metal buildings, while other windows remain cloaked in darkness. Down by a set of sports equipment, Seneca notices citizens engaged in conversations as they waft smoke from their cigarettes. The entire scene and its acrid scent of recycled air helps create an atmosphere that accurately represents the hardships faced by these families.

Marco continues explaining how the situation unfolded about three years ago, shortly after his election. The Empire barged in one day with military forces. They 'congratulated' Pyre for being forced annexation into their domain. When faced with such overwhelming force, Marco swiftly dismissed any thought of resistance and the residents reluctantly complied to preserve stability. However, the people remain on edge and need change.

With a weary tone, Marco delves into the challenges they've faced ever since. Under Imperial rule, Imperial Lord Simon has meticulously controlled every aspect of their existence, including their financial affairs. Their hard-earned wealth had to be directed according to rigid Imperial mandates, leaving them with barely enough to maintain their current operations. The Empire's intervention indefinitely shelved their aspirations to expand the colony. Now, Imperial bureaucracy and oppression ensnares Pyre Mining, cruelly dashing their hopes for a brighter future.

* * *

Ilana furrows her brow. "I understand your complications, governor. I will ensure Lord Simon becomes aware of the people's plight and more funds are necessary for you to thrive."

Marco responds with a grateful smile. "Thank you, Princess, but this is the first in a series of problems. At this point, we need more money than just our own."

Over the next few days between Ilana addressing the citizens, Marco continues to show them around the colony, elaborating on a laundry list of issues. Many parts of the colony require repair because of years of wear and tear, including critical life support systems that keep the colony with stable artificial gravity and oxygen generators. The aging mining fleet, the backbone of Pyre's faltering economy, also needs new ships and repairs to the older ones. However, the most pressing concern is the disruption of shipping. Pyre Mining, caught in the rebellion's crossfire, strives to maintain a sense of normalcy and neutrality. Unfortunately, this leaves their shipping lanes vulnerable to rebel attacks, causing difficulties in transporting goods and relegating the ability to produce income to a halt.

Ilana reassures Marco that the Empire is not turning a blind eye to the problems caused by the rebellion. She speaks with her trademark brand of empathy and understanding, easing Marco's worries.

"Thank you," Marco expresses gratitude. "The people of Pyre hold you in high regard, princess, even if we don't agree with your government. I wish the three of you safe travels. Please take a few days to rest here and enjoy yourselves. We aren't lavish, but we are welcoming."

Later, in a bar within the recreational district of the colony, the trio relaxes exchanging jokes while sipping on a modest amount of alcohol. The friendly people of Pyre insist that Seneca and company drink for free, but despite their attempts, Seneca continues to pay for their drinks as the night progresses. Ilana eventually stretches and excuses herself to visit the bathroom. As she departs, her hand flirtatiously brushes against Seneca's shoulder, causing him to meet her eyes with a smirk as she strolls away.

Throughout the tour, Seneca noticed that Ilana's interactions with him had become increasingly tactile. Her friendly demeanor has taken on a slightly flirtatious edge on multiple occasions, though it remains subtle and not drastically different from the norm. They would even find themselves alone occasionally, engaged in conversations that delved into personal subjects regarding one another's ideal partners or what they find romantic. Over time, Seneca has slowly grown more accustomed to these exchanges, though subtle unease lingers after the fact.

He recalls one evening on the tour, as they strolled through the dimly lit corridors of one of the many space colonies they've visited, Ilana's laughter rang out like music, and she playfully nudged his shoulder while sharing a childhood memory. Another time, when angry crowds angrily hurling rotten fruit at her on arrival, she reached out and grabbed his arms for reassurance, her touch indicating a sense of deep trust as she bid for confidence. There was also one long evening on the Solace where Ilana had fallen asleep against his shoulder as she vented her frustrations regarding the plight of the citizens they visited. These instances left Seneca both exhilarated and anxious, a mixture of emotions he can't quite decipher yet.

Seneca and Serena watch Ilana walk away from earshot. Serena suddenly utters, "I swear to god, Seneca."

Seneca responds in shock, "What?"

"Do you really have walls *that* thick? Are you stupid? What. Is. Your. Issue?" Serena asks, flailing her arms around to make her point.

Seneca stammers, "I'm confu—"

"Shut up! Listen! Ilana. Likes. You," Serena asserts, clapping her hands with every word. "Make a goddamn move or turn her down or something. Shit, I'll bring you back to my room on *the Solace* and ride you myself just to see if I can understand what she sees."

Taken aback by another one of Serena's heated and crude outbursts, Seneca tries to explain, "I had a feeling, but I work for—"

Serena interrupts again, "Listen. To. Me. She needed a security head to do the job. There were others qualified. She could be arguably safer with others, especially since you refuse to work with others and do this as a solo op. The only reason you are as involved as much as you are at this point is because she likes you. She doesn't *need* you for a lot of the shit you sit in on. She just *wants* you there."

Seneca attempts to respond, "Wait—"

"Shut. Up!" Serena interrupts once more. "*Please.* I don't know what your deal is, but you aren't the only one here with eternity at your doorstep. You choose to be lonely, but just understand Ilana's never had that luxury of choice until now."

Seneca leans back and lets out a frustrated sigh. "That doesn't mean I owe her anything."

"You owe her the truth," Serena asserts sternly before ducking her head. "I can't read you; half the time you goggle at her like a dog looking at food, other times you hide from her because you're afraid of yourself. I don't know your past, but I'm not dumb."

Silence overtakes them momentarily before Serena continues, "Look. If I have to listen to Ilana talk about dancing with you in her cabin one more time, I'm going to scream. Make a move; it's free real estate—*or* tell her you aren't interested, but we both know that's not true."

Seneca ducks his head and shakes it side to side. He sets loose another sigh. "Look, I don't know if I can, Serena. I'm not exactly known to stay in one place for long. Shoot, I'm still here. That's progress for me…"

Chapter 17: If You Can't Beat Them, Buy Them

The remainder of the tour passes much like the rest. Serena did not confront Seneca further regarding his relationship with Ilana. It doesn't go without mentioning the lasting impact it had on him. Thoughts about Serena's stern words have plagued him since into the present day. Hopefully, the upcoming proceedings regarding the captive Whisper official will keep him distracted. If not, they'll keep Ilana busy. Given the atmosphere in the palace upon their return, she'll have her hands full and won't have time to tempt him.

She's met with continued cries for retribution. They sit in long conferences listening to the lord's testimonies while Ilana insists that sparing the Whisper official will garner some step towards peace. The lords wholeheartedly disagree, believing mercy to be a sign of weakness that will further encourage the rebellion. Lord Marc Antony stands out among other lords for his extreme stance—he vociferously advocates for the public execution of anyone remotely connected to the rebellion and calling for martial law Empire-wide. Thankfully, most lords do not share his zeal, yet they still fervently agree with a televised execution of the rebel.

The days progress and the window of opportunity for Ilana to find a solution narrows inexorably. Another day marked by relentless attempts to quell the Imperial lords' bloodlust concludes, and Ilana retreats from the conference hall, her frustration and disappointment evident to Seneca, who watches from the sidelines of his job. The nature of the lords tests his temper as well. He still holds no true allegiance to anyone other than himself, but the manner in which the lords conduct their business is loathsome to his personal values. Deep down he remembers at one point in his life being a guardian of freedom and justice who served as his nation's sword and shield, and such service garnered him respect for morally sound authority. There is no justice for the oppressed in the dystopia the lords have created, and they are not subject to consequence.

After noticing Ilana's prolonged absence, Seneca approaches Serena to ask her for help to locate Ilana.

"She's probably on the eastern balcony. She goes there to watch the sunset on… days like this," Serena says, watching Seneca walk by. "She knows she's going to need a miracle… or help to save the rebel."

He takes her input in stride and, true to her prediction, he finds her on the east wing's balcony watching the sun fall. Seneca walks out, and the sullen look on her face encourages him to say something. "You need to talk?"

"Yes," she says without hesitation, and sighs, "I don't know what to do. We may lose a chance to get any step toward resolution…"

"That sucks…" He says, lost for further sentiment.

Seneca waits as she cries "… So many people are suffering…dying for freedom and I'm…" she pauses "… Not in the best position to help anyone."

Seneca watches her dry a tear with her hands as it rolls down her cheek. "I don't imagine it's easy to care… I guess it's why I usually choose not to."

"I'm trying so hard to get them to listen…"

"I guess it's off topic, but why don't the Whispers turn to the Confederacy?"

"Some do," she answers, "but joining the Confederacy is a lengthy process, and the Confederacy will not liberate systems already annexed by the Empire. By the time some of these systems know they are on the radar for annexation, it's too late."

Seneca senses Ilana is concealing something. She obviously holds little faith in the lords, but it almost seems as if she supports the rebels directly. However, he still understands too little of the Imperial government to form a realistic view. All he knows is the royal family are just faces of the government, public figures, and utilized for diplomacy. The lords hold true power. Should there be a reason the lords question her loyalties, it would not be farfetched to believe they might take drastic actions to strip her of what limited power she has.

"Listen, Ilana, if I can help, let me know," Seneca says.

She dons a half-smile and gently pokes his chest somewhat flirtatiously. "Just tell me tomorrow will be better… like you did in Myanmar."

"Tomorrow will be better… I promise," Seneca says, flashing a smile.

She flashes him a heartwarming look with her dark green eyes that cuts right through him like a hot knife through butter. A mild chill moves up his back as she walks away, completely unaware of how dangerous her alluring nature is becoming… Furthermore, he does not make promises he does not intend to keep, and the one he'd just made is a round in a chamber given the *look* that Ilana just gave him.

He's out of bed before the sun rises after a sleepless night. Seneca has little time to make good on his promise. Though Ilana only wanted kind words, he knows words are not enough to help her. Unlike Myanmar, he won't be able to rely on shouting at the fat cats and firing a pistol in the air to get compliance. He brainstorms potential means of garnering agreement from the Imperial lords, knowing they aren't easily swayed.

* * *

He remembers a conversation he'd had with Serena regarding lordship appointments. Serena had told him The Empire wanted him on their side—or at least the appearance of him being on their side. Obtaining lordship might be possible. Maybe becoming a fat cat to persuade other fat cats… A deplorable thought, but all things considered, he's in this adventure for the long haul. Like Serena suggested, he'll ride the wave to see where he lands. Using his connection to Ilana, he should be able to buy his way in…

He shoots a UniCom message to Ilana and her reply comes quickly in a single word: "Why?"

Seneca responds to her message, "Couldn't tell you, but I'd like to help."

"It's not going to come cheap," she replies.

Money is of no concern. Seneca has deep pockets accumulated over a lifetime of investment income, paid contracts, combat missions, and bounty hunting across the galaxy. Many of these endeavors earned him substantial capital. The income from them continuously trickles into his bank accounts, resulting in a constantly replenishing fortune. His financial resources are partially because of his ability to earn in high risk, high reward combat campaigns, and partially a byproduct of his longevity; after living over two centuries, if he weren't rich, something would be very wrong.

If the lords prioritize monetary gain over everything else, Seneca can utilize his personal wealth as a tool to purchase support for Ilana's side, but he needs the "in". He receives no further reply, and he isn't sure if Ilana will go for it or not.

Later, however, Ilana finds him outside the conference hall just before another repulsive round of debating begins. The presence of a distinguished gentleman, emanating an aura of authority, accompanies her as they walk together.

"Seneca, this is Lord Simon," she says, introducing the man. "He's a lord who governs over four imperial territories. I spoke with him, and he's agreed to sell over lordship over Pyre Mining for twenty-two million."

Seneca takes a deep breath. There is no excitement to commit to the political arena, yet circumstances have him, albeit reluctantly, willing to brave the previously unexplored frontier to help Ilana save a life for her pursuit of peace.

"Done," he replies and offers a handshake.

Lord Simon, without uttering another word, firmly shakes Seneca's hand. Once funds promptly appear in the lord's bank account, Simon proceeds to swiftly execute the series of necessary paperwork on a kiosk tablet. Then, as if by magic, Seneca finds himself now bestowed with the title of Imperial lord as they enter the conference hall.

"Welcome to the party," she says with a slight hint of concern in her tone.

"Thanks, now let's make today a better day," Seneca tells her, patting her shoulder.

Serena arrives just in time for Ilana to explain what had just happened as she looks at Seneca with a baffled expression and a confused smile. "Yay, now he's useful when we aren't in danger of being kidnapped, I guess."

"Gee, thanks," Seneca chuckles as the three of them walk into the conference hall to take their seats.

As Ilana's last chance to stay execution of the rebel official begins, everyone takes their seats. No sooner does the meeting come to order does the loudmouth lord of Moniear stand. "Fellow Imperial patriots. Let's make this a quicker day. We know what we want, and what the Empire needs. Let's get our vote in and—"

Seneca stands up. He's heard enough from the arrogant man in the last several days and now has the ability to open his mouth. "Shut up."

"Excuse me," the lord replies, "Major, who are you to silence me?"

"Newest Imperial lord, badass combat pilot with more money than you could ever hope to see. Plus, I'm the only one in the room packing heat, so I'm telling you to shut your damn mouth."

Ilana's face bears an expression somewhere between horrified and impressed by Seneca's lack of tact. The room is silent as Seneca resumes speaking, "Here's what I propose. I will *pay* every other lord to vote in support of Ilana."

"You can't just *buy* our support," the lord thunders in frustration.

"You can bet your ass I can."

The room falls into an expectant silence; the air growing dense like cold soup. Whispers float among the lords, their faces betraying a range of emotions. Some gather in hushed clusters, discussing the turn of events in low voices. These murmured conversations weave a tapestry of intrigue throughout the assembly. Seneca then finds himself under the scrutiny of various expressions—scowls of disdain, incredulous laughter, and thoughtful contemplation. It is as if the room is holding a collective breath, waiting for fate to swing definitively.

Finally, skepticism gives way as the lords nod before Lord Marc Antony speaks again, saying, "Show us the money *Lord* Mason: eight million for each lord in the room, with eighty of us... that's six hundred forty million. Then we will entertain the Princess' plan."

"Done," Seneca says without hesitation.

Serena whispers in his ear, "You have that much money?!"

Seneca leans over and whispers back, "I have *way* more..."

"Alright, you'll fit in here well..." she chuckles.

Ilana assists Seneca in the chore of dispersing a ludicrous amount of money to a bunch of already rich bureaucrats. Faces of disbelief flood the lords in the pews surrounding them; they did not believe he'd be able to pay up. However, they finish dispersing funds, and true to the agreement, the silver spoon council casts their votes in unanimous support for Ilana; proving their temporary support can indeed be bought. Consequently, he makes good on his promise to help Ilana whether or not she expected it. They step out of the conference room once the event draws to a close and go their separate ways, while Ilana returns to plan the next steps.

Later that evening, Seneca receives a knock on his door. He opens it to find Ilana. This is a first for him. She's never come to his door at night in the palace, let alone in her pajamas. The soft, silky fabric of her V-neck pajama outfit is a deep shade of crimson, a color that complements the hues of her hair and eyes. The material drapes gracefully over her form, offering a hint of her delicate curves. Seneca discreetly tries to avert his gaze, not wanting to appear overly interested in her appearance. His curiosity piques. Not only because of her attire, but also what has brought her here at this hour.

"I'm fine. I just wanted to talk." She smiles.

"By all means," he gestures into his room, and she walks in. Before he shuts the door, he catches Serena peeking from her doorway with a devilish grin, making kissing faces again, as well as a very crude gesture with her hands; to which he replies with a hand wave and a brief scowl.

"Things are getting harder and more tense..." she sighs, voicing her concerns in the process of seating herself at the foot of Seneca's bed. "At first, keeping the peace wasn't too tough, but the lords test everything I do. They test the boundaries of what people will tolerate."

Seneca says, offering a suggestion. "Well, push back. The people of the Empire respect you. The people will listen to you; make change with them, not the Lords."

Ilana chuckles lightly and leans back. "That's a thought..." She looks at him, and the glance she shoots yet another piercing gaze. "I won't keep you long, Seneca... I just wanted to know... what prompted you to do all this to help me?"

He knows where the conversation is headed, and her question frightens him. Between Serena's heckling and his internal curiosity to explore the chemistry he feels with Ilana, he cannot deny a growing sense of attraction. He hates witnessing her upset or seeing her hard work being ignored by those who should respect her. Her ability to connect with people astounds him and has been chipping at his walls since he'd met her. There's nothing less than amazing about this woman that does not call his name.

Ilana breaks the silence, sensing Seneca's hesitation. "I'm sorry. I don't mean to push you or anything. I just... I don't know. The moment I met you, something felt... Different."

Seneca sits down, trying to calm his nerves. "Was that the only reason I got this job, though?"

She shakes her head. "No. I had and still have genuine needs for your skills."

Another heavy silence follows. His heart drums heavily in his chest and his hands are sweating like a horse. He rolls the dice and speaks up. "Ilana. I can't lie... I feel something. I'm not very articulate and I'll speak right to the point. You make me feel emotions I haven't felt in a long time. I don't know how to handle them though. I see you and want to be around you. I see your passion and I want to chip in. That's all I can tell you…"

She smiles and her face takes on a bright red hue as she approaches him and gives him a hug. It's a tight embrace—different from any physical action she'd initiated before. It speaks more than her words as she lets go and says, "Goodnight, Seneca. I'll see you tomorrow."

Chapter 18: Wise Men Say

A new day dawns and Ilana has the daunting task of returning to Vista and negotiating with the rebels for the release of their military official. Seneca isn't entirely certain about Ilana's expectations for these negotiations, but she seems confident in her diplomatic abilities. She holds a belief that she can negotiate some sort of agreement, not peace, but *something* in that direction—a baby step of sorts. Unfortunately, the details are to remain a mystery to him.

According to Ilana, reaching out to the leader of the Whispers is a challenging affair, as the true leader remains hidden from the public eye. Only a select few within the Whispers of Freedom are believed to know the leader's identity, but nothing is confirmed. Negotiations for the release of the captured official will occur through untraceable video conferences between Ilana and a third-party spokesman on behalf of the true leader. Ilana is solely responsible for managing the envoy and circumstance has cast it behind a shroud of secrecy, leaving Seneca with time to visit Pyre Mining. After which, he'll return to Vista to spend time on the mountain estate with Ilana after she handles negotiating with the rebels.

He touches down at Pyre's deteriorating spaceport once again, traveling alone for the first time since he'd embarked on his adventure as Ilana's security detail. Marco greets him as friendly as he had the first visit, and they take a rail-shuttle to the government complex in the center of the colony. The colony's center is a lively area. Dozens of towering high rises stretch towards the sky, reaching for the colony's transparent dome. Among them sits a rectangular building with a humble blue-steel colored exterior and dark tinted windows that look out over the colony's port. The inside is an organized system of hallways and corridors with various office spaces within. Up the stairs on the third-floor rests Marco's office across the hall from a conference room.

Marco ushers him in and continuously offers him coffee and snacks until he can no longer decline. "So, my friend, you're replacing Simon?" He asks Seneca.

"Yes. I'm aware of your situation and I'm not the uptight prick that he is."

Seneca replies, taking a sip of coffee.

"Let us hope so. Simon was not a friendly character. He made many unreasonable demands."

"On that note, I don't need your money. In fact, I'll send Pyre five million a month. Use that to replenish your fleet, make colony repairs, and pay out bounty rewards on anyone attacking your shipping. That should help you get back on your feet."

"Such generosity. We will make it up to you."

"Don't worry about it. Rule yourselves and such. Just make sure the taxes get paid, so the council stays off my back."

Seneca spends another several days on Pyre doing public appearances and letting Marco introduce him to his new constituents. Though the citizens are still apprehensive about Imperial rule, Seneca's role in overseeing them buys them some optimism for their future, especially when Marco informs them that Seneca will supply financial support. Grateful citizens extend warm thanks and express their hopes for the future. It's a pleasant change compared to the exasperating endeavor of sitting through council hearings he'd recently endured with Ilana. After concluding his business in Pyre, he returns to Vista and waits for Ilana at the royal mountain estate.

Serena joins him on leave during Ilana's continued preoccupations in the palace. As winter tightens its grip on the region, the cabin becomes a haven of both tranquility and occasional unease, as they spend most of their days indoors. Serena's penchant for teasing Seneca about his previous conversation with Ilana is undeniable. Despite Seneca's repeated assurances it is none of her concern, Serena playfully engages in banter, bringing entertainment and levity to their interactions.

"Why don't you pester Ilana to make a move and leave me alone about it?" Seneca suggests to Serena as they watch through the emperor's collection of rare Disney "purple diamond" VHS tapes, whilst the fireplace keeps a steep difference in temperature than that of the outside world.

"You're so dense," Serena scoffs. "Ilana doesn't want to rush you past whatever emotional fluff you have… Also, these movies suck. Who falls in love in three days?"

He's unlikely to receive any respite from Serena's teasing, and she doesn't understand the nuance of the Disney renaissance. Instead of arguing with her about Ilana or the plot quality of the films, he seeks other means of shifting the conversation. At that moment, Seneca finds a rubber band wedged in the couch and stretches it out between his fingers and thumb until the tension on the rubber carries it across the room and hits Serena's thigh.

"Ow! you fucking jerk," she yells, grabbing the rubber band and unsuccessfully replicating the action.

He laughs as she gives up and hurls pillows at him during his escape attempt. "Relax, girl! I'm just playing."

* * *

She calms down and plops back down on the couch, hoping it's safe to do so. Seneca returns to his seat as well.

"I just think you both deserve to be happy, and—"

"Both?" Seneca says, sitting up with a smirk.

"Fuck you, Seneca. We're friends, okay?" She scoffs.

"I'll buy that for a dollar," he chuckles. "I guess it's nice to have friends... even violent ones like you."

A pillow hits him square in the face as Serena tells him to shut up once more.

Three more sunrises and a snowstorm pass before Ilana joins them on the snow coated retreat. Ilana had been under tremendous strain while serving as a mediator between the rebels and the Empire in the palace. The Imperial military council and a select group of lords had proven to be quite unyielding, strongly advocated for the complete dissolution of the rebellion. Conversely, the Whispers of Freedom remained steadfast in their position, refusing to back down as long as the Empire continued annexing free systems. It took her a significant amount of time to mediate between the two groups because they couldn't communicate directly with each other. The representative for the Whispers had to relay lengthy messages to the actual leader, which created a chaotic logistical situation that Seneca is grateful he didn't have to deal with. (Although he is curious why the other lords did not include him in the lordship council meetings.) In the end, the results turned out notably favorable.

The priority is to bring the military official back to the Whispers at a secure location in a timely manner, using a third-party transport for added secrecy. In return, the rebellion has agreed to accommodate an eighteen-month ease-fire so long as the Empire refrains from annexing any further territory. During the temporary armistice, the Whispers will temporarily suspend any and all liberation, evacuation, and acts of aggression. In addition to the hiatus of conflict, they've requested an audience with Ilana to further discuss permanent resolution. It's not peace, but it affords everyone ample time to work toward it; that is, if the Empire cares to do so.

Once Ilana and Serena wrap up a debriefing about the current political climate, Seneca seizes the chance to have a conversation with Ilana. They find themselves on the back porch of the cabin, overlooking the picturesque snow-covered mountain ridges.

Seneca leans against the rail beside her. "How are you?" he inquires, gazing out at the horizon.

"I'm good... I think," wisps of her warm breath escape into crisp winter air as she replies.

Seneca offers, "Do you want to talk about it?"

She grins, her gaze shifting to him. "Actually, for once... I don't. I just gave Serena the whole spiel, and I'm pretty sure you were listening anyway. I'd rather take you down to the springs and talk with you about...something else. Serena's gonna hang back.”

Ilana had intended to show Seneca the springs during their previous visit to the estate, but the unexpected events perpetuated by Imperial stubbornness cut it short. Despite the crisp winter air, the springs remain inviting, thanks to their geothermal heating. The only challenge is that Seneca lacks a bathing suit. Unbeknownst to him, Ilana had bought one for him at some point, and she now hands him a standard pair of swim trunks; trunks that sport a less-than-ideal neon hot pink coloration.

“Get changed,” she laughs, tossing him the trunks.

Before Seneca can protest the color of the bathing suit, Ilana swiftly runs inside and ascends the stairs and subsequently disappears into her room. Serena approaches him as he walks inside and pats him back with a sly grin. “You heard her stick jockey, and when you get to the springs... behave if you can.”
    “Behave? Serena, what are you two do—”. Serena too disappears up the stairs without minding his request for clarification.

After Serena makes her escape up the steps, Seneca is left alone to contemplate what lies ahead. It’s typical for these two women to have their own covert schemes, and occasionally he desires another male companion in the group to help him comprehend the situation. Unsure of the fate that awaits him, he too traverses the steps and enters his room to change. As he exchanges his usual grab for the grotesque swimming attire, he contemplates staying in his room to avoid whatever sinister plot might be at play. Nevertheless, once he’s prepared, he descends the stairs to meet Ilana, whose outfit appears to be ill-suited for a hot spring experience. Her outfit consists of a jacket, leggings that cling to her like paint, and boots that will certainly keep her feet toasty.

“I thought we were going to the springs,” Seneca remarks, standing shirtless and barefoot in the foyer, wearing only his trunks.
    “We are, genius, but it's freezing out. Maybe go put on a jacket?” Ilana replies with a chuckle, “I’ve got my suit on *under* this.”
    Seneca glances out the window to see snow falling once again. “Oh… yeah…”

Seneca had been so preoccupied with his thoughts about the impending “trap” at the springs that he forgot to consider the weather. Taking environmental conditions into account, along with the fact that they must walk to the springs, he dons his pilot jacket and a pair of shoes before joining Ilana as she walks out the door.

It’s rare for him to be affected by the weather. When worn in its entirety, his suit provides him with comfort in any weather, thanks to its innovative engineering. Despite wearing a jacket, his exposed legs are vulnerable to the icy chill, allowing the cold to penetrate his muscles. Seneca can't help but comment on the frigid conditions on their trek through the trees and down the steps to the spring. “Holy shit, it’s cold! How much further?” he exclaims as he shivers ferociously.

* * *

Ilana chuckles at his reaction as they follow a narrow gravel trail through the pines down a hill. "Maybe, another five minutes. What, are you cold or something?"

Seneca endures the five-minute walk down the narrow path through the snow-laden pines. Time seems to slow its pace, worsening the numbing sensation from his legs to his fingers. Finally, they reach the spring, and he wastes no time hanging his jacket on a nearby post designed for draping garments. He almost forgets his shoes as he approaches the spring in a rush to escape winter's breath but catches himself and removes them as well. Without further delay, he plunges himself into the warm and steaming water of the spring. It's refreshing and helps him recover from the frigid walk down.

Ilana, still fully dressed, remains on the edge of the spring. Seneca looks up at her as he leans back in the water. "You comin' in?"

"I am, but could you close your eyes or turn around?" she asks.

"I thought you had a bathing suit on?" Seneca replies curiously.

She blushes. "I am, I just haven't... ugh. I've never had a guy see me in my swimming attire before."

"Lucky me, I guess," Seneca winks and leans back.

"Are you flirting with me, Seneca?" she asks, unzipping her jacket in a teasing manner.

Though Seneca had recently expressed his growing attraction to Ilana, circumstance had not afforded them much time to interact since. Outside a few flirtatious messages, he has done little to act on his intrigue.

"Maybe a little. Flirting, I'm good at. Expressing my feelings, not so much."

"Hmm," she says, taking her jacket off and peeling the leggings off. "Enjoy the view then."

Seneca watches Ilana prepare to join him in the warm water. He can't help but feel an acute awareness of the vast gulf between them. Underneath the discarded layers of winter attire she'd worn, she reveals a striking red and black bikini. The suit top gracefully cradles her assets, her alluring form on display, without giving in to immodest exposure or excessive movement. Her flawless skin gleams on her subtly curved midsection, seamlessly transitioning into her hips just above the bottom of her suit. The bikini bottom, while not overly snug, hugs her form with a tantalizing absence of loose fabric. As Ilana senses Seneca's intense gaze upon her, she playfully executes a slow, teasing turn, allowing him a tasteful glimpse of her equally enticing backside. The charged atmosphere between them crackles with unspoken desire as their eyes lock, sparking a captivating dance of unfulfilled longing.

"Didn't your parents tell you it's rude to stare?" she laughs, splashing him and snapping him out of his trance.

He wipes the water off his face. "They may have mentioned it, but they never did much to prepare me for you."

Ilana laughs, her cheeks turning bright red. She sinks into the pool of warm water and sits across from him before changing the subject. "I love coming to this spot. It's so relaxing, especially during winter."

"It is pretty nice…"

While immersing themselves in the warm water, they spend time conversing with each other. The surrounding atmosphere is pristine. Delicate snowflakes drift gently down through the gaps in the towering pine trees, where some cling to the branches. With the passing of time, sounds of branches gradually relinquish their icy burden, interrupting their chatter. Small, glistening ice crystals adorn the nearby rock formations, casting a wintry enchantment over the mountain ridge above them.

Taking the breathtaking scenery and Ilana's company into account, his heart races as he allows himself to delve into his emotions. He's yet to have another soul since Kelsea set his heart on fire like this, nor has he had another person he could trust to share his pain and past with. At this point, the desire to open himself up outweighs the fear of grief that used to imprison his heart.

He meets her gaze as she eases into the warm water. His eyes wander across the serene winter landscape surrounding them. "You know this place kinda reminds me of home…"

Ilana inches closer to him in the water, her curiosity piqued. "Where is home? I've never heard you mention it before."

He offers a casual shrug. "I don't really talk about it much. Home is… where I lived with Sophie and Oliver before they died."

Her expression shifts to one of sympathy. "Oh, I'm sorry… I didn't mean to —"

He cuts her off gently, not wanting her to dwell on the topic. "Oh, no. It's fine. On Earth, I've got some land that I loved too much to let go of, but it was too hard to stay there alone…"

She leans in, her eyes locked onto his, as he describes his Earthly roots. The land he owns was once a bustling summer camp for children, a place where he himself spent his youthful summers. Nestled in the mountains of western South Carolina along the Chauga river, the camp became akin to a second home to him. The same family had run it for generations and the camp remained a significant part of his life, even after the HLEP. As more and more individuals left Earth to venture into space, the planet enacted rules that restricted permanent residence and imposed regulations on visitation to maintain a sustainable populous and protect the traditions that remained on Earth. This action unfortunately led to the decline of the camp's attendance and eventually its closure. Not wanting the history of the camp to be lost, Seneca purchased the property and lived there for years with his first wife and son, hoping to one day restore its purpose of bringing children close to nature.

"That's so neat," Ilana remarks, inching closer to him in the warm water.

Seneca hesitates for a moment before suggesting, "I could take you there if you want."

He misses home dearly. The memory of mountain air adorned with scents of white pine lingering, dear summer night skies, concerts of cicadas and whippoorwills echoing across the valleys, and freeing sensations of bare feet running through thick summer grass all tug at his heartstrings whenever he thinks of them. Yet, he has never returned, fearing painful reminders of everything he's lost. The prospect of facing his emotions frightens him, but if Ilana accompanies him, it might make the journey more bearable.

"I'd love that," she says, moving even closer to him, their shoulders almost touching.

He considers the logistics and says, "We could probably go sometime this week unless we have places to be soon."

Ilana's eyes light up, and she smiles playfully. "Nope," she replies, her gaze locked with his and painting a portrait of desire and longing. "But I'm only going with you if you give me a *good* reason to go with you."

Seneca scratches his head, a hint of flirtatious uncertainty in his expression. "Define a 'good' reason."

Ilana leans closer once again and says in a low voice. "I want to know how you feel. *Specifically*. You told me you feel something. I want to know what it is."

Seneca pauses, taking a moment to gather his thoughts. He can no longer suppress his growing desire to kindle the spark between himself and Ilana, nor does he want to. While fear of loss still lingers, it no longer justifies ignoring his intuition. Opting to be brave, he decides to take the leap.

"You know that light feeling in your stomach when you're falling?" He pauses, and Ilana nods, a sultry smile creeping across her face. "I feel like that whenever you're around."

She wraps her arms around his neck, shifting to sit in his lap. Suddenly, the warm spring water is no longer the hottest thing embracing him. "Name that feeling for me, and I'll go to Earth with you," she purrs, her voice laced with longing and her face mere inches from his. He can taste her breath moving over his tongue as her lips slowly close in.

"Falling," he responds, his voice sincere, his eyes locked onto hers. She giggles softly, causing water to ripple around her body, just before she presses her lips sensually against his. It's a passionate kiss, a promise of the intense connection between them, and the decision to go to Earth together seems definitive.

Chapter 19: Homecoming

Serena politely declines an offer of passage to Earth, flashing a knowing smile. She asserts she has no intention of becoming a third wheel on Seneca and Ilana's trip, and besides, *the Phantom* isn't designed to carry more than two passengers in some degree of comfort. The journey from Vista to Earth stretches over two days, and the Seneca and Ilana settle onto the small sofa in the quarters while the Phantom's autopilot takes over the piloting duties. There, they indulged in "watching" movies. Thanks to Serena's absence, they can spend entire durations of films with their lips pressed together in tender displays of affection.

Their passage through Federation space to Earth is uneventful, but the transition to flying into Earth's airspace differs vastly from much of the rest of the galaxy. Earth still employs the same air traffic control system that was in place when Seneca left. Once they enter Sol, Seneca almost forgets that he needs to file an S-EFR (Space to Earth Flight Rules) flight plan with the Port of Charleston as their destination. Luckily, he remembers just in time. After he files necessary flight plans and receives approval from Earth ATC, they are then transferred to the appropriate radio frequencies, guiding the spacecraft through the solar system all the way to the Port of Charleston.

The sight of Earth in his canopy fills Seneca with a bittersweet sense of nostalgia. He hasn't set foot on Earth since his move to Phoebe. With the blue and green ball of humanity's origin growing in size before him, memories transport him back to similar moments during returns from early colonization missions. As they continue the approach for landing, the brilliant blue of the planet gradually gives way to the lush green of the land below. The Phantom's communications radios abuzz with instructions from ATC as they make the final descent. The scent of Earth's oceans and forests, carried by the wind, wafts through the ventilation system, igniting his senses. Eventually, Seneca brings the Phantom down for a landing at the Port of Charleston, where the vast expanse of the ocean meets the welcoming embrace of the land.

* * *

For the first time in more than a lifetime, Seneca steps out into the summer sun—the sun of his people—on the planet he once called home. He offers his hand to help Ilana down from the ladder of *the Phantom*. "Welcome to Earth," he says, leading her away from the spacecraft.

The scent of the Atlantic Ocean drifts over the port, its salty fragrance gently kissing the cobblestone streets at the far end of the port. Ilana observes the sights of cranes stretching to the sky, cargo ships wading in the water, and tugboats moving about with childlike awe as Seneca leads her to the customs office. Earth's architecture has seen little change despite the ever-marching progress of mankind elsewhere, thanks to its heritage site status declared by the UF. If someone were born on Earth today, it would look remarkably similar to the world Earth-born HLEP survivors knew as children. Those who remain on Earth resist change staunchly, preserving the planet's traditions and resisting the transformation of humanity into space-faring beings. Buildings, roads, and vehicles, some electric and others running on imported chemical alternatives to fossil fuels, still maintain their familiar appearance. If only time had been frozen in the nineties and not the 2030s...

Customs clear them for entry, and they walk through the pathways of the port as Seneca sifts through a set of keys he'd dug out of a drawer in *the Phantom*'s galley. "It has to be on this chain..." Seneca mumbles quietly.

Seneca is on the hunt for the key to a storage unit at the port. The storage unit itself has been located—being only a short stroll across a street just north of the customs office, but the key lies buried within a jingling bag of keys that has been sitting, gathering dust. It takes a few more frustrating moments for his determined search to yield success. He finally finds the elusive key and places it into the rusty padlock that's keeping the tin unit closed.

He unlatches an extremely rusty padlock and proceeds to open the door. The sliding open of the garage-style door piques Ilana's curiosity. "What's this?" she inquires, her eyes falling upon an object shrouded beneath a tarp.

Seneca, with a grin of nostalgia, reveals the antique vehicle hidden beneath the tarp—an early two-thousand model Toyota Tacoma. "This..." he taps the hood with a satisfying metallic *thunk,* "...is my old truck. Hopefully, it still runs... might take a minute..."

Ilana, intrigued by the vehicle, takes a leisurely stroll around it. Her face reflects back at her as she admires the glossy black paint (littered with a fair amount of scratches) as Seneca uses a toolbox in the corner of the storage unit to perform some maintenance. "It looks somewhat like the vehicles on other planets... Except they don't smell like this."

Seneca, ever the knowledgeable human, explains, "Well, most vehicles in the galaxy are electric or radiologically powered. This thing used to run on gasoline, but now it operates on a synthetic fossil fuel substitute that burns cleaner... however still has a mechanical smell to it." He delves into a brief explanation of how a four-stroke gasoline engine functions while he finishes changing the pickling oil with regular motor oil and swapping out the battery. Finally, he closes the hood, and they hop into the vehicle and fasten their seat belts.

"Old technology..." she says as she takes in the scent of carpeted upholstery inside a hot vehicular interior fills their nostrils.

Seneca himself takes a moment to examine his old transport. It's eerie how the truck is in the same state he left it in. Old empty bags that once concealed spicy snacks lay crumpled and stuffed in the door cup holder by his feet. His outdated insurance card hangs, clipped to the visor. Cards of well wishes and condolences from Sophie's family that were mailed to him after she passed still sit in the center console, in mint condition as well untouched by the light of the sun for centuries... Seneca stows them quickly and pushes the thoughts to the back of his mind.

"... and the keys should be in that little compartment right there in front of you," he says, pointing toward the glove box.

"How does this thing even still work?" Ilana asks, laughing as she hands him the keys.

"If it does..." Seneca scratched his head as he put the old truck into gear. "It's because I preserved it well enough. Before that, it's practically been rebuilt several times. I used to work on it myself when I lived here..."

Seneca details the nature of his abilities to keep such an outdated vehicle in working order. He purchased the 2008 Tacoma in Colorado right after he had graduated from the Air Force Academy and developed a sentimental attachment to it akin to the current sentiment he has toward *the Phantom*. He'd always kept it running through the help of good friends who made engineering their calling and machine shops that could produce discontinued parts as needed.

With a hopeful prayer and a couple of attempts at turning the engine over, the old truck roars to life, its engine revving for the first time in an extremely long time, filling the unit with disgusting black smoke.

"Oh shit! Is it on fire?!" Ilana asks, startled at the sight.

"Nah, just been sitting for... damn... I don't know... a long ass time."

Seneca grabs the wheel, skillfully maneuvering the truck out of the storage unit. He hops out and secures the unit and steers the vehicle through the cobblestone streets of the city and up Interstate 26 west towards the mountains, excitement on his breath as he embarks on a drive to his long-abandoned home. It's nice to be behind the wheel of a vehicle after so long. The feeling and smell of the vehicle's air-conditioning cooling the stuffy, humid air.

The vehicle, despite its age, performs up to standard as it continues the drive up to the mountains; unfolding just as he remembers it. They cross the Santee River, leave behind the sandy flatlands of South Carolina's low country, gradually ascending into terrain marked by undulating hills until they find themselves along scenic highway-11. A beautiful winding route at the Appalachian foothills that consumes more time than taking interstate-85 but treats its travelers to a beautiful snaking road that follows the contours of the mountains as they rise and fall.

Ilana's endless curiosity prompts her to pepper Seneca with questions about every detail they encounter on the ride. Seneca guides them through familiar landscapes, passing through quaint towns like Inman, Campobello, and Cleveland. As they approach Walhalla, the last town along their route, Seneca marvels at how everything appears frozen in time. Like all the towns before it, brick buildings and diagonal parking spaces still line Walhalla's streets, exuding a welcoming southern charm. Houses scattered around the outskirts further enhance the small town's familiarity; the resident's wave as he drives past.

Amidst Ilana's curiosity and the waves of nostalgia washing over him, Seneca can't help but sport a wide, joyous smile that stretches across his face. The last stretch of their drive ambles up the foothills on a winding two-lane road that meanders about the contours of the mountain ridge. It's always been a comforting journey, signaling his proximity to home. He rolls the windows down, allowing the scent of the mountain summer to fill the cab. Lazily drifting cumulus clouds adorn the hazy summer sky, and damp pavement serves as evidence of traces of rain showers that have blown through. Sounds of distant thunder reverberate as a low rumble from an unseen storm hidden away by the hills stretching above them. Wild grasses along the roadside blur past as they drive.

Soon, he turns the truck onto a red dirt road, navigating around the occasional obstacle like large branches. Despite his absence, Seneca ensures local governments maintain the road and property while he is gone (for generous annual donations added to maintain the nearby state parks and trails). The land still holds deep sentimental value for him and the care of it is no small matter. They reach their destination, marked by an old, rusted gate that he clears of kudzu before driving through.

Continuing through, the road veers left, passing below the ridge a grassy field roughly the size of a major league baseball field atop a hill. Ahead of them, around the corner of the hill, there sit rectangular, rustic cabins with tin roofs. Beyond them, a slope leads down to a lake, with two more rows of cabins on the descent. Seneca steers the truck to the left, driving it among other structures to his left and right before the road forks; once bustling with activity as craft huts, activity centers, and storage sheds, now these equally rustic buildings stand preserved, yearning for the joyous laughter of children to grace their interiors once more. After several hours of driving, he finally parks the truck beneath a metal carport beside a gray cabin that has a spacious front porch offering a serene view of the lake nestled at the bottom of the hill. Small ripples, stirred by bass and bluegill inhabiting its cool mountain waters, serve as evidence that nature here is thriving as it always has.

As they swing the doors open to exit the vehicle, the familiar scent of clean air, flourishing grass, and white pine greets his nostrils, just as it always has since childhood. Seneca's breath grows heavy as he exits the truck alongside Ilana, overwhelmed by a blend of happiness and sadness as memories of his childhood, his late wife, and Oliver flood his mind. The summer Appalachian breeze carries with it a familiar symphony of rustling leaves and buzzing insects, evoking a profound sense of nostalgia.

"This place is beautiful," Ilana remarks, taking his hand. "You okay?"

Seneca fights back a tear, struggling to put into words the intense bittersweet emotions surging within him. "Yeah, I'm okay. Just being back is—well, is tough."

Ilana doesn't press him with more questions; instead, she envelops Seneca in a tight hug. Taking a deep breath, he concentrates on the soothing weight of her hug, surrendering to the waves of pain that were destined to wash over him the moment he parked his ship. His pride crumbles, and he finally allows himself to confront the grief regarding everything he left behind on Earth. Gradually, waves of anguish consume him, forcing him down to his knees. Tears flow freely from his eyes as he murmurs repetitive phrases, swallowed by a torrent of emotion.

Kneeling on the grass, memories wash over him. He recalls lazy summer days drying in the sun, his son's laughter echoing as they tumbled down grassy hills. He remembers the warmth of his wife's smile when they'd sit together on the porch watching Oliver fish, and comforting embraces of camp friends gathered around a crackling campfire the night before they all parted ways. It's as if a floodgate has opened, engulfing him in a tidal wave—the inexorable passage of time crashing over him forcing him to acknowledge the irreplaceable void left by those he cherished and lost.

Ilana remains by his side, her silent support a lifeline amidst his emotional tempest. In this moment, Seneca slowly catches his breath and gradually realizes that facing these emotions, painful as it may be, is an essential step in healing and moving forward, though it's incredibly difficult. The unavoidable truth that those days are now mere history, his family forever beyond reach, and time ceaselessly marching forward weighs heavily upon him. The pain is deep-seated, likely to endure, but with Ilana by his side in this moment, he finds comfort in knowing he's not entirely alone in his journey of self-discovery and reconciliation with the past.

After the flood waters of his demons settle, Seneca regains the composure of his breathing. Inhaling, holding his breath, and slowly exhaling until he is able to return to his feet. Catharsis, for once, fills a void once full of affliction, even if only for the moment it's welcome.

"Sorry," he says, drying his face with his arms.
    "Don't be," Ilana says, helping him reset.

Seneca continues returning to a state of normalcy, despite intermittent post-cry convulsions and sniffles, as he guides Ilana onto the front porch of a house he once occupied. He unlocks the sliding glass door and steps inside. The familiar smell of an old wooden building invades his nostrils as he breathes, and Ilana steps inside behind him.

* * *

"This is home... kinda," he says as he shows her the different rooms and pictures on the wall. A wardrobe of shirts that he owns hangs nearly in a long closet in his old bedroom.

He takes time to tell her stories, some old, some new, of being a kid at the camp as well as stories about Sophie and Oliver that do not relate directly to their untimely death. She listens intently and holds his hand, asking the occasional question. The day passes as he takes her on a tour outside, showing her around the grounds and continues the nostalgic stories of what was and who he used to be.

Chapter 20: The Song of Nature

A long summer day gives way to a setting sun as evening sneaks up on them. Time seems to fly by. The night sky fades into view, adorned with the millions of stars Seneca has patrolled over the centuries he's been in space. Seneca and Ilana lie on the hillside by the large lake that occupies the valley of Seneca's property. They talk and watch stars come into view as bullfrogs, crickets, and cicadas crescendo into song.

Ilana breaks up a brief silence. "It's hard to believe we live up there, and there are millions of people—-the bulk of humanity living out there when they all came from places like this…"

Seneca laughs and replies, "Shit…imagine being a little kid laying on this hill looking up at those stars and how foreign the idea of people flying spaceships was hundreds of years ago."

She turns her head toward him. "It's crazy to think, as beautiful as Earth is, why people would leave."

"I guess it's like when they discovered the Earth wasn't flat and distant shores were to be found. People left their homes to find themselves somewhere else. Somewhere new. Somewhere to challenge themselves and make themselves into legends."

"Is that why you ravage the stars with your piloting skills?" She says jokingly.

"Truth be told, I never intended to make space home. I lost myself out there after Sophie. I recovered a bit when I found Kelsea but watching her take a natural course of life that I won't—I don't know… kinda caused me to abandon what was left of myself. I figured I'd never make it back, but now maybe there's hope." Seneca says, taking her hand.

He pulls her close, their shoulders pressed against each other on the side of the hill by the lake. As he kisses her cheek, he watches her face light up with a smile, and together they marvel at the stars twinkling in the night sky. His display of affection and solitude around them inspires Ilana to position herself on top of him. With a smile on her face, she gazes down at him. Her beautiful ocean blue hair tickles his face as it drapes at the mercy of gravity.

* * *

"Hi" Seneca responds playfully to her change in position.

She reciprocates a playful greeting and kisses his cheek. As their lips met in a subsequent kiss, she slowly leaned into him, her weight pressing down on him, while her red clay dusted feet lightly brushed against his legs. The kissing between the two becomes less playful and more passionate as the two roll about on the hillside. Ilana has seen a moment of vulnerability in him and capitalizes on it with no intention of mercy. The confines underneath Seneca's pilot jacket become a playground for her exploring hands as the romantic rendezvous intensifies. Using her soft and nimble fingers, she expertly unfastens his belt, leaving it loose and ready to be removed—an action that alerts him to her intent to further escalate the intimacy.

"Madam, what do you think you are doing?" he asks, grabbing her wrist with a flirtatious grin on his face.
"Shut up and listen to the frogs or whatever they are." She says.

In the heat of the night, Seneca and Ilana sensually undress each other by the lake, their lips locked in a passionate embrace throughout. The grass tickles his bare skin as he lies on his back, the sweat making the red clay of the southern soil cling to him. But in the throes of passion with a beautiful woman, he doesn't even notice.

The sparks of their connection finally burst into a flame, blazing brightly and beyond their control. Seneca, now bearing the weight of Ilana's body, softly caresses her arms and eases the tension in her back through gentle, rhythmic movements. Inquisitively, he takes the opportunity to trace the intricate contours of her form, savoring the varied textures and intricacies that adorn every inch. Just like the cabin on Vista, their bodies move in sync with rhythmic motion, harmonizing with the chorus of sounds that fill the night. While nature's music steadily grows in intensity, Seneca remains fully attuned to his body's sensations, the rhythmic sounds of Ilana's heavy breathing, and the tactile experience of her bare skin pressed against him, all in harmony with the nocturnal chorus. It's a cherished melody that two enjoy together as one. Ilana tightens her body as the night's song crescendos to its peak and slowly returns to a soft, unorganized harmony of bugs, frogs, and a whippoorwill joining in late into the performance.

Even after Seneca and Ilana had finished their contributions to the night's symphony, it continues to sing its verses, surrounding them with the sticky embrace of a humid summer night. He kisses her one last time, weakened from fleeting ecstasy, and the lovers fall asleep on the grassy hillside several yards down from where they began their liaison.

Seneca awakens from his slumber due to the soft sting of the morning sun. His and Ilana's bodies remain uncovered—their naked forms exposed to the morning, coated with dew and dirt. Seneca smiles as he looks at her sleepy smile before he gently wakes Ilana with a motion for her to come into the cabin. Seneca and his lover scale the hill in silence, their footsteps barely audible as they make their way to his cabin. Once inside, they take a refreshing shower together in a very aged tub-shower, rinsing off the dirt from their bodies. Afterwards, they change into comfortable summer clothes, ready to relax. He digs up an old iPod and connects it to the house's speaker system to play an old playlist of mixed era country music. Pleasantly surprised it still works, he turns on a coffee maker and brews some coffee he'd found in his cupboard.

He takes a second to take in the surroundings of his cabin. The rustic interior has old 1970's style wooden paneling, creaky and scratched wood floors that show their age and use. The kitchen is small and has a wall with a cutout so you could see the tv while you wash dishes in the ceramic sink. The bedrooms are at the back of the hall just after you pass a staircase that takes you to the den in the basement. The cabin is older than Seneca is and was where family of the camp directors would live when the property was in its prime years. The furnishings within, such as the old piano and plaid couch, look as if they were plucked from a 1970's catalogue.

Propping his feet up on the antique coffee table in his quaint living room, he says to Ilana as she joins him, "So that was fun."

Ilana turns red as a cherry, covering her blush, she says, "Shut up..."

Seneca laughs as Ilana's embarrassment subsides, and they proceed to exchange stories about previous romantic experiences, being careful to maintain a level of privacy appropriate for their new relationship. To Seneca's astonishment, he finds out that Ilana is completely inexperienced, having only engaged in such intimacy for the first time the night before.

"But you're, what one-hundred and sixty, how?" Seneca asks in disbelief, "How am I your first?"

Another embarrassed expression plasters itself onto Ilana's face as she giggles. "Yeah, but I'm also royalty and can't just *date* you know. Also, it's not like I was fascinated in anyone until I met you..."

"Why not?"

"The only people I could find myself around were flashy, trying to impress me, or otherwise full of themselves in attempts to sell themselves to me." She pauses to sip her heavily sweetened coffee before continuing. "I wanted someone who would not be a constant reminder that I'm a princess. I want a less complicated experience, like my parents told me they had when they were young. Imagine being royalty for your whole life. There's no true freedom, there's no peace. It's all complicated."

Seneca digests her sentiment. Details regarding Ilana's lack of romantic experience tell him she's picky for one, but also apparently pines for a simplistic life. She describes a book that she found in her father's personal bookshelf called *Where I Come From*, by a southern man named Rick Bragg. Seneca doesn't know the book but recognizes the author.

"I can understand how you feel. Sometimes I've wished I could've just come back here and stayed..." he sets loose a heavy exhale. "But I never have since I'd have had to be here alone"

"You aren't alone now," Ilana says. Seneca feels the warmth of Ilana's hand in his as they get up to get going.

Though he'd love to stay in the rustic three-bedroom cabin he calls home, Ilana is a non-resident visitor with only granted ten days of visitation, so they waste no time getting on the road for the day. The two of them spend the next several days exploring Seneca's old haunts across Georgia, Tennessee, North Carolina, and, of course, South Carolina. The itinerary consists of several locations that hold sentimental value to Seneca. Simplicity of Earthly living—the sights, sounds, and smells enthrall and captivate Ilana. Even the uniqueness of living somewhere where there is no synthetic food fascinates her—especially when she saw a live cow for the first time.

While they spend the days exploring the southeast, they return to Seneca's cabin at night, embracing each other's bare company. They take turns teasing each other and joking post intimacy before drifting into conversations about what they think the future may hold for them. Ilana even openly begins fantasizing about running away from her role as a princess and spending every night here, with Seneca, like this. He enjoys listening and dwelling on that prospect himself. How fun would it be to return to normalcy with kids, farm animals, and other accouterments? Unfortunately, at least for the time being, it's not a possibility. Seneca knows Ilana will not abandon the people of the Empire when they look to her for aid. Still, it's a fond thought.

On their last day of their Earthly visit, Seneca and Ilana hike old trails that Seneca pays to keep maintained. These trails see few visitors nowadays, but Seneca ensures that funding is available should people want to enjoy them. The particular trail he's chosen is one of his favorites, a beginner-friendly hike leading to a two-tiered waterfall named Licklog falls. Both levels of the falls have shallow pools at the bottom that are perfect for swimming, and Seneca plans to take Ilana up to the upper pool. It's a picturesque sight where a log sits above the cool water—a spot where he received his first kiss when he had snuck off with his camp girlfriend when he was a teen… It was a romantic backdrop then, and he doubts the appeal would have degraded over time.

A mix of deciduous hardwoods and pines forms a thick green canopy surrounding the trail, keeping them shaded from the summer sun on their trek. Their conversation intermingles with the sounds of songbirds calling out to each other. Unmistakable sounds of a mountain stream cutting through the forest soon dominate the soundscape as they cross old wooden bridges and make their way between the poplar tents to the falls.

As the falls appear, Seneca and Ilana are relieved to see them, seeking respite from the summer heat. Despite the shade from the sun, the warmth and humidity of the region's summer afternoon leaves them both decently coated in sweat. They change into their swimsuits and hold hands as they make their way into the water.

This time Seneca had access to his personal collections of aged camo colored swim trunks while Ilana boasts an ivory one-piece suit.

"Cold!" Ilana squeaks, jumping back out as the mountain water's chilly embrace wraps around her feet.

"Oh yeah," Seneca chuckles. "It's like this year-round. The water comes out of groundwater springs and hasn't seen sunlight in decades."

They continue to inch into the water, their bodies slowly acclimating to the cold temperatures. Finally, Seneca musters up strength, inhaling a deep breath to prepare himself, and then fearlessly jumps into the frigid water. Ilana, however, hesitates to follow his courageous lead and continues to inch in slowly. Seneca's patience wears thin, and after teasing her a bit, he maliciously decides to help her adjust to the water. As he approaches her, she desperately tries to flee, but her feeble efforts are in vain. Seneca swiftly grabs her and tosses her into the deeper water, causing a resounding splash and drenching her in the refreshing coolness.

"Seneeecaaaaa!" she shouts, standing up in the waist deep water.

Both of them burst into laughter at her brief discomfort, noticing one another's bodies graced by anatomical responses to the cold. Seneca suggests, "I guess we need to be close for warmth," standing behind her and pulling her toward him.

"I guess so," Ilana agrees, leaning into him.

He guides her to continue, and they climb up the moss-covered rock wall to the upper pool beneath the upper waterfall, where the water is deeper. The upper fall cascades whitewater over a log that has been there for centuries. Seneca and Ilana, satisfied with its weight-bearing capacity, settled down together, enjoying the mist from the waterfall that adorned their faces and hair with small droplets.

"This is beautiful," Ilana smiles, wiping the water from her face and brow. "It might even rival my family's mountain estate..."

"Yeah, it is. My granddaddy gave my dad hell when he moved to Atlanta away from Hendersonville just northeast of here. Though it was more so because Dad didn't want to be involved in the 'family business'. However, it was more about my dad opening a bar downtown with a buddy of his."

"What was the family business?"

"Moonshinin'. distilling and running corn born whiskey to folks without paying the tax collector their fair share—or at least what the revenue man believed was their share. Us Mason's ain't too keen on government feeling entitled to the people's production..."

Ilana laughs as they sit, taking in the roaring falls beneath the shade of the poplars, hemlocks, and oaks. "Sounds like you aren't the first outlaw in the family, then."

"Nope." He shakes his head. "Though Dad didn't get involved in the business, he eventually returned to Appalachia when he retired... Makes me want to do the same."

"Maybe someday we can," Ilana says, grasping his hand.

* * *

With little regard to their tender moment, time trudges forward cruelly. Seneca does his best to ensure that they do not spend the remaining time in vain as he sits with Ilana perched on the log. Conversations lead to kissing, and kissing leads to further romancing. Seneca, fondly remembering how the fires of passion feel, begins rediscovering a long dormant aspect of himself there with Ilana. Unfortunately, time is still his enemy, and forces another sunset upon him before they make their way back to his truck.

The sun rises the next day, bringing upon the advent of their return to required duties among the stars. They pack up shortly afterwards and depart from his mountain property. As they drive back to the Port of Charleston, conversation naturally steers toward Ilana's future plans.

"I think we should visit some of the rebel-controlled territories," she proposes.

Seneca feels slightly surprised. "That's risky… Any particular reason why?"

"First of all, I owe them a visit per the previous negotiations. Plus, with the ceasefire, I should be safe, especially with you by my side. I just… have a feeling it's the right thing to do," Ilana explains, her voice laced with determination.

"The visit was technically supposed to be within a neutral territory though." Seneca says, reminding her.

"I know, but… I want them to know that I intend to pursue change…" she says.

He's concerned but has unwavering trust in Ilana as he nods. "Alrighty then. We're off to see the rebels."

Chapter 21: No Caution for Time

From the moment Seneca arrived back on Vista with Ilana in tow and informed Serena of Ilana's plan to venture into rebel-controlled space, she's been up in arms with relentless protests.

"*Absolutely not*! No! Why? I don't know what sort of gas you inhaled in Earth's atmosphere that makes you think this is a good idea!" Serena exclaims.

"Nothing is going to get better unless someone continues pursuing resolution. The rebels are Imperial citizens and deserve to have their voices heard! Somebody has to reach out for peace. Serena, please..." Ilana says, pleading with an irate Serena.

"No! This is dumb! What if they kidnap you? What if they hold you for ransom? What if they kill you on sight?!" Serena interrupts Ilana, bombarding her with an endless stream of "what-ifs."

Serena shares a plethora of concerns that have also crossed Seneca's mind. Curiosity fills him as he contemplates the intentions driving this venture, mindful of the unknowns and hazards that await. While the possibility of catastrophe exists, he trusts his abilities to perform his job duties, and he trusts Ilana. Furthermore, he believes that his reputation alone should be a powerful deterrent against anyone who might consider being aggressive towards Ilana. Ilana's decision is driven by love for her people and a steadfast devotion to pursue peace, and it's enough for Seneca to align himself firmly with Ilana in this audacious endeavor.

"The Imperial lords would never allow it anyway," Serena says in a frenzy, trying to talk sense into Ilana.

"I don't need their permission. I'm going to do it anyway," Ilana says and then looks at Seneca. "Besides, I know one Imperial lord sanctioning the trip."

"Ilana. You know that doesn't count. Seneca commands one vote, and he didn't exactly have a great first impression..."

Ilana crosses her arms and looks at Serena, unwilling to back down. Serena sulks and throws her hands up in surrender as she stomps away. "Fuck it then, send it. Let's fucking go get fucking kidnapped or some shit! God damn it!"

With Serena's reluctant "support" secured, the three of them invest considerable time in planning their ambitious "unity tour," as Ilana has dubbed it. The girls carefully plan out destinations and discreetly communicate with governments willing to engage in diplomatic talks. Their overall strategy entails spending a week in each rebel-controlled region, engaging in public speaking and meeting with local leaders. The goal is to gather the wishes of the Whisper territories and present them to the lordship council. Seneca believes this task is ultimately pointless, though he keeps his thoughts to himself.

His doubts won't alter his role as the vigilant protector. He takes time to study relevant information thoroughly in order to ensure the party's safety and refining his marksmanship skills in Vista's shooting range. They will probably encounter more hostility than ever before, so honing his accuracy with a pistol is a must to ensure his skills are up to standard (though he suspects Ilana will impose restrictions on its use). Additionally, he meticulously creates security protocols and contingency plans, ensuring to the best of his knowledge that he accounts for every potential situation and leaves nothing to chance. Finally, he also recognizes the advantage for enhanced security and recommends the addition of another agent to the team but wants someone who Ilana trusts with the… specific nature of their trip.

Ilana readily agrees with the suggestion and quickly finds a suitable person, introducing Jesper into the group. Evidently, Jesper used to have the same role as Seneca, but he was particularly skilled in intelligence-related functions, so Ilana moved him into Imperial intelligence.

Jesper's tall and slender figure, with his short curly hair and darker complexion, adds to his debonair. His muted but friendly demeanor conceals a keen intellect with prior experience in the role, making him a solid choice for the new opening. With a pilot certification of his own within the Imperial ranks, Jesper will be able to help safeguard Ilana aboard *the Solace* and other locals they will traverse.

Seneca introduces himself with a formal handshake. "I'm Seneca. Nice to meet you. Hope you're ready for a fun vacation."
"Jesper Thompson." he says, introducing himself quickly.

The group wastes no more time as they finalize their preparations and begin their uphill battle to achieve peace in the Empire and depart the next morning. The onset of the expedition unfolds just as Seneca expected it would. A three-day trip across Imperial space takes them to Daryl, where they'll be visiting the three major cities that lie within. Upon landing in Caissoux, the capital of the system and largest city on Daryl-4, they encountered air filled with the sounds of shouting and the sight of angry mobs, which makes it difficult for Seneca to secure the landing pad. Seneca finds himself at a standstill as port security declines to offer support or establish boundaries, leaving him restricted by the limitations on the use of force to preserve the fragile ceasefire and project an image of genuine diplomacy.

* * *

To make matters worse for him, the citizens here feel betrayed by Seneca. Angry chants and expletives fill his ears as they hurl rotting food and other unsanitary debris at him. It's a stark contrast to the times when many had regaled him as a beacon of hope, arriving to save their homes from Imperial influence. The disdain emanating from the type of people who formally celebrated the sight of him, and *the Phantom* is unsettling, creating a distracting atmosphere for him as he tries to focus on the task at hand. His efforts to disperse the crowd prove futile. The crowd doesn't thin out until they have thoroughly coated Seneca, his ship, and *the Solace* in the city's refuse. Eventually, Ilana, Serena, and Jesper can safely leave, although there are still a few stragglers who have held onto some garbage that they successfully throw at Ilana before Seneca can react.

They finally enter the ground shuttle transport to the lodging that Serena had arranged. They all give a collective sigh. Seneca is the first to speak "That. Was not fun."

"What were you expecting?" Serena replies, "This isn't the first time we've been somewhere *this* bad. You're lucky they weren't throwing rocks…"

Ilana remains silent, her usually expressive face now stoic and composed despite the soiled diaper in her hair. She takes deliberate breaths, giving the impression of being the most composed among them. Seneca had expected her to be more upset by the hostile reception, but her face and calmness have shunted those expectations.

Amidst the silence, Seneca gazes out from the shuttle at the sprawling urban landscape unfolding before them. Impressive glass exteriors adorn intricately designed skyscrapers that dominate the city's skyline, while streets and walkways below boast generous decorations of trees and planted gardens. The opulent facade makes it hard to believe this is a society torn by war and oppression.

They clean themselves within the confines of a quiet, shared hotel suite. Although there is an undeniable tension lingering in the air as if something is ready to strike at them, hidden from view. Serena's earlier warnings about the potential pitfalls of their plan echo in Seneca's mind, now validated by the hostility they faced in Daryl. He grapples with internal doubts, questioning whether he'll be able to fulfill his duties, given the constraints on the use of force he's now acutely aware of. He couldn't even keep Ilana from getting trash thrown at her… What if it's not trash next time? Those thoughts pave the way for a rough night of sleep as Ilana curls up beside him and drifts off.

A furious sea of chanting citizens hurls insults and debris at Ilana the next morning. Daryl's government has agreed to let her speak, and amidst the surrounding turmoil, she steps onto a platform set up in the city center to address the enraged citizens. The cacophony of hate only subsides when Ilana signals Seneca's permission to fire blanks into the air. The buzzing metallic noise of plasma fire momentarily captivates the audience, allowing Ilana to speak.

* * *

"People of Daryl," she begins, her voice cutting through the tension, "I hesitate to call you Imperial citizens, for I recognize that this title is one you never asked for. Take your time. Throw your trash at me. Send your message. Make your voices heard, for I am here to listen."

While her opening remarks make Seneca nervous, the citizens eagerly embrace her invitation. Attendees waste no time showering her with detritus and filth as she outstretches her arms to the side and bowing her head in acceptance. The occasional hard object makes worrisome contact, causing her to flinch and leaving noticeable red marks. For over an hour, an endless deluge of hatred floods the stage, nearly burying her beneath its weight. Finally, they run out of trash and resort to simply booing her.

She gracefully wipes her face and brings the microphone to her lips, undeterred by the sludge on it and resumes her speech

"I *hear* you. I come to you with an open heart and a listening ear, recognizing the depth of your grievances and the validity of your aspirations. My presence here is not symbolic; it is a testament to my commitment to acknowledging your voices and effecting change…"

Seneca, as well as the sea of Daryl's inhabitants, listens silently as she weaves words together covered in garbage with no animosity, discourse, or anger in her voice. Serena echoes his impression in an exchange of glances as Ilana captivates those before her. Her speech almost sounds like something between an apology and some sort of call to action. Whatever the case is, her words soothe the crowd.

"…As we navigate this path forward, let us remember that genuine change requires not only understanding, but also action. Let us harness the power of unity to dismantle the barriers of oppression and injustice, forging a society where every voice is heard, and every individual is valued. Together, let us write a new chapter in history—one defined not by division and strife, but by cooperation and progress."

She concludes her speech as gracefully as she began, signaling for Jesper and Seneca to assist her in stepping down from the podium. As she navigates through the mountain of filth before her, an unfathomable occurrence takes place. To Seneca's astonishment, the previously angry crowd erupts with applause and praise, and nearby citizens step forward to help her off the stage. He's never witnessed such a dramatic shift in the mood of a crowd.

"How?" He mutters as they make their way back into the hotel to clean up prior to meeting with the local leadership.

Ilana, with a couple bruises on her face, just whispers back, in almost a cryptic tone, "I listen to the whisper."

Seneca, confused, nods as he thinks silently to himself, "*What does that mean?*" He takes a moment as they walk back up the city streets to really analyze what Ilana had said in her speech. Her words definitely would not sit well with the lordship council, and almost seemed to side *with* the Whispers. He shrugs it off and chooses to remain oblivious to her political motives since he cares little for the government game. Thankfully, the remainder of the stay in Daryl goes smoothly, with no additional litter being tossed their way.

It is on the eve of their departure when the four companions unexpectedly come together in the hotel room, where they spend the night engaged in animated conversation that stretches well into the darkness. Ilana's familiar demeanor is on full display, radiating with pride over the noticeable sway she has over the citizens of Daryl and the resulting atmosphere.

Chapter 22: A Calm Before the Storm

Receptions in the subsequent star systems they encounter continue to start with angry mobs and protests greeting the entourage. Seneca faces a constant challenge of resisting urges to use his pistol for crowd control, but he continues exercising restraint for Ilana. It's not an easy task, and it tests his character, but it's been worth it thus far. With each system they visit, Ilana's ability to win over rebel communities becomes more apparent as enthusiastic applause replaces their initial hostility. Employing the same empathetic and passionate approach she used on Daryl; she wins them over one system at a time. Occasionally, Seneca finds himself wondering if Ilana has the capability to bring a swift conclusion to the rebellion.

As part of her routine before leaving any system, Ilana arranges meetings with local leaders to actively engage with them and collect their aspirations and demands for the Empire to meet the mission of their envoy. She assures them she will make sure the Empire acknowledges their desires. Most of the rebels demand nothing less than absolute liberation, while others are satisfied with receiving appropriate support and assistance for their population. Month after month, Ilana's commitment to being an attentive listener is unwavering, regardless of the specific demands imposed.

Eventually, the group's journey leads them to Trinity, a bustling port city located in Origo Liberatis, which is known to be one of the most infamous strongholds for rebels. Much to their astonishment, a remarkable serenity greets them at the port when they make their way down the stairs of *the Solace*. Autumn has set in the region. Trees line the edge of the port with amber and yellow-colored leaves that the wind carries up into the planet's clear red sky. The hue of the atmosphere comes from abundant neon and argon in its upper atmosphere. Although the urban landscape stretches far and wide, only a small number of people, including a well-dressed gentleman with dark hair, stand awaiting them at port. MagLev rail bridges and skyscrapers adorn the skyline as a slight chill rolls across Seneca's exposed hands and face. It's somewhat eerie compared to the usual mobs, but Seneca appreciates the relative calm...

* * *

They stroll down the port together to be greeted by the dark-haired gentleman, who, as it turns out, is the local leader of the rebels. They exchange professional formalities and introduce themselves. The gentleman, who remains unidentified, politely declines to reveal his name but proceeds to lead everyone to a port-side conference area, which Seneca finds somewhat undesirable due to its proximity to the ships. The conference area, designed to evoke the charm of a small airport FBO, is housed in a humble wooden building. Attendees can catch a glimpse of the port through the building's windows, which are tinted in a deep shade. Inside the small lobby, there are several facilities available, including restrooms, a flight planning area, and kiosks that provide convenient payment options for fuel and ship services. Conference rooms line one hallway, and the leader gestures them into the first one they come to.

The room is standardly equipped for conversation and discussion. Off-white walls surround a token conference table with a small holographic screen in the middle. Synthetic leather chairs sit neatly tucked under the rim of the table until they're utilized for seating by the party. Without delay, Ilana and the unidentified leader begin conversing. All the while Seneca permits his eyes to wander across the walls and examine the plaques inscribed with different Latin phrases that elude to the Whispers' fight for freedom. He hears Ilana's voice grow as their conversation seems to veer to the subject of the ongoing rebellion.

Her tone is diplomatic yet earnest, and she takes moments between exchanges to swap words with Serena. Seneca shifts his focus to the mission at hand as he hears Ilana say, "I understand your concerns and the grievances of your people. The cease-fire is an opportunity for change, a chance for dialogue. We want to ensure that the will of your people among the rest of the Whispers is heard by the Empire."

The leader, a weathered man with a determined look, responds with caution, "Princess, we've been fighting for our freedom for so long...."

The leader details their unique, yet eerily similar story...Prior to the unwanted intervention by the Empire, they were a prosperous independent nation. The tale of the weathered leader tells of educated men and women who worked in a white-collar economy that was renowned for designing self-improving AI-helper software (think like digital butlers or secretaries that could assist families and businesses with menial tasks). Poverty was low and people were happy, fed, and thriving. Like any society, they had their share of problems, but they were afloat without the influence of larger governing agencies like the UF, COS, or the Empire. Before the Empire decided they owned the system, they were on the verge of expanding into neighboring unoccupied solar systems. Life there was a paradise for most.

However, like many independent systems before them, the Empire arrived to "save" them. In reality, the Empire sought to assimilate the defenseless but profitable state into their ranks to exploit the reward. Unlike most Whisper rebel states, Origo Liberatis, previously named "Isila-11", immediately retaliated and fought from the onset of Imperial occupation. The Empire had nearly silenced

their resistance before the Whisper rebellion as a whole surged into existence and re-energized the efforts of Origo Liberatis to fight against Imperial rule. Other Whisper states recognized the notoriety of the state and quickly began rallying behind the renamed aspiring nation.

Ilana nods empathetically as he finishes divulging the details of their unique struggle. "I know. Furthermore, I cannot promise change overnight, but I promise I'll do everything in my power to address your demands and make this peace lasting. We're not here to impose; we're here to listen and understand."

The leader nods and continues to make amicable conversation with Ilana as Serena leans in closer to Seneca and whispers, "She's good at this... I still don't understand where she's going with it though..."

Seneca looks over at her, slightly confused, and raises his brow. "Huh?"

"I'll tell you later..."

Ilana and the rebel leader continue their conversation. All the while, Seneca and Serena can see a change in the leader's posture. He seems genuinely curious about Ilana's sentiment, and his expression seems to soften for the moment as they discuss the possibilities of a more peaceful future. Though Serena's cryptic statement leaves him with doubts that the leader has any real optimism regarding the envoy at hand, and with the trip ending shortly after this final stop, how Ilana plans to make good on her efforts to appease the Whispers into peace.

The conversation draws to a close as Ilana, with her characteristic empathy, places a hand on the leader's shoulder, a gesture of solidarity. "I believe in a future where this rebellion can conclude with the people's interests in mind. It won't be easy, but I want to be committed to taking the first steps."

The leader takes a deep breath, contemplating the potential outcomes. "We'll need guarantees, Princess. Words alone won't sway my people."

Ilana nods understandingly. "Of course, I'm prepared to negotiate with the Imperial lords tooth and nail and provide assurances however I can. Let's work together to find a path that benefits everyone. This is the opportunity for you to make your voice heard. I can make sure it is."

He cracks his neck side to side, "Princess, if our voice were enough to liberate us, we wouldn't need guns..."

This valid point serves as the catalyst for another in-depth and significant conversation between the two parties involved. Following several additional hours of conversation with the rebel leader, they finally find themselves in possession of Origo Liberatis' demands, and the group proceeds back out onto the port to return to the Solace. Seneca, Jesper, and Serena accompany Ilana outside, and her thoughtful expression suggests deep contemplation.

"Do you think we could stay a little longer?" Ilana asks Seneca. "I just... need a moment to stand out here."

"By all means," Seneca says, thankful for a calmer day in the last few months. "Cool."

* * *

Seneca and Jesper settle together on the steps of *the Solace*. Jesper, a quiet and reserved individual, follows orders diligently, but has yet to engage in casual conversation with anyone other than Serena.

As Ilana continues her conversations with individual citizens who have since made appearances to service their ships, Jesper turns to Seneca. "Ilana is brave as shit, man."

Seneca, surprised by the sudden conversation, turns to Jesper to reply, but before he can, Serena joins them. "She sure is. This whole let's-visit-the-rebels thing is going to cause issues for us when we get back... I don't know exactly what's going to happen, but I know the lordship council is not going to take whatever document Ilana is writing lightly... nor are they going to care for the sympathetic nature of her speeches."

Seneca tilts his head in acknowledgment of their valid concerns. They haven't made a return to Vista in the past few months of parading about rebel space to avoid whatever disdain awaits them in the palace. Seneca, though, remains resolute. "Whatever happens, we'll be with Ilana," Seneca asserts, their attention still fixed on Ilana as she brings smiles to the faces of those who come to interact with her.

Jesper speaks up once more. "I've been working in the Imperial government for a very long time. I wouldn't have a very positive attitude if I were you man. Our ruling class is as famous for being vindictive as you are for flying."

It's a chilling and harrowing remark from someone who speaks so little. The caution remains active in Seneca's mind as the visitation of rebel territories comes to an end two months later. Ilana's mysterious initiative completed as she now holds compilation of a massive list of demands the rebels desire from the Empire; transposed into a well written diplomatic document that bears Ilana's desire to entertain the ideas or liberation to convert the cease-fire to a permanent peace.

While he's proud of Ilana for her steadfast devotion to her cause and personal quest, Seneca still can't shake the belief that the document they carry will probably fall on deaf ears and could even incite anger and feelings of betrayal from the lords. Furthermore, as they board the ships and get underway for the return to Vista, Seneca receives correspondence from his fellow lords revealing that they've finally discovered why Ilana has been absent and unavailable for their errands. This news, coupled with the revelation of a suspected traitor within the Imperial ranks, only serves to heighten his anxiety on the journey home.

Chapter 23: Grounded

For the first week upon returning to Vista, they avoid going near the palace. During this time, Ilana invites everyone to join her at the mountain estate to spend a day before they make their appearance in the capital. She clearly expects a harsh welcome and thorough investigation when the lords find out about the group's discrete return. However, for the moment, there's a fleeting sense of peace and quiet.

Seneca finds himself on the porch cabin, silently watching the melting snow shimmer in the sun as spring begins a slow arrival to the Vista mountains. Jesper interrupts the tranquility of the moment by approaching to strike up a conversation. Seneca and Jesper had spoken little before Origo Liberatis aside from small talk and job functions, so it once again strikes him as peculiar that Jesper is electing to speak with him in this particular moment.

The conversation starts with typical greetings and generic small talk when Seneca finds an opportune moment to learn more about his comrade.

"So, Ilana tells me you used to have my job. What happened?" Seneca asks, intrigued.

Jesper nods "Yeah. Stopped around the time that the rebellion started. Ilana felt I'd be better off with Imperial Intelligence due to my background in anti-sedition and military intelligence."

Seneca nods, acknowledging the connection. "Sounds interesting. How'd you get into that?"

"My father sent me off to the Imperial military academy when I was young, and I majored in the field during the career track selection. After I graduated, my dad pulled some strings to get me the job with Ilana." Jesper replies before shifting the conversation to a more personal note. "Serena tells me you and Ilana are a couple? Good job on that. You may be the first guy she's ever seriously been interested in."

Seneca, amused by Jesper's sudden interest, dodges the question with a playful smirk. "You've been quiet and reserved during the entire trip, and now you're suddenly diving straight into personal inquiries,"

"Sorry about that. Serena warned me you were a closed box." Jesper chuckles as he tilts his head. "I'm more interested in Serena, personally. Just never had the courage to talk with her outside of work."

Seneca raises a brow, about to offer advice, but as he draws a breath to speak, Ilana and Serena join them on the porch, both clearly anxious about their upcoming visit to the capital. News has spread that the Empire is intensifying its efforts to investigate internal breaches of critical information following a recent leak of post-ceasefire plans. Inconveniently, the leaked information details planned attacks aimed directly at several systems they had just visited. The update is ambiguous regarding any specific measures the lords are taking and whether or not this is in direct relation to the group's unsponsored enterprise is still a mystery, but it seems like the two are likely linked from the headlines the girls are sifting through. They'll find out in the morning when they arrive at the palace.

The girls' concerns are justified by their reception in the capital the next day. Numerous high-ranking Imperial security officials are present when the group steps out of the limo onto the palace steps. News crews keep their distance while armed personnel are present throughout the vicinity. The new vehement measures apply to everyone as agents scan anyone entering palace grounds for weapons, strip them of UniComs, and inspect them for potential treason.

Ilana, Serena, Jesper, and Seneca all get separated by Imperial security and escorted to undergo individual interviews, inspections, and debriefings regarding their endeavors over the last several months, which amplifies the pandemonium. Seneca's interviewer introduces himself as "Agent Maxwell," although Seneca privately dubs him "Baldy," a more fitting moniker.

With his tall stature, well-defined muscles, and bald head, the agent gave off a strong, intimidating aura reminiscent of a bouncer at high-end clubs on Earth. It's evident that his imposing presence is meant to intimidate, as Seneca's firearm is temporarily confiscated upon entering the palace. Inside, the agent escorts him through the halls into a room that has two opposing sofas and a coffee table, creating a sense of symmetry.

The agent pulls out a kiosk tablet and wastes no time scrutinizing Seneca. "We understand you and your associates were involved in a four-month-long diplomatic venture that was not officially sanctioned by the Imperial lordship council. I am here to interview you and ensure that no critical information was compromised," the agent states. "I'm sure your fellow lords have made you aware that critical operational plans were leaked two and a half weeks after your visit in Daryl occurred."

"Yes," Seneca answers, sporting his best poker face.

"To your knowledge, did you bear witness to any of your associates leaking classified information to any persons associated with the whispers of freedom?"

"No,"

"Did you yourself, through either malice or erroneous intent, divulge any information that could be used against the Empire in a military campaign?"

"No," Seneca states once again

Seneca's deep distaste for government interactions is well-concealed, but as the interview progresses, frustration becomes apparent in his curt, one-word responses. Most questions continuously receive a simple "No" as an answer, yet the interrogation continues for hours, to his dismay. The focus of the questioning eventually shifts to Ilana and the others, with inquiries about whether Seneca witnessed them engaging in any actions or conversations that could compromise the Empire's intelligence. Once again, Seneca responds with a series of "No's.". — even if he had witnessed such behavior, it's not like he'd divulge it.

Finally, the agent concludes the interrogation and offers Seneca the opportunity to ask questions. Seneca responds with sarcasm and a degree of confusion, "If you had suspected me of anything, why didn't you ask more probing questions rather than questions that were simply 'yes or no'?"

The man scowls. "Trust me, Lord Mason, you've got a history as a pest to the Empire, but we know subversion is not your style."

Just to antagonize the agent, he says, "You only think you know me asshole," as he exits the room and retrieves his pistol.

Outside the conference hall, Jesper and Serena engage in hushed conversation, waiting for Ilana's interview to conclude. Their faces bear nervous expressions as they wait... The fact that Ilana's interview length is longer than his own is an intriguing matter, and the others believe that this is because her interviewer has been thoroughly analyzing the rhetoric in Ilana's extensive hours of speeches.

He's worried little about what suspicion may befall Ilana. The lords can't be dumb enough to suspect she's committed any espionage. Instead, Seneca's concerns revolve around being viewed as a possible suspect in the Empire's witch hunt. He questions the wisdom of his playful remark to the agent, considering a long track record of interfering with Imperial invasions, smuggling, and manipulating the Empire's bounty system through anonymous errands. However, it doesn't concern him much though as he could leave and take everyone with him if need be. Fantasies about escaping with Ilana and their friends to retreat to his camp on Earth swim through the oceans of his mind.

The sound of heels tapping the tiles beneath their feet resounds through the hall as Ilana joins them moments later, appearing just as apprehensive as the others. He is curious as to why the Empire is investing their time in her instead of focusing on other matters. The Empire's citizens hold her in high regard, as she is beloved by them, and her support is of utmost importance for maintaining the stability of the government. If she were to be accused of any wrongdoing, it would cause a multitude of borderline systems to crawl towards the Whispers.

Ilana silently motions for them to join her in the conference hall. As for what awaits the group inside, he anticipates a thorough lecture from the Imperial dignitaries.

* * *

They enter the pit of the hall once the doors swing open. A profound silence in the room allows the creaking sound of the door to take center stage as they walk through the threshold. There's an ominous atmosphere within the conference hall as he, along with his companions, are seated at a table sitting in the center of the hall. Surrounding the circumference of the dome-shaped room, Imperial lords occupy the stands, their murmurs filling the air. The emperor stands above them in the arena's epicenter, his left hand holding a tablet illuminating the collective voice of the Whispers establishing their price for peace.

Standing head and shoulders above the others in the room, the emperor exudes a commanding presence. His fiery red hair is neatly swept to one side, adding to his strong and masculine appearance, which is enhanced by his well-maintained facial hair. Prior to his corporate career with Benzet Enterprises, he had served as a Marine Drill Instructor, maintaining impeccable physical fitness that lends him a muscular build. His furrowed brow deepens as he carefully examines the document before him, occasionally glancing at the group below with a penetrating gaze. Seneca, who is not easily intimidated by an individual's appearance, can't help but think silently that Ilana looks nothing like her father aside from the striking green eyes they share.

The room is silent before the emperor speaks. "Ilana, what were you thinking?" He asks calmly yet sternly before escalating the weight of his tone. "Cease fire or not, hopping around in rebel space, basically unprotected during the worst rebellion in the history of the Galaxy, for what? A list of *demands*?" He finishes by throwing the tablet to the side, condemning the document that Ilana had risked so much to compose.

    Ilana opens her mouth to speak, but he interrupts her. "We already know what they want, Ilana! You can't give them liberation in response to a temper tantrum. They need the Empire's leadership, and the Empire needs their loyalty! Stop trying to play peacekeeper before you dig a deeper hole for everyone else who has to clean up the mess you make! Do you realize how bad this looks amidst the wavering security?"

The emperor's scolding persists, his words laced with stern reproach. He reprimands Ilana for what he perceives as lapses in Imperial security, chastising her for putting her own safety at risk, which could have potentially jeopardized the fragile cease-fire Ilana herself had worked so hard to achieve. All the while, he emphasizes the critical importance of her continued support in order to stem the tide of rebellion that threatens the Empire.

Observing Ilana's reaction to the emperor's harsh tone is uncomfortable. Her body tenses, and she flinches at the way he accentuates certain words to underscore his disapproval. It's evident that this scolding is taking a toll on her, and Seneca can't help but feel a desire to speak up on her behalf, though this is not the time.

The emperor points at Seneca in a condescending tone, "And you!", he says, catching Seneca's attention. "Do you think we would just forget about your previous intrusions against the Empire because you wear a rank and have lordship over a struggling rock-pile?" the emperor asks Seneca in a condescending tone, catching his attention. "Do you really think you are *that* important?!"

Ilana inserts herself into the emperor's condemnation of his existence "I do!"
"Ilana, quiet."
"No. Dad. You can't deny the asset that Seneca brings to the Empire." Ilana shouts, interrupting her father, "I vetted him. I hired him. He performs this job better than any agent the council has *ever* appointed. On multiple occasions he's proved worthy of Imperial recognition like his actions protecting us in Malachi's Arm, where he fought off two pirates single handedly, one of which commanded a vessel substantially larger than his own. That action would have earned anyone else a medal but not a single word of thanks and had anyone else been flying escort, I wouldn't have survived the trip…and you know that!"

Murmurs fill the room and scowls descend upon Ilana from the fat cats surrounding them. Seneca pats Ilana's shoulder reassuringly and gives her a nod before turning his attention to the emperor. His voice is steady, carrying a hint of defiance, as he addresses the ruler of the Empire. "Go ahead. Finish yelling at me, Byron. Tell me how it is, but don't think for a second that I've forgotten that we came from the same place."

At the mention of his real name, instead of a formal title, the emperor's face contorts with anger, his complexion growing flushed. Seneca can't help but find it somewhat absurd that this man, who used to be a corporate executive at Benzet's electronics facility in Wilmington, NC, now holds immense power as the emperor, completely disregarding his humble upbringing. Seneca recalls the time when he and Byron would even watch the Carolina Panthers play a season late while they worked together on Mars, among other enjoyable aspects of being human and on Earth.   That Earthly aspect of Byron appears to be long gone.

Byron thunders a response, chastising Seneca for his use of informal language, "Don't use informal addresses when speaking to me, Lord Mason! If it weren't for the merit my daughter sees in you, I'd have you ejected from Imperial space. As her security agent, you saw no issue with visiting the rebels?"
Seneca meets the emperor's gaze unflinchingly and retorts, "No because I'm the most dangerous thing behind the controls of a spacecraft, because I trust Ilana, and because she signs my paychecks. I will do what she wants."

With an annoyed huff, he turns his attention to Serena and Jesper, speaking to them in the same condescending tone he had used with Seneca and Ilana. Seneca suspects that the raised voice, shouting, and insinuations are merely a reflection of the lords' anger, rather than the emperor's genuine emotions, since all the lords in the room seem to sport a different facial expression. Byron looks angry, maybe even…scared like a father would be if his child ran into oncoming traffic. The lords look overjoyed though—they must be the traffic.

Finally, the Emperor concludes his tirade and issues frustrating instructions for the four of them. "Since, for the time being, none of you can be trusted to make sound decisions, any business you conduct must be approved by the council. Otherwise, none of you are to leave the planet, including you, Ilana."

Seneca seizes an opportunity to secure a lifeline to avoid confinement in some capacity. "What about my obligations with Pyre Mining? I owe them a visit since it's been a few months."

Byron considers for a moment before granting permission. "Granted. You have one week, starting at the beginning of every month, for your visitation and political obligations. Otherwise, you and your ship best remain here. If you can abide by that, you'll demonstrate your loyalty. But don't entertain any misguided notions while you're out and about, Seneca. We'll be keeping a close watch, and should you test us there will be no bounty reward in the universe that will protect you."

With that, the emperor stands, signaling the end of the meeting.

Chapter 24: Room to Grow

Ilana, her eyes brimming with tears, darts from the hall, with Seneca and the others hot on her heels. Seneca witnesses her visible tremors, a strong temptation to speak rising within him, but he's unsure of what to say. He knows how much the past few months meant, the weight of the promises she'd made, and the heavy burden of responsibility for the people she cared for. Yet, in a cruel twist, the lords and her own father callously discarded her work, leaving it to wither and fade away. In the process, Ilana's hard-earned respect from the rebels will shortly return to the effervescent cauldron of hate it had been before the tour. The whole group can see it in Ilana's eyes.

They make their way quietly and solemnly, like scolded teenagers out of the palace; content to spend their days grounded in the solitude of the mountain estate. The ride up the mountains in the limo is filled with an eerie silence, occasionally broken by the sound of the electronic drive straining against a steep hill. Seneca's attention is drawn to Ilana, who sits slumped in her seat, staring at the sky, lost in profound reflection.

Once again in the solitude of the mountain estate, they exit the limo and bring their bags into the cabin, and Seneca takes a moment to approach Ilana. Gently tapping her shoulder and offering words of encouragement. "I'm proud of you. You stuck your neck out and did something you believed was important and could help. It's not your fault that your desire for peace is being overlooked by everyone."

"Thanks, but I really don't need your pride," she replies in a solemn tone. "I'm not trying to be cross, but I need change. I just wish I knew what to do now. I only get to do what they want... I never wanted any of this..."

Offering a reassuring sentiment, Seneca replies, "I know. Don't forget it. You're able to do something huge that I haven't been able to do in a long time."

Frustrated by Seneca's engagement, Ilana asks, "Yeah, What's that?"

"You can give a damn about something," he responds. "I've been stuck in a cycle of doing things selfishly for my own interests for decades now."

Her mood seems to calm as her furrow smooths to an impartial smile.

"Thanks, sorry I don't mean to sound angry with you... I'm just so powerless and I don't feel like I can change that anymore. I used to, but after being cast aside by my own father, what hope do I have?"

"Make your own," Seneca says as he gently brushes her hair back.

Ilana smiles but says nothing further and joins Serena and Jesper inside. Everyone seems to have calmed their nerves by this point, though nobody felt like talking at first. By dinnertime, the energy among everyone appeared to return to normal as conversations once again take place among them as they eat. Thus, the silver lining to the confinement order becomes clear as Seneca realizes everyone will be able to bond "regular people" for a while without the barrier of work clouding their lives.

Days pass slowly, Seneca and Ilana find themselves with plenty of time to walk together on the estate's hiking trails, talking in great detail. Exploring the springs or caves beneath the waterfalls on the property is a worthwhile way to spend time alone and make the best of a less than desirable situation. He knows Ilana's sense of purpose is eating at her, but for the time, she's forced to shelf her aspirations of peace and is content to be with him.

Paying close attention, Seneca has been able to discern Jesper's unmistakable infatuation with Serena, and it is highly probable that Serena feels the same through her equally awkward reactions. The two are a sight to behold when they interact as they have developed an awkward "flirtationship"; Ilana claims the dynamic between the two has persisted for years since they've known Jesper. Serena, despite her crude jokes and direct nature towards Seneca, is apparently far from the type to make the first move when confronted with genuine chemistry. Jesper, true to his word, is far too shy to take the initiative. It's both entertaining and cringe-inducing to watch them flirt, but neither actually expresses emotion (not that Seneca is one to judge on that front). As a result, Seneca contemplates helping Jesper make his move, although clueless as to the best approach just yet, since he doesn't know Jesper as well.

Seneca remains with Ilana and the rest of the crew until the month comes to an end, and he's finally permitted to travel to Pyre Mining. Though it's rather frustrating that he cannot travel with his companions, he's internally relieved to have a temporary hiatus from confinement.

Seneca arrives at Pyre Mining once more, welcomed by the familiar grandfatherly presence of Marco. They engage in conversation while riding on a rail-shuttle, discussing the ongoing issues faced by Pyre Mining, particularly those related to the transportation of goods. On his previous visit, Seneca had requested additional security support from the Empire, but the Empire did not grant it, citing profitability thresholds that Pyre Mining did not meet—and would not meet without the aid.

"My friend, if this continues, we may have to align ourselves with the Whispers, I wish to give you a thorough chance to secure our future, but I must listen to the voice of Pyre's people," Marco muses as they complete their walkthrough and enter a conference room in the government complex. "Your investments have greatly aided in colony repairs, and our fleet is recovering as well, but it's all in vain if we can't move our goods. The cease-fire was helping at first, but they have found a loophole by paying privateers to attack our shipping."

Seneca nods, his gaze shifting to a galactic map of the area projected on the conference room table. He looks it over for any ideas and suggestions. "Have you considered altering your shipping routes to stay within higher-security star systems?" he suggests.

Marco nods in response. "We are surrounded by systems with high security, but most of these systems were annexed by the Empire without their consent. Support for the Empire is shallow here. It is a shame that we are in the same boat yet they shun us… Many system security agents ignore our distress calls because they know our ore goes to the Empire's bottom line. If only you were able to help them the way you're helping us."

"Trust me, they don't like me right now, either." Seneca scoffs as he retells the numerous systems they visited where he was bombarded with garbage.

The situation remains desperate, despite Seneca's financial assistance. Poverty is still widespread within Pyre, and the system continues to bleed money. The Empire demands profitability before committing to additional security units, though their lack of security is largely to blame for the lack of financial accomplishment.

Something else Seneca notices in his study of the galactic map that has gone previously unobserved is that Pyre Mining also occupies a strategic choke point; ships in a certain quadrant of the galactic disc must pass through to access major Imperial shipping lanes. This makes Pyre a perfect location for imposing passage tolls (ships can be charged automatically by electronic ID, even at warp).

Seneca formulates a plan as he thinks. "Here's what you can do…."

He suggests to Marco that Pyre should vary shipping routes every time, even if it doesn't seem logical. It'll make their movements and shipments harder to predict to anyone seeking to attack them. Additionally, imposing toll fees for those passing through Pyre. For those seeking to move between shipping lanes, Pyre offers the only route unless they want to risk running out of fuel in dead space. That should drastically increase their revenue and give them more than one option for income. Finally, Seneca decides to raise his monthly contribution to five million so Pyre can use it to build up their *own* security and escort fleet since the Empire won't commit security.

Marco agrees with a nod. "That might work, but how do we create new routes if we're one of only three systems with access to these shipping lanes?"

"Use AI to generate solutions," Seneca suggests with a wry smile. "It's a tactic I used to outsmart Imperial security when smuggling goods into places like this. Shit, instead of selling ore to the Empire, you could also sell it to the COS, UF, or even the Whispers for all I care. Again, if the taxes get paid, and the council leaves me alone, I don't care."

* * *

Seneca dedicates the remaining week to formulating a list of essential projects and exploring potential improvements in Pyre Mining's operations. First, he collaborates with Marco and the shipyard director to place an order for faster cargo ships, designed to be coated with the same stealthy paint used on his Phantom vessel; enhancements that aim to reduce the chances of being intercepted during cargo transportation.

The second initiative, though expensive, involves terraforming the planet within Pyre's goldilocks zone, using their own abundant ore resources. Instead of selling all the ore they mine, keep 20% for themselves and employ it for construction and manufacturing purposes. Terraforming the planet as originally intended will yield more economic prospects through real estate sales to the system, allowing them to branch from blue collar economies to a mixed blue- and white-collar economy. He reaches out to engineers in nearby systems willing to assist with this ambitious undertaking for delayed compensation.

Additionally, Seneca takes part in establishing curriculum and training programs to equip Pyre with its own combat pilot militia. Given the uncertainty of support from the Empire, it's imperative for Pyre to be capable of self-defense. Expert flight instructors are summoned from around the galaxy to commence training immediately, and orders are placed for training craft as well as combat-ready medium fighter-class ships, newer models of the Raytheon SF-33. While these ships may not match the cargo carriers at warp speed, they contribute to bolstering local security.

Despite Seneca's considerable resources, he realizes the staggering amount required to make Pyre self-sufficient. Many of the newer Imperial lords lack the financial means to invest in a system like Pyre, leading them to neglect its potential. Systems such as Pyre Mining could flourish if the Empire would remove oppressive taxes and bureaucratic obstacles. It's evident why resistance is mounting against Imperial control in these struggling regions.

With his business concluded in Pyre, Seneca returns to Vista. However, he is ordered to report back at the palace before returning to the mountain estate, following an obnoxious arbitrary rule imposed by the Empire. Upon arrival, he's guided to the familiar room where he had been debriefed before, accompanied by the same bald agent. In contrast to before, there were a few additional Imperial lords in the room, which intrigued Seneca as he observed silently. Was this going to happen every time?

'Baldy' finally speaks, "Major, this debriefing is to verify you were indeed on Pyre Mining and for you to report your dealings."
 "Yes." Seneca replies to the point.
 "And your dealings there?" The man asks, "Per your suggestion, this is not a yes or no question."
 "Investing." Seneca replies with a shrewd attitude.
 "Can you be more specific?"

"No."

The agent's voice adopts a tone of frustration as he asks, "Were the funds allocated to Pyre from their Imperial allowance or your personal accounts?"

Seneca matches his tone to the frustration of the agent. "Yes."

"It wasn't a yes or no-"

"I paid the deficit in their Imperial allowance and added sufficient funds from my own account."

One of the other lords, an unfamiliar aged bureaucrat in traditional Imperial garb, interjects himself into the conversation. "It's not typical for us to invest personal funds into our holdings. Their budget problems are theirs, not the Empire's or their appointed lord's. We can't have you setting a standard—."

"Ohh. So, you assholes already knew I was spending my own money, and that I was there; what's this debrief for?" Seneca asks sternly and confused, "I was led to believe I need only check in with Imperial security and then go on my marry ass way, not sit through this. I'm not doing this every time I come back from Pyre."

"To make sure you know which side you're supposed to be on. If Pyre falls to the rebels, you're practically arming them and preparing them to fight," the disgruntled lord utters in a condescending tone. "From now on—"

Seneca cuts in abruptly once again, his voice filled with defiance. "Oh, kiss my ass."

"I beg your pardon," the baron responds.

Seneca continues, his words laced with anger and frustration. "I will spend my money how I damn well please. I didn't fly your ancestors into space, so some rich pricks like you could tell me how I will live my life. Maybe if you and other stuck-up lords would actively lead the people you rule over instead of screwing them over, you wouldn't have this rebellion on your hands."

"Careful Major," agent Maxwell says, "I wouldn't adopt Princess Ilana's way of thinking. It's significantly more dangerous for you than it is for her."

A heavy silence follows as the room's occupants cast scowls in Seneca's direction before he adds one last jab, closing the distance between him and the agent. "If you want to threaten me, take my gun next time morons. Don't think I don't know this is because other systems will look at Pyre and resent their own lords for ignoring them."

The pervasive greed among these Imperial lords infuriates Seneca. His face is red, and he can feel heat escaping from his head as he exits the palace. What's worse is he hates playing stupid political games, and he stews while he waits for his ground transport to arrive and take him back to the mountain estate. The scenic drive through Vista's countryside as spring is now in full effect, offers a calming respite from the tense encounter and slowly qualms the boiling thoughts within his mind.

Ilana is there to greet Seneca as the limo drops him off. Once the transport is out of sight and the two of them are inside, she throws her arms around his neck and kisses him.

She asks, her lips parting from his, "How was your trip?"

Seneca sighs, his affection for her dear in his gaze. "It was okay until I got back."

"Oh?" she says playfully.

"Don't worry, I missed *you* the whole time I was gone. It's not your fault," he confesses, "but when I got back, some lords and the bald asshole were trying to hassle me about the way I rule Pyre."

"What?!" Ilana exclaims in shock. "That's so backwards... They just don't want to help their own holdings."

"I know... but for now, there's not much they can do. Hopefully, Pyre will be able to get on their feet before they do find a way to stop me."

Seneca updates Ilana on everything that happened on Pyre, including Marco's kind words and good wishes. She listens patiently as he talks. "That's great news. I'm glad you care about people enough to change things..."

Care was a strong sentiment that may not necessarily be representative of his actions. Seneca responds with modesty, saying, "I guess..."

During his absence, not much has changed for the others, which doesn't come as a surprise for a mere week. Jesper and Serena have been their usual awkward selves. Ilana has apparently resumed her diplomatic ventures through virtual means, though not all of them Serena has weighed in on. Ilana's happy to delineate the luxuries of being royalty and being able to negotiate through unmonitored teleconferences.

Time continues crawling slowly during Seneca's confinement to the surface of Vista. Ilana and the others make daily trips to the palace, leaving him to his own devices at the estate. Although he has little insight into their activities down at the palace, he assumes they'll inform him if anything significant happens.

With the start of each new month, Seneca embarks on his trips to Pyre to work with Marco and continue their progress. His actions slowly show positive results across the months, enabling Pyre to start exporting highly profitable amounts of ore. The attacks on Pyre's shipping abruptly ceased without any apparent explanation, and they haven't needed to rely on random shipping routes—almost as if someone called the attacks off entirely since his first visit.

Besides restored shipping, the efforts to terraform the planet Pyre-3a, has generated thousands of jobs. With the planet now known as Fortuna, there has been a significant surge in demand for educated engineers, increasing educational initiatives accordingly. Thousands of people from all over the galaxy have already purchased millions in value of pre-ordered real estate in the planned communities of the first city on the planet. In just five months, society has experienced a remarkable and rapid transformation from the verge of collapse. They are eagerly anticipating the opportunity to sincerely repay Seneca for his generosity, which was instrumental in facilitating their unexpected growth.

* * *

Seneca's actions have also inspired a small number of other lords to invest in their holdings (even if only to avoid their holdings from joining the Whispers), generating both support with some Imperial holdings and backlash in different systems where the governing lords are unwilling to follow suit.

Through their indefinite confinement, Seneca maintains his cycle of visiting Pyre and returning. He and Ilana spend quality time together. He's nervous to think that what they have is love, but it's the closest he's been in a long time. During the spring days, they hike and immerse themselves in the sounds of birds chirping and the scent of blooming flowers, all while dreaming of a tranquil life far from the chaos of politics. In the stillness of the starlit nights, they find solace on the porch, gazing at the heavens, hoping to catch a glimpse of a shooting star, while finding comfort in each other's embrace.

They've opted to keep their relationship shrouded in secrecy for the time being, letting it be known only to Serena and Jesper. Despite not breaking any laws, they've opted to exercise caution and remain discreet in order to prevent any further unwanted focus from the esteemed dignitaries and lords of the Empire, who would likely view the love affair between the princess and ex-outlaw with disdain. Nevertheless, Seneca knows where his heart is leading him and has recently taken a significant step forward by purchasing an intricately designed ivory ring on one of his trips to Pyre. At its heart lay a captivating ocean-blue sapphire... He doesn't know when he'll need it or be ready... but he has it.

Chapter 25: Ultimatum

Seneca has nearly lost count of how long they've been grounded, and still the Empire and Whispers haven't reached a resolution. The dreaded end of the ceasefire arrives with the rising of a cruel sun and brings with it an ultimatum issued by the Whispers as conflict resumes. They've allotted the Empire no less than ninety days to liberate a mile-long list of held territories that were forcibly annexed, or the Whispers will declare formal war (as if they weren't fighting a war already). In Seneca's view, the letter indicates intent to actively engage in attacking the Empire rather than seeking to liberate territory.

Despite the threat, the Empire remains unmoved and reacts minimally, opting to release a statement instead. Their dismissal emphasizes that only a sovereign entity can officially declare war and asserts that the threat posed by the opposing party is merely a continuation of their lawless and reckless course of action.

In addition to the "threat" (or lack thereof) of war, conflicts are arising throughout the Empire as Imperial security forces attempt to stop mass evacuation operations conducted by the Whispers of Freedom, who have resumed efforts to assist citizens in fleeing from annexed societies. Following the ceasefire's end, the sudden surge in rebel activity has overwhelmed the emperor and the security council with military meetings. Consequently, the council has assigned Ilana back to diplomatic duties and lifted the group's confinement.

Ilana eagerly resumes short travels and diplomatic duties on behalf of the Imperial government, all the while pressuring the lords to change their ways and either aid their people or liberate them altogether. Serena has been urging her on their first few trips out and back to keep her expectations in check. Regrettably, the lords cannot comprehend the challenges faced by the commoners and working class, as they were born into privilege and lack the ability to empathize with their fellow citizens. They lack the understanding of the determination, intelligence, and unwavering dedication needed to turn celestial bodies into livable and sustainable environments for humans.

* * *

Seneca is well aware that with some investment, these systems would be less inclined to rebel against the Empire. Pyre, under his lordship, has made an unprecedented turn for the better. Despite the end of the ceasefire, Pyre is still getting ore and metal where it needs to be—even if it's not in Imperial refineries. People are not departing Pyre in droves, like elsewhere within the Empire, and the economy is booming thanks to his efforts. In the months leading up to the end of the ceasefire, they've finally begun turning a profit from his massive investment. Although he declines to profit from Pyre's people, Marco insists he at least accepts a break-even amount.

It's yet another grievance the lords have with Seneca's methods of ruling that they bombard him with in council meetings. The events are nauseating occasions, and he hates them, a sentiment he does little to hide. He's stomping out of the most recent of these meetings as Ilana approaches him with a full awareness of the toll these encounters take on him. The lords' greedy and selfish nature is difficult for Seneca to endure as they continuously criticize his methods.

Seneca sighs as she joins him by his side, and they make their way through the corridors of the palace. He can't help but express his frustration to Ilana as he leaves one of the lordship council meetings, saying, "Makes you wonder why more of them don't just do what I do; willing to bet it would probably stop the rebellion."

Ilana teases him, poking his arm, and replies, "We can't all be amazing like you."

He chuckles and pokes her arm back and smiles silently.

Changing to a more serious tone, she continues, "So we got our next 'assignment'…we're visiting the rebels again."

Seneca's head snaps to the side but before he can protest, she urgently proceeds, "*This time*, with *explicit* orders from the lords."

His brow furrows. Perplexed, he adds, "funny, I don't remember being part of that conversation."

"Well, regardless, we're going back to Origo Liberatis. They want me to… caution them against continued escalation…"

A sense of discomposure creeps over him. From his viewpoint there is little that will come of this as he's seen the resolve of the Whispers firsthand in his travels with Ilana and their newfound confidence in threatening formal war is nothing short of affirming this notion. Furthermore, he is confused why the other lords hadn't informed him of this. He voices his concerns, saying, "I thought they weren't taking the threat of war seriously? something's not right…"

Ilana pauses her explanations and asks, "What?"

Seneca elaborates, "The rebels are not going to take well to you changing from princess empathy to shaking an iron fist."

Ilana shrugs, "I don't know what to tell you…"

"Don't tell *me* anything," Seneca says thoughtfully, "Tell the lords to kick rocks. They have to know how much danger you'll be in."

* * *

Ilana says nothing and glances to the side. Clearly, the statement incited some degree of sentiment; whatever it may be is not expressed before Ilana replies. "Well, they must really trust that you'll do your job, and besides, this is something we need to try to achieve peace..."

Her words do little to comfort him and by the way she's talking she doesn't seem to believe her words either. All he can do is nod as the group assembles in one of the palace's many meeting rooms to plan the trip itinerary and security measures. Jesper, now a permanent member of the group, also joins in, assisting with contingency plans for various scenarios before they depart the next morning.

Something about the situation is amiss, though Seneca can't pinpoint the specifics. He can't ascertain whether the trap is meant for Ilana or himself, but he is aware that he wasn't involved in the decision to send Ilana back to the rebels and that he and Jesper will possess minimal capability to safeguard Ilana in the worst-case scenario.

Just as the sun beats down mercilessly on the desert, the anxiety surrounding the situation weighs heavily on him. He fidgets nervously alone inside *the Phantom* as the trip out feels all too short—soon finding himself back in the Whisper stronghold of Origo Liberatis for the pre-arranged meeting between Ilana and the Whisper military leadership.

The reception is ominously quiet as he escorts Ilana down the boarding stairs from the Solace. Jesper and Serena keep close behind him as their ground transport awaits them. Once again, the calmness of the place is palpable, but now there is a faintly unsettling undertone carried by the soft breeze. The port is eerily empty, devoid of any signs of life or even the slightest trace of sound.

Down the eerily empty streets of Trinity, the ground transport moves silently, the only sound audible being the faint hum of the ground transports electrical hum. From the windows high above the street, snipers that could be hidden behind them provide advantageous positions with a direct line of sight to Ilana's seat. As the ride continues, it feels like time slows down, adding to the Seneca's worry of impending danger. The streets are absent of signs of life or moving vehicles, just as the port had been. Darkened lights in the high-rise buildings add to the umbrage emanating from the atmosphere.

Uninterrupted by other traffic, they arrive at the stronghold headquarters. It's unknown where the center for rebel operations rests, but this location would certainly fit the proverbial bill. With its imposing presence, the building exudes a corporate aura, resembling a grand brick structure. The dark tinted windows and armed guards stationed at the entrance give it an air of authority and importance like the pentagon on Earth has. Ever since the revelation of the original news of the enterprise, an unsettling feeling has lingered in the back of his mind, refusing to dissipate, and is now magnified by the armed escorts approaching their transport to corral them inside. Unsettled, Seneca anxiously verifies that his firearm is fully loaded and switches it to lethal mode... just in case.

* * *

Inside, the building maintains the atmosphere of a typical corporate office, complete with a small fountain and a plaque on the far wall. The plaque displays a quote in what appears to be Latin, possibly poorly translated, saying "Hoc Ubi Libertas Ingreditur Est" or "Where freedom finds its way" (Seneca isn't certain, it's been over 200 years since he'd taken Latin in high school). From the lobby, the rebels usher them down a winding series of hallways into a conference room with a lengthy table. They find several individuals already seated around the dark wooden ensemble in black leather chairs. Among the faces are a couple whom Seneca recognizes from the previous visit, though their lack of excitement is apparent in the scowls and faces of disdain that aim their way. The same leader from the previous visit speaks, asking, "I assume, Princess, that you're here because of our ultimatum?"

Ilana answers calmly, but also likely deviating from the script the lords assigned her. "Yes, and while the Empire is willing to accommodate some concessions, at this time there is no plan to liberate any systems, and only a sovereign power has authority to declare war. I'm afraid I could not sway the lords on this matter."

The leader scowls. "That is unfortunate. I'm afraid your visit here is fruitless then. We will accept no concession. Our demands to the palace were absolute, ninety days or we will declare formal war. You have sixty-two remaining."

Eying the room for signs of aggression and choosing his words carefully, Seneca's makes his voice heard, "You are aware that if the Empire really wanted to expend the money, your rebellion could be over in a matter of days? You are hilariously outgunned."

"That wasn't your tone when you helped the Whispers in the past, Seneca," he replies, looking at him. "Are you truly an Imperial now?"

"I am who I am, that's it. The past was different, that was preventing an annexation of independent systems that had a strong security force and pending memberships with the COS. They also were not challenging the full might of the Imperial fleet."

Ilana brings herself back into the conversation and engages in a dialogue with him, alternating between speaking and listening, in an effort to find common ground and potentially reach a peaceful resolution. Meanwhile Seneca looks the leader up and down with care. He's undeterred, unwavering, and resolute. He can't help but wonder where this sudden confidence is stemming from. They definitely don't have the setup to fight one of the largest existing militaries in the galaxy. Anyone with the slightest knowledge of military tactics doesn't have to strain to see it. Why the confidence? He continues watching the conversation unfold, hoping to find something to satisfy his curiosity.

"Even if we wanted to make concessions," the leader continues, "I am not at liberty to make them. I am not the voice to the whisper, nor is anyone visible to you or myself. Our namesake is derived from a subtle and quiet call to action from someone longing for freedom. They beckoned us in secret to start this fight. Begrudgingly, they still choose not to reveal themselves to the public but..."

* * *

He delves deeper into the enigmatic nature of their unknown leader. Although it was widely recognized that the Empire had no information about the rebel leader's true identity, there were persistent rumors suggesting that the leader operated secretly, remaining unknown even to fellow rebels. However, this meeting appeared to support those speculations and conclusively prove that the rebellion had a mysterious, unidentifiable leadership.

"All we know of our leader is they are feverishly on our side against all odds. Their ideals harken back to the founding principles of mutual prosperity, and they speak with eloquence of a prophet." The leader says.

Serena tugs on Seneca's jacket from behind. "What?" he whispers in response.

Serena doesn't reply, but she gestures behind them, using her eyes to communicate that a few armed individuals had made a stealthy approach with their weapons ready to fire. To ensure they were on the same page, Seneca exchanges a quick glance with Jesper before following his lead. He unholsters his pistol and prepares to raise it as the leader continues deliberating with a distracted Ilana. He needs to regain control of the situation, so he aims the pistol at the leader and halts the approach of the potential assailants.

"Hey pal," Seneca says, commanding attention, "If your goons shoot at us, they'd better kill me."

"Oh?" He says confused and slightly surprised, "Forgive us and please stand down. They're just going to escort you back to your ships. Save the bloodshed for the battlefield... and Princess," He pauses as Ilana looks back at him standing from her seat, "Please don't make us any more promises you can't keep. We know all too well your government won't look kindly on you for that, and if they turn on you, we will not shelter you."

Seneca reluctantly drops his firearm with additional assurance from the leader before the armed men at the back escort them, as promised, back to the ground transport. Even though the leader declared a commitment to non-violence, Seneca's senses remain alert, and he is unable to shake off his uneasiness. Why would the Empire have sent them here? What was the true agenda at play? His anxiety is evident in his restless eyes, as if he's constantly bracing himself for an imminent attempt on his or Ilana's life.

"Dude, chill," Serena says through gritted teeth as they get into the ground transport to return to the ships.

"Sorry," Seneca murmurs as the ground transport's doors close, "I just have no idea why we are here. There is no way the lords thought this would do anything."

She shares a glance with the others before she says, "It's a bit. They do this shit as bait. It wasn't necessarily a trap, but they definitely wouldn't have been surprised if we all got killed. The lords were baiting the rebels into harming us so they could have grounds for scorched Earth retaliation and quell the rebellion."

Serena elaborates that ever since the rebellion started, the duties given by the lords have become progressively more dangerous. From the moment Ilana hired Seneca, the lords have been using their diplomatic missions to eliminate her as a political adversary. From the trip through Malachi's Arm, traveling through the Empire's rioting systems during the loyalty tour, negotiating with Clemson, and the current expedition all share a common thread: they are exceptionally dangerous with escalated risks to their safety.

"That's why Ilana needed someone as notorious as *you* for security, and we hit the lottery by finding *you* on Oberon. You are likely the only reason we are still here." Serena continues her frustrated rant. Ilana's growing popularity and her alignment with the people's views have made her a formidable rival to the Imperial lords. "If any of us, especially Ilana, were to be killed, not only do they have just cause for scorched Earth, but they also eliminate political adversaries. It's why the lords are always united with each other... until you came along."
  "And the Emperor allows it?" Seneca asks with disbelief in his voice.

Serena once again nods. "He doesn't really get a choice. Again, he no longer holds any ruling authority. The only reason he exists is to be a scapegoat and to keep Ilana in check. If the royal family outlives their use, they're gone."
  "Did you know this?!" Seneca asks Ilana in shock.

She responds with a nod, knowing that she's been bait for a while now. Seneca shakes his head furiously in utter disbelief "Then why not tell them to kick rocks?! That's insane. Why on Earth would you all allow this?"

Ilana briefly snaps. "Look Seneca, *you* might be able to just run and hide from shit like this, but *we* can't. I'm fucking royalty whose family depends on not getting assassinated to stay alive since we hold *no* real power, Serena knows the inner workings of the government, so she's stuck with this for life, and Jesper's fucking father is an asshole whose bullshit started this *whole* rebellion. It's better to chance getting killed doing what they want, while trying to change things in the process! If it bothers you, get in your ship and fight off the Imperial bounty hunters. Go back to whatever you were doing before, but we're in this life!"

He freezes in shock as Ilana bursts into tears and sobs hysterically. Her calm demeanor shattered in an instant, surprised him, as he had never witnessed her lose her composure like that. Jesper and Serena share equally surprised expressions as the usually positive member of the group suddenly erupted into an outburst. A hidden force must be at play within her mind. Seneca's no expert on psychology, but he's been alive long enough to smell a fire burning. The profound silence lingers for a moment as he tries to discern what it could be but chalks it up to the pressures of trying to survive against a cruel ruling class seeking to destroy her.

"I'm sorry Sen..." she says, wiping a tear out of her eyes. "This whole fucking rebellion is a result of the corruption within the government. The only way I can change it is… reaching the end of my capabilities and my hands are tied. I have no ability to tell the lords to stop, and they are ruthless."

He, apparently, wasn't the only one with walls guarding deeply buried emotions. While he had been hiding from his past, Ilana had been protecting herself from the present. Seneca wishes so badly that he could help her run, but he knows Ilana well enough to understand that she doesn't have the personality of a runner; she would likely decline any such offer if he were to put it on the table.

"No. I'm sorry. I didn't know." Seneca tells her calmly, as he puts a hand on her shoulder. "I'm not running from this. I'm not leaving you."
Ilana calms her breathing after a moment and looks up at him before Serena interjects. "Fucking gross, why are you so corny?" she asks rhetorically, swatting his arm down.

Ilana bounces back ever so slightly with light laughter at Serena's action. They head back to the port, and Seneca is now acutely aware of the weighty implications of the information disclosed during their encounter with the rebel leader. This serves as a strong indication of the lengths that certain individuals will go to in order to maintain a profitable status quo, showcasing the harsh reality of their actions.

Seneca maintains his guard as he escorts everyone onto *the Solace*, and they depart in their usual flight formation of two ships. The trip amounts to nothing significant in terms of tangible progress or agreements. However, it had sparked an outburst of emotion from Ilana, where she and Serena had revealed the sick and heartless nature of those who rule over the welfare of others.

Soaring through the starry expanse of space, Seneca's head is full of a sense of anticipation for the challenges that await. War with the rebellion is ahead, though Seneca does not expect it to be a particularly long campaign. From his perspective, the rebels will soon realize, to their great disappointment, that they are not adequately equipped to confront the full military might of the Empire. Nor would they ever…

Chapter 26: Off to Fight the Rebels

The group persists in their diplomatic attempts to calm down the enraged Whispers, and as a result, two more months sneak by. The unsuccessful nature of every trip weighs heavily upon Ilana's shoulders (and subsequently Seneca as he watches her struggle). Tension builds with each failed attempt. Even in his own holding of Pyre, the desire for the Whispers to make a stand fills the air; even with Seneca's benevolent leadership. On the ninety-first day since the rebels issued their ultimatum, the Imperial palace receives a shocking revelation—*two* declarations of war. The Whispers of Freedom, as the anticipated source, presents the first declaration. However, the second proclamation stems from an unprecedented and fresh entrant into the entire affair—the United Federation.

The United Federation's unexpected alignment with the Whispers of Freedom reverberates across the galaxy, stunning all with its implications. After a half-century of peace with the Empire, the UF's decision, purportedly influenced by the enigmatic rebel leader, marks a monumental shift. By framing the Empire's expansion as a violation of its values, the UF lends credibility to the rebellion's cause, showcasing the rebel leader's remarkable political savvy. This alliance not only legitimizes the Whispers but also tilts the power balance in their favor, empowering them with resources and diplomatic clout to challenge the Empire's authority. As a result, the galaxy now stands on the brink of all-out war, with the rebels and the UF united against the Empire, reshaping the political landscape in unprecedented ways.

The news of this uncanny alliance spreads across the galaxy and violently casts a shadow of uncertainty and tension amongst the Imperial leadership Vista palace, who had no reason to suspect the UF's sudden involvement. The very ground seems to tremble beneath the weight of this monumental discovery as it lands on the emperor's desk, justifying the haughty confidence of the rebel governments Ilana attempted diplomacy with. In response, Ilana and the crew are called to Vista Palace to participate in the scramble. The only one seemingly not blindsided by the news, curiously, is Ilana.

* * *

The four of them stroll down the corridors of the building, exchanging hushed chatter as they walk in and out of meetings and debriefings with various lords, generals, and security officials. Describing the palace to be in shambles would be a drastic understatement. Military officials are running everywhere, and their cyan and golden uniforms do little to hide their frustration. The group maneuvers among the chaos to their next meeting, which happens to be with the emperor himself. Stepping into his office, Seneca can see his face is stern and annoyed. The room is opulently decorated with portraits of the royal family—examining many of them, Seneca can see that Ilana bears a striking resemblance to her mother, Winter McClain. A huge cyan stained-glass window dyes the sunlight a cool hue of blue as it filters through and paints the occupants. Despite the frustration on his face, he greets Ilana with a hug as he says, "Ilana, I'm sorry it's come to this. I know you held a much more hopeful view of the course of the rebellion."

They exchange a few more pleasantries before he instructs the group to sit. "The rest of the council thought it best *I* give you this news… For the time being, Ilana, you and your group will all be confined to Vista once more except for absolutely essential business. The climate of this rebellion—war… does not allow for risk… nor am I willing to… accept the ones that might afford you travel."

The emperor runs his hands through his short red hair as he delineates the nature of their restrictions. Without a proper military escort to secure locations, Ilana will only be permitted to perform diplomatic ventures remotely. Before any diplomatic endeavors take place, they'll require approval from the Imperial security council since cyber-attacks against the Empire's communication networks are already increasing tenfold. Ilana seems disappointed but offers little reply in protest. The emperor then turns his attention to Seneca.

"Major, you have done the Empire—and myself—a great service by keeping my daughter safe…"

The sudden praise towards him immediately puts Seneca on high alert as he attunes his ears to listen intently as the emperor continues.

"Were I to find out sooner than I had, I probably would not have allowed her to put her faith in you. Your attitude and demeanor are nothing short of rash and inhospitable… but for whatever reason, your sense of duty brings my daughter home safely time after time. Thank you."

Seneca nods and simply thanks the emperor for his kind words but knows something more is coming. He can see it as the man inhales and looks down, just as Ilana does before delivering bad news. "We need more from you. You bear a rank in the Imperial Space Fleet. You're being called in for service—"

"Dad. No." Ilana protests before Seneca or the Emperor can relax, and before he knows it, a fiery debate ensues between them.

Nothing would bring Seneca greater displeasure than to fight his home government while serving the regular Imperial military, and he is silently weighing options as Ilana and her father exchange heated words. Running means losing

Ilana forever but fighting the UF puts his holdings on Earth in jeopardy. The federal government could potentially seize his home, history, roots, everything Earthly he holds dear. However, what was it worth without Ilana? What would happen to her if he ran? Is there a future with Ilana if he does? He knows the answer is definitively no, so he remains quiet as Ilana and her father's voices grow louder. All he can do is hope his legacy veteran status will be enough to protect his livelihood back home.

"Ilana! There is nothing in his contract the prevents him from traditional military service. That's why you're being confined, since he won't be able to perform his normal obligations."

"It's supposed to be my job to determine the details of his contract and my authority to change them as I see fit."

The emperor's patience finally breaks as he slams his fist on his desk. "That was true until war broke out, Ilana! Tell me why you don't want the best combat pilot in history fighting to protect your home and your people!"

Ilana's face turns, absolved of expression as her eyes dart to meet Seneca's before returning to her father. Some internal voice beckons Seneca to speak on her behalf and profess his feelings then and there, but also knows the time is not opportune. Instead, he watches Ilana sink back into her seat. There's no further debate before the emperor dismisses them and they make their way to the mountain estate. It's a quiet ride up through the familiar countryside. Serena makes a few attempts at consoling Ilana and coaxing her to talk but is unsuccessful as she exchanges a solemn expression with Seneca. Once in the cabin, Ilana locks herself in her room for several hours, leaving the other three to their own devices.

Later she finds Seneca downstairs. She's still (understandably) furious and quickly begins pacing restlessly around the cozy living room as she talks to him. Her frustration is evident in every step she takes, and her words cut through the air like daggers. "This isn't fair," she huffs, her voice tinged with exasperation. "You work for me as *my* security. Your commission was meant for pay grade and paperwork, not for throwing you into the mainline space fleet and their battles.... Plus, I can't guarantee the lords aren't just trying to kill you." She pauses and sits by him. She stares at him sincerely. "I've made my mind up... I just want you to run Seneca. Please. Go home back you your mountains."

"No. If I run from this, I'll be labeled a traitor, and that would shatter any hope we have of making this work."

She doesn't take his dedication lightly and soon Seneca is embattled in a similar debate she'd had with her father. Circumstance has forced them into a complicated crossroads. Seneca does not want to fight the Empire's battles. His hate for the Imperial corruption and love for Ilana are at odds with one another, but his emotional investment has pulled him too deep to comply with Ilana's request. She fervently advocates for Seneca to resort to self-preservation and wait out the war back on Earth and just hope things will sort out... it sounds like a perfect situation to send him back into a downward spiral—a position he makes clear.

* * *

Ilana rebuts with a frustrated shout, "But this isn't your fight!"

"Ilana, look, I've flown in hundreds of war campaigns. I'll be fine. Don't worry about me. Worry about working toward peace so we can move on from all the war and rebellion." He remarks

"I know, but flying for the Imperial military is different. They don't care about strategy. They send enough troops, win the battle. Casualties don't matter to them," she says, fighting back tears. "You'll be a pawn Seneca! Major is field grade —"

"Ilana! I will be fine."

She shakes her head and continues expressing panicked sentiments. Throughout this conversation, Ilana pleads with him to do anything else other than comply. He knows she can see it in his eyes that he doesn't want to. After all, he doesn't owe any true allegiance to the Empire. However, Ilana represents something more significant in his life. Everything he's been entangled in—this war, the Imperial lordship, and all the political games—is a facade to keep himself close to her.

Silence overtakes their debate. Ilana stands quietly, leaning against the doorway between the living room and foyer, tears falling from her face as she cries. He walks up behind her and massages her shoulders. "Ilana, I love you. I will be okay," he says as he takes her hand, confessing his true emotions verbally for the first time. "I'm not about to give that up either."

A halfhearted smile replaces her frown before she wraps her arms around him and kisses him. "I love you too."

Stomping from above interrupts their moment before Serena yells, "Fucking stop! Y'all are so corny!"

They both laugh as Ilana places another kiss on his face. "Now I really don't want you to go."

"I'll come back. I promise." he says, with a false smile on his face.

Accepting the inevitability of war with a sense of resignation, Seneca takes time to prepare himself to fulfill his military responsibilities. His position as a squadron leader means he will fly into combat, directing Imperial units towards specific objectives, and no longer receiving the payment per kill that he usually receives as a mercenary. UniCom messages revealing his deployment schedule add an extra layer of difficulty. The schedule is relentless, with eight months on duty followed by just four months off, and he's due to leave soon for his first tour. As such, he and Ilana make the most of the time they have before he departs for Phalanx station.

Chapter 27: Two and Seven Off Suits

He arrives at Phalanx Station the following week, a formidable military stronghold nestled three days' warp away from the bustling hub of Vista. Serving as the central nerve center, this installation is crucial for the Imperial Special Operations Command (SPECACT), operating in a manner akin to the highly skilled Navy SEALs or Army Rangers of Earth. Here, the most perilous and clandestine missions demand specialized expertise, and Phalanx stands as the bastion of those skilled enough to undertake them.

With a sleek, ring-shaped structure, Phalanx stands out in the emptiness of space, serving as a fortress tailored for pilot training exercises and drills to produce forces ready for the most dangerous mission profiles Imperial pilots will face. Within its halls, the hum of activity resonates as personnel prepare for the next high-stakes endeavor. Most would consider it a great honor to walk the halls as the elite of the elite, but not Seneca. Instead, he reluctantly finds himself thrust into the role of squadron leader of a detachment tasked with combatting key federal targets. During his indoctrination and in-processing, he encounters his new commanding officer, Colonel Shari Graas—a disgruntled and unpleasant individual.

She's a short stocky woman with short red hair and peppered with freckles across her stern face. "Oh boy. They gave me you…" she says as Seneca steps into her dimly lit mono-hue office space, "Any chance you salute me shit-stain?"

"Not with that attitude," Seneca replies crossly. "I'm still an Imperial lord."

"Your fellow council members warned about your anti-authoritarian bullshit… You're not even wearing an Imperial uniform… tell me, Major, why are you here? Do you plan on deserting?"

"If I planned on deserting, I would have done so already." Seneca scowls as the woman steps towards him. "As it so happens, my commission doesn't regulate me to Imperial monkey suits and my orders come directly from Ilana. I'm where she needs me to be serving her people."

"The citizens of the Empire haven't been *her* people for over a century, but she has their support. I'll give you that." The cocky woman sneers before continuing,

"Take this kiosk. It'll fill you in on your first mission. I sure as hell don't care to help you. Now get out." She groans as she thrusts a kiosk into his hands.

Stepping out in silence, Seneca absorbs the mission details from the kiosk, his expression growing darker with each revelation. The cards dealt to his squadron are far from favorable, resembling a rigged poker match where folding seems the only prudent option. Ilana's suspicions about the Empire's intentions now appear justified. Their mission: to attack a heavily fortified UF shipyard, devoid of cruiser support. Furthermore, his unit will face a larger squadron of heavy-class fighters, similar in size and shape to Clemson's *Rot*. Despite Seneca's comfort aboard *the Phantom*, his squadron's standard Imperial light fighters pale in comparison. Their agility may be their only advantage against the formidable opposition, as the rules of engagement strictly focus on hitting the shipyard and disregarding UF forces entirely—a scenario tailored for maximum casualties.

The photos of the target shipyard reveal a massive metallic jungle gym-like structure, where UF cruisers are manufactured and repaired. Metallic scaffolding and cranes stretch upwards, creating a striking sight against the backdrop of space. If they manage to reach the target without being picked off, the exposed structure leaves it open to being rendered inoperable. Situated on the periphery of an asteroid field surrounding a small red gas giant, the yard may seem like an easy target at first…if not for the formidable defense force that safeguards it.

"We're twenty smaller fighters against thirty-four federal heavy defenders, there's no possible way we're hitting the shipyard *and* surviving…" Seneca mutters to himself as he ambles through the installation to the hangar. "They're actually trying to kill me…"

With each stride, Seneca's mounting anger reverberates through the steely corridors until he finally arrives at his destination. Shoving the door open, metallic walls hold up a high ceiling decorated with LED lights in neat rows that illuminate the floor below where the sight of nineteen freshly graduated lieutenants greets him. The air is tense with nervous anticipation as they occupy the cold metal chairs in neat rows, their faces displaying a mixture of unease and anticipation, all while waiting to meet him. The sight is enough to launch his heart into the pit of his stomach. Without a shred of doubt, Seneca sees this as nothing more than the lords' attempting to eliminate him as a political competitor.

"You're fucking joking!" He curses before using the full might his left leg could muster to relocate a stray metal chair to the other end of the hangar, its clanking echoing his fury to the ceiling. "Okay, this is how it's gonna be…"

They have no business being assigned to a unit like this. Their lack of decorations on their uniforms, the youth in their faces, and undeniable signs of fear amongst them betray their inexperience. They're fodder. Seneca runs his hands through his hair and huffing as he says, "Everyone, I'm Seneca Mason. Don't fucking call me Major or Lord or anything… I'm going out on a limb and assuming none of you have any combat experience."

* * *

The room of young men nod in affirmation to confirm his suspicions and Seneca continues, "Out-fucking-standing... Gentlemen, I'm not one for inspiring speeches. If you want inspiration, listen to Princess Ilana. I'm not going to sugarcoat this either, the Empire is basically sending us on a suicide mission..." Seneca tersely reveals the nature of their mission, addressing questions sporadically as they arise.

For a moment, a twinge of guilt washes over Seneca as he considers how many young men The Lords threw to their deaths by sending them into his gunsights over the years. In the past, he may have disregarded the people at the receiving end of his weapon's fire, but now, having witnessed the Empire's brutality, it is deeply troubling for him to realize that he has taken the lives of many individuals who were undeserving of such a fate. He'd never have suspected a socialist government that was supposed to be a beacon of prosperity would treat its military members as mere pawns, but he now stands among them as the same within the uncaring hands of a corrupt government.

 The room grows tense as he describes the enemy and their capabilities, the weight of fear almost tangible, as if he could reach out and grab it. Their legs shake and some of them look pale and sick; He pauses as needed, allowing some to rush to a waste bin to empty their stomachs. His heart goes out to them as he continues speaking, finally dismissing them to board the carrier ship already loaded with their fighter craft and *the Phantom*. At dawn, the carrier will transport the squadron 80 kilometers away from the imminent deadly encounter.

Seneca too boards the carrier ship, meandering through the dimly lit narrow halls of the ship to settle into his quarters for the evening. In the cramped room, he lies down, and his gaze is drawn to the off-white ceiling, which lacks any illumination. The beige walls surrounding him feel suffocating, like a prison cell, as he tosses and turns, consumed by thoughts of the young men assigned to die alongside him. He knows he will not allow himself to fall victim to any attempt on his life, and his future with Ilana mandates a perception of ignorance. Should he speak up, they might try harder and force him to withdraw from the endeavor out of self-preservation. The question at hand is, how can he save the young men under his command?

The question has him tossing and turning all night until an alarm signals the carrier's impending arrival at its destination—it's time to go to the hangar and ready his ship and squadron. Seneca gathers with his young followers once more, giving them one last mission briefing. Their faces are pale, and they tremble vigorously, some even vomiting once again as Seneca stands before them. He furrows his brow for a moment... *"you're not an Imperial, don't act like one... fuck their rules of engagement..."*

 He dons a halfhearted smirk as he delivers concluding remarks, "...And listen, guys. Don't break ranks. Keep a tight formation. Keep your speed up. Hit the target. I will do everything in my power to bring every. Single. One. Of you back safely. A long time ago I was twenty-three flying my first combat mission. I know what's going through your mind. I'm going to be here *with* you. Now get to your ships and get engines running. We launch in twenty."

The young pilots perk up a bit and emulate Seneca's resolve as he readies *the Phantom* once more, preparing to spit fire and bend metal in the vast expanse of space. Time ticks by, and soon his flight of twenty is left to navigate through an asteroid belt, utilizing the rugged floating rocks for cover as they approach their target eighty kilometers away. The deafening silence amplifies the tension as the minutes pass, bringing them within view of their objective. Their presence doesn't go undetected as heavy fighters and flak are already rocketing toward them at blinding speed.

Seneca makes a radio broadcast to his squadron. "Alright everyone, do as I say, not as I do. Hit the target and get back to the asteroid field. You have the advantage there and can outrun their fighters back to the rendezvous point!"

After issuing the command, Seneca breaks formation, throttling ahead into the enemy squadron. Setting maximum power to his lasers, he defies the rules of engagement, engaging the opposing fighters with relentless fire. Upon close inspection, they appear outfitted with fixed weapons that don't have targeting assist systems giving Seneca the ability to out maneuver their flak cannons, leaving only seeker missiles to worry about. It does not come as a surprise when his AI alerts him of incoming missiles as he deftly maneuvers, weaving between enemies. While most deploy flares or countermeasures, Seneca lets the missiles follow him, expertly placing opposing ships in their damage path. Since these ships rely more on heavy armor than shields for protection, Seneca's method of turning their weapons against them proves to be an effective retaliation.

He forces them to break formation and cease using seekers to prevent further abuse of their weaponry, and it will take most of them careful planning and maneuvering if they want a shot at him. Carefully watching his shield integrity by using shield charges and boost charges as necessary, Seneca's plan is keeping the attention of the enemy and protecting his squadron as the first wave of his comrades hit the shipyard. He couldn't care less about the importance of the mission for the Empire's purposes. All he wants to accomplish in this moment is to protect the nineteen other souls, even if that means all guns on him.

He continues his maneuvering, jousting, and efforts to distract the UF's defenses. He's too lost in the moment to have given much thought to the passage of time, but as the second wave hits, his shield's integrity is down to thirty percent. It's intense tracking thirty or so bandits trying to pin him down and, thanks to the laid-back job of protecting the Princess, his physical capacity to shoulder combat of this level has reduced. Fatigue is creeping in on him with every sharp turn and pitching moment. Despite exhaustion and dwindling shield integrity, he maintains aggressively engaging the enemy to ensure the safety of his squadron and drive out the UF's pilots.

* * *

Thankfully, he's returned the pressure in kind upon the heavy fighters trying to take him down, and whenever their shields fall to Seneca's Phantom, they bug out and disengage. It takes some pressure off him as one by one he forces them to retreat and relieves the burden of tracking targets. A silent prayer escapes his lips, hoping they aren't simply recharging shields at a medic-drone before reengaging. There's not much left in this confrontation, and the third wave of his squadron approaches. He stays focused, corralling the opposing ships where he needs them to be and peeling them away from his young followers.

In the last moments of the battle, his shields give way, but he remains relentless, taking aim at the engines of any who dare to look away from him to redirect them. Despite his sore arms and armor now taking some damage, he remains resolute, ensuring the success of his squadron's mission and allowing his companions to deliver the killing blow to the shipyard.

A shaken voice of one of his troops sounds on the radio. "Seneca, we got it!"

"Get back to the rendezvous point. They're going to keep chasing us for a bit. Good job boys," he answers excitedly, performing a quick turn and accelerating full speed toward the asteroid field.

Seneca tallies up a whopping total of zero kills against the UF. It's a rarity for Seneca to leave a confrontation without reaping at least one life (though he boasts no desire to dispatch UF pilots if he doesn't need to). A head count over the radio as the squadron evades into the asteroids reveals they sustained no losses. Celebration erupts among his young followers as they reach the rendezvous point—an unforeseen impossibility made reality thanks to Seneca's expert flying and the resolve of those who followed him. The ride back to Phalanx is joyous, with his troops chanting his name and firing champagne corks about the main hangar of the carrier ship's bowels. "Alright, y'all," Seneca shouts after being drenched in champagne. "Listen, we did good, but I need you all to be self-sufficient. We're going to be spending every waking moment training for our next go around when we get back. I suspect this won't be our first bad hand and I need to be able to trust this group to be able to fight back."

The unit nods in unison and spends the remainder of the trip building camaraderie. Upon returning to Phalanx Seneca storms into Shari Graas' office.

"Mission successful. Target destroyed. No UF casualties per the ROE parameters." He spouts before she's able to acknowledge his presence.

"That's good to hear..." she pauses as if awaiting something "and *our* casualties?"

"None."

"*Really?*" she asks in disbelief. "How's that possible? Given your ROEs—"

"Fuck your ROEs," Seneca spits as he turns to exit. "Remember, I make my own rules. If you want casualties, they won't be me or my pilots."

He leaves her office without another word and with no fear of retribution. He has more important matters to attend to now. True to his word, he spends weeks at a time between missions training with his squadron rigorously. Aware that his defiance won't go unnoticed in future missions, he knows these young men must be prepared to face challenges without him. Once an excellent instructor pilot in the latter part of his Air Force career, he knows exactly how to hone their skills to ensure their survival. Dogfighting, maneuver drills, and simulation exercises are all employed liberally to sharpen their abilities.

It takes time, but Seneca's dedication and expertise pay off. What began as an inexperienced group of fodder, seemingly unable to fend off threats without Seneca, gradually transform into skilled pilots. As suicide missions continue to come their way, they overcome them, maintaining an unprecedented streak of no casualties...notwithstanding a few close calls. Over the remaining months of their tour, they complete over seventy-two missions, much to the dismay of their commander. Whoever it was... or is... trying to kill them will have to try a different tactic on his next tour, lest they find themselves reluctantly giving his squadron of pilot's medals again as opposed to death certificates.

Chapter 28: Suspicious Activities

The eight-month tour has flown by, and Seneca is sitting with his young followers in a quiet lounge of Phalanx station. Engaged in conversation, they collectively shoot jokes at one another as they play cards. Seneca smiles as his mentees pick at him as well, and he silently acknowledges how they've grown on him. He still struggles with their actual names—a side effect of calling them by callsigns they'd earned throughout their time together, but the progress they've made as pilots and the camaraderie among them is typical of a military group. Being their last night together for the tour, they drink the night away.

"Hey Seneca," one of the young lieutenants, Caimen, says as they drink to their own survival.

Caimen, one of the element (formation) leaders Seneca had appointed earlier for his ability to remain calm and take command in high-pressure situations, has a new aged style haircut that complements his calm face to boot. When it comes to combat, Caimen displays exceptional composure and is undoubtedly one of the top performers in the group.

"Yessir," he acknowledges the lieutenant.
   "You think we'll fly with you again on our next tour?"

Seneca knows it's likely his next tour will not include a squadron of proficient and deadly combat pilots. In truth, he has little due what lies in store when he returns to service after the four-month hiatus ahead. "Can't say for sure, but if y'all ever want to fly with or for me again, make your way to Pyre Mining. You have jobs there if you want them. I'll fly with you boys anytime." he replies.

With the night drawing to a close, he dedicates time to personally honor each of them with a firm handshake, acknowledging their exceptional abilities as pilots in the galaxy. He genuinely desires to meet them again, preferably as allies instead of adversaries. With goodbyes exchanged, temporary freedom arrives at dawn, and he makes a beeline for Vista to reunite with Ilana.

Anticipation soars until their joyous reunion ensues. Ilana's face lights up with excitement as she catches sight of him stepping out of the limo that carried him to the cabin. Waiting for the limo to leave is challenging, but once the sound of crunching gravel is out of earshot, she embraces him tightly, tears of happiness staining her cheeks. He hadn't been at liberty to talk with her on deployment, so he doesn't imagine it's been easy for her to await either his return or word about his death. As such, her appearance is somewhat weathered and exudes telltale signs of prolonged stress.

"I've missed you Sen!" she says in a voice that's somewhat sobbing, yet joyful. Seneca reciprocates the sentiment with kisses before she continues talking. "I'm so glad you're safe. When I learned where they assigned you... I feared they were lining you up to die... especially because I didn't think you'd fight so hard against your own government."

"Well, it sucks that I'll have to wait until the war is over to get my Earth pass back, but my research and discussions with a lawyer tell me it's a protected status... Also don't forget my only allegiance is to you."

She blushes. "Oh yeah, I forgot... Mr. Outlaw," she teases, kissing him once more.

They spend the first few days together in...blissful comfort...naked...within the confines of her room. However, new peculiarities in her behavior do not go unnoticed—something is amiss. For instance, normally, Ilana leaves the windows of the estate wide open to allow ample sunshine to fill the rooms. They've yet to be withdrawn since his return. Her demeanor is off as well. Ilana, typically talkative and eager to engage in conversation of any type, lacks her trademark enthusiasm and passion. She's anxious, quiet, and evasive when he asks about her recent activities during his absence. The few times they've ventured down the mountain to the palace, she's on edge and easily startled.

He tries to chalk it up to the stress of the war as the days pass, but concern eats at him as he watches her stare off into the evening sky. It's been a couple weeks since he'd returned, and it's time he makes an attempt at determining the cause of her strange shift in behavior. "Ilana," he says as they sit on the back porch overlooking the summer-soaked mountains. "You don't quite seem yourself. Is there something going on?"

Ilana hesitates, her gaze remains astutely fixed on the setting sun that is currently burning the sky with amber and golden colors. "I don't know Sen. It's... complicated... and I can't really discuss it right now. Certain things have gotten out of hand and now...I'm just so scared all the time," she finally replies, her voice barely above a whisper, "let's just say I don't get out much anymore because things... haven't been the same since you left..."

"What do you mean?"

"I don't know how to explain it."

* * *

Ilana shuts down the conversation by kissing him on his cheek and making her way inside and up the stairs to her room. The kiss was genuine and appreciated, but it does little to prevent his concern from deepening. While he respects her boundaries, it's very unusual for Ilana to retreat into discretion and secrecy. While the war may have altered what she's comfortable divulging, the sense that something more significant remains unspoken is undeniable.

Driven by an insatiable curiosity, Seneca's resolve solidifies as she sets out to unravel the truth, starting by seeking answers from Serena. He's confident that her candid and direct demeanor will offer him assistance when he notices her engrossed in the dining room, reading the latest headlines.

He speaks up, breaking a profound silence that has engulfed the cabin's atmosphere. "Serena, I need to—"

Startled, she jumps in her seat and knocks the kiosk off the dining table. "Holy shit Seneca, you scared me, what?"

"Geez, you're as jumpy as Ilana."

She gets up and peeks out a nearby window and shuts it before returning to her seat. "The Empire has a traitor. The entire palace is like this. Things aren't exactly sunshine and rainbows right now…"

"I just don't get it, you guys hardly go outside anymore, y'all don't talk with each other much, hell, Ilana hardly leaves her room."

Serena looks down and slowly raises her head. "I… I'm sorry Seneca. I don't know."

Unfortunately, it's apparent whatever is affecting Ilana is also pressing Serena. He gives her a silent nod before venturing up the stairs to Jesper's room with shallow hopes that he may offer some insight to share regarding the proverbial dark clouds intermingling in the cabin's atmosphere.

"Hey man, can we talk?" he asks, knocking.

Jesper opens the door and extends Seneca an invitation to have a seat at the desk on the left side of the bedroom. "Things are different. I know what you're going to ask," he says hurriedly in a low voice. "I'm wondering the same thing so…" His voice remains the same, but his demeanor shifts as if suggesting something cryptically, "If you want some fresh air, the weather outside is nice right now."

Whatever message he's trying to send escapes his perception, and he asks, "What?"

Jesper says nothing in reply, and just shrugs with side-to-side head motions. An even larger dead end, but with an accompanying cryptic message.

Days continue to snake by quietly. He's happy to be home with Ilana, but he wishes normalcy would overtake them to distract him from his looming duty as an Imperial officer. All he's been able to get out of Ilana is they hadn't been traveling and they won't before he returns to duty for his second tour. She reassures Seneca she's fine, but the group's abnormal behavior troubles him. The shadow lurking among them casts a pall over their moments of respite, making it difficult to fully savor the reprieve from the war. Despite his efforts, he remains unsuccessful in unraveling the root cause of their anxieties.

One morning, the darkened living room is occupied by Seneca alone. He fights the urge to align his actions with the past. When he'd normally open the curtains, everyone else insists on the shades remaining closed... apparently as a means to maintain a pleasant ambient temperature. In his silent solitude on the couch, he checks his UniCom to find that all nineteen of his former troops have taken his advice and are now flying as security pilots in Pyre, bringing a temporary smile to his face before he lets his mind wander for a moment. At least something made sense...

Darkness around him gives way to sunrise and prompts him to start a path toward the back porch to get some air... 'Fresh air', he thinks... He takes mental account of Jesper's expertise in anti-sedition and his own understanding of hidden messages.

"Go outside..." he thinks as he redirects his venture to the front door before strapping on his pistol before he opens the door to go on a walk. Birds sing into the sky and a gentle breeze engulfs him as he steps into the solitude of the estate's serene surroundings. A stroll on one of the many hiking trails that snake through the estate is in order as he sets out to discern the cause of negative aura surrounding his friends—he doesn't know what he's looking for, but the air is fresh indeed.

Early morning walks that precede the awakening of the others become a habitual part of his daily routine. In an effort to be unpredictable to whatever entity is pressuring Ilana and company, he ensures he randomizes the routes of his early morning outings. Some mornings, his departure from bed will wake his lover and coax Ilana into venturing out with him, though she remains stoic and silent, citing the desire to take in the beauty of nature. Alone or accompanied, no event of notoriety rears its head. It goes on like this for weeks.

He finds himself awake another morning like many before, feet crunching on the gravel in the driveway, preparing to begin one of his walks. It's a cool summer morning. The cool dampness of the summer morning dings against his face as he strolls alone in the front yard, his thoughts wandering amidst the tranquil surroundings. Suddenly, a disturbance in the tree line across from him seizes his attention. His eyes lock onto it immediately and scan the area carefully, knowing that Vista's natural beauty never conceals large fauna. Something caused movement in the nearby trees and was of large size. Approaching the site of disturbance silently, he narrows it down to two possibilities: either one of his friends managed to slip past him unnoticed, or an uninvited guest is lurking on the property. Given the group's aversions to venturing outdoors, he doubts it's a mere prank.

"Fresh air..." he mutters.

With measured steps, Seneca continues toward the point of disturbance in the tree line, keeping his senses on high alert. The ground beneath his boots is still damp from the previous night's summer rain. An examination of the littered leaves on the forest floor betrays signs of a misstep, which is further evidenced by broken branches on a nearby tree.

Seneca's heart rate increases at the sight, and he reaches for his pistol. "Good call Jesper," he mumbles quietly to himself as he inspects the disturbed ground.

The boot print indicates someone's presence had passed through, but there are no further tracks, suggesting that the intruder knew not to leave a trail. Seneca raises his pistol, ready to fire, and cautiously proceeds deeper into the woods. The morning is eerily silent, save for the occasional rustle of leaves in the warm morning breeze and the sound of his own breath. He advances carefully, his eyes systematically scanning the forest floor and the canopy above for anything awry. To his dismay, nothing seems amiss and the chances of finding a clue to the group's anxiety seem to be drying out as his time is running short.

Just before abandoning his search, a peculiar detail catches his eye—a perfect ninety-degree angle in the pattern of leaves. In nature, such angles are exceptionally rare, and Seneca squints, focusing on the anomaly... Then there it is, as clear as day: a camouflaged tent enclosure, barely twenty yards into the woods. It's nestled in a perfect spot to see most of the downstairs area of the cabin, save for the dining room and the back porch.

Seneca shifts his pistol to a non-lethal setting. He calls out a demand, "Show yourself by order of Imperial Security!"
    He listens and waits momentarily for a response. Receiving none, he shouts his command once more with his pistol aimed at the tent's center of mass, "Show yourself! I saw you, asshole!"

Again, after receiving no audible evidence of life, he fires three rounds of non-lethal plasma into the tent. A loud yelp shatters the silence, followed by the collapse of the tent. A man, dressed in technologically sophisticated optical camouflage, now rendered useless by a plasma blast, falls backwards from the structure, convulsing in pain and trying to recover his balance. With lightning speed, Seneca rushes the suffering individual, forcefully knocking him down with a swift kick and pressing his weight down on the victim's chest with his foot.

Switching his pistol to a lethal setting, Seneca aims it at the intruder's face. "I really hate it when people make me shoot them. I don't like wasting charges. Identify yourself and tell me why the hell you're on the royal family's private estate spying on us."
    The man winces, his voice strained. "Stand down, Major. I'm with Imperial intelligence."

The man peels off the mask of his suit, revealing his sharp facial features as he grunts in pain. Seneca doesn't recognize him. How long has this guy been out here? Why is he here? A swarm of questions buzz about his mind but now at least he has an answer to why the group has been so weird.

"Okay, that's cool. Tell me something I care about and answer my damn question. Identify yourself and tell me why you are here, or I can fire another shot and put you out of your misery."

The threat prompts minute cooperation, as the intelligence officer stops struggling and raises his hands. "I'm here by order of the Imperial Intelligence Authority. Any and all government members are subject to observation until we can find out who is betraying the Empire."

Seneca allows the officer to stand up, but he keeps the firearm trained on him. "Tell your boss that if they want to observe us, they can talk to me first."

The officer pants. "They don't answer to you, Major.

Seneca's tone is resolute. "Like hell they don't! I'm going to check this area again tomorrow. If I or other security detail ever catch you or anyone else here again, lethal plasma rounds will send them home in a body bag. So, piss off back to wherever you came from."

The intelligence officer slowly recovers from the endeavor. Seneca's eyes never leave him as he packs up and finally leaves. The morning sun continues skyward, bathing the canopy in a warm golden glow that casts long shadows. Meanwhile, a heightened curiosity fills his thoughts with endless inquiries. He doesn't understand why an intelligence operative was here, but he now comprehends the depth of the group's paranoia. Seneca decides to keep this unsettling discovery to himself for the time being. In order to ensure the estate is free from unwanted onlookers, he tirelessly patrols the property for hours on end before returning to the cabin.

Chapter 29: A Face to the Whisper

Over the next few weeks Seneca continues to patrol the property for lurking trespassers, even going as far as studying topographic imagery of the property and identifying any points where someone might erect observation blinds. Evidently, Imperial intelligence took his warning seriously; He's found no further evidence of Imperial observation attempts. Maybe it's Seneca's diligence and presence... maybe it's a coincidence all together, but his friends have perked up as well. Things are unfolding much like times before the war. Seneca and the others chat idly about random topics, engage in group games, and do their best to distract themselves from the deteriorating world around them.

Improvements are not absolute, however. While Ilana is more talkative and at ease than in previous weeks, a lingering anxiety and bouts of hyper alert tendencies still perpetuate through her interactions. Seneca's concern is reaching a critical point, his desire for answers growing insatiable. The past eight months of the war have been taxing on each of them, but since he returned from Phalanx, he's been interacting with an incomplete version of her. It's as if something is eating her from the inside.

Seneca seizes a chance after dinner one evening alone to probe her for information. Seeking to break the tension, he teasingly pokes her nose, a playful gesture accompanied by a warm smile. It's a familiar gesture, one that used to make Ilana burst into laughter and playfully respond—Ilana's giggles briefly, but it quickly dissipates, leaving Seneca feeling somewhat disappointed but not surprised by her lack of engagement.

They're standing alone on the porch, bathed in the soft, silvery glow of Vista's moon, which casts a pale-yellow hue over the mountains. The heavy silence enveloping them mars the beauty of the scene. It's the variant of silence that speaks volumes, revealing the depths of whatever is weighing on her mind. Seneca's gaze lingers on Ilana, his face revealing the degree of his concern as he grapples with the words, he desperately wants to convey yet hesitates to articulate.

* * *

The uneasy silence remains before Seneca massages the tension off his face and says, "I'm going to miss you when I have to go back," breaking the oppressive silence.

"I wish you didn't have to... I've never felt so alone and powerless," Ilana replies, sinking into a rocking chair and placing her chin into her hands with her elbow resting on the chair's arm. She looks down, and a sigh brings her face behind her hands and her hair sulks forward. She looks up and quickly glances inside where Serena and Jesper have mysteriously ambled out of sight, as if she were verifying the coast is clear before speaking in a hushed tone, "I'm sorry I haven't been myself lately... it's probably not the best idea right now but you deserve to know why..."

With a halfhearted chuckle, he attempts a joke to lighten the mood. "If you're pregnant, I'm out."

Ilana smiles halfheartedly, shaking her head. "No... if only life were that simple."

Despite her attempt to hide it, Seneca can't help but notice the apprehensive expression on her face as she leans in for a kiss. It's difficult to describe, but she always makes this face before delineating bad news. He braces himself, feeling a sinking sensation in his stomach.

"Every single time you kiss me and make that face, you're about to hit me with bad news," Seneca comments.

Ilana nods and hesitates for a moment. The weight of the pressing truth at hand is evident in her hesitant movements and wincing, her mouth opening and closing a few times before she finally finds the courage to speak as she says, "I know who the Whisper's leader is, and I've known for a while..."

This revelation catches Seneca off guard, as he was expecting something more personal and related to their relationship. Momentary relief comes over him. That knowledge would explain the heightened paranoia Ilana's been shouldering. If the Imperial government suspects that she knows or has had contact with the leader of the Whisper rebellion, they would make significant efforts to obtain that information. Now a completely new set of questions streak through his mind. How long is 'a while'? Who is the leader? What does she plan to do with that information?

Ilana pauses, and Seneca can feel her heart rate increasing as he gently places his arms over her shoulders. "I'm so afraid to talk about this out loud. Imperial intelligence has followed people everywhere, including me and my father. They monitor everything now. This is the one place I feel safe enough to speak, but even here I feel like I'm always being watched."

Seneca recalls the encounter with the intelligence agent he chased away and responds, "Why?"

"Because they know the leader is... inside the Imperial government and everyone is a suspect" Ilana stops abruptly, gripping her hair. "I think they've figured out—if they know who the rebel leader is—I don't have much time left."

"What?" Seneca's concern deepens, and he urges her to continue. "I don't understand. What's going on?"

Ilana's eyes reflect fear and dread, and she trembles as she mouths words. Seneca tries to read her lips, but the absence of sound and the changes in her facial expressions make it difficult. He reassures her, "You can trust me. If you don't want anyone else to know, the only allegiance I have in this fight is to you."

She nods and takes a deep breath, finally exhaling. "I'm the..." she pauses and gags, almost throwing up. "I'm the lea—"

This time, after she fails to articulate, she hurries to the rail and vomits over the side. Once she's sufficiently emptied her digestive tract, she looks at Seneca. "I'm the leader of the rebels. I have been leading them in secret since the beginning."

The insanity of her statement leaves him stunned in disbelief, but her face is absent of signs of a lie. The weight of the revelation hits him like a ton of bricks, and he questions her sanity as he recalls their past interactions with the rebels. There was no obvious sign that Ilana supported or opposed the rebels, leaving him utterly perplexed but gravely concerned.

"You? What?!" He shouts in a confused fashion, causing his voice to echo in the surrounding hills.

She repeats herself, pointing at her chest. "I'm the leader of the rebels."

Seneca meticulously pieces together the puzzle in his mind, focusing on every sign he's noticed and fitting them into the larger picture. It begins to make sense: her initial refusal to halt the flow of refugees from Moniear to Myanmar, her relentless determination to secure the captured rebel official, the tense and fiery negotiations for the ceasefire, the unity tour, her impassioned speeches, her willingness to endure perilous trials orchestrated by the lords, and numerous other seemingly unrelated moments all start to align, forming a coherent narrative of conspiracy. Everything he's witnessed has all played for the benefit of the rebels, while being well disguised by vigorous diplomacy.

"Holy... Shit... Well, that explains a ton," Seneca finally responds at the realization; a weakening sensation overtakes his knees. The consequences for this will be dire if it's discovered.

Ilana raises an eyebrow. "Was it obvious?"

Seneca shakes his head vigorously. "No, but now the prolonged, unrealistic diplomacy from the Empire makes sense."

"You aren't mad?" Ilana inquires.

"No, impressed actually... How?" Seneca says, standing and subsequently taking a seat in a rocking chair behind him.

With each detail of her carefully orchestrated plan, Ilana pulls Seneca deeper into a web of intrigue, his mind buzzing with connections. Her actions, once enigmatic, now unfolded before him, revealing a purpose that had remained elusive until this moment.

It all began because of the New Genoese system, once under the rule of Jesper's father, Mylos Thompson. The Empire forcibly annexed New Genoese, despite a narrow vote against joining. With over two million residents and a thriving medical research community, the system was renowned for groundbreaking medical advancements. Shortly after their annexation, cutbacks and Imperial imposed shortcuts in research caused a catastrophic pandemic, known as "The Genoese Sickness," during an attempt at curing leukemia. Despite the system's expertise in treating illnesses, the sickness rapidly spread, causing widespread devastation, extreme poverty, and the implementation of strict quarantine measures.

Scientists managed to develop an effective vaccine for the deadly illness, but it came with an exorbitant price tag to produce in the necessary quantity to save their society. Considering the system's crippled economy, Jesper's father blocked funding for the vaccine's further production. His decision condemned the remaining citizens of "Hope," the lone planet in the system, to permanent quarantine, a place now known as a desolate wasteland where no one dared to tread lest they encounter disease carrying survivors. The plight of these condemned citizens, left to their own fate, put the Empire's ruthless obsession with wealth over human lives on full display and enraged millions throughout the galaxy.

Jesper was working for Ilana at the time, and her apparent lack of response to the Genoese pandemic left him both angry and confused. He was only familiar with the military aspects of the Imperial government, so he didn't fully comprehend its inner workings. He confronted his father about the atrocity, and as a result, his father disowned him. Then he redirected his anger towards Ilana, interrogating her at gunpoint, erroneously believing she could wave her hand and bring about change. Through Ilana's careful explanation, she had convinced Jesper of her sincere disgust with The Empire's behavior and vowed to help him. Together, they crafted a daring plan to incite change from within the very heart of the Empire. Ilana, using her connections within the government, relocated Jesper from her security detail into Imperial Intelligence, positioning him to warn systems vulnerable to annexation and motivating them to resist the Empire's clutches.

Over time, Jesper successfully recruited others who shared their cause, operating covertly within the Empire's secretive intelligence network. They collected crucial information from deep within the heart of Imperial Intelligence, and Ilana, disguising her true intentions as diplomacy, covertly identified potential rebel sympathizers for Jesper to subsequently call to the side of the infant rebellion. Their intricate communication code, employing complex ciphertexts, allowed her to maintain the secrecy of her leadership while ensuring secure communication with the growing rebellion. It was through these clandestine efforts that the Whispers of Freedom were born, a namesake for the silent and secret manner the rebellion first began.

Seneca listens to Ilana's revelation and feels a sense of awe and admiration wash over him, along with respect for the intelligence required to keep it secret for so long. The immense sacrifices she's made shows her unwavering dedication she's poured into this rebellion. The significance of her tale and the magnitude of their mission settle in as the details of her leadership draw to a close.

"Everything ever since the Genoese Sickness that was performed as diplomacy for the Empire was placing pieces on a chessboard," Ilana explains. "Jesper—and now you are the only ones who know."

A long silence ensues as Seneca wrestles with the revelation and a flurry of questions float around his mind. Has he messed up her plans? Has he done something that would give it away? What now?

"Are you sure you aren't mad?" Ilana asks, reflecting continued concern Seneca may not take the news gracefully.

Seneca, still in shock, reassures her, "If I were I wouldn't have a right to be... Just wondering what this means for us now. The Empire has me on the wrong side of the fight you've risked everything for."

Ilana explains Seneca wasn't supposed to get involved in the war at all, he was originally supposed to ride it out with her on Vista. While he's been gone, she's been working diligently to ensure that his role in the war won't interfere with the Whispers' activities. Hence, his opposition has been the UF and not the rebels.

Seneca probes further, "When were you going to tell me?"

She reveals, "I was going to tell you the day after war was declared, but with you getting sucked into the war, it changed the circumstance. You, being a massive political rival to the lords made it too dangerous for you to know anything."

As they continue discussing their situation, Seneca drops another concerning piece of information, "on the topic of knowing something... on my walks I found an Imperial intelligence agent camping out on the property. He was wearing an optic camp suit. Practically invisible. I have no idea how long he's been there or what he knows."

The revelation horrifies Ilana.

"What?!"

"You're too important to the people of The Empire. They wouldn't spy on you here unless they know something that would turn the people against you..." Seneca adds, "Ilana, you have to run. I can take you, all of you. Clemson still owes me a favor we can get passage to—."

"I've told you before Seneca, I. Can't. Just. Run!"

The Empire is likely closing in on her... his admiration for her accomplishment slips away into panic, thinking about what happens when the truth comes out— and it will. This secret is too big for anyone to keep. It's now Seneca's turn to be sick. He barely makes it to the rail before the contents of his stomach escape under the weight of reality. Once more, he's poised to lose *everything* again. Disbelief fills his mind; he'd finally allowed himself to love again, only to lose it so soon. "No... Not this time..." he mumbles as he picks his head up and wipes the bile from his lips.

Ilana sits silently and plants her face in her hands, overwhelmed with fear. She explains that if she runs, her mother and father would also be at risk. Seneca watches her spiral into panic, talking to herself under her breath. Should the truth come out, the consequences will ripple far beyond just Ilana herself. It's not just her life on the line…The royal family, once beloved by the Imperial citizens, would lose the support and trust of the very people they had ruled for generations. The lords would put all of them on trial for treason. Without the support of the people, it would be a shocking fall from grace for a family that had held the highest position of honor in the Empire for centuries. Ilana's situation is nothing short of a powder keg, ready to explode, and it's quickly spiraling out of control. Knowing the situation is slipping further from her control, Ilana mouths to herself repeatedly as she struggles to fight the urge to cry.

Seneca needs her to focus if he's going to do anything to help. He's panicking internally as well, but the mark of a true pilot is working through it. "The lords are showy. How is treason normally exposed?" Seneca asks.

Her voice is barely above a whisper, laden with anxiety and fear. "They do a security convention where enough evidence exists to make an accu—" she freezes in response to their UniComs buzzing with a startling message regarding the very topic Ilana was about to elaborate upon. The look of existential dread rears its head from her breathing.

She unleashes an ethereal shriek in response. "Seneca, they fucking know! They're holding a security convention the day you report back to Phalanx! They know you're loyal to me… Seneca, what do I do?!"

Her frantic cries reverberate off the nearby ridges. For Ilana, she's experiencing fear of death for the first time in her immortal existence… For Seneca, however, rage is all he feels as he reads through the message. On the *hour* he's set to return to Phalanx, Imperial intelligence and the council of lords will hold a security convention to bring forth evidence against a "rebel conspirator" operating within the government. The timing is deliberate; likely to prevent expected protest from Seneca.

The prospect of punishment has Ilana trembling, her breath coming in short gasps and her body uncontrollably convulsing. No matter how hard Seneca tries to calm her, nothing seems to have any effect. He waits helplessly, watching her lose all control of her emotions. It feels like an eternity before she finally tires out enough for him to get a word in. "You can't do this alone anymore."

He slumps down and leans on the house, pulling her close. Ilana shakes her head. "I know, but I don't know how or what to do," she says as she struggles to keep from returning to her state of hysteria.

Another silence befalls them, only broken by Ilana's sobbing. Seneca's not ready to lose her… Not yet… Not without a fight… For once, he has a chance to forestall loss and the agony of grief. He wasn't there to drive Sophie home the night a drunk asshole ran her off a mountain. He couldn't cure Kelsea's cancer. He *can* save Ilana. Drawing in a deep breath and setting it loose with a heavy sigh, knowing there was no caging his thought once it's out, he says, "Let me come out publicly as the leader, you keep low for the rest of the war…"

"No!" Ilana interrupts angrily.

"You've done amazing Ilana, bringing all these people together; You convinced the UF to engage in war with a much stronger military, and you are a guiding light to rebel and Imperial alike."

"But this is my fight! I can't lose you!"

"Ilana, listen to me." He says, grasping her shoulders and sprinkling in a bit of a lie, "It's a war now. Let me fight this battle. I know, given time, you'd win. But you are out of time. Let me take the fall."

She continues adamantly refusing before she begins to panic once more. "Your face will be on every bounty poster in the galaxy. I can't protect you if you do that and the Empire will hunt you down—"

Seneca grabs Ilana's hand, attempting to calm her. "They have to fight the war first, which *we* can win—"

She shouts in reply, "It's not like you'll ever be able to come into Imperial space ever again. You'll be a traitor and—"

Seneca interjects with a hint of frustration, "I've never been anything less, Ilana!"

"I know Seneca! But that doesn't mean we'll ever be together again!" Ilana yells and shakes her head, tears flying around like shrapnel.

"I want to protect you, Ilana. I haven't felt this whole in centuries. I'd rather die feeling like this, knowing I fought for this, then live like I was before I met you. If I have to be alone for the rest of time, I'll eventually find happiness knowing you're safe."

He doesn't believe everything he's saying but Ilana's tears flow like a torrential rainstorm, soaking her shirt and leaving her gasping for breath… he can't let her suffer. Seneca watches her with a heavy heart, the helplessness eating at him as he witnesses the emotional storm that has engulfed her. He briefly wonders what Serena and Jesper are up to, suspecting that Jesper is keeping Serena away to shield her from the immense burden he and Ilana have been carrying.

Gradually, Ilana's sobs subside, and she regains enough composure to speak again. Her voice trembles with the remnants of her emotional turmoil as she whispers, "Okay." between erratic breaths.

Seneca helps her up, and they sit down together on the couch inside the living room, enveloped in a dismal silence that hangs in the air like a specter. In the dim light of the room, their silhouettes dance on the wall opposite the dying fireplace. As time passes, those elongated figures draw nearer, eventually converging into a single silhouette as the fiery blaze transforms into smoldering embers.

Exhausted from the emotional release, Ilana finally drifts off to sleep, her head resting on Seneca's shoulder. He holds her tightly, feeling the rise and fall of her breath, as they find solace in each other's presence amid the darkness of the night. He's only going to get so many moments like this...

Chapter 30: Trials and Tribulations

Vista's sun rises the next morning and Ilana gently sends Serena off to spend time with her family, sparing her from the burden of their heavy secret. To ensure her safety, it's best if she doesn't know about the deceitful plot at hand. In Serena's absence, Seneca, Ilana, and Jesper come together at the dining table, meticulously mapping out the transition from Ilana's hidden leadership to Seneca's public control.

"The first hurdle we have to overcome is convincing the Empire it was you the whole time," Jesper says, "…all the way back to the beginning."

Jesper warns that if the Empire accuses Ilana as predicted, convincing them otherwise will be challenging, despite Seneca's track record of disrupting their efforts and his recent reputation for non-compliance. Moreover, Ilana is a bigger political target than Seneca, and the lords would eagerly seize the opportunity to eliminate her and her family from the political arena.

"Just claiming to be the secret leader won't be enough… especially considering your relationship…" he finishes.
    Ilana interjects. "We've never given anyone a reason to believe our relationship was more than professional, though."
    Jesper nods and replies. "Yes, but time after time Seneca has showed unshakable loyalty to you."
    Seneca thinks for a moment, "What kind of statement do I need to make?"
    "A big one… Something the lords can't sway public opinion on. Just appearing at the convention should draw a massive portion of attention, but again, you need to make a huge scene and lie like you believe it. You'll need to improvise and make it convincing." Jesper says.

It's a vague first step. There are no finite rules at hand, so Seneca will need to use his big personality to… persuade The Empire he is the rebel mastermind without contradiction. Planning shifts from the security convention to the rebellion's overall approach to the war. Seneca stressed a change in strategy. Ilana's eloquent tongue is as adept at weaving words into inspirational calls to action as it is at kissing, but she has no military mind. The strategic means by which she and Jesper have the Whispers fighting is too traditional for a rebel fighting force. Seneca suggests shifting strategy accordingly to fight like the rebels they are.

"Military targets are too well defended and making ground in the war will take forever. I suggest we focus on hitting economically significant targets. Precious metal mines and refineries, shipping lanes, anything that generates Imperial dollars." Seneca says as he analyzes the assets available to the rebels and the UF.

He awards the plan the name "Operation 1929", referencing the stock market crash of 1929 that kick started the great depression. Hitting the economic targets per Seneca's suggestion should put pressure on the wallets of the lords. Money, being their motive that caused the rebellion, should force them out of it once the financial cost of the war reaches an unacceptable threshold. In the meantime, let the UF fight the traditional battles and maintain pressure on military targets. The duality of the approach will spread the Imperial military thin between defending both economically significant targets and the more traditional military targets.

"Won't that incur civilian casualties?" Ilana asks.

"Jesper?" Seneca looks to him for guidance.

"That's complicated... We can take measures to keep them minimized, but they're possible. Especially at first. It's war Ilana. It's not like civilians in the rebel systems aren't being harmed."

"That's true..."

"The shorter this war is, the more lives that are spared." Seneca adds.

"Agreed." Jesper nods.

Seneca couldn't help but wonder how he had come to this point, entangled in a web of rebellion and subterfuge... he just wanted to flirt with someone in a bar on Oberon and now he's going to be the leader of the largest civil war in galactic history. The path ahead is fraught with danger, and the future is uncertain. Yet within this space, Ilana's eyes convey to him he is the beacon of hope she has yearned for. He is unafraid to stand with her in defiance of an oppressive Empire and possesses the resilience to confront any forthcoming challenges—even though, as far as Seneca is concerned, it's solely for the sake of Ilana.

"This could work," Ilana sighs, a faint smile finally gracing her lips, finally able to shed the burden she's been carrying for years. "I just wish you didn't have to go away again..." she says, turning to Seneca.

"I'll come with you too, Seneca," Jesper adds as they finish up the session. "You'll need someone who knows both sides to help you."

Seneca nods, recognizing that in this upcoming campaign, having a known ally by his side will be crucial. Although he hasn't vocalized it to Ilana, the fear of losing another loved one is at the forefront of his mind. He's not adept at processing negative emotions in a healthy manner. When Kelsea died, he spent three years exacting his anger and grief on the Orinian military without remorse or respect for life, including his own, before roaming the galaxy aimlessly.

Jesper excuses himself to make his own preparations for the upcoming challenges. Seneca and Ilana embrace the fleeting nature of their time together. Acutely aware that their separation could last for years once Seneca leaves, they treasure each moment. They commit every kiss, every gaze, every sensation of each other's touch to memory, cherishing the time they have left. With the uncertainty of the future looming, they hold on to each other tightly, knowing that an undefined number of sunrises and sunsets await them before they can be reunited.

Before Seneca knows it, an emotional farewell with Ilana is in order; the day of reckoning upon them. It's a disheartening moment that seems to have arrived all too swiftly. Time, a capricious companion, has both favored and challenged him. Now, they all must depart, separately, for the Imperial palace. Seneca puts on the false facade of journeying to his own ship, in reality donning Imperial regalia as a disguise to help him keep a low profile and stealthily enter the palace shortly after the Ilana and the others.

Humid summer air entices his skin to sweat underneath the uncomfortable monkey suit, and the sky is laden with remnants of overnight showers as the sun continues skyward. He watches Ilana, Serena, and Jesper head into the palace among other pretentiously dressed dignitaries, lords, and security personnel. As of yet, nobody but a few lords and Imperial security know who's to be accused, nor the crime they're to be charged with. Silent anxiety and confusion are evident in the expressions of the attendees, making it easier for Seneca to melt into the crowd. Walking into the familiar arena-esc courtroom, his heart pounds with anticipation. In order to stay ahead of the moments to come, he ensures his weapon is ready for lethal action if needed, all while shrouded in a darkened corner of the hall.

Armed guards are everywhere, and he nervously ponders how he intends to escape. He'll need to improvise that as well. He doesn't have enough time to concoct a flawless plan before the room reaches capacity. Before long, the space is full of pretentious individuals who are ready to present their evidence against an undisclosed individual, though glances at Ilana by whispering dignitaries tell him everything he needs to know. Tensions in the room thicken as Ilana settles into her customary seat at the center of the room without him. Seneca's gaze remains fixed on her from the nosebleed position he occupies, his senses attuned to the joyful and haughty attitudes of Lord Marc Antony as he chats with Agent Maxwell. There's an air of arrogance amongst them that would rival his own attitude.

Finally, the convention ensues and despite the importance of the meeting at hand, Seneca's mind wanders almost immediately. Some thirty minutes pass while lords voice concerns about the loyalties of their constituents in the occupied territories. Periodically, both Ilana and the Emperor interject with questions or requests for additional information. Much of the briefing is as dry as most political slough he's sat through, and he waits for the proverbial "main event" for some time longer. In the lull of all the bullshitting, Seneca can't help but observe Agent Maxwell. His smug demeanor and his growing anticipation to speak is hard to ignore, especially when Ilana engages in the conversation.

Seneca's limited familiarity with the bald agent extends only to their previous interactions, but now, in his dual roles as a private security member and a romantic interest in Ilana's life, he is scrutinizing the man for his reactions to Ilana during the unfolding briefing. Ilana must be noticing as well, as her trademark confidence in her speaking is waning. Clearly, he possess some type of knowledge he is eager to share, and his trained eyes, along with those of others in the room, keenly observe the subtle shifts in Ilana's facial expressions and her escalating unease.

Finally, the moment of action is drawing near. With determination in his eyes, Agent Maxwell takes the floor, ready to expose the evidence that points to the individual's betrayal of the Empire.

"Esteemed compatriots," he says, his voice dripping with gravitas, "It is no secret that the rebels have been operating with assistance from within our own ranks. For too long, we've endured the loss of Imperial interests and the erosion of our security, all due to the treacherous actions of those who have forsaken their loyalty to the Empire's principles. After dispatching our *dear* princess..." He pauses for a dramatic effect, a sly smile gracing his lips. "...on a series of diplomatic ventures, we hoped her efforts would quell this disloyalty and remind our constituents of the Empire's generosity and glory. However, our department now has reason to believe she may not have been entirely truthful about her allegiances."

As he speaks, the bald man projects a slide show from a ceiling mounted holographic projector. "Behold item 1, this very document is an example..."

The document he's displayed on the holographic projection at the center of the hall is the concession agreement granted to Idalia. The gentleman details how she intentionally misled COS governments and secured protection for 'fleeing convicts who shamelessly abandoned their duties'—Suggesting that it is an odd sentiment when one considers the refugees were all civilians.

"Item 2, transcripts and recordings of various speeches. None of which truly promote Imperial rhetoric, and many that subtly promote rebel sympathy and some even inciting rebels to join the cause..."

Some of the speech transcripts in the presentation preceded Seneca's involvement by several years, amplifying the difficulty of redirecting the lord's fury. How is he going to explain that? He needs to make it so that he doesn't need to...

Continuing his analysis, Agent Maxwell meticulously dissects Ilana's rhetoric, comparing compiled data that reveals spikes in rebel activity after her speeches. Unfortunately, The Empire has done an outstanding job in ensuring every detail of evidence is well analyzed and incriminating. There is no fallacy in their presentation, nor anything to which any witnesses of the events could protest. Everything is objective fact and not conjecture or speculation; it makes for a captivated audience and draws scowls from the lords. The event is also being televised as well, so there's no doubt that citizens are forming their own opinions of Ilana at this moment.

The agent transitions from analyzing speeches and rhetoric to present photos that align with statements from captured rebels, who were coerced via torture and drug into revealing Ilana's habit of whispering in the ears of those she conversed with. 'I listen for the whisper,' a famous statement of the rebel alliance is cited as evidence. Seneca too has heard her say this once on Daryl. Images presented as evidence dated back to the loyalty tour, with data indicating a subsequent surge in Whisper activity following their visits. Other photos of Ilana whispering to rebel leaders are sourced across a variety of the group's diplomatic visits with accompanying audio recordings that are picked apart by forensic analysts.

Seneca can't help but steal a glance at Ilana, whose complexion had turned ashen, and at her father, whose expression currently wrestles with a mix of anger and fear. Serena, too, looks pale, eyeing her best friend hopelessly. The nerves prick vehemently at Seneca as well, and he can't shake off the shame that he had been completely unaware of the extent of the surveillance. It was his job to protect Ilana —his job to ensure her safety and security. It's a frustrating internal fight he wrestles with. Ironically, the only aspect of their lives that hadn't been captured on camera was their relationship—a detail they hadn't *actively* sought to conceal.

The agonizing presentation and explanation of evidence goes on for three more hours before agent Maxwell points his finger at Ilana, "Lords and generals, it appears as if our own princess is the result of the loss of stabilization of our nation. Princess Ilana, from this moment you stand formally accused of treason and conspiring—"

Chapter 31: Cold Blood, Hot Plasma

Suddenly, deafening sounds of a plasma weapon firing fill the hall, with its metallic buzzing echoing off the walls. Agent Maxwell clenches his chest as the rest of the room stands frozen, consumed by fear and confusion. Before Maxwell could finish his speech, Seneca had made his grand statement; he had drawn his weapon from the dark corner where he stood and fired five rounds into the man's back, piercing through him and burning deep holes in his chest. Time to make a scene...

"Oh, please..." Seneca says sneering condescendingly as the man's body thuds upon the floor, dark red life force oozing from the wounds left by Seneca's pistol.

Shock maintains its grip on everyone, making for a silent and dramatic scene for Seneca's stroll down to the basin of the hall. No one seems to have fully processed what just occurred. Shedding the Imperial attire, he adopts a fake smug expression, holstering his firearm in a flashy manner, resembling a character from a western film. Loud shouts and chatter fill the space as they realize Seneca's identity.

"If you honestly believed Ilana was betraying the Empire, you're all just as stupid as I'd hoped," he declares, addressing the room.

"Major!" The familiar voice of lord Marc Antony echoes through the chamber, "What are you doing here? You were supposed to report to Phala—"

Without hesitation or remorse, Seneca brandishes his weapon once again and fires a lethal round into the shoulder of the arrogant lord. The man shouts and the rest of the hall echoes the distress of the man as he screams. He's in no mood for distractions—no state of mind to entertain anything from the lords at the moment. Murder in cold blood under the eyes of the galaxy... there's no turning back, and he's got a job to do. The love he feels for Ilana is his only anchor and he's praying it's strong enough to carry him through. Until then, he channels his anxiety into anger.

"Yeah...on that note..." Seneca says, unpinning his Major lapel from his neck and tossing it to Ilana, "I resign my position and commission. Sorry princess, I don't really have much use for you anymore." He does his best to sound condescending and snide.

She catches it and just nods, avoiding further eye contact, and Seneca redirects his attention back to the lords while armed security runs into the room. He needs to buy time, and to do so he aims his weapon immediately at the nearest lord before addressing the armed guards. "Stay right there, assholes. I got shit I need to say and if we're going to start shooting, I'm going to paint the room with brains and viscera. Y'all best let me finish."

They stop in their tracks without a word. The only sound in the room is the continued screaming of a bleeding fat cat in the stands above. "Listen here. The Empire has had this shit coming for years. Time after time, decade after decade, you greedy barons take and take and take. When that wasn't enough, you *stole...*"

Seneca waves his pistol around, keeping it constantly trained on anyone of importance as necessary to sell his false narrative as he meticulously dissects the deceased agent's litany of evidence. A twisted tale of deceit rolls off his tongue, expertly unraveling the carefully constructed narrative that pinned the blame on Ilana.

"... I'd met the princess *years* before she'd found me on Oberon. Naively, she believed me when I told her if she didn't follow my instructions to a tee, I'd come to Vista and assassinate the royal family..."

With every point, he weaves a complex framework of context, revealing the "truth" behind her actions. He artfully deconstructs Ilana's speeches. Instead of it being of her volition, she spoke under duress. Moments witnessed by Imperial security were nothing more than moments when Seneca's cunning deceived them. He spoke of her as nothing more than a puppet, who was so good at lying on her family's behalf, appeared to have adopted the rebel's beliefs herself. Every piece of the puzzle falls into place, and none of these actions could have been initiated by Ilana herself; they were all orchestrated by Seneca. All the while, he has to discipline his emotions carefully, preventing precious moments from replaying in his head. He hates speaking ill of her in this manner, but it's all in the name of protecting her and what she's worked so hard for.

"Then she convinces one of you *morons* to make me a fucking lord! It was too fucking easy. I guess decades of me fucking with you didn't command respect. Do I have it now?!" He shouts angrily.

The room is silent for a moment, many too unsure to speak or nervous. Seneca's own face is red from emotion. If they didn't buy his story, Ilana's life remains endangered, and Seneca won't be able to protect her after this.

"I'm not so convinced..." a familiar voice says behind him.

"I'm sorry, what are you unsure about?!" He shouts, turning around to meet the origin of the voice to find the female voice speaking up and standing staring at him—Serena.

"Your *friendship* with Ilana." She says.

He flashes a glance at Ilana and at Serena. Is she serious? Is she helping him? Does she understand he's trying to help? Why would she risk this plan? He hadn't intended on her, Jesper, or Ilana speaking up, but at this point, he takes a risk and aims the pistol at his friend. Serena doesn't flinch but the eye contact they make silently communicates everything he needs to know.

"Friendship?" he says calmly. "I told you long ago, I don't have friends. It's just me. I don't attach. I only trust myself."

"Then why defend her? Why not let her take the fall?"

"She's served her purpose, and unlike *your* government, *I* don't kill the undeserving. We all know—" Seneca pauses to look around the room and locks his gaze on the emperor's furious expression "That the royal family holds no actual power anymore. Everything rests with the lords."

Serena sits down slowly. Seneca can feel the tension bearing on him like a magnifying glass scorches ants. The faces in the room are buying what he's selling, and Serena has helped immensely.

Jesper takes a false stand as well. "We trusted you... the Empire trusted you!"

"Ha!" That statement elicits *actual* laughter as Seneca asks, "When have they trusted me? They never did, and rightly so. I am *the* one true leader of Whispers, and y'all should have listened... Mark my words, we will gain our freedom or burn the Empire trying."

"Enough!" Byron's voice thunders. "You have committed treason and unforgivable transgressions against the empire and personally against me and my family. I will see to it you receive death for your actions, Jesper, arrest him!"

Byron's threat looms large, and his intentions are clear. Unbeknownst to the Emperor or Imperial lords, Jesper is the perfect choice to carry out the "arrest." Backed by the additional security officers who have been waiting to pounce, Jesper propels himself forward from behind the table where he had been standing to engage Seneca in a false struggle. Seneca fights back against Jesper and the Imperial goons who are frantically grappling for Seneca's pistol. Despite Seneca's apparent efforts, Jesper and the others overpower him, bringing him down. Amid the chaos, Seneca shares a final glance with Ilana. She's sobbing and watching the scene unfold as Serena pulls her away from the sight and attention of the Imperial lords, now sheltered from their wrath. Now that she is out of danger, it is time for him to focus on himself and winning a full-scale war against the most powerful military in all of human-occupied space...

Jesper yanks Seneca up from beneath the dog pile and huffs through his teeth, "I'll transport him to the prison myself. I wanna see it when they lock him up..."

The other agents easily buy into Jesper's plan, watching him drag a resisting Seneca from the hall. Seneca maintains an appearance of struggle. To continue selling the ruse, Jesper thrusts Seneca aggressively into the rear of the vehicle, covertly tossing him a key card to disengage the cuffs along just before he slams the door. Now that they're safe and underway in the police transport, Jesper tosses him his pistol as Seneca escapes the unlocked cuffs.

"You're one good actor" Jesper says now that a moment to catch their breath presents itself "They definitely bought it. You even got the emperor to react. Holy shit, that was awesome!"

"Thanks… a girlfriend in high school talked me into doing drama and improv dub…" he replies with minimal enthusiasm.

The dastardly duo drives the transport straight up to *the Phantom*. To their relief, security is yet to arrive on scene to impound it, believing Seneca to be safely in custody. Swiftly, before anyone becomes wise, he lowers the boarding ladder from the entranceway, and the two make it into the belly of the craft. With hands steady on the controls, quickly brings his ship roaring to life and sets a course for Pyre—a place where the people support him and where a formidable militia stands ready to defend against any Imperial squadrons.

Jesper settles into the copilot seat as Seneca prepares to take off. The ship is ready to depart and a route to Pyre is ready in his navigation computer. Seneca's just about to go when his emotions surge forward, threatening to overwhelm him. Ilana is safe, but he wishes he'd taken one more look at her face or found another way to say a proper goodbye. The weight of his feelings hits him like a tidal wave. It's been over a century since he'd allowed himself to love, and now he's thrust into a war to protect himself from grief again. He refuses to shoulder the blame alone; the Empire bears responsibility, and they will pay dearly for their actions against him.

Seneca's pain morphs into seething rage. He channels his anguish into fury. Instead of taking off bound for Pyre, his fist pounds on a panel above him. The force of his blow shatters the plastic cover, sending the shards of plastic littering the floor below, revealing a multitude of hidden switches connected to various auxiliary combat systems. Each switch represents a different tool in his arsenal, a means to unleash the full force of his ship's violence upon his enemies. In this crucial moment, Seneca's attention is on two switches. He flips the first one, turning on a radio jammer that broadcasts heavy metal music throughout the range of VHF frequencies. The noise serves as a distraction, covering his movements and jamming Imperial air-to-air communication.

Seneca swiftly flicks the second switch, activating a unique feature of his ship—the "Atmospheric Combat Mode." As he does, the ship undergoes a remarkable transformation. Dimensional thrusters are covered, lasers disappear into the wing structure, and additional flight control surfaces extend from hidden compartments. Panels on the ship's belly open, opening a venturi for four concealed turbojet engines that eagerly gulp in air as they spool up to power. In moments, the craft transforms from a space-faring vessel to a sleek fighter jet, ready to soar through the atmosphere using traditional flight control surfaces. Quick verifications confirm that the ailerons, elevators, and rudders move under his command.

"Uhh Seneca, what's going on? We need to get moving before they figure out what's going on."

Seneca ignores Jesper's question as *the Phantom* completes its transformation. He's not leaving Vista without turning something into a smoldering pile and the ACM capabilities of the ship will give him an unparalleled advantage should anyone show up to do battle with him. Before Jesper can further protest, Seneca burns a boost charge to perform a rocket assist take off from a standstill. *The Phantom* flies smoothly at nearly mach-speed toward a planet-side weapons cache north of the palace.

"Seneca, we don't have shields in this configuration."
    "Nothing other than missiles is getting through my armor before we get out of here."

Music playing through his jammer echoes his anger to every radio receiver within thirty kilometers of *the Phantom*'s location. There's no initial resistance; after all, he isn't supposed to be airborne, and he arrives over the weapons cache in a matter of minutes. Anti-air weapons fire at him, but true to his words, the flack does little damage to the armored hull of the ship as Seneca pitches the nose down and strafes the weapons cache with his guns.

Gunfire peppers the ground and structures below, kicking up dirt and debris into the air. His guns tear through buildings, volatile cargo concealed within exploding into fireballs, creating an unexpected chaos to those below.

"Seneca, this wasn't part of the plan. They'll have a squadron of fighters here to intercept you if we wait too long."
    Seneca is growing mildly impatient with Jesper's constant input. "Can they be configured for atmospheric combat?"
    Jesper hesitates for a moment before saying, "No."
    "Then I don't care."

Most ships lack the capability to maneuver aerodynamically and rely solely on thrusters. While thrusters are essential in space, they lack efficiency within an atmosphere's gas ocean. Even if they had ACM, controlling a ship with flight controls is extremely different from flying with thrusters; the accompanying skill set is equally rare.

He banks the ship ninety degrees and pulls back on his stick smoothly. The horizon moves steadily across the window as the nose comes back around to his target, exerting more than 7gs on the occupants. It's a familiar maneuver for a former Air Force pilot to set up for another strafing run; a maneuver he repeats until the cache is a smoldering pit on the ground.

He pulls the nose up into a vertical climb after the last run, aiming his nose into the sky just as onboard radar detects a squadron of 20 ships barreling towards him.

"Alright Seneca, no shields. What are we doing man?"

He depresses another switch on his auxiliary combat system panel. This one reconfigures his missile targeting system to select multiple targets, locking onto their unique ship ID as opposed to a heat signature—a highly illegal system. His AI targeting locks onto twelve of the twenty ships descending to punish him and he depresses the thumb switch on his stick; all twelve of his missiles begin an unrelenting pursuit of their targets. Just as the gap between the enemy craft and himself close in upon one another, the missiles force them to scatter and break their formation. Seneca ascends paying no attention or making any effort to engage the other eight fighters, who are preoccupied with rescuing their comrades from Seneca's missiles.

He reaches maximum service altitude of his ship's aerodynamic capabilities, where he promptly reconfigures the ship for normal space ops and officially begins the trip toward Pyre. The escape is complete, and Ilana is safe. If only he could calm his nerves…

Chapter 32: No Small Task

In the dim blue glow of warp, expansive space stretches out, quiet and cold. The weight of his actions sets in, and an overwhelming sense of loneliness gnaws at his core, replacing his anger from mere hours before. This form of loneliness... he hasn't experienced since the day he first purchased his faithful vessel. Now the feeling is once again threatening to consume him entirely. What's worse, the most challenging trials lie ahead, and the fear of never seeing Ilana again haunts every corner of his mind. He has to maintain the alliance with the UF and lead a rag-tag rebellion against the strongest military force in the galaxy. Logically speaking, odds are not on his side. He has no idea how the UF is reacting to his public... announcement, nor does he know if they will maintain the alliance. If they don't, the rebellion is as good as over.

Jesper's voice cuts through the deafening silence, interrupting the internal shouting of the voices within Seneca's mind. "I'd say you got the Lords's attention. Ilana definitely isn't their priority anymore..."

"Hopefully you're right," Seneca replies, his voice betraying none of the turmoil churning within him.

"I'm more than certain. There's already bounty contracts out for both of us on the bounty compendium. They're offering *lordship* and eighty million for your head. My bounty reward is less impressive, but still high." Jesper chuckles.

"Oh."

"You don't seem impressed?"

Seneca cracks a small joke of his own. "Well, I figured I'd be worth more..."

Humor breaks the negativity for a couple of moments, temporarily bringing relief to Seneca's inner turmoil and altering the atmosphere in his psyche. Though Jesper and Seneca have not known each other long, they've steadily become what most would consider friends. It's a relief to have such company given the insurmountable task at hand.

"They're relatively sure you're headed for Pyre," Jesper says as they calm their laughter, "Not an incorrect assumption on their part, but that's going to leave us only a day or so to prepare for incoming imperial squadrons, less if we get intercepted multiple times enroute."

"Unless they have an entire fleet between here and there, I doubt they'll pick a fight with us. Any spare pilots out here will be in small numbers or alone and incapable of combatting us."

"Maybe, but they could be just used as speed bumps." Jesper replies.

Seneca nods. It's not outside the realm of possibility... The Empire frequently uses their own troops as pawns and could just be tossed at him to slow him down. Thankfully, the journey is short and without incident. However, the news of Seneca's public announcement reached Pyre faster than *the Phantom* could carry him and a standing ovation greets him at his former holding.

The port area, typically a desolate expanse dotted with parked ships, service equipment, and fuel trucks, now pulses with life. Bodies of Pyre's citizens crowd the landing pads, creating a riotous atmosphere. A sea of cheering faces engulfs them, and chanting voices ring out as he navigates through the lively crowd, their energy electrifying the air. Despite the overwhelming reception, Seneca's gaze searches for Marco. It only takes a brief moment for him to locate the familiar face as they wade through the enthusiastic crowd.

Marco shakes Seneca's hand enthusiastically. "Sir, we've heard the news. Pyre stands with you and the Whispers. We owe our prosperity—"
Seneca interrupts him, his tone firm. "You and your people owe me nothing. Pyre is free as far as I am concerned."
Marco nods and continues. "My friend, Pyre would not be here without you, and we are prepared to lend our resources unconditionally to the Whispers."
Seneca, Jesper, and Marco walk together as they head for Pyre's government complex from the usual rail shuttle station. "Fighting the Empire is a massive undertaking, Marco. Make sure the people understand. At least hold a vote of some kind to make certain this is their will."
"It will be nothing more than a formality, sir, but I will ensure the people are properly informed," Marco says with a joyful smile as they walk into the old conference room. "Tell me, though, how were you able to keep it under the nose of the Empire for so long?"

A fair question... Seneca expected he'd need to recount the story again. Hopefully, he remembers to tell it the same way he'd told the lords to keep a consistent narrative should the conspiracy ever come under scrutiny. He dives into the lie once more, his words flow like a river of deception, each sentence crafted with precision as he spins his intricate web of lies, just as he has done before the lords. Just as he had before, he weaves a narrative of cunning strategy and calculated moves, portraying himself as the mastermind orchestrator of the rebellion's clandestine operations. His voice remains steady, his demeanor confident, as he paints a picture of his alliance with Ilana as a strategic partnership, a clever exploitation of the Empire's vast resources to further the cause of the Whispers of Freedom.

* * *

They continue their way to the government complex while he delves deeper into the convoluted narrative. Seneca struggles to remember certain details, yet he maintains an accurate and believable tale that would fool most. Occasionally, he pauses or adjusts his wording to sustain consistency. Marco, his attentive audience, nods in approval and offers encouraging smiles throughout the elaborate fabrication. Seneca can see the genuine interest in Marco's eyes, but as he nears the conclusion of his tale, a subtle hint of doubt flickers in Marco's expression and his stoic face seems to see right through Seneca. Surely, though, he had been certain in his words enough to convince him though? Is Marco a skeptic or merely about to play devil's advocate?

"Crazy mantle to undertake for Ilana, no?" Marco's inquiry lingers in the air, challenging Seneca's carefully constructed narrative.

Seneca chokes and coughs at the way he mentions Ilana, his mind racing as Marco's unexpected insight leaves him grappling for a response. Marco is perceptive and patient, nor would his skepticism cover malicious intent, but Marco's insight leaves Seneca stunned.

"What? Where did you get that impression? She was never the rebellion leader. I told you everything." He sputters amid a flurry of coughs and wheezes, trying to regain his equanimity. His voice carries a note of incredulity, attempting to downplay the assertion.

Marco's reply is calm and perceptive, offering little room for evasion. "Please, my friend, I know the actions of love when I see it. Ilana's a deeply caring individual whose words are inspiring and don't carry the tone of duress, and I know the look of fear and pain in the eyes of a friend," he says with an understanding gaze.

Once more, Seneca loses composure. His direct nature makes talking himself out difficult. "Love? It's not—"

Seneca's thoughts spiral into a whirlwind of uncertainty as he reflects on his first visit to Pyre. The walls of the government conference room they occupy close in. Marco's astute observation lingers in the air. Doubt grips his mind... Could others, too, have since detected the concealed emotions that had simmered beneath the surface during their encounters? The mere possibility sends a shiver down his spine, and he can't shake the unsettling feeling that their well-guarded secret might not have been as impenetrable as he requires.

Seneca leans in closer, a hint of urgency in his voice. "I won't lie to you, since you clearly know that what I said isn't the truth. But I need to understand how you figured it out so I can ensure nobody else has caught on."

Marco's gaze remains steady, his expression unwavering. "My father," he begins, his tone measured, "held a Ph.D. in forensic psychology and was renowned across this section of the galaxy for his ability to investigate and read people. He trained me in the field as well. It was no small task for me to deduce through your inadvertent cues that you're protecting Ilana, just as you have been since I met you." He pats Seneca on the back. "My question is why would you do so? Fighting the Empire is no small undertaking and drawing their wrath to yourself? One would only do such a thing for love, especially one such as you."

Seneca finds comfort in this knowledge; relief replaces the worry that previously dominated his expression. The likelihood of another possessing Marco's skills is as rare as it would be for Seneca to encounter a pilot better than himself. Furthermore, he need not worry since the wrath of the Empire is indeed enroute to bear its weight upon his shoulders. Ilana need only keep low and hope the Whispers can win the war.

Marco then smiles and grabs Seneca's shoulder firmly, rocking him from side to side. "You, my friend, are in love. There's no nobler cause."
    Jesper joins Marco in teasing Seneca. "Ay, not that you can blame him. I'd go to war for her too if I were in his boots."

The lighthearted, humorous sentiments ease his worries as Seneca laughs along with them. Further banter will need to wait, though. There's a lot to be addressed and the Empire is on its way. They all take seats around the oval oak table in the middle of the conference room, boasting a holographic display with an accompanying computer as its centerpiece. "If you two are done, we've got work to do..."

The others nod and begin analyzing Pyre's resources. The fleet in Pyre, while proficient and powerful, currently lacks larger support vessels such as cruisers and destroyers. As a result, Seneca tasks Jesper with contacting the governor of Myanmar. It's likely that concession payments to them are about to end due to the dramatic change in Imperial politics, even though refugees are still arriving there in droves. The Whispers will probably be able to strike up a deal for some ships and weapons in exchange for monetary compensation. Furthermore, refugees that Myanmar is still struggling to accommodate could aid bridge the gulf in manpower that Pyre lacks, and Seneca is willing to pay refugees in earnest to join the fight.

"...Any other refugees are welcome within Pyre, and future refugees can take up residence on Fortuna."
    Jesper raises an eyebrow. "That's actually genius."

Next comes the matter of settling ties with the UF, who, in light of Seneca's eight-month campaign against their military assets, might make for a confused and bitter ally. Using the computer on the table, Seneca initiates a teleconference with the president of the UF, Tessa Jackson—another stern-faced redhead with a condescending attitude who answers the call.

"Seneca Mason," President Jackson says as her face illuminates the holographic projection, "Never would have expected you were the one to rope us into this war. Of course, using people for your own game is consistent with your history."
    "A simple hello would have sufficed, Madam President," Seneca chuckles.

"Lighten up. I strictly remember voting for you."

"Certainly, doesn't help me right now. I've got forty-odd shipyards destroyed under your command."

"A debt I'm more than willing to repay," Seneca pauses before providing clarification "…in monetary compensation, that is."

"Just help me understand everything, and I'll see if we are still interested in maintaining our alliance. This isn't the first time you've backstabbed your own people, but Imperial aggressions need to cease, so I'm willing to hear you out." She sighs impatiently.

Unfortunately, Seneca's history isn't on his side at this moment. While he's primarily known for combating the Empire's agendas, he's also had numerous encounters with the UF. From pirating weapons to smuggling and taking part in quasi-wars siding with the COS, he's been a source of concern for Pentagon security back in Washington D.C. It's not in Seneca's nature to comply with a government whose morals or ethics he disagrees with. As such, negotiating with leaders he's not at liberty to intimidate, his options are low. Without Ilana's eloquent abilities and personable demeanor, he's got to pick and choose his words carefully.

Seneca, sensing an uphill conversation, utters a generic phrase beloved by the Whispers, "All people are my people, Madam President…"

Somewhat tense negotiation between President Jackson and Seneca unfolds, with anecdotes and statements from Jesper and Marco aiding in conveying the rationale behind Seneca's calculated decisions. Despite Seneca's efforts to navigate the conversation smoothly, President Jackson appears uneasy during the early stages. In order to help her understand, he reiterates the fabrication of his role as rebellion leader from the fabricated onset, delivering his sentiment with more confidence than he had with Marco. He adeptly combats any skepticism and shifts the focus of the conversation to the future of the alliance as the president empathizes with his decisions and rationale.

It takes over an hour, but eventually, they shape a tentative agreement to maintain the alliance. In addition to monetary compensation for past damages, Seneca proposes offering advantageous trade deals to the UF at the outset of the conflict (should The Whispers win). This move secures continued support, eliciting a sense of relief from Seneca. Fighting the war without the UF's allegiance would have been impossible.

Tessa Jackson finishes her side of the negotiation as they sign an agreement on the holographic screen. "…and once the war is over, we will reinstate your Earth resident pass. Despite your… rebellious tendencies, The UF cannot deny the asset you posed as a legacy service member within the US Military Armed Services."

"Thank you, madam president. Marco and Jesper will be points of contact for your generals. Feel free to call anytime." Seneca says before signing off.

The call ends and they've successfully preserved the Whispers and UF's alliance.

Following this pivotal moment, Seneca now faces the daunting task of conversing with hundreds of rebel leaders. Amidst the chaos and the weight of his new role as a rebel leader, Seneca can't help but wonder how Ilana is coping with the situation. However, he finds himself too preoccupied with settling into his newfound responsibilities to dwell on his emotions for more than a moment between calls to fellow rebel leaders.

Chapter 33: Pilots and Pirates

Imperial combat squadrons descend upon Pyre, as expected, aiming to squander the rebellion by capturing Seneca. However, Pyre's well-trained militia, accompanied by the unwavering loyalty he had earned from its people, has been more than capable of rising to the challenge. The Imperial forces, expecting an easy fight, have been unsuccessful thus far and have suffered heavy losses in their relentless assaults. Against all odds, Pyre continues operating valiantly, defying the Empire's attempts to bring it down. However, they can't win the war until they win this prolonged battle. They need to do so before the Empire starts taking them seriously as well.

Thankfully, they're gaining footing in the right direction. Jesper, though not nearly as adept at diplomatic endeavors as Ilana is, still impressively secures three cruisers from Idalia and other COS members willing to lend aid in the form of ships, weapons, and refugees willing to fight to retake their homelands. However, the Empire's blockade is difficult to get through and will take some time to circumnavigate. In the meantime, Seneca has to find creative ways to replenish Pyre's small losses from the consistent engagements.

"We're not *completely* blockaded, but we can't leave the safety of our battle stations and system defense grid." Seneca sulks in one of the daily strategy meetings he holds with Jesper, Marco, and other appointed leaders. "The nearest rebel fleet is currently tied up defending their own system and the UF's forces are half a quadrant away. What do we have here and now?"

"Plenty of ships, sir, but pilots are the problem. We have no constitutional draft in place, and it could take some time for that legislation." Marco says, "Pilots are being trained as we speak."

"We need pilots with combat experience, though."

Marco scratches his head. "If you trust such things, there are pilots we have in our impound. Some are pirates and Imperial space fleet pilots…"

Seneca's attention diverts away from inventory spreadsheets and snaps onto

Marco's face. "Space fleet pilots?" He asks.

"About nineteen of them. They all showed up in a group about four months ago. Actually, they claimed they knew you, so we hired them. However, they're all Imperials so we locked them up as a precaution."

"*Holy shit*! Why didn't you tell me sooner?!" Seneca jumps from his seat. "Come on!"

Seneca feels a twinge of guilt as he realizes that the chaos of the past few weeks has caused him to push his former squadron members to the back of his mind. Marco leads him across the colony to the impound. It's a fairly decent sized structure close to the government complex. Inside, the thin halls are cool and quiet, aside from the hum of the environmental control systems. Their hurried steps echo on the metal grate flooring as LED lights cast a bright light on the blue metal walls. Turning left around an intersection of corridors, he finds cells that have his former squadron mates paired up except for one who shares a cell with a pirate named Parker. Their expressions reveal confusion and anxiety, as recent weeks have left them completely unaware of the reasons for their confinement. Sporting white jumpsuits, they occupy various furnishings within their respective cells.

"Seneca!" One of his former lieutenants, a skinny blonde named Payson, exclaims. "What's going on?"

"Easy guys. We're going to go into the mess to chat..." Seneca says, calming the young man. "Marco, let'em out."

Marco obeys and then leads them through the corridors of the prison, the air heavy with the scent of disinfectant and metal. The sound of their footsteps echoes against the sterile walls as they march to the heart of the impound, where the impound cafeteria is located. Entering the cafeteria, his group of former squadron mates follows Marco and Seneca with a mixture of apprehension and curiosity. They move with a sense of hesitance, uncertain of what awaits them in this unfamiliar environment. The cafeteria itself is a stark space, its blank white walls offering no comfort or distraction to its residents. Rows of empty metal benches line the room, their surfaces gleaming dully under the harsh fluorescent lights above. Without a word, the boys find seats on the cold metallic benches, their expressions a mixture of resignation and resolve as they prepare to hear what Seneca and Marco have to say.

"So. This is awkward, and you all know me well enough to know I don't skip on the things that are hard to say... I'm the leader of the rebellion. The Empire was going to blame the Princess before I murdered an Imperial agent and shot another lord before I came to Pyre to make a stand against the Empire. The Empire never truly trusted me, and I needed to infiltrate their system to benefit the Whispers."

He looks down, slightly guilty for the position he's placed his comrades in. They only came to Pyre by his recommendation. He knows what's at stake for them, but he knows what the rebellion needs as well. Silence dominates the spaces between them as he examines the contemplation on their faces. They all still owe loyalty to the Empire, bound by military contract. Should they do anything less than kill

Seneca, the Empire will brand them as traitors and persecute them as such. It makes it difficult for Seneca to continue his speech.

"Now, sparing you the details of a rather long and complicated story I'll cut to the point—I need pilots like you."

It's silent for a moment. He's made a weighty request to companions... Caimen is the first to speak up. His family works as financial liaisons for various lords, and his ties to the Empire are weighty. "Did the Empire know you were the leader when you were assigned to lead us?"

"Potentially," Seneca lies. "However, they were going to accuse the princess first. Likely because the Lords believed she'd protect me."

He nods. "I see. I guess that explains the suicide missions they sent us on... but... why fight with us so fervently against your own cause? Why train us to fight the way we did?"

"Deep cover and a ruse like this demand calculated sacrifice. I trained you all because you were undeserving of dying the death the Empire meant for me. You all did not—do not deserve to be pawns. You deserve a fair chance at life in this galaxy."

They look at him, their undivided attention on his face. Payson's voice asks the question weighing on all of their minds. "So, what now?"

"That's up to you all. I know if I return you to the Empire, and you aren't persecuted for treason, we will likely meet as enemies on the field. If you want, you're welcome to seek asylum here free from the Empire's use, but truth be told, I'd be grateful if you'd fly *with* me again. Fly for Pyre and the Whispers."

They gaze at Seneca, their faces revealing a mix of emotions as they're all collectively lost in thought. Far from the terrified boys he encountered a year ago, each of them has grown into skilled pilots who would be invaluable assets to the Whispers. Seneca's personal connection to them leads to a preference for them to act as allies opposed to enemies. It's likely The Empire knows of the bond he shares with them and would gladly exploit it. Seneca anxiously waits for an answer as the group huddles in muted conversation.

Caimen finally says, "Guys, what do you think?"

In that poignant moment, they all rise to their feet, their movements synchronized as they salute Seneca. "You may be a rebel and the cause of this war, but you saved our lives. We'll stand with you, Seneca," Payson says, his voice brimming with gratitude. Seneca returns the salute, a silent acknowledgment of their loyalty. They lower their salutes and dissipate tension that becomes replaced by a chorus of agreeing chatter.

Seneca shakes each of their hands, ensuring they feel welcomed and valued. He meticulously ensures that they are all settled into their quarters in the barracks and grants each of them commissions as captains, fully prepared to lead in combat. It's a lengthy endeavor that eats much of the day. Unable to stay and chat with them any longer, Seneca and Marco make their way back to the government complex.

He's secured nineteen highly experienced pilots to aid them in the coming conflict, but they need more to help while recruits are being trained...

They arrive back in the confines of the conference room. Indistinct sounds of quiet deliberation fill the air as the scent of coffee and carpet blankets the occupants with talking slowly ceasing as Seneca returns to his seat.

"Alright, there's nineteen pilots... we need more. Any more ideas?" Seneca asks, scratching his scalp in deep thought as he thinks.

Jesper raises a hand and tosses him a kiosk displaying a recently decoded cipher text, "Hey Seneca. I told a 'fellow ally' about our predicament. They suggest you call in a favor. I'm not sure what that means..."

"Favor?" Seneca pauses to read the kiosk. He knows the fellow ally is Ilana but has no idea what she's inferring. He thinks for a few moments more and it hits him. "Oh my God! Yes! Gotta love 'fellow allies'."

Ilana's message was to remind him of the favor he'd won from Clemson some time ago. Not only can Clemson lend his own formidable strength, but his reputation also lends him heavy influence within the Revenge of Teach—An asset that could rally more pirates to the fight... for generous compensation on Seneca's end. Pirates, while stone face in their willingness to take orders, respond enthusiastically to the promise of a fortune, and there's no denying the combat prowess that many notorious pirates like Clemson possess. Even if they don't fight directly under Seneca's command having the Revenge pillaging the Imps... it's perfect. Dissolving them strategically into Pyre's fighting force would be of great use to their cause.

"Jesper, call this contact." Seneca says, forwarding an encrypted contact to Jesper's UniCom. "When you get an answer, say 'Seneca's net is snagged, and he needs more rope'."

"Sir?" Jesper says, confusion illuminating his face.

"It's pirate code. His response *should* be 'in what waters can he be reached', then patch him through to the room. If he says something else, let me know."

"Why don't you call him."

"Two pirate captains never make direct contact. It's just not how things are done."

Jesper, still confused, nods and exits, leaving Seneca to continue deliberating with the other leaders until. His instructions to Jesper yield correct results. Within minutes, Clemson appears on the screen. "Cashin' in so soon, Seneca? I heard you made a fool of the Imps." He pauses to laugh. "I love it."

"Well, Clemson, we could use pilots in this fight. If you'd be able to make your way to Pyre with some of your buddies. I can make it worth your while to stick around, too."

"Aye, a favor's a favor. Even better when there's loot to be made. State the nature of your venture."

"Help us for the duration of the rebellion. I'll pay you generously for operational ships and munitions. Anything you want to keep from the Imps is yours. I'll pay you for every month of service per head you bring to fight with us. Also, if you could sick the rest of the Revenge on the Imps, I'll do you a favor later."

"Aye sounds good. What of the sunrise on the horizon?"

(What he means is what happens after the war). Facial expressions around the room look bewildered by Seneca's… fluency in pirate slang. It's not all that hard for the average individual to discern with some effort, however Seneca deftly navigates the conversation without asking for clarification.

"We'll ensure smooth waters and settle any bounties you *currently* have with the UF and COS. I won't guarantee tailwinds post-squall."

Clemson smiles and runs his hands through his beard. Even though Clemson is bound by favor and Seneca could have just made him help, Seneca wants 'full service' from Clemson and the Revenge. Seneca's offer, which includes a reciprocated favor, should be sufficient to get the most out of Clemson's aid.

Finally, the rugged pirate smiles and says, "Deal," before signing off.

Seneca smiles as well. Others in the room look less eager to conscript the aid of a feared pirate organization, and some raise concerns. However, Seneca doesn't care.

Chapter 34: If You Bait Them...

Days turn into weeks. Seneca's critical role as rebellion leader, according to Jesper and other council, necessitates he avidly avoid combat, but on many occasions, he finds himself immersed in skirmishes alongside Pyre's forces. Jesper scolds him for it, but he persists in joining his fellow pilots to escape his greatest enemy—himself. In too many instances, he's found himself internally toiling with impatience and frustrations regarding the tasks at hand. Fighting The Empire... Reuniting with Ilana... Returning Home... Each time he asks himself how it's going to happen, he worries about when... It all invokes too many questions lack finite answers, and he is not the type to accept the uncertain.

During unwanted moments of respite from his duties when he cannot slip past Jesper to take flight in *the Phantom*, Seneca finds himself confined to the loneliness of his makeshift quarters. Once a storage area and bathroom for the neighboring conference room, he's since transformed it into a living space, furnished with standard bedroom fixtures. Beige walls blend seamlessly with the rest of the building's interior, while the rugged black carpet adds little warmth to the atmosphere. A solitary window offers Seneca a glimpse of the colony below, its view illuminated by the distant glow of Fortuna, several light-years away—a waypoint he fixates his gaze upon when he needs to clear his racing mind.

Ilana is everywhere when nothing else demands his attention. He has a steadily growing anxiety about what the war could mean for his future. He envisions disastrous scenarios where the Whispers suffer defeat, leaving him to endlessly evade the Empire's relentless pursuit, or the haunting possibility of Ilana facing persecution by the lords torments his attempts to find peace. Frantic calculations regarding the war's duration drain his energy, leaving him unable to push aside his darkest fears. He'd rather focus on anything else, so he frequently launches into battle against Jesper's wishes.

Today is one of those days where he'd successfully made his way unnoticed past Jesper undetected and joined the ranks of the latest defensive effort and spared himself from torment within his own psyche. Fighting in battles such as the ones persisting as of late is merely a casual endeavor to him. Demanding no significant amount of attention from him as he effortlessly maneuvers and engages in combat with enemy ships and denies a request by Jesper to exit the battlefield.

"Jesper, what kind of leader would I be if I didn't fight with the troops?"

Clemson, who has now been on scene for several weeks now chimes in as well, "Aye Jesper, Seneca's no observer. He's a leviathan destined to remind the unaware who owns the skies."

Jesper, from the safety of a nearby command post, sighs over the radio before saying, "Why do pirates talk like that?"

Clemson's laugh echoes over the radio as he keeps Seneca's six o'clock position free of unwanted pests. "Started as a joke when they first formed the Revenge... then it grew as symbolism until all us piratin' types took to it."

"Let's focus up," Seneca says, performing a barrel roll to dodge a railgun round fired by an enemy ship. "As much fun as repelling Imps can be, I'm getting less than patient. Hence why I'm taking control of the field. We need Pyre's forces to group with the rest of the Whispers."

The faster Pyre becomes part of the larger battle, the quicker the rebellion turns the tide. Across the Whispers campaign against the Imps, the need for Pyre to achieve victory is the central focus of every conversation he has with tactical leaders. Much like Pyre, they lack resources to actively go on the offense, but unlike Pyre, they didn't have years to assemble a strong militia capable of repelling attacks as efficiently as Pyre does, nor are they as "fresh". The Whispers seldom regain control to territories they lose, and The Empire has been aggravatingly effective at preventing the UF from reinforcing Whisper fleets. Unfortunately, until something changes, they cannot put "Operation 1929" into full effect.

Seneca uses his gatling guns and lasers to strafe an enemy cruiser as they deliberate. Sparks fly and brilliantly colored lights shimmer on the surface of the cruiser's shields in response.

"Listen." Jesper says, "Right now, just focus on pushing this wave out."

They follow Jesper's suggestion and finish out the battle, focusing on disabling the shields of the Imperial command ship until they order a retreat. After the battle, they convene in the conference room. Clemson and Seneca crack up passing jokes back and forth with each other and praising the other for their performance. Were Clemson...in a different "line of work", Seneca would outwardly consider him a friend and not just a "professional contact". The complimenting personalities between the two leads them to natural friendly conversation, and sharing the same passion for flying gives them a foundation for a bond to form. Their banter and jokes continue until Jesper files in with Pyre's militia leaders. His smile fades now that the less exciting part of his job demands his attention as he takes his seat at the head of the table to start deliberating.

* * *

"So, picking up where we left off from our conversation on the battlefield, did anyone think of anything?" Seneca asks.

Jesper, always quick to offer insights, is the first to speak up. "Honestly, Seneca, there may not be much we can do right now, until we can make an invasion of Pyre look utterly pointless..." Jesper pauses for a second... "or—"

Seneca furrows his brow, his mind racing with questions. "Or?"

Jesper smirks and tilts his head slightly. "Well," he continues, "You've fought them out of systems before. You know the Empire values its image and its wealth. Either make the battle so expensive that they leave or embarrass them. If we can manage both, it'd be even better."

Seneca hadn't thought of it like that before. Usually when he fought the Imps as a mercenary IC, it was on a paid-per-head basis. He got monetary compensation for every ship he destroyed, with bonuses for sticking around. Pushing them out usually meant the end of the adventure, so he never placed much emphasis on the timeline until now, nor did he take notice of what would inspire the Imps to withdraw.

Marco, who rarely interjects on strategy, speaks up "Jesper's advice strikes a chord. It's just like the overall plan. The Empire likes money."

Seneca thinks for a minute. The seeds of an idea are taking root, but the legality of his plan may raise concern. "How...constrained... by galactic laws are we?" Seneca queries.

Jesper considers the question. "That's complicated," he responds. "The Empire does not recognize us as a sovereign entity, and we haven't signed any agreements regarding galactic laws of conflict. However, the United Federation and Confederacy would likely raise objections if we blatantly exceeded their limitations consistently."

"Ok... and how much longer until the cruisers arrive from the COS?"

"They're technically ready now and waiting on the edge of Pyre's border, but the confederate military council has to vote to allow their use. The vote should pass in a day or so."

Seneca nods, recognizing the complexity of their situation. He leans forward, his eyes focused as he lays out his idea to the room.

"I've got an idea then." He says "We bait the Imps. Mock them publicly and dare them to send the 201st fleet..."

The 201st is one of the premier fleets in the quadrant. Three of the new Rayett-class destroyers, boasting what the Empire claims to be impenetrable armor and state-of-the-art AI controlled shielding systems, support a fighting force of one hundred Imperial medium fighters. The fleet has a reputation for squandering rebel activity across the galaxy and is the most expensive and capable unit employed by The Empire.

* * *

"...and instead of meeting them on the edge of our system like we usually do, we draw them into the center of our defense grid..."

Pyre's defense grid is a checkerboard like pattern of high-powered railguns that are spaced every seventy kilometers on the orbital plane of the system. Each railgun can fire munitions at mach-four with deadly precision. Marco had it developed at the onset of the war years ago, anticipating a heightened need for self-defense—a surprisingly convenient decision demonstrating Marco's intuition and leadership skills. They've chosen to keep the defense grid hidden from The Empire up to this point since they'd been faring well without it—conveniently concealing it for an opportune moment. A moment that Seneca believes is upcoming.

"...Only once their destroyers wander into the middle does the grid reveal itself and open fire. They claim those destroyers are impenetrable, but I think we know better. Once their shields are down, which shouldn't take too long considering the amount of rail guns firing at them. They'll either retreat or surrender."

"That might do it. The 201st is both expensive and the jewel of the quadrant right now, but do you think our pilots can hold their own?" Jesper asks. "The 201st's pilots are among the best in the Imperial military."

Seneca walks up to the panoramic window in the room and looks out at the landing area beneath the complex. He has no reason to doubt Pyre now. "Absolutely."

He pauses. If they succeed in baiting the 201st into Pyre, it will be the first high-stakes conflict he's overseen as the rebellion leader. Winning would boost the Whisper's morale across the war and allow Pyre's forces to go on the offense. Additionally, they'd be able to take control of The Empire's destroyers to fill in their need for support class ships. Losing, however... He sidelines that thought before he resumes speaking.

"Plus," He says, "The Imps don't know that the COS has leased us cruisers. They'll come in overconfident and complacent. Once their command ship loses its shields, we can force a surrender."

"And if they retreat?" Jesper asks.

"Remove the option." Seneca says with a mischievous grin. "If they retreat, we give chase. Clemson can track ships through warp, and we'll pull the destroyers from warp. The rest of the fleet will drop with the destroyers. We pick off what we can before they jump again—rinse and repeat."

"That's incredibly illegal." Jesper says. He looks like he's debating the merits of challenging Seneca's plan but apparently decides against it. "But it will send a message and accomplish the goal."

"And what of prisoners?" Marco inquires, "we aren't outfitted to hold exorbitant amounts like that."

"Offer the pilots the ability to change sides. Otherwise, have labor camps constructed on Fortuna and put them to work farming food. They're to be treated humanely. Bring the commander to me," Seneca finishes.

* * *

Seneca opens the floor for objections, comments, questions—anything that might poke holes in his plan. Yet, to his relief, nobody raises any objections to his morally ambiguous strategy. Instead, strategists immediately delve into the process of refining the operation, discussing specific details—who will be where and when and how to corral the retreating Imperial forces, and the primary targets: the Rayett-Class destroyers. Hours of tactical brainstorming give way to a well-refined plan, and Seneca concludes the session by establishing a teleconference with Lord Marc Antony—the perfect hotheaded lord who will be easy to gaslight into sending the 201st.

The holographic screen illuminates and the lord's image is coming through clear as day. "Howdy." Seneca chuckles, "How's the shoulder?"

"What do you want, Seneca?" the lord asks, clearly annoyed to be bothered. "Are you ready to answer for your crimes?"

"Hardly. In fact, we're getting bored with your pathetic attempts to take Pyre. How about sending the 201st our way—unless they're as incompetent as the rest of your military?" Seneca taunts.

"Your arrogance isn't worth the effort. Your infantile fleet would be incapable of combatting such force. It's a waste of our time and money."

"Or maybe you're too poor to fund it. I guess I can try to call some of the wealthier lords in the council."

Taunting the lord's image and wealth does it. He begins shouting incomprehensibly and even re-injures his shoulder in the process of throwing his temper tantrum. After a few more taunts and carefully targeted jokes, the lord promises to give Seneca the fight he wants before he signs off.

"You want the 201st Seneca? You'll have it, and then I'll have your ass cooked in front of the entire galaxy you arrogant fossil!"

Seneca just smiles as the lord hangs up and concludes the meeting, dismissing everyone. Bodies file out, chatting amongst each other as they go. The stillness returns, wrapping him in its uneasy presence once again. He waits in the conference room, hoping someone will return and engage in friendly conversation to keep his mind distracted, but his prayer goes unanswered. Silence bids Seneca's mind to once again echo negative and unwanted rhetoric. What if the plan doesn't work? What if operation 1929 fails? What if? What if? All the disastrous scenarios his cruel brain concocts all end with him losing Ilana... He paces around silently dwelling on these thoughts until the desire to silence them overcomes him. He can be confident in the face of others' lines of questioning, but he's not the type to be able to convince himself of anything.

With no one coming to distract him with further discussion and no other solution in mind, he strolls through the empty halls of the complex and exits to find a local liquor store down the street. There, he buys a case of Keplar fire whiskey and returns to his quarters. In an effort to drown out the voices and find sleep, he pops the cork on the first bottle and drinks until the world fades away.

Chapter 35: ...They Will Come

Careful observation and reconnaissance operations discreetly monitor the approaching 201st fleet. It's both according to plan and a toll on Seneca's nerves to anticipate the oncoming attack force that will arrive in a couple days' time. Though he has full faith in Pyre's capabilities, he's still choosing to drown silence induced doubt with strong drink. The debate at hand is now regarding whether or not Seneca will be on the field for the engagement. Jesper argues adamantly for Seneca to remain off the field and command the unit from safety. Seneca, for his own reasons, would rather be in his ship fighting.

"We need every pilot we can out there attacking those destroyers!" Seneca shouts at Jesper.

"No. The railguns and defense grid will do that. Plus, If you die, the rebellion dies along with you! All the work that Ilana has done is wasted! Do you want that on your hands?"

"That's not going—"

Jesper interrupts him. "It could! Why are you so hell bent on throwing yourself into the enemy?"

"I just need to! I need to contribute!"

Jesper huffs and says, "You are contributing by being a leader. That's what this rebellion needs is a public figure with no collateral the Empire can use, but if the Empire manages to kill you, they kill the morale of our forces... I thought you trusted Pyre's pilots?"

Seneca remains silent, averting his gaze to the side. He resists the urge to let his emotions surface, unwilling to expose the growing pain welling up within him. He senses Jesper's gaze fixed upon him, awaiting a response that he refuses to give. Silently, Seneca makes his way to the window of the conference room, cursing the window and walls under his breath as he yearns to escape elsewhere.

"Look, Seneca, you need to be the face of the war, not its spear. Stop giving the Imps a chance to take you out."

"Damn it, fine…" He says with a defeated sigh. Seneca, though he doesn't agree with Jesper, respects his request to remain off field for this engagement.

In the past few days of preparation, Clemson and his crew of pirates assisting them have amassed an impressive collection of EMP railgun ammunition—munitions that impart powerful electromagnetic pulses strong enough to disable city power grids. They'll help them quickly drop the shields of the destroyers. Once their shields are down, they'll call in the three cruisers on loan from the COS.

The Confederate Cruisers, roughly half the size of the destroyers, boast remarkable agility for their size. Their design resembles that of a stingray, adorned with a long, two-pronged tail structure. For their size, they boast a wide array of weaponry, such as defense turrets, long-range missiles, and laser guided hell-fire rockets. The crown jewel of their arsenals sits at the tip of the tail structures, which can pivot upward to launch harpoons capable of piercing through nine feet of titanium. Once attached, the cruisers inject corrosive plasma through the cable into the interior of their target—a feature ideal for the current mission since they'll be aiming for the engines.

With the decision to keep Seneca leading from the ground, he tasks Jesper with briefing Pyre's defenders on their enemies and their assets and ensures that their forces are adequately prepared. The might of Pyre's militia gathers in traditional military formation to listen to Jesper address them from a podium positioned beneath *the Phantom* on the apron of the colony's station. Seneca stands in the corner listening to Jesper's briefing, but in the midst of the speaking and on-screen presentation he finds his mind wandering… He dwells on cherished memories and wishes he had made more of the time he had with Ilana. If only this war didn't exist… He's dying to resume his life, yet subtly wishes he'd never let himself get so deep—will the pain ahead be worth it? When the pain starts, it's hard for him to escape it without inebriation or sufficient distraction.

Jesper's speech eventually pulls Seneca out of his mind and back into reality. "Now Seneca will take it from here. He's going to outline the training and exercises parameters for the remainder of the day."

Seneca sheds his frown. Donning a false smile in order to project the image of a strong leader, he trades places with Jesper on the podium. "I'm not one for public addresses, so I'll keep this short…"

He divides everyone into the groups they'll be flying with. Their force is eighty strong for the engagement to be divided into four squadrons with two elements of ten each. For training, three squadrons will skirmish together with one team at a two-to-one disadvantage. A single squadron must fight off two others while causing enough damage to a mockup destroyer. It mirrors the odds they'll be performing against in the coming days. The squadron that is not skirmishing practices high-speed connections with the shield charger of the COS cruiser, a necessary skill to ensure speedy returns to the engagement. Practice will make proficient for an already experienced fighting force.

* * *

Though he won't be in the battle, Seneca participates in the skirmishes, taking care to humble those whose abilities may not be as good as they perceive them to be and mentor those who lack confidence. He holds a deep admiration for Pyre's pilots throughout their training, particularly his nineteen former squadron juniors. They've wholeheartedly embraced the Whisper's cause—even more than Seneca has. Without hesitation, they've been more than willing to bear the responsibility of guiding the less experienced, reflecting Seneca's own dedication when he trained them just a year ago.

Training exercises persist for the next few days as their deep space scanners 'ping' the approaching Imperial fleet, now only eighteen hours out. By this point, Pyre's fleet is either prepared or they're not. Continuing with any further exercise would waste energy, and it would be better to spend the remaining hours resting.

Seneca lays awake in his quarters staring at a ceiling fan as it spins, disrupting the air in the room and moving it in turbulent downdrafts over his exposed face. Observing it, his mind becomes scattered like the air in the room, and he daydreams about Ilana and how deeply he yearns for her. What he would give for her to roll into this bed and place a kiss on his cheek. Some nights he'll struggle to find sleep for hours as her ghost haunts his mind, and his thoughts wander into forsaken thoughts of losing her... Thankfully, this is not one of those nights. Without tossing and turning endlessly or needing a stiff drink to lure him, he falls asleep.

Alarms awaken him and the rest of Pyre. The 201st Imperial Fleet is three hours away and Pyre's members are needed port-side to preflight their ships. Seneca watches from his window as hundreds of people scurry about the port in anticipation of the arriving force. From his perch, he can see Clemson and his crew mates smoking and drinking beforehand (Seneca wouldn't advise drinking and flying, but they're pirates and do what they want). Continuing his scan, Caimen's face stands out among the crowd as he passes words of encouragement to his brothers in arms. The bustling scene beckons Seneca to join in taking up arms, though he's promised to remain in the safety of a command station with Jesper.

Seneca independently makes his way to the port in order to meet the fighters and, in some way, shape or form, establish a connection with them. He steps out of the complex and boards the rail-shuttle. Amidst the brave souls assembled to fight for freedom, his face draws cheers and his name echoes in chants throughout the crowd as he walks among them. The energy of the legion is inspiring and heartwarming to know that they believe in him—even though he doesn't deserve it. The pressing need to join them on the field pesters him and he eyes his own ship. His walk slows as he internally measures the merits of betraying his promise to Jesper before dismissing the idea and pressing onward to the command station at the far end of the port.

The command station bears a striking resemblance to an air traffic control tower one would see at a bustling airport back on Earth. It towers high above the surface of the port and sports a viewing station with reinforced windows that give it a 360-

degree view. However, instead of directing air traffic, they're armored and serve the purpose of monitoring space in the vicinity of a port and make for the perfect location to direct Pyre's forces during conflict. The building has its own shield generator and defense turrets to protect it from attacks, though one would need immeasurable luck to stray several kilometers from the battle without being intercepted inbound.

Once inside, Seneca enters an elevator that climbs several stories and deposits him at the top where Jesper is awaiting him within the hexagonal shaped space. Tinted windows also act as integrated displays to follow radar targets and sophisticated cameras can superimpose their observations upon them. A console in the center of the room projects a three-dimensional holographic display that televises the vitals of their pilots and their ships as well as a radar display to track spacecraft. Nevertheless, what truly piques Seneca's interest right now is a coffeemaker. He may have been able to sleep, but to say he felt truly rested would be a lie.

"Thanks for sitting this one out," Jesper says, greeting him.

Seneca shoots him a disapproving glance, "Don't rub it in or I'll change my mind…"

He takes a sip of his coffee and ambles over to a monitor displaying the 201st fleet's ETA. Destiny is a mere ninety minutes away. Even though the battle itself will likely last less than twenty minutes, the time spent watching fights feels longer compared to being actively engaged within it. Seneca wishes he were in his ship…

"Oh, by the way," Jesper interjects with a hint of cheer in his tone, "you've got a cipher addressed to you. It's from a friend."

"That's good… Y'all haven't showed me how to decode those yet," Seneca replies.

It's the first personal correspondence Ilana has sent him. Grateful and thoroughly eager to read it, Seneca is also aware of the emotional toll the letter is likely to have. Furthermore, he doesn't yet know how to decode the ciphers. He's attempted a few related to war matters, to no avail, and thus far he's had Jesper decode any of importance.

Jesper nods. "I'll give you some tips later. They're just as hard to write."

Time ticks away as they chat idly about last-minute expectations for the battle. Finally, the time to issue commands arrives. Thirty minutes before the enemy's anticipated arrival, Seneca calls the fleet to initiate startup sequences. The monitors come alive with pilot vitals, dots on the radar, and radio chatter. Ships alight into the void, organizing into formations akin to a well-rehearsed marching band performance ready to meet the incoming attacking force. Pyre's militia parks themselves beneath the protection of the defense grid with minutes to go.

A sigh escapes Seneca's mouth as he says, "Here we go…"

* * *

The 201st arrives, dropping out of warp and materializing before their eyes and leisurely approaching the colony, unaware of the trap that awaits them. The Rayett-Class destroyers are indeed imposing, their cyan paint adorned with golden accents, but their lack of battle scars indicates that this is a test run for these ships. Smaller fighters are harder to make out with the naked eye from the distance so the occupants of the command room must utilize the camera and radar to view them. It's time to turn the tide of the war, and get him one step closer to home...

Chapter 36: Fish in a Barrel

The sight of the 201st is impressive. They advance closer to the colony but stop short of Fortuna's gravitational influence. Prior to the first shots being fired, the Imperial commander makes contact. It's a surprising turn of events. Attacking Imperials rarely observed customary formalities such as pre-engagement communication. Unfortunately, Seneca finds himself confronted with the image of an unlikable character on the screen. Shari Graas, his former commander at Phalanx, apparently now commands the 201st. He groans at the sight of her face.

Speaking with all the callousness her foul nature can muster, the ill-tempered woman on the display sneers at him as she says, "Ah, the traitor. You never reported for duty."

"Oh, I'm sorry. I guess being sent on suicide missions breeds a little resentment." Seneca says in reply, disdain present in his tone. "Plus, the decades of Imperial expansion aren't exactly welcome either."

She scowls before she taunts, "Do your fellow *criminals* know they're wanted now? Two hundred thousand a piece and a bonus of two million if someone gets all nineteen."

Seneca yearns for her physical presence. He eagerly awaits the opportunity to fulfill his fantasy of spitting in her face, a hope that might come true today. With no consideration for formalities, he uses the center console to signal Clemson to fire a rail gun munition directly at the bridge of the command destroyer, distinguished by a golden phoenix painted on its side.

"I'll give you the chance to surrender now and save yourself the embarrassment." He replies just as Clemson's round contacts the shields of the command destroyer; the sudden flash of shimmering lights audibly startled its occupants.

"Please. Your ragtag rebels aren't a threat. By the way, thanks for the promotion. They'll probably make me an admiral when I drag your ass back into the palace." Shari Graas says, unmoved by Seneca's attempt at intimidation. She's carrying the overconfidence that Seneca's relying on for a smooth engagement. She does not know about the trap they've set.

She concludes her taunting with those final remarks, then signs off, while Seneca observes the other displays. Unaware of the intricate network of railguns precisely aimed at the distinct ID signals of the three destroyers, the enemy fleet blissfully resumes their approach; their impending clash growing near. Despite the Imperial fighters' numerical advantage, Seneca's forces maintain their composure, remaining stationary to draw in the attacking invaders. He can feel his heartbeat quicken as the 201st wanders carelessly into firing range of the defense grid.

He takes a deep breath and as soon as the defense grid opens fire. The monitor displays the battle scene in vivid detail. Patterns of small red-mushroom shaped explosions pepper the Imperial destroyers, and he clears Pyre's militia to engage. The militia is quick to comply; swiftly launching into action, carrying out their well-practiced strafing maneuvers against the destroyers whilst pushing back opposing fighters and preventing them from leaving the range of the defense grid. With each vessel in perfect formation, the mesmerizing sight of vibrant colors and flashes of light becomes a captivating light show of tracers, laser, and explosions.

Inside the command station, the radios buzz with activity, conveying urgent commands from squadron leaders immersed in fighting the battle at hand. With a watchful eye, Seneca monitors the enemy squadrons' every move, ensuring that Pyre's forces are well-informed and strategically maneuvering to exert the highest possible pressure on the destroyers—not that it's wholly necessary. The 201st could not have been more unprepared for the defense grid. Their formations struggle to hold, and the destroyers target the grid as they've engaged full reverse thrust. "What a pitiful sight…" Seneca thinks to himself as he watches and questions why he was so worried.

The command center fills with a soundscape that echoes the actions of the ships on the field, which are coordinating chaotically. The rehearsed nature of the occasion is unmistakable, as the fighting force moves with precision and composure. It's not without losses on their end, however. Red X marks appear sporadically over ship vitals, each one a heavy symbol of a lost soul who paid the ultimate price—undeniably something that weighs on Seneca and sharpens his desire to be on the field. While his investment in the war is strictly on Ilana's behalf, Seneca still cares about the welfare of all those who die in the fight for freedom. He also has friends in the fray and he's eyeing the status of his fellow Imperial deserters with care. To his delight, his comrades are alive and well; their determination and combat prowess are on full display to those involved in the confrontation.

"Someone give me a scan of the destroyer's shields. We need that data in here." Jesper commands via radio broadcast.

Clemson acknowledges the directive and complies. "Oi, Jesper, scan data comin' to you. Seneca, you ought to be headin' into the fray. Fishing's good right now." He says, charisma oozing through the radio.

"Maybe some other battle. Good fortunes out there." He replies in a plasë voice.

Collected shield data is a positive sight to behold. The rail guns are rapidly depleting the shields of all three destroyers, and the ongoing updates from Clemson's strafing runs inform them that the plan is working. All without their own fleet suffering significant casualties against a seemingly more powerful enemy in the process. The 201st is becoming more frazzled by the minute, and by scrutinizing their movements it's clear they have forced the Imperials into a disordered struggle to stay alive. Despite the possibility of surrender or retreat that a wiser leader might consider, Shari Graas, driven by her unwavering determination, continues to stand her ground without yielding.

"Hey Seneca," Payson radios in with a bit of concern in his breath, "any chance those cruisers can make their appearance? Shields are thinning out here."

Seneca's attention diverts from the struggles of their enemy once again to the status of Pyre's own fleet. Despite the destroyers being at a disadvantage with low shields, the 201st still has an advantage in numbers. Ten minutes in and Pyre's fighters are running low on shield resources. To keep the battle in their favor, it *would* be a highly advantageous moment to deploy the cruisers from the COS, as it would effectively compel the enemy to retreat or surrender. In addition, it would provide Pyre's forces with a valuable opportunity to recharge their shields.

Seneca exchanges a glance with Jesper, who nods. "Affirm, we'll send them in."

He depresses a button on the center console to issue the call to the COS' cruisers, summoning them into the midst of the action. They swiftly materialize before them, wasting no time in lending a hand to help pressure the destroyers. Cheering and whooping fills the radios. In addition to providing additional supporting fire, the ships can recharge shields of Pyre's fighters. It's time to finish the fight out. The Imperial destroyers have gone from merely reversing thrust to pointing their noses away to retreat.

"Alright Whispers, let's end this."

The fleet obeys Seneca's directive. With precision and coordination, the well trained and choreographed dance of destruction unleashes a barrage of munitions on the center destroyer, taking turns one by one. The latest scan conducted by Clemson has produced updated data, offering a detailed insight into the moment when the shields on the command vessel falter and allow the ship to be damaged directly. At that moment, Imperial fighters form up around the destroyers—they're about to retreat.

"Cruiser Alpha, you are green to fire harpoon. Target the engines of the command ship. Cruisers Bravo and Charlie prepare to chase the other two. All units clear to engage retreating units."

They shift the camera's attention to follow this poignant moment that is unfolding. The intended purpose of the harpoon is to knock out the engines of the overconfident craft, which, if accomplished, would prevent any attempt by the command ship to escape even if the other destroyers escape. However, in the unfortunate event that the harpoon fails to do so, it might spell disaster since it places the cruiser close to the heavily armed opponents. The cruiser makes its calculated moves; spectators hold a collective, anticipating the moment when its tail lifts to unleash the harpoon. The harpoon flies through space and pierces the rear starboard side of the command ship, tethering the cruiser to the command destroyer. At the moment, corrosive pseudo-plasma is being flooded into the engines of the main destroyer as the cruiser applies thrust to pull it side to side, using it as a bludgeon against its own comrades. Unless Shari Graas is a complete idiot, the battle is over.

Seneca watches as the flicker of the ship's lights shows the extent of the damage that Pyre's attack had dealt by this point in the battle. The engines of the destroyer, once powerful, are now disabled, causing the ship to list sideways as the thrust systems fail. Demonstrating mercy, he commands the fleet to cease their attack on the disabled behemoth, enabling the opportunity for a surrender order to be issued before completely wiping out the opposing fleet. The preferable course of action would be their surrender, as it would enable them to make use of the imperial's weapons for their own purposes instead of annihilating it.

Though the command ship is out of commission, the other two destroyers jump, followed by the rest of the 201st's fighters. The other two cruisers and bulk of Pyre's militia race into warp after them. Radio silence prevails while Clemson and Pyre's forces chase down the retreating vessels. Hopefully, it will inspire some cooperation to realize that surrender would be better than annihilation.

Finally, a screen on the north monitor comes to life, featuring the face of Shari Graas, who appears visibly frustrated. She's a competitive spirit who is sensitive to losing and ungracious in defeat.

"Something you want to say?" Seneca chirps.

"Fuck you." She replies, "You'll have your day on the execution block yet, you fucking thorn. You can't attack ships in retreat! That's against galactic law!"

"Not sure if you noticed." Seneca chuckles, "But I don't give a shit. Issue the surrender and we'll stop. Better hurry, you're going from an embarrassing defeat to a complete annihilation."

She stares at him with fury in her eyes. Meanwhile, the second of the three destroyers has been disabled with the fleet hot on the tail of the third. Seneca smiles as looks back at Shari Graas. "One destroyer left. I'm taking it too, surrender or not. Plus, unless I get a surrender, we'll board your ship with guns blazing."

Shari Graas grits her teeth, seething with anger as she grunts, "I issue official surrender and I'm seeking parlay to negotiate terms of the surrender."

Seneca's face lights up with a smug grin, his nod signaling to Jesper that it's time to issue the stand down order. In the course of events to follow, they compel enemy pilots to land outside the designated POW labor camps established on Fortuna, while Clemson being tasked with the mission of retrieving Shari Graas and bringing her to him while the COS cruisers tow the destroyers back to Pyre. To maintain security and prevent any potential disturbances during the negotiations, they deploy a group of armed foot soldiers to occupy the inside of the destroyers and escort the Imperial officers to Pyre's impound.

The day is theirs. In part due to the careful planning of Seneca and his fellow leadership, but also because of the habitual nature of the Empire to underestimate what Seneca is capable of. While a single squadron of ships dedicates its efforts to escorting the surviving Imperial fighters to the surface of Fortuna, the rest of the squadrons start their journey back to the port where Seneca is patiently waiting for their arrival.

The feeling of elation is overwhelming for many, celebrating victory and the hope of finally attaining freedom looming within reach. Others lookout at the boundless field of stars beyond the port; Seneca overhears their muted prayers, grateful for having endured and silently expressing their thanks. Despite the prevailing jubilation, there is a distinct somberness that lingers in the atmosphere, as many mourn their fallen comrades in solemn reverence. It is a solemn sight to witness pilots kneeling in homage, their tears a testament to the deep bond they shared with their departed friends, at the very parking spots that now remain empty.

Seneca's heart is filled with elation as he catches sight of Payson and Caimen, who have returned to the port with all their companions in tow. They performed admirably during the battle and, over the course of previous engagements, have received particular notoriety among the rebel fleet. Becoming known as 'The Nineteen,' the group reunites, celebrating their triumph with the camaraderie of a football team, cheering and embracing each other in joyful solidarity. Seneca moves among the port, taking in the bittersweet mix of victory, sacrifice, and loss, sharing in the collective experience of the rebels he commands.

Amidst the raucous celebration, Clemson's ship lands, bringing Shari Graas along. With her head bowed in shame, she has to endure the weight of the crowd's boos and insults pressing down on her as Clemson escorts her to Seneca. He looks forward to what promises to be an interesting conversation with the haughty colonel.

"Impenetrable armor, huh?" Seneca taunts her as Clemson nudges her towards Seneca. "Seems like the Imp's lies have no end."

Shari has no other response to his taunting other than asking, "Terms of surrender?"

"We'll talk about that inside, but first we need to make a little promotional material. Smile, colonel, you're about to be *real* famous back in the capital."

Chapter 37: Baby Steps

Although it was not initially included in the victory plans, Seneca takes the initiative to assemble a camera team on the port and capture footage of the disabled ship in the distance, as well as the visibly embarrassed Imperial commander. The last second idea serves a dual purpose. Firstly, it will make for phenomenal propaganda to showcase the Empire's vulnerability to boost morale throughout the Whispers. Additionally, it should provoke anger and frustration among the lords and send a message regarding the strength of the Whispers. If nothing else, it's guaranteed to rile up the lords and generate captivating headlines across the galaxy.

After successfully capturing the propaganda footage and securely housing the crews of the destroyers in the impound, Jesper joins Seneca and Clemson in the conference room of their government complex to negotiate with Shari Graas. Seneca's already gotten what he needs out of the 201st, but he wants her to identify economic targets to expedite Operation 1929. Realistically, this will be more interrogation than negotiation...

Nobody speaks at first, with the four occupants all sporting different facial expressions. Jesper is serious and patiently awaiting someone else to initiate conversation. Clemson is disinterested in the politics and outcome but is likely waiting for Seneca to give him the go ahead to loot any adrift wreckage floating around in Pyre's space ways. Seneca is eyeing the defeated commander with a smug attitude evident in his face. He looks over at Jesper and a hand motion offers him the chance to speak first; Jesper shakes his head side to side, deferring to Seneca.

Seneca breaks silence by saying, "Still think the lords will make you a general after this?"

A warm glob of spit contacts his right cheek as she grumbles. "State the terms of the surrender so I can be on my way."

Seneca wipes the spit from his face and fights the urge to reciprocate. He takes a deep breath before he replies, "Well, we are going to keep all your shit. That's non-negotiable. What are you willing to divulge to keep yourself and your officers out of a work camp?"

Shari says, "You can keep my officers for all I care. Surrender is my concession."

Her comment catches Seneca off guard. She's still in a delusion that she's in control over the situation. "*Really*? You think *you* deserve to go home, but your officers and pilots don't?"

She sneers. "They lost. They failed the Empire."

Memories of his tour at Phalanx surge forward. This woman… has the audacity to criticize the performance of her pilots? Seneca may be willing to pull the trigger against an Imperial pilot and take their life, but he still respects the work it takes to hone the craft. Her lack of accountability enrages him.

"No, colonel, *you* failed. It is *YOUR* job to ensure *your* units are combat ready. *You* lost because *you* failed. So, if you want to leave this room alive, I will tell you what we want, and your *will* comply."

"I'm not going—"

Seneca abruptly interrupts her, thrusting his pistol between her eyes. Maybe it's his bottled frustration from remaining on the ground for the battle. Maybe it's rooted in a vendetta against her for viewing people as instruments. Either way, it's time she learns accountability for her actions and stops mirroring the leadership of the Empire. He's made up his mind, and he's going to extract the information he needs. Jesper, however, interrupts with protest just as he is about to resume making demands.

"Seneca, that's against galactic laws of conflict. You cannot threaten her like this," Jesper says with concern taking over his.

"Clemson, pull up a map of the Empire's holdings." Seneca yells, ignoring Jesper as he keeps the anodes of his weapon placed firmly against the forehead of the now terrified colonel.

"Aye Cap." Clemson replies before turning to Jesper. "Oi Jesper, ride the wave on this one. It's not like the Imps put much wind behind the sails of galactic law. 'Sides, Seneca's smart enough to get out of any trouble he causes."

Jesper looks horrified while Clemson raises the map on the screen. Seneca swiftly takes hold of Shari's shoulder and thrusts her towards it, positioning her in close proximity to interact with the screen. Seneca expresses, "I can get the information I want from other sources, so your life is not completely necessary. However, I don't want to make a mess."

"I don't—"

Seneca clicks the weapon from non-lethal to lethal, the sound interrupting Shari's voice. The sound profoundly affects the previously callous colonel, reducing her to tears out of fear.

"Seneca!" Jesper shouts.

* * *

Seneca momentarily directs his attention to Jesper and says, "Jesper! Shut your ass up and sit down! Let me do my damn job. I should have been flying, but you want me to lead. Let me lead *my* way!"

Jesper, although still disagreeing, backs down. Seneca returns his attention to the sobbing imperial "Start talking! Identify any economically significant target, diamond mines, precious metal factories, bank servers, whatever I don't care. Do that and I *won't* kill you."

"They'll have me executed; you know that!" Shari replies in fear.

"All the more reason to fuck them over. Tell me what I want to know!" he shouts.

Seneca's point is loud and clear. Anyone who knows him and his reputation also knows he doesn't bluff. She folds under his threats and begins to comply. Gradually, she embarks on the task of identifying various locations of economic significance that, if destroyed, would significantly impact the Empire and cause widespread distress. In just under half an hour, she sobs as she provides them with over thirty-six different locations within one hundred light-years of Pyre.

"Thank you! Holy shit, you imps only respond to one thing." Seneca says activating the safety of his firearm and stowing it "Don't worry, *colonel*. I'm not an Imperial. I'm not going to knowingly send you back home to your death, but you'll stay here with your pilots and officers as a leader should. Pray I don't send your former subordinates a recording of this conversation."

Seneca addresses Jesper, "Take her to the impound. Then come straight back. We need to hash out our next moves."

Jesper unleashes a heavy sigh and swiftly aids the colonel to her feet and escorts her out.

Over the next few weeks, a critical moment in the war unfolds. Although the Empire has not made any public response regarding the defeat of the 201st, no further attempts at attacking Pyre have surfaced. Now, the Empire is aware of the presence of a formidable defense grid and the recent battle has provided them with enhanced firepower, making it highly improbable for any follow-up attacks to occur. The fleet commanded by Pyre can now proudly showcase three cruisers alongside the three destroyers (which do need repairs but should be returned to service under the Whisper's command in a matter of days.)

The pause in hostilities has presented Seneca, Jesper, and the other prominent leaders with an invaluable opportunity to dedicate themselves to formulating a comprehensive strategy for their first offensive moves as part of Operation 1929. In line with the usual pattern, tempers often flare during these discussions as every participant takes their turn to provide valuable knowledge and expertise. Seneca frequently experiences apathetic thoughts as his mind drifts away, mainly because he considers the political aspect of leadership to be the least attractive part of the endeavor, especially whenever he encounters conflicting perspectives. However, Jesper serves as both a blessing and a curse for Seneca, helping him manage his emotions and providing reminders of what is lawful and prohibited.

Finally, they settle on a plan. The fleet will divide their forces into two factions. One faction will be responsible for actively attacking targets within one hundred light-years while taking control of the nearby trade routes that the Empire relies upon. Concurrently, the other faction will focus on aiding and empowering additional Whisper fleets, enabling them to advance towards an offensive position and ultimately break free from the oppressive onslaughts they're enduring. A smaller contingent of the fleet will stay ready and prepared within Pyre, training to relieve deployed squadrons.

On the eve of their campaign, a crucial conversation between Seneca and Jesper takes place, setting the stage for the upcoming operations to commence.

"Well. We're finally moving out of Pyre. Much faster than I thought it would, too. You should be happy." Jesper says, giving Seneca a firm pat on the back.

Happy… He meditates on that sentiment. After the battle, their sole focus has been on devising plans, which has resulted in him spending a significant amount of time by himself. Consequently, he had a significant amount of time for his thoughts to overwhelm him, creating a strong desire to find a way out. In his attempt to redirect his thoughts to the present, he exhausts all possible methods, and by far the most effective method is indiscriminate consumption of alcohol.

"I'll be 'happy' when this is done. I want to go home." He sighs.

Jesper, being the realist and logic minded individual that he is, reminds him, "You gotta be patient, man. There's going to be allot more than just winning the war before you and Ila—."

"I suggest…" Seneca quickly interrupts him before Jesper repeats a thought that already prevents him from sleeping, "…you don't finish that sentence."

Despite achieving consistent success, Seneca continues to experience unrelenting anxiety. He is conscious of the fact that there are endless possibilities, and he has experienced firsthand on multiple occasions how merciless time has been for him. Instead of speaking about it further, he stands silently in the room and tries to keep his face from betraying his inner turmoil. Jesper knows all too well that Seneca's fight is for Ilana and not necessarily for the Whispers. The silence envelops them, and Seneca can sense Jesper's endeavor to comprehend the impassive look on his face. He longs to have a greater capacity for communication or the confidence to be more open, but he lacks both. He finds it challenging to act with such courage and vulnerability, especially when he is experiencing pain.

Jesper decides to break the silence and says, "Sorry. Shit, speaking of Ilana, let me show you how to decode those cipher-texts."

A sense of relief engulfs Seneca, soothing his troubled mind. Not only do the ciphers allow him to communicate with Ilana, but the recollection of the pending communication also offers him a way to escape from the conversation. On the screen, Jesper presents a codex and proceeds to provide detailed instructions to both him and Seneca's AI assistant on how to decode the cipher. The ultimate goal is to enable Seneca to establish proper communication with Ilana.

Chapter 38: Delays and Dogs

Three months have come to pass since Operation 1929 officially began. In an ongoing display of dedication (and reserved reluctance), Seneca has steadfastly remained in Pyre's conference room. Agonizing as it may be, he's been continuing to lead the rebellion while consciously refraining from participating in battles to respect Jesper's… nagging. In fact, it's *only* out of *immense* respect for his friend that earned his compliance; any less significant individual would lack the necessary influence to persuade him away from the battlefield. However, because of his hiatus from combat, he is often alone to handle ongoing correspondence with rebellion leaders. Jesper's gratitude does little to ease his ongoing emotional distress.

For the past two weeks, his duties have been non-stop and have effectively confined within the government complex, affording him no opportunity to escape its encroaching walls. Day after day, the walls continue to inch closer, magnifying the sense of loneliness as progress slows to a crawling pace. While Operation 1929 is functioning effectively, the Whispers are yet to witness tangible results. Despite the effect of ongoing negative economic impacts, the lordship council from within the palace seems to have a stubborn nature that remains unyielding. More needs to be done before Operation 1929 moves from an unwanted sore to a crippling detriment to Imperial operations.

With their successful turnaround in the war, the Whispers wasted no time in eliminating eighteen targets, but these were all space-based metal refineries, mines, etc. However, not all the key targets they need to destroy are based among the stars. Some economic targets Shari Graas directed them towards sit upon planetary surfaces—places where the Empire remains formidable. On terrestrial surfaces, the Whispers are significantly lacking in terms of firepower and ground-based equipment. Consequently, Clemson and his gang have been deployed with the dear objective of procuring weapons for ground forces, but finding heavy weapons like artillery guns, tanks, and weaponized levitating craft is a challenge due to the rare presence of them in *space*. The fact that a considerable portion of the ground forces cannot meet their objectives reveals a major weakness in the rebellion's efforts, slowing their progress and frustrating Seneca.

"Jesper, I've told you, boots on the ground are your area of expertise. I fly and shoot a pistol. Directing an army isn't something I've ever done." Seneca says after Jesper probes him for suggestions.

Jesper, speaking to him via teleconference from a much more interesting location, sighs and says, "We just don't have the weapons. Clemson's delayed and the COS will only sell us so much without risking drawing too much attention from the Empire."

"What about the UF?" Seneca asks, hoping for any alternative.

"Seneca, they're fighting just as hard as we are and need all the equipment in their arsenal. We need them to keep pressure on military targets so this plan can work. You want progress? We need weapons. Nothing's going to change until we get a proper arsenal."

Jesper signs off, allowing silence to overtake the room. Seneca, frustrated and enraged, hurls an empty whiskey bottle at the wall. The bottle dents the drywall and explodes with a loud bang, sending shards of glass flying in all directions. "God *damn* it!" he exclaims.

It's far from the first time his frustrations have erupted into an outburst, sending bottles helplessly accelerating into destruction against a solid wall. Like clockwork, bad news creeps up at least once a week, overwhelming any positive news and compacting his emotional turmoil. The last time he felt like this was during Kelsea's distressing—losing battle with cancer. He'd hold a brave face in front of her, but when out of her sight, he was a self-destructive drunk; a status this war and its potential consequences have brought upon him once more. Leading this confounded campaign from a desk is maddening, leaving him struggling.

"Fuck this!" He shouts, kicking the door open between the conference room and his domicile, and lays down on his bed.

Unable to grip his emotions, he releases a frustrated series of expletives and shouts while his eyes remain fixed on the ceiling, adorned with intricate details that he has unknowingly committed to memory. Cupping his hands on his face, he grinds his teeth, trying to direct his mind to more productive thoughts. He needs to source weapons and war-fighting equipment for the Whispers, but where? The UF and COS cannot supply any more than they already have. Independent systems are not going to cross the Empire, and none of the systems within Whisper control have facilities to manufacture weapons en masse. Even if they did, almost every able-bodied soul without children to care for is involved in the rebellion.

"You could rob the Empire... You've been stealing their destroyers and ships at every opportunity," he thinks to himself just before he opens another bottle of whiskey. That's a thought... though, the only weapon caches he's aware of are planet based in the heart of Imperial space. The idea has potential, but Jesper is occupied in

some far-off place with limited contact, so Shari is the only one who can offer the valuable insight he needs.

The mere thought of talking to the woman fills him with disgust. Captivity has made her more cooperative when they need information, likely because she now has a personal stake in the rebellion's victory since she's a condemned traitor. However, she remains harsh, haughty, and annoying to converse with. Regardless, visiting her at the impound is his only choice at the moment. Taking a deep breath, he composes himself and makes the trip to the crowded impound, which is now filled with Imperial officers.

"Colonel Graas," Seneca says, tapping on the window of her cell.

"What?" she replies with disdain in her voice.

Seneca sighs. "I need your help with something. I'll make it worth your while."

Once more she replies with her usual hateful attitude, "Ha! What are you going to do? Bring me some fucking ice cream?"

He tries not to take the bait and asks, "I need ground weapons. Tanks, hovercraft, artillery. Where can I steal it from the Imps?"

"Aww. Seneca didn't know he'd have to fight a war on the ground?"

Following several more sarcastic exchanges that test Seneca's waning patience, he finally manages to make some progress. Shari's generous offer includes sharing the transponder ID of one of the Imperial military's mega-carriers. These colossal structures are ingeniously engineered to facilitate the transportation of supplies equivalent to those needed by entire colonies during interstellar travel. Their speed is impressive, and the secrecy that surrounds their movements makes intercepting them different unless you know their unique ship ID. If the Whispers could commandeer one carrying military cargo, it would greatly enable them to shift the tides of the ground war. They just need to win one or two battles before they'd be able to procure more equipment from surrendering Imperial units.

"What's your price?" Seneca asks, thankful to have kept his temper in check.

"I want my dog." she replies, a rare sincerity in her voice.

"Your…dog? Where is it?"

"He's in a kennel called 'Woof'n' in Vista Capital…he's a pointer named Beal."

"*Shit*," he thinks, scratching his head. "I'll see what I can do…"

This isn't an ideal complication. The act of going to Vista, especially in *the Phantom*, would entail a significant level of risk. His ship is too easy to recognize visually, even though he's taken his transponder offline. This is yet another obstacle he's got to overcome, but he's not going to delegate this to others. He'll take care of this himself. Once he retreats back to his quarters, he scribes a ciphertext for Ilana. She might be able to do something or give him direction.

Ciphertexts have been his only means of communicating with Ilana. The time-consuming task of decoding or writing takes hours depending on the length, but the outcome justifies the effort. Typically, she'll send him a ciphertext once every few weeks. Receiving them tends to be the highlight of his month, and he's happy to hear she's doing well for the situation. She's revealed to him that she prefers to spend her days in isolation at the mountain retreat. Occasionally, Serena will take breaks from being with her family to join Ilana, but with the state of the war, they aren't traveling. Knowing she's safe and in relative comfort keeps him going.

Starting with a heartfelt greeting, his message to Ilana shares how he is doing and expresses his deep love for her. Typically, this is where he concludes his communication. However, in this instance, he elaborates on the needs of the Whispers. Doing his best to make the message serious, since it sounds ridiculous. He tells her about Shari Graas' knowledge could procure weapons and acquiring a dog at a kennel will satisfy her enough to share information. Once he finishes composing the message, he sends it to Ilana through the secure channel they use for communication.

Ilana responds eight hours later. Apparently, Serena's family has a connection with the owner of the place, so she has since 'adopted' the homeless dog, considering the owner's presumed death. Ilana will coordinate with a spy who will transport the dog to a location precisely midway between Vista and Pyre—unfortunately still in Imperial space. Following that, Seneca will need to rendezvous with the spy. Ilana cautions him against his choice of vessel, since Imperial forces will intercept any ship without a transponder ID immediately.

Seneca reclines back in his chair, propping his feet up on the desk and staring thoughtfully at the ceiling. He has a way to get weapons, but he can't get the dog without a ship that won't attract Imperial attention at the border checkpoints. Any captured Imperial ship is certainly blacklisted, and without a transponder, he'll get intercepted for sure. COS and UF have embargoed the Empire, so one of their ships traversing their space would be suspicious. He needs something guaranteed to slip by unnoticed. A sudden knock on the door breaks his concentration, causing him to shift his weight and stand up as Marco opens the door.

Marco cheerfully greets him, "Hello my friend. How are you doing today?"

"I'd be lying if I said great, Marco." Seneca replies.

Marco frowns at Seneca's trademark pessimism and asks, "What's the situation on this occasion?"

"I need to fly a non-blacklisted ship into Imperial space to retrieve a dog from a spy," Seneca says as he rubs the tension out of his forehead.

Marco looks puzzled. The sound of the statement is just as bewildering as the way it feels to say it. "Quite the predicament. I apologize, I have no solution. I have come simply as a friend to wish you well. Your presence is missed among the people of the colony when you stay in here like a hen on the roost."

"I'm not one for good company right now. Too much to do and I need to get progress going." Seneca says as he returns to his seating position.

"You cannot rush things, my friend. You must let your heart rest knowing you're doing your best. Please come with me to dinner."

* * *

Rejecting Marco's kind offer for dinner never yields positive results. Marco's culinary creations are simply outstanding, with each dish bursting with flavor. Furthermore, Marco will continue to insist without pause until he gets compliance. With no prospect of achieving solitude, he opts to go along with Marco.

Marco lives among the people of Pyre in the barracks, though with a larger suite consistent with his position as governor. Stepping into his home, a cozy and quaint atmosphere greets those who enter. Tan wooden floors harmonize well with the light green walls. A dining room at the back of the apartment buzzes with the cheerful chatter of guests eagerly anticipating the meal, while children giggle and play on the sectional, engrossed in cartoons. The image evokes a sense of nostalgia, transporting Seneca back to the joyous family gatherings of his younger days.

The aroma of a perfectly roasted hen fills the air as Marco presents his masterpiece —a colorful plate of stuffed bell peppers, rice, and tender meat. Taking an empty seat at the table, Seneca engages in conversation with Marco's family and friends, savoring the taste of the delectable food. From chatting about their day-to-day routines to discussing their aspirations for the future, the conversation topics at dinner are diverse and random. Evidently, Marco has set his sights on moving to Fortuna after the war is over. His ambitious plan involves acquiring a significant piece of land to establish an ostrich range, which may strike some as an unconventional choice.

"Why ostrich?" Seneca chuckles at the mental image of Marco in a cowboy hat wrangling a flock of ostriches.

"They're red meat, healthier for you than beef, and easier to keep in places where grass isn't plentiful." he replies.

Seneca laughs and wonders what other absurd things Marco has in store for his future. "What else are you wanting to get into after the war?"

"I'd love to start a non-profit medical transport enterprise. Not all systems have the capabilities to treat all ailments, you know. The paperwork for medical transport ships is extensive, though. One might expect such measures for operations that have exempt ID."

A light bulb goes off in his head as he realizes he has a solution (and like many of Seneca's ideas, illegal) as he says, "Wait. Exempt ID?"

Marco elaborates and a solution to his predicament presents itself. Pyre has an infirmary with a medical transport vessel Marco had purchased to transport injured workers between Fortuna and Pyre colony. The ship has a medical exempt ID; it has galactic exemptions from wartime scanning and can travel freely without being stopped if it is not behaving as a combatant—not that the necessary purpose would be technically lawful, but the ship is fast and won't draw Imperial attention. Seneca jumps up quickly and asks, "How many do we have?!"

"Just the one, my friend," Marco says, smiling.

"I need it."

Marco nods before he says, "Take it, my friend. See what good comes from eating among your people?"

* * *

After expressing his gratitude to Marco, Seneca wastes no time in making his way back to the government complex. His footsteps echo as he runs through the halls to his quarters to update Ilana on his progress in acquiring the dog and to provide the spy with the necessary details for their meeting. He sighs… he's at least one step closer to being one step closer to Ilana.

Chapter 39: Whaling with Pirates

Seneca was relieved to find that retrieving the dog turned out to be a straightforward task, with no issues arising once he had acquired a vessel that met the requirements of his mission. The legality of using a medical transport vessel for subversion is a matter open to scrutiny, but what does it matter if you don't get caught? It's not like Seneca is overtly concerned with the law. He successfully acquires the white and chocolate spotted dog from the spy during a discreet meeting at a secret location. Without any delay, he quickly returns to Pyre's impound to retrieve the crucial information he desperately desires.

He strolls through the impound to Shari Graas' cell and opens it to reunite the dog with its owner. Shari experiences a touching moment with her beloved hound, and her speech is brimming with astonishment. "You actually got my dog?!"

Overwhelmed with happiness, she softly cries tears of joy while the dog affectionately licks her face and wags its tail from side to side in complete bliss.

"I did." Seneca says, leaning against the wall of the cell awaiting Shari to hold up her end of the bargain.

"Thank you. I mean that. I never thought I'd see him again." She says happily, embracing the pet, "Give me a kiosk. I'll give you the ID of the Empire's mega-carrier."

With complete transparency and no ulterior motives, she divulges the information. Seneca expresses genuine gratitude to her and departs, leaving her to enjoy the company of her loyal four-legged companion. Instead of going back to his office-prison, he makes his way to *the Phantom*. He has classified transponder ID for the mega-carrier and the name of the port from which it departs. He doesn't have a proper plan, but he's longing for a respite from his leadership duties. Now he has a valid justification to occupy his time in his ship as opposed to painstakingly playing out timelines in his head. It's a welcome event for him to engage in a mission conducted by the seat of his pants.

* * *

Once he boards his ship, he plots a course for Yvelli-72, which is a solitary star located along the trade path Shari Graas said the target vessel frequently travels. Grateful to be behind the controls of his ship, he brings *the Phantom* roaring to life once more and thrusters blast him off the landing pad of Pyre's space port. Prior to losing the connection on his short-range radios, he reaches out to Marco, informing him about his temporary departure and asking Marco to take control until he comes back. He's enroute when he realizes he may require aid to commandeer the mega-carrier, so he promptly reaches out to Clemson through a UniCom call.

Clemson answers with a hearty laugh, "Aye, Seneca. Every time you call, I hear money callin'. Where do you need us?"

"I'm whaling and need a fellow with a harpooning. Coordinates inbound. I'll pay you and your crew *generously*." Seneca says reciprocating Clemson's joyful demeanor.

"A whale, you say? How's the condition of the seas?"

"Be a mystery. Are you coming aboard?" Seneca asks with a devilish grin painting his face.

"Aye, but what of Jesper's thoughts on the ordeal?"

"Under the cover of nightfall, my sails won't be visible," Seneca says. (He doesn't intend to tell Jesper.)

Clemson chuckles and readily agrees, and based on their respective locations, the two of them should meet up in Yvelli-72 within a few hours of each other. With the destination in mind, Seneca sets *the Phantom* to warp, feeling a rush of excitement as the stars blur into streaks of blue light. He takes extra precautions to guarantee that his journey to Yvelli will keep him undetected by setting the nav computer to avoid Imperial ID checkpoints before he makes his way back into the crew suite of his ship.

Upon entering the room, he looks around before sighing, "Oh…yeah."

The room is a mess. Such things happen as a result of the heavy atmospheric maneuvering he'd done months prior. His mattress tipped on its side, its blankets haphazardly caught in the tubing along the wall, and cushions from his sofa tossed about. Former contents of cabinets and drawers adorn every inch of the floor. With several hours of spare time available before he reaches his destination, he dedicates a portion of it towards resetting the room to a satisfactory level of tidiness. Once the room reaches an acceptable level of cleanliness, he plops down onto his bed and quickly drifts off into an expected peaceful slumber.

It's strange how easy it was to drift off to sleep, despite struggling to fall asleep most nights as of late. There have been numerous instances in recent months where he experienced restlessness, tossing and turning throughout the night, only to realize that the morning hours are fast approaching before he finds a moment of satisfactory rest. The bed of *The Phantom* is nothing more than a glorified twin mattress, lacking the comfort of his most cozy sleeping experiences, but its familiarity is undeniable. Before he'd met Ilana, this bed was where he would spend most of his nights sleeping. Sleep was a pleasant and peaceful experience up until the moment he is unceremoniously tossed out of the bed, jolting him awake.

Disoriented from sleep, Seneca's heart races as he fights against the ship's lurching and shuddering, desperately trying to reach the cockpit. If Imperials have intercepted him enroute, there's likely four or five ships about to open fire. Dashing into his seat and buckling the harness, he grips the controls ready to engage the bandits… Nothing… Confused; he looks around, pointing the nose in all directions to find the assailants. Afterward, he directs his attention to the radar, but it shows no signs of any bogies. Nothing still. Maybe stealth craft?

He scans *the Phantom's* status panel in front of him, his eyes darting across the screen, searching for any clue about what transpired. He takes a moment to glance at his navigation computer and realizes that he had reached his destination, yet he couldn't help but feel a sense of unease. The autopilot was not what dropped him from warp and the telltale sensation of being pulled leaves him confused. As he continues his anxious search for clues around his ship, his eyes catch a failure message on the flight management screen, bearing an answer to the peculiar situation. Due to a malfunction in his autopilot's auto-drop feature, he was stuck in a high-speed orbit around Yvelli for three hours before someone pulled him out.

Suddenly his radio crackles with laughter "Seneca, you're late! You kept us in the doldrums for an hour too many! Found your ship flyin' in circles!" Clemson says.

"Y'all scared the shit out of me," Seneca says, laughing as he sighs in relief. "Any sign of the mega-carrier?"

"Aye, it appears we're just in time. One of my wingmen scouted ahead. Reported it 'bout an hour away with light chop."

Clemson's crew's assessment means a light escort. It makes sense; the Empire has no reason to expect an attack on this carrier, as it is situated at a significant distance from the primary campaign and shouldn't be known to the Whispers. It's pleasing news; even though Seneca and Clemson would make a formidable duo that would rival the capabilities of most fleets, Seneca is hesitant about *the Phantom* sustaining any visible damage that might tip off Jesper to his buccaneering escapade. He'd never hear the end of it—though he and Ilana are not immune from occasional bickering, Jesper turns out to be the "wife" in his life right now.

The light escort makes the stereotypical pirate mission rather easy. They don't need to physically board the ship, rather Clemson need only plant a hijack drone. By eliminating the mega-carrier's shields and providing protection for Clemson, he can make a close approach and successfully launch the probe. Following deployment, hijack probes use a drilling mechanism to penetrate the ship's hull and establish a link with the navigation computer. Once that happens, it'll slave the carrier's navigation to follow Clemson's instructions. It's a standard hijack, just on a massive ship. They take the moment of calm before the storm to discuss the minutia of the plan before Clemson decides to probe Seneca for information about Ilana.

"Seneca color me excited to score a mark with ye again. Also, forgive me for asking, but how's your ol'boss?" Clemson asks.

"Couldn't tell you." He lies. "She's probably doing alright. I don't know."

"A fine spirit that one has. It'd press on my softer side to spend too much time in her presence." Clemson replies.

Seneca doesn't reply other than grunting over the radio. Clemson's current expression of emotion is quite surprising, considering his usual reluctance to participate in personal discussions. Fortunately, the attempts at engaging in further personal conversation cease. Their prey is closing in, and the two alter conversation to plans to get drinks when they meet up later in the month.

"And there's our whale," Clemson remarks as he engages his warp disrupter to pull the ship. "Let's get her out of warp so we can harpoon the beast."

Seneca watches a massive ship suddenly appear with blue streaks of energy pulsing around it as the ship sways from its inertia. Clemson strategically pulled only the carrier, leaving its small escort force moving through warp away from them. His skillful action affords them an extra minute to attack the shields of the carrier without worrying about its fighter support.

This colossal wonder is a sight to behold with its massive size and slow, lumbering movements. With its typical cyan paint, the imperial vessel catches the eye, but it is the unconventional design that captivates—a mile-long tube with sizable containers fixed along its belly. The rear and front ends of the ship resemble triangular shapes, pointing away from the center in opposite directions. Its appearance is a stark contrast to the sleeker designs of smaller ships. They waste no time and throttle up toward the unprotected super-structure.

"What's it carrying Clemson?" Seneca asks over the radio as he takes an eight o'clock position off *the Rot*.

Clemson replies after a moment, "Plenty of what ye need. Scanner shows plenty of useful stuff to the land-bound forces."

"Good. I need some good news."

With lightning speed, Clemson, Seneca, and the rest of the pirates sweep across the ship, their gunfire creating a chaotic show. Due to the excessive amount of concentrated firepower directed at a ship that is relatively unprotected, the shields suffer a substantial amount of damage in just one pass. Seneca silently nods to himself. Their chances of successfully stealing the ship are high. It's a relief. Getting these weapons means ground-war has the chance to progress. It'll get them that much closer to winning the war and getting him one step closer to Ilana. The mega ship prepares to jump back to warp, causing the surrounding space to ripple and twist as they maneuver for another strafing run.

"Alright, let's back up and pull her as she jumps." Clemson instructs.

* * *

Seneca, along with Clemson and his six wingmen, reduce throttle to avoid getting caught in any jump-wake. Clemson once more prevents the ship from escaping. They quickly regroup and form a straight line and launch another strafing run along the entire length of the ship. Escorting fighters finally arrive to defend the mega-carrier, whose shields are hovering just above fifty percent as Seneca and company complete their strafing run. Although it's inconvenient, it's not significant enough to require a retreat. The seven Imperial heavy fighters barrel toward them, their spearhead shapes granting them an imposing appearance, but limiting their lateral maneuverability.

"Lads, keep'em in a maelstrom while Seneca and I reel in the catch." Clemson says, instructing his crew mates.

The other six pirates, each commanding a different model heavy fighter, break off to engage in combat with the Imperial pilots, allowing Seneca and Clemson to remain unchallenged as they press forward with their assault on the carrier.

On their next approach, Clemson directs a question to Seneca. "Seneca, what tackles' on the rod?"

Seneca replies as the ship grows before them on their approach. "Thermal pulse, like usual. Unfortunately, the UF doesn't want me using PDDs anymore."

"Well, those be well suited for this endeavor. The ship has four shield sections. I'll hit the front two with the rail gun. You hit the back with all of your missiles. That should drop all the shields and let us finish this quickly."

Seneca and Clemson coordinate their maneuvers to fulfill Clemson's command. Seneca effectively utilizes his multi-target system, dividing his missiles to target the aft two shield segments, while Clemson's railgun proves its precision by striking the junction between the forward two segments. The shields drop to zero percent and give way, allowing Clemson to move in to deploy the hijack probe. Meanwhile, the other pirates have been effectively preventing the escorts from interfering. In fact, three out of the initial seven imperial fighters are now disabled. It serves as dear evidence of the peril that comes with crossing paths with a renowned pirate and his crew, regardless of the quality of one's own vessel.

Clemson laughs over the radio while Seneca watches him. Clemson's ship deploys the probe, and it quickly drills into the mega carrier's hull. "Barrel is in the whale, boys. Disengage. Seneca, will ye be joining us for the delivery?"

"Unfortunately, not. Jesper won't be too happy to see *the Phantom* show up. Just get those supplies where they need to be. Your loot will be in the coffer by the time you get where you're headed. Good fortunes until next time!"

Clemson bids him farewell and they all go their separate ways for the moment. Seneca back to Pyre, and Clemson to deliver a mega carrier full of weapons necessary to fight a ground-based campaign at Jesper's current location outside an Imperial diamond mine.

* * *

The proficiency and skills exhibited by Seneca and Clemson's crew contributed to the successful completion of the operation, making the process seem almost effortless. If all goes well, Jesper will remain unaware of Seneca's involvement when the carrier arrives with weapons and equipment. However, he wouldn't be surprised if he had to bribe Clemson to maintain his silence.

Chapter 40: The End Approaches

Despite sluggish acceleration, unmistakable shifts in the war's trajectory have favored the Whispers. Seneca's efforts guided Whisper contingencies and are finally advancing into Imperial territory. The UF's sustained conventional military tactics, coupled with the Whispers' ever-growing war-fighting capabilities, enable them to engage both planetary and space-based targets; whittling the Empire down one inch of battlefield at a time. Operation 1929 is decimating economically vital infrastructure, and the Whispers have slowed the Imperial economy to a grinding halt. There's not so much as a functioning lemonade stand or stable Imperial trade route beyond a meager fifty-lightyear radius from Vista.

Yet, no reprieve is in sight. Despite the Empire's faltering economy, their prehension on rebel territories remains firm, underscoring their unwillingness to be defied. Conflict rages on, month after grueling month. The Empire's military, stretching ever thin by relentless pressure by Whispers and UF alike, faces dire financial straits. However, months stretch into years to Seneca's frustrated dismay. His longing for Ilana deepens, stinging like a festering wound that won't heal. Neither he nor his liver can accept that two and a half years have crawled by since he'd last seen Ilana's face.

Pungent odors of alcohol hang in the air, mingling with the sight of Seneca, visibly intoxicated, sprawled out on the floor of his sty. He's drenched in spilled libations and desperation, and anxiously poring over his collection of ciphertexts from Ilana. His determination is waning in the battle of wills against the Imps, and his spirit is at breaking point. These messages are all that anchor him to a dream he's unsure if he can actually realize... this war—his involvement was never supposed to drag on like this. He knew from the moment he saw Ilana's ethereal fear of death that he would do anything to protect her... subsequently he knew there were to possibilities to this gamble: he won the war, or he losses everything for eternity. At this rate, it appears that the Empire is just waiting for the Whispers to exhaust themselves.

* * *

226

He curses his attachments and his weakness. Giving into Ilana… this pain… it's not unfamiliar, yet it's new at the same time. The notion of returning to an easier form of life without the need to confront his emotions poisons his thoughts. So, he slouches on the floor drinking whiskey to derail his mind, listening to music to cover his inner voice, and focusing entirely on the only connection to Ilana he has now—reading and weeping, he holds on tightly to Ilana's words. She misses me… She loves me… She's waiting for me… Don't give up… Across the hundred or so ciphertexts that he tirelessly reads, these messages resurface repeatedly, evoking only a feeling of helplessness.

He chokes down the remnants of a bottle of Keplar fire-whiskey, coughing from the burning sensation in his throat. He casually tosses the empty container towards a trash can in the corner, where it joins a mountain of discarded bottles that have completely filled the space. It simply falls to the floor, shattering and adding to the pile of broken glass.

"My friend, not again." Marco says stealthily entering the room, startling Seneca.

"I'sorry Marco. Jus tryin'ta sleep." He slurs, trying to wipe tears from his face, knowing Marco will once again question why Seneca feels the need to numb himself.

Marco grabs his shoulder and urges Seneca, "One only subjects himself to this for a limited number of reasons. Talk with me Seneca. Share your pain."

"Marco I ca-" He stifles his stomach's attempt to rid itself of whiskey as he says, "I can' jus'tel people Ilana's secres…. fuck…."

Seneca recognizes the full extent of his mental haze, as he is typically proficient in keeping secrets safe. Now, thanks to another 750ml bottle of Kepler fire whiskey, he had lost all inhibitions and blurted out the most significant secret he has.

"Ilana?" Marco says, confused. "Tell me, what secret does she keep?"

"God dammit… jus close the door an'lock it" He replies. Marco may as well get the full story now.

With no further hesitation, he slurs his burden to Marco, his words punctuated by his own occasional choked sobs. He goes beyond just Ilana's role as the true leader of the rebellion (Seneca is too drunk to remember Marco already knows). He doesn't stop there though. He goes on and ensures that Marco comprehends his entire past—Sophie onwards—in order to avoid being excessively judged based on his current situation. It's a long story that involves drunken backtracking. Marco proves to be a ferocious listener, though, nodding along as Seneca talks.

"…an thas why you come in'ere, and see me on my ass with loud music drowning out the soun'of my 'dest'u'tion." Seneca says, airing the last of his demons out.

Marco pauses, meditating on the convoluted narrative, before he says, "You carry a heavy burden, my friend. It's not easy venturing back into the woods once you've found your way out. Perhaps, though, you're lost alongside another right now and it's too dark to see?"

"What'n the hell's that mean?" Seneca grumbles, shaking his head.

Marco is a brilliant mind, unreasonably patient, and unnervingly positive in his outlook on life. However, from Seneca's inebriated and emotionally biased perspective, Marco cannot comprehend the extent of his emotions. Marco does not know the pain of having two-hundred-year-old memories of his parents, or an accompanying long-term regret that he never got to say goodbye. Marco cannot grasp the scars of losing a child because Seneca had been thousands of miles away, instead of driving his son home from baseball practice. How could Marco, in his short life, have any idea how bitter someone can become with their own existence, when their wife withers from a disease that was five years from having a cure? Furthermore, what makes Marco qualified to understand that Seneca is poised to lose everything again?

"It means," Marco says calmly, "That you are choosing this isolation and to carry this burden alone—"

"No shit." Seneca sneers, interrupting Marco.

"You don't have to, my friend. Across the galaxy, and here in particular, you have friends that you can trust."

"This isn't news." Seneca sighs.

Seneca's struggle has nothing to do with trust in others—rather a lingering distrust in himself. It seems as though whenever he follows his intuition, nothing but ill fate follows. Why is it, after decades of apathy, that the first instance of connecting with others throws him into a literal war for the fate of the galaxy? A war he would never have got involved in, were it not for his personal investment in another attempt at love. Every decision he's made since that night on Oberon has dug him into a deeper and deeper hole. If he can't trust himself, what good would trust in others serve?

"I cannot ease your pain, my friend… nor can I pretend to understand. However, you and I know there's a reason you are here. One day soon, you'll be telling me why that is."

"Will I?" Seneca scoffs sarcastically.

"If there wasn't a reason for you to be here, you'd have left already." Marco says, disrupting Seneca from opening another bottle of whiskey. "I want you to think about that. Instead of listening to echoes of regret, ask yourself why you are still here."

In his mind, Seneca is still here only for Ilana. No larger purpose comes to mind. He stays silent, thinking about what Marco said. At the very least, it stopped Seneca from drinking the rest of the evening and calmed Seneca enough to steer the conversation elsewhere. Regarding Seneca's drinking, Marco's wisdom is unlikely to present much of a roadblock, but Seneca agrees to *try* and lean on his friends more —provided they find him before he starts drinking. Marco remains by Seneca's side throughout the evening, ensuring his comfort until Seneca finally finds his way to bed, where Marco leaves him to rest, at least for the night.

The next evening, however, Seneca is returns to using stiff beverages to numb his racing mind. All too inconveniently, Jesper arrives to bear witness… from the urgency in his voice, it doesn't sound like he's here for chat.

"Sen-" Jesper says, dodging glass shrapnel as he opens the door to find that Seneca is ill company.

"Sorry. I didn't know you were coming in." Seneca lies. "Now's not a good time. What's so god damned important?"

"Clemson found something. Get cleaned up and be out here in fifteen." Jesper replies, unmoved by Seneca's tantrum.

"Great! More bad news…" Seneca scoffs. "Add it to the pile."

Frustrated, Jesper comes over and jabs Seneca in the shoulder with 'hangover-be-gone' before huffing disappointment.

"Motherfucker!" Seneca yelps in response to the sharp pain in his right shoulder. "I hate when you do that!"

"Damn it, man." Jesper grabs Seneca's shoulders, "Shut up. Stop hating yourself. You're doing good here. This is the closest some of these people have been to freedom in decades. Stop looking at your promise to Ilana as a curse!"

Seneca simply shrugs and pushes Jesper's arm away as he turns to say, "I should have just left well enough alone… whatever Jesper. If you wanna do the happy preachy shit, you gotta catch me before I pick up a bottle. What do you need?"

"Clemson captured an Imperial science officer. He needs to speak to you—urgently." Jesper says.

Seneca continues rapidly recovering from his excessive drinking. However, before he can respond to Jesper, the medication kicks in, forcing him to hastily rush to the bathroom to violently rid his stomach of any alcohol that hasn't been absorbed. His timing is seconds short, and he soils the clothing he's wearing with regurgitated whiskey, necessitating a shower and quick action of quickly washing his suit.

Fully recovered, although his parched throat reminds him of his thirst, he returns to Jesper, looking clean and no longer drunk. Taking a deep breath, he mentally prepares himself for whatever news awaits him in the conference room. The doors swing open, and he walks out of his quarters with Jesper to find Clemson standing with an Imperial science officer in custody. Seneca examines everyone's expressions, trying to gauge whether they heard the commotion on Seneca's side of the wall before his gaze falls upon the disheveled Imperial.

The science officer is middle-aged, maybe in his lower thirties, adorned in the traditional Imperial cyan military blues. His brown hair, longer than one would anticipate for a military officer, matched the unruly state of his uniform. As Seneca looks at him, he can't help but notice the speckled pattern of bruises on the man's worn face. Adding to the overall dreary status of the man, he's emaciated and smells awful.

* * *

"Geez, did we mark his face up?" Seneca asks Clemson as he examines the officer.

Clemson shakes his head in reply. "Negative. Found him like this in the brig on a ship haulin' weapon parts and platinum. Says the other imps beat him when he was tryin' to defect. Lucky fella, we took the ship 'bout the right time."

Seneca gestures for the weary soul to sit down and requests someone to bring him water and food. He trembles as Seneca takes the seat across from him, fear lacing his nervous stuttering as he speaks "F-f-forg-g-ive me. T-t-they tell us you k-ill without mercy or warning s-s-so..."

Seneca raises an eyebrow. At this point, he has a reputation for being trigger-happy among Imperial circuits. He takes a scant breath and says, "On rare occasions, but generally not people who run from the Empire. I hear you got something important to tell us."

"Ye-yes..." he takes a breath to calm his nerves. "The Empire is manufacturing dark matter weaponry—ballistic missiles capable of erasing entire star systems."

"Where?!" Seneca asks, his voice reflecting deep concern.

The Imperial science officer calms his nerves enough to abandon his stutter as he says, "Aboard the Empire's two capital vessels, they've moved them to defend Argi-Pecun, the last remaining platinum mine that you haven't destroyed."

There it is. The worst in a long line of bad news. The Deitus-class capital ships, *the Pantheon* and *Echelon*, are super-massive ships, rivaling the size of space stations in excess of two kilometers long. Shaped like horizontal monoliths with a half-moon arc situated on their aft ends, they boast the normal assortment of offensive and defensive weapons capable of repelling entire militaries. While the standard arsenal alone makes them imposing threats, the crown jewels of their deadly capabilities are two particle accelerator cannons (PACs) located at the tip of each end of the half-moon structure. The PACs, when fully charged, can reduce planetary continents to crates by accelerating particles at unfathomable speed.

However, the Deitus-class ships are only tools to protect something far more sinister. While they're powerful vessels capable of widespread decimation, they pale in comparison to the destructive capabilities of dark matter weapons. The Orinians, in a singular instance, employed a dark matter weapon to make their presence in the universe known. With just a single warhead, they eliminated an entire planet inhabited by humans, leaving no evidence or traces of their once-thriving existence. After the Orinian war, the bloodiest war in galactic history, galactic laws henceforth barred anyone from using or creating dark matter weapons because of their capabilities for complete decimation.

The specific science of dark matter and the derived weaponry far exceeds Seneca's limited understanding, but the Empire is, apparently, growing desperate. No doubt, this is why the Empire's been hanging on so long... It's smart. Creating the weapons on their capital ships, paired side by side... The Empire is hysteric and stopping them without sending the entire might of the rebellion and its alliance with the UF will be nearly impossible.

* * *

There's not a hopeful expression in the silent conference room as the officer continues. "The weapons will be ready in less than a year, eight months at the earliest. It needs to be stopped. Once warheads are ready, they'll be able to be launched at every single UF and Whisper stronghold including Earth and Pyre."

Seneca stays silent, his knees buckle as he attempts to stand from his chair. Seneca knew their plan was hemorrhaging the Imperial economy—Many Imperial lords, who were once wealthy and powerful, are now facing bankruptcy due to the decline of economic output throughout the Empire. Thus, the luxurious existence that the people of the Empire once indulged in was substituted with impoverished communities struggling to make ends meet with rationed food supplies. It was a desperate situation for all involved. Despite this, Seneca could not have foreseen that instead of surrendering, the Empire would resort to dark matter and genocide. Unfortunately, it seems that the remaining lords are desperate, and they do not intend to lose.

"That... sucks..." is all Seneca manages to say.

The unbroken silence in the room is deafening. Seneca's motives for drinking stand before him justified in their existence. A massive torrent of emotion welling up, his face cherry red with anger. Thankfully, before his meltdown ensues, the Imperial science officer presents a kiosk tablet.

He turns on a projection from the kiosk as he presents a glimmer of hope to the room. "I stole schematics for the capital ships, engineering, and CAD drawings. It is highly classified information. I can help you. If you don't stop them, billions will die. I supported the Empire with every breath I had at one point, but this... is inhuman."

Inside knowledge is an incredible asset, but with the scenario at hand, victory is fifty-fifty odds at best. In a fit of rage, Seneca's emotions explode at the realization, inciting him to stand up and hurl the office chair with incredible force, shattering it against the drywall.

"I didn't sign up for this!" Seneca shouts. "Everyone, just get out! I'll call you when I'm ready!"

With the odds of victory feel as if they have vaporized before him, so have his hopes of a life with Ilana. The voices in his head erupt. His existence will be relegated to forever evading the Empire's wrath with no statute of limitations on his transgression. He'll never see Earth, his home again. Despair engulfs him, fueling a rampage that fills his room with the sound of frantic yells, curses, and the shattering of objects.

Hours pass before his anger yields enough for him to recall everyone and the Imperial science officer into the conference room. Now, the debate at hand is whether or not the Whispers should surrender given the change in circumstance.

Victory is assured if they successfully attack the Empire, destroy the dark matter manufactories, and eliminate the last major economic target. In the event of failure, the Whispers will be defeated. Seneca doesn't know where he sits either...

"Seneca, they'll have every bit of force they have left there. Argi-Pecuni is the largest platinum mine in the galaxy and our last big target." Jesper says, pleading with Seneca to maintain his resolve.

Seneca slams his fist on the conference room table as he says, "*Fuck* the platinum mine Jesper! We aren't taking out dark matter manufactories or mines with *two* of the strongest ships in the entire galaxy *side by side*!".

"We have to try. If we don't, we lose the fucking war. We have our victory." Jesper reciprocates the action of slapping the table, "Right. There. This is what you've wanted this whole time!"

"If we fail, the rebellion and war are over. I'll issue a surrender before they fire those weapons..." Seneca says with a defeated breath.

The debate goes back and forth. The fate of the Whispers rides on one key victory, an all-or-nothing engagement to affect the fate of the galaxy. Seneca's mind, clouded by fear, cannot see a realistic scenario where the Whispers come out on top. Jesper believes the threat of dark matter weapons should compel the COS to join the war in some capacity, but Seneca is skeptical and does not want to rely on this idea.

"What would *they* want you to do?" Jesper asks Seneca, pointing out the window to the port, seeming to gesture the rest of the Whispers but clearly implying that "*they*" is synonymous with Ilana. He knows what she'd want him to do...

His voice, hoarse from the yelling and shouting, "Fine! Jesper," Seneca yells, "But if we fight this battle, I'm *on* the field. I at least need the illusion of control, and we will need every pilot possible to be on the field."

Jesper nods. "And if you die? You have *people* counting on you after the war."

Once again, Seneca understands the implication. Ilana would be crushed, feeling the profound grief that he had felt when his own loved ones died. He wouldn't want Ilana, or anyone else for that matter, to be in such a state of mind. Nevertheless, in the event of their defeat, if Seneca chose to stay on a command ship rather than engage in the fight, his own guilt would haunt him. To avoid such sentiment on his conscience, he needs to feel like he exerted maximum effort in the war. Even if that means dying in battle.

"Then God and I finally have our day in court."

Chapter 41: Knights, Pawns, and Queens

In the weeks following the harrowing news, Seneca has been working with rebel leaders to covertly spread the news regarding the Empire's intended use of dark matter weapons through communication channels. They have collectively reached a consensus that it is advantageous for them if the Empire remains unaware that they know of the Imp's heinous plan, as it may potentially encourage them to accelerate their destructive timeline. As such, the Whispers slowly trickle the majority of their attacking forces to prepare for the next steps in the war.

Tiresome conferences plague Seneca's sober moments he has to endure with the UF and COS. The news has created significant worry for both UF and COS, and unfortunately, neither of them has a constructive strategy to address the issue. Thankfully, through tactful diplomacy on Marco's and Jesper's part, the UF reluctantly remains resolute in their alliance. The COS's military co-op, however, expresses little desire to draw attention to themselves. According to their contention, the Empire's wrath is presently directed solely towards the Whispers and the UF, while member systems of the COS remain unaffected.

Claxton Evahns, the current head of the Confederate Military Council, speaks to the point, "We understand the position this places you in, and we will continue to sell you weapons and provide indirect support. However, we are not an offensive military. It is against our values to participate in offensive campaigns."

The COS has long held the stance of neutrality in the realm of galactic conflicts. They had the luxury of being born after the Orinian war and have not been drawn into previous conflicts between the Empire and UF. To Seneca's recollection, the closest thing to war the COS has ever participated in was an indirect quasi-war with the UF. It was short-lived and over trade agreements and was eventually dissipated through diplomacy without escalating into a full-scale conflict. The COS's articles of confederation permit their military to declare war, though only through means of unanimous vote across its members or automatically in response to being attacked by another sovereign entity. Either way, it is imperative they explore every possible avenue of potential military aid for the upcoming altercation.

"Understood, commander," Seneca says, fighting the frustration out of his voice. "But if we lose, what message is that going to send? If you allow these weapons to exist in the galaxy, you condemn its future to uncertainty. The Empire's greed has no end, and the COS is rich with resources. It is ignorant to believe the Empire will not come after you next—when there is nobody left to stand beside you."

"I personally do not disagree with you Seneca, but I represent the collective ideals of our members..." Claxton says in response.

Jesper frowns and interjects, hoping for something. "What would it take then? What has to happen for you to help? It's *one* battle. One critical moment..."

Claxton's face portrays regret, but he firmly maintains his stance that holding a vote is the only viable course of action, but he acknowledges that the historical precedent in the COS raises doubts, as no vote has ever successfully passed a declaration of war. Nevertheless, the debate persists for days, wasting valuable time that Seneca and Jesper could spend on strategizing and analyzing the weaknesses of the Empire's capital ships. Eventually, Claxton holds a vote throughout the COS member states, and in affirmation of his reluctance, the vote is strongly in favor of declaring war, but *not* unanimous.

While the COS maintains its position of not committing to declare war, the overwhelming dissent towards the Empire among COS members has prompted Claxton to grant permission for individual member leaders, including himself, to contribute pilots and ships to the battle. It's a bittersweet compromise. While they could receive aid from the COS, the quantifiable force that will assist is unknown if it happens at all. Furthermore, the COS are reluctant to be seen moving units en masse into rebel territory so they won't take part in any training exercises alongside the rebels and UF. The participation of the COS is a wildcard that they cannot rely upon...

With no further concessions to be earned, Seneca and Jesper return to Pyre, where they call for a meeting to make plans for the upcoming battle. Keenan Vehrs assumes a significant responsibility for educating rebel strategists on critical information regarding the capital ships during a critical planning session.

"The weapons are being created here." Keenan gestures to a large cargo bay on a holographic display of capital ship schematics. ", it's a stadium sized cargo area converted to stabilize dark matter for the warheads. You'll need to access it here..."

He points to the mid-ship hangars. It appears they'll need to deploy foot soldiers to attack from the inside, since the manufactories are far too deep within the bowels of the ship to be destroyed externally. Foot soldiers will need to fight their way through the ship, which has hundreds of Imperial soldiers and armed crew inside, into the cargo area to detonate explosive charges and destroy the facilities...

"Okay... in order to do that, the shields need to be down..." Seneca says.

"Yes, there's no way around it..." Keenan replies.

"What's the shield strength then?" Jesper inquires.

"The mid-ship shields, fortunately for you, are the weakest—however, they can still sustain two hours of steady fire from your forces. The forward shields are the strongest sitting at ninety tera-ohms. I'd avoid wasting much energy there."

Seneca clenches his fist, frustrations well, and he wished he had a drink... without an additional fleet from the COS, they won't be able to last that long... "Are they linked shields, or do we have to destroy each segment individually?"

Keenan looks annoyed, as if offended by Seneca's question, but answers. "They're linked to save power for the PACs. However, the forward shields have a secondary independent generator."

Jesper and Seneca exchange a concentrated glance, pointing at the surface mounted generators of the capital ships and chat quietly for a moment. They only need to destroy the mid-section generator and all the shields will also drop... easier said than done.

"We don't have the firepower. The capital ships will eliminate half our fleet before we make a dent..." Seneca says with a sign.

UF President Tessa Jackson interjects. "We can commit our three super-battlecraft. They can force the Capital ships to divert shield power to the front end."

The Hercules class super-battlecraft, with their colossal dimensions, are sights to behold in their own right. Although they are significantly smaller than the Imperial capital ships, their presence in the battle would greatly shift the odds in favor of the rebels. Just like most capital ships, *the Appomattox*, *McHenry*, and *Normandy* also possess a standard arsenal. However, what really distinguishes these ships from others is the fact that they are equipped with the most powerful rail cannons in the entire galaxy, with barrels that span the entire length of the impressive football-shaped super structures. The speed at which these weapons can launch nuclear warheads is truly astonishing, as they can reach hypersonic velocities.

More frustrated expressions morph Seneca's face. "That's well and good, but the Empire still has more destroyers, carriers, and cruisers than we do, and every bit of firepower will need to be concentrated on the Empire's capital ships."

Jesper nods in agreement as he contributes to the discussion. "That's true and not only that, the PACs can eliminate most of our support ships without fully charging, and that's what the PACs are going to fire at first."

The weight of the overwhelming odds they stand against is bound to buckle their knees and overpower them. They have no method to disable the capital ship's shields. Hence, their dropships can't land in the mid-ship hangars and carry out the deployment of foot soldiers. They have no ace...

"The Imps want to curb the moon an' sway the tides in their favor. I say we do the same. Why don't we use jumpers?" Clemson suggests.

"Jumpers" is a term used for small, guided missiles that are capable of micro-warping through a target's shields and detonate directly on the surface of a ship. Although the weapons have low damage output, they possess the unique ability to completely bypass shields. Deploying enough jumpers to target the shield generators would destroy the shields without directly attacking them. Although the idea seems promising, jumpers are widely regarded as illegal because of their tendency to cause significant collateral damage. In the past, there was an incident where jumpers were employed to harm civilians, resulting in their subsequent prohibition under galactic legislation. Now their use is limited to select terrorist organizations.

Tessa Jackson, who continuously encourages strict adherence to galactic law, tries to interject, "Out of the question—"

"I'm going to have to stop you, ma'am," Seneca interrupts President Jackson's attempt to uphold galactic law, "Clemson's right. Our fighters, equipped with jumpers, would make this a fair fight. There aren't civilians involved. It's justified force, especially since the Empire is *already* breaking galactic law by manufacturing these weapons."

Jesper reinforces the idea to Seneca's surprise. "I agree Madam President. I think the solution has merit. In fact, breaking the rules may be the only way we win this. If we play by the rules while the Empire doesn't, we leave too much to chance."

President Jackson quietly diverts her attention, seeking input from her own military advisors. After a nod of agreement, she chooses not to provide any additional comments on the matter. Seneca appreciates her conviction and acknowledges the immense bravery required to defy it. Given the intricacies of federation politics, it is very likely that her decision to permit such weapons could have serious political consequences for her re-election prospects.

"Clemson, I assume you can source enough jumpers for the engagement?" Seneca meets the unscrupulous gaze of Clemson.

"Aye, coulda fought the whole war with how many I keep. Let us borrow that mega-carrier and we can have 'em here soon." Clemson says with a chuckle.

Seneca nods, dismissing Clemson with a sense of cautious optimism. It seems that they have a way to shift the balance even more in their favor for the upcoming battle, even if it is only a slight advantage. Even though things are still far from favorable, their willingness to bend the rules has granted them a fighting chance in their battle against the Empire.

The conversation gradually shifts towards the finer nuances of strategy. Time will be a formidable adversary in combat, on par with the four PACs. The Whispers have access to a diverse and powerful fleet, which includes not only three super battlecraft from the UF but also a handful of destroyers and cruisers, and twenty fighter squadrons. When combined, these assets amount to a staggering total of over three hundred ships. In contrast, the Empire holds a clear advantage due to its double number of support vessels and a one and a half to one ratio of fighters.

The Empire's overwhelming numbers advantage guarantees that there will be substantial losses.

Hence, they conceive a plan that consists of three basic yet indispensable steps. The initial phase of the plan involves deploying sixteen squadrons, each of which will initiate an assault by unleashing a barrage of missiles. These missiles, ranging from three to fifteen per ship, have a precise objective: destroy the armored mid-ship shield generators. By implementing a three-minute time on target strategy, the aim is to maximize the impact of the attack. Two waves, consisting of four squadrons each, will carry out strafing runs. These runs, lasting a total of six minutes, will be supported by the rail cannons positioned on the battle's outskirts, and should neutralize the shields of the capital ships.

In the meantime, squadrons that are not assigned to bombing runs will escort the "bombers"; actively engaging enemy fighters to guarantee the secure delivery of the payloads. As soon as the bombers deploy their missiles, they'll alter their primary objective. While escorts circle back to defend the next wave of bombers, the first wave will focus on the Imperial support ships.

Once the second wave destroys the shields, the escort squadrons will circle back once more to defend the dropships on their way to the mid-ship hangars. The dropships deploy foot soldiers who will have to navigate to the cargo bays and plant timed explosive charges. Afterwards, the foot soldiers will have five minutes to get out. It seems simple enough, but by this point up to a minimum of thirty minutes may pass. Considering the potential outcome of the war, it is crucial for the Whispers fleet to prevent substantial losses. Even if they lose their dark matter weapons, the Empire could capitalize on any weakened state, and enduring a confrontation against all odds for thirty minutes can seem like an interminable struggle.

To ensure the fleet gains some valuable time, Seneca and The Nineteen will separate and focus on the maneuvering to the four PACs, employing PDD missiles to destroy them. By this point they'll likely be close to a forty-minute mark—the fleet will be running low on shields, and by forty-five minutes they could expect an exponential rise in Whisper casualties... Without a reliable source of reinforcements, conservative estimates tell them that they'll lose half their fleet by the one-hour point... by which time the dark matter manufactories need to be destroyed, or the Whisper surrender. It's a hefty gamble...

Everyone but Jesper files out after the hours of planning. Seizing the opportunity, Seneca walks behind him and pats his shoulder. "This will easily be the deadliest battle of my career. I'm good, but I know I'm not invincible... Jesper, if I don't make it all the way through, you're next in line. Just... let *everyone* know how much they meant to me in the short time I've been with them." Seneca says.

Jesper nods silently and firmly grasps Seneca's shoulder. The war's end is on the horizon. Chess pieces are being set. Seneca is ready... whichever outcome may await him.

Chapter 42: The Dealing's Almost Done

The Whispers have organized their plans, and the chessboard is set. On one side, the titanic might of the Empire; on the other, the resolute voices of the Whispers. The upcoming battle, potentially the deadliest in galactic history, will test the collective strength of the galaxy. Leading the operation are Seneca, The Nineteen, Clemson, and his crew, among the fleet's elite combat pilots. They will serve as the primary defenders during the battle and, for now, as the main training resource.

Since the inception of the plan, Seneca has recalled the Whisper's military to Pyre, and the UF has committed units to hold the current line—at least units that aren't training with the Whispers. In the shadow of Fortuna, fighter squadrons engage in rigorous combat training scenarios, simulating war-games against Seneca and the Whisper elite. "Bombing" squadrons, tasked with carrying the payload to take out the shield generators, are pushed to their limits as they practice evading Seneca's squadron to strike their targets.

Despite lacking the same level of combat prowess as the prime squadron, they receive no mercy from Seneca, who believes failure teaches more valuable lessons than success. Knowing the Empire will show no mercy, the training is intense. To ensure the bombers reach their targets within three minutes, defending squadrons must protect them during exercises against Seneca and the prime squadron. Hopefully, training against the best pilots in the galaxy will enhance their skills and put them on par with the Imperial elite.

Jesper, like Seneca, imposes high expectations on the foot soldiers tasked with invading the capital ships. Utilizing VR systems equipped with AI-generated opponents, they experience realistic simulations of the ships intricate inner workings. Although there's no specific time on target requirement (outside the universal one-hour time mark), it's crucial for foot soldiers to move swiftly in all scenarios to maximize chances of victory. They're the determiners, the ones who will ultimately win or lose the war.

* * *

Rigorous practice continues daily from reveille to lights out. The fleet cannot strike Argi-Pecun until pilots consistently meet or exceed target times, and foot soldiers can navigate and handle any situation that may await them. Idleness could be deadly, as billions of lives hang in the balance. All this training, all this preparation, yet the bombers struggle to meet time constraints, resulting in high simulated losses. Concerns regarding the escorts squadrons' ability to defend bombers' gaslight many progress briefings... All the while, foot soldiers take an average of one hour to attack the weapon manufactories on the capital ships, which is too long for a successful assault.

While the fleet struggles to meet the goals as the first month of preparation draws to a close, Seneca's hopes plummet. Exercise after exercise, the fleet falls short of standards, sending Seneca into a panic. He's just about to reach for a bottle of whiskey when Marco—a savior on nights like this—enters his quarters.

"It's been a rough month, but surely you haven't given up now?" he asks, grabbing Seneca's wrist just in time.

"I don't know any more Marco." Seneca says, gripping his poorly groomed hair in his hands. "How are we supposed to win this? I'm asking the impossible from the Whispers..."

Marco changes the subject. "Have you thought about what I asked you? Would you still be here if you truly believed it was impossible?"

"No."

"And what of your issue of trust? Do you not trust the Whispers? Jesper?"

"It's not that Marco."

"Perhaps you don't trust yourself?"

Seneca's face snaps up—his mouth open and speechless. Marco smiles. "My friend. Tell me, why."

"I did this..." Seneca gestures around him and points to the bustling activity outside. "...I front this lie, for Ilana—because I love her, and this is all to protect her... but I may never see her again... so I don't trust myself..."

Seneca hesitates. He knows the myriad of reasons that he doesn't trust his own judgement, but he's less than willing to express the chief among them. Marco urges him to continue.

Seneca shakes his head. "I'll just say my heart's not in the right place..."

"Well, alcohol isn't going to put your heart where it needs to be."

Marco makes it a habit to meet Seneca in his quarters daily as time continues to trudge ever onward. His... persistence helps keep Seneca away from liquor but does little to curb Seneca's inner machinations... A grueling five months of briefing, training, and debriefing, the fleet is finally experiencing consistent progress.

In fact, as of late, the squadrons consistently exceed eighty percent payload delivery, while also ensuring that they reach the target within thirty seconds of the time requirement. Through nothing short of a shared determination by the fleet, it's been a miraculous transformation that demonstrates the true resolve of the Whispers. Nothing can change the reality in Seneca's mind, however. He knew the Empire had capital ships from the moment he left Vista, and Operation 1929 was supposed to subvert the need to combat them. After all, if the Imps couldn't afford to operate them, what use would they be—what a miscalculation... Seneca's seen *the Pantheon* and *Echelon* in action before—people will need to forgive his lack of overt optimism.

Even so, the steady advancement of the fleet in comparison to the projected completion time of the Empire's dark matter weapons poses a complex dilemma. Do they try to get even better? Would further training matter? Is the iron hot enough to strike? Per the usual deliberations, squabbles and disagreements are plentiful. Jesper asserts that time is running short, and that the fleet is ready; Seneca disagrees.

"We're seeing consistent results from our pilots, and with only three months left before the weapons go operational, we can't afford to wait any longer," Jesper urges, his voice carrying the weight of urgency as he addresses hesitant military leaders. "Furthermore, with our fleet tied up here, the Empire is starting to push the UF's smaller forces back."

"That won't matter if we jump the gun before the fleet is appropriately ready, Jesper." Seneca argues. "We cannot waste that time to assure that the fleet is as good as they're going to get."

By now, Seneca is all too accustomed to being on the opposite side of a decision as Jesper. Whether it's playing devil's advocate, or his more reserved nature, Jesper always finds a reason to oppose him. This time, Jesper's perceived impulsivity surprises Seneca, since Seneca is usually the more aggressive of the two.

"If we fail, there's still time to bounce—"

"No. If we fail, that's it. I thought you understood that?" Seneca interrupts.

The two stare at each other. Though neither utter a syllable, their gazes communicate everything. Jesper's been working for this moment for so long and he's ready to risk it to achieve the freedom he's been fighting for over nearly a decade. Seneca is holding back because he's not ready to lose. Marco's words and questions about trust penetrate Seneca's thoughts and persuade him enough to soften his poker face. Jesper doesn't disappoint.

"Seneca. I know what you're going through. I know what's at stake for you. You'll never be ready for what might happen, but it's time to face it. Let's do this..."

It's ironic. Not long ago, he drank himself silly, waiting for the war to end. Now that he sees the end, he's not ready. He's known for many things. To some, he's a ruthless killer. Others, he's a legendary hero. What he's not, is a gambler. Leaving life to chance has never been his forte. Following inverse advice from a song by Kenny Rodgers, you can't lose if you don't play. Now his hand is forced, and running isn't an option. Fate, whatever it may be, awaits him, whether he likes it or not, and Jesper's right, but admitting it to himself terrifies him.

"I know..." He replies. "Give us one more month to prepare... not necessarily to better the fleet, but for me to... try and find peace."

Jesper nods and departs without another word. Now alone, Seneca whispers to himself, "I used to be ready for fate, but now… I have something worth living for…"

The remaining month, as if to torment him, seems to pass faster than any other month in the war thus far. There's no noticeable improvement in the fleet's performance or Seneca's mindset. However, time stops for nobody, not even those who elude time's influence. All too soon, Seneca, along with the combined forces of the UF and Whispers, are aboard the Appomattox. It's a three-day trip from Pyre to Argi-Pecun, and Seneca's mind is far from at ease. It remains uncertain whether they will receive support from COS members upon their arrival, or the extent of support they can anticipate. There's no guarantee that the Whispers will perform to the necessary standard. Despite all the training and preparation—all the strides and achievements the Whispers have accomplished—nothing is certain. An inescapable fact remains: the fate of him and the Whispers hangs delicately on the outcome of the next three days.

Seneca is trying to maintain a sense of internal peace without succumbing to the temptation of reaching for a bottle. It's hard work. All he can do in his moments of weakness is trust… just as Marco has been urging him to do. Trust that the COS will come through unexpectedly. Trust that their forces will achieve the victory they've fought for. Trust himself enough… to keep himself alive on the battlefield. A ghost of himself is calling, and he wishes desperately to drown out its utterances with liquor. Circumstance, however, demands sobriety…

Chapter 43: Destiny Inbound

It's into the final day of the three-day trip and Seneca's forced sobriety has tortured his racing mind since they'd left Pyre. Thankfully, remaining sober on the final evening is not an endeavor he has to undertake alone. Jesper joins him in t*he Appomattox's* hangar as he sits in contemplation underneath *the Phantom.* There's a wide range of emotions plaguing Seneca, and unfortunately, he's not able to hide all of them at one time.

The hangar bay of *the Appomattox* is a vast expanse, so large that it could fit three football stadiums. It's appropriately filled to the brim with ships tightly arranged in diagonal formations. Some three stories above them, bright fluorescent lights illuminate the ceiling with a subtle buzz. Echoes of power generators, forklifts, and a constant hum of workers fill the air, accompanied by the distinct aroma of fuel and fumes of various fluids. A sense of haste and urgency surrounds everyone aboard the formidable craft, as the ship carries the Whispers through space.

Jesper's voice carries an optimistic tune, resonating with confidence as he speaks, "Almost done."

Seneca's voice, on the other hand, carries the weight of weariness. The weight of the last few years catching up to him, making everything feel like a whirlwind. His nerves are higher than they've ever been, and he freely shares the sentiment with Jesper, "Yeah. I don't think I've been this nervous about a battle since my first combat op over Tawian in 2025."

"How'd it go?" Jesper asks, curious about Seneca's past.

"Allot better than tomorrow is going to go…" Seneca says, frowning. "My wingman and I went in, took out three J-20's before they ever saw us."

There isn't a soul aboard who believes the battle will be easy. It's not a difficult assumption that most won't survive the ordeal. The weight of guilt pulls at him as he acknowledges that his motives in this battle are driven by self-interest, still, he holds great admiration for the brave individuals in this room who are prepared to lay down their lives in the pursuit of peace. Jesper nods, acknowledging the risky game they must play to ensure the Whispers' victory in the war.

"There's nothing I can say to ease whatever is racing through your mind, but you got us farther than Ilana and I could ever get on our own. It's not that we weren't smart enough to, but because Ilana had too much to lose," Jesper says.

"Well, I *do* have something to lose now." Seneca sighs. "That's what sucks the most…"

Jesper nods, "True, but. You're sparing Ilana from losing her life and her family because you know that pain. That's a genuine act of love if I've ever seen one."

Seneca stays silent as he internalizes the sentiment. Loss is a familiar experience for him, even though he strongly wishes to avoid it. For hundreds of years, he had roamed through space alone, living a life that felt incomplete… so incomplete he wished for an escape from it. Ilana somehow managed to revive not just his desire to form relationships and experience love once more, but also rediscovered his motivation to live for a greater purpose. Once he learned of Ilana's involvement in the rebellion, he faced two options: flee the situation, leaving the Empire to accuse Ilana of treason and persecute the royal family; or stand his ground, fighting for the reignited spark for life he'd found, regardless of the potential consequences.

Seneca continues silent contemplation for a moment more before he says, "Love… love got me in this mess."

Jesper shoves Seneca in a brotherly manner. "Yeah, it does that to people."

Jesper stays by him and chats until mandatory rest goes into effect. Their arrival impending and the fleet needs adequate rest for what the day ahead will bring. Seneca bids an unusually sentimental goodnight to his friend. Climbing up the boarding ladder of the Phantom, the stark reality that this could be their final conversation weighs heavily upon his shoulders. Quiet descends upon him as the access door shuts beneath him and he ventures to the crew suite to try to rest. Strangely, for the first time in weeks, he finds himself in an unexpectant calm. He takes a moment to consume an adequate meal and hydrate appropriately before settling in his bed. It doesn't take long before he's lulled to sleep, where a vivid dream greets him.

It's a typical summer afternoon at his camp. The summer sun bathes him in its warm glow as he and Ilana rock side by side, accompanied by the soothing scent of a passing rain shower and the nostalgic fragrance of white pine trees. Songbirds turn the hillside into an amphitheater as a lumbering cumulonimbus cloud obscures the sun with virga. It's a serene image from his subconscious that he longs for desperately.

He hears Ilana speak. Her characteristic bubbly voice interrupts the serenade of the birds as she says, "You're nervous, Seneca."

He turns and immediately his attention is drawn to her, his eyes fixed on her blue hair tied up in a ponytail, with the wind playfully flinging strands of it about. Her face, now confined only to his memory, is as beautiful as ever.

A sadness lingers in his speech, betraying his anxiety. "Yes. This war is ending tomorrow. I'm afraid of losing the war because that means losing you… not only that, for the first time I—I'm afraid of…"

Ilana looks at him brandishing a curious expression. Even through the veil of a dream, Seneca can feel the magnitude of Ilana's lasting impact on him. He'd not known this uniquely mortal, primitive, basic instinct for some time. In fact, not long before Ilana, he considered it in a much different way. He'd successfully avoided opening up to Marco, but Ilana's his safe listening ear.

"What else?" Ilana asks while gently stroking his hand.
"Dying…" Seneca says nervously.
She grabs his face, stroking his cheek gently with her thumb. "Sen, listen to me. We have an eternity ahead—you have eternity ahead. Regardless of how this turns out, our hearts will find their ways home."
Seneca chokes down the urge to cry. "How do you know?"
"Because you're ready to live again." Ilana smiles.

With a sound that resembled both laughter and crying, he nods and flashes a smile. The way his eyes light up when he sees her reveals the deep affection and peace she brings into his life. Together, within his dream, they sit hand in hand, enjoying the serenity of the Carolina summer. The sound of thunder echoes in the distance, finding its way closer to them. Its approaching thunder soon takes on a disconcerting quality, with rumbling beginning to resemble the echoing buzz of alarms. The surrounding dream begins slowly dissolving as he tries to relish every moment. He breathes anxiously as he tries to study the fading image of her face.

"Go Seneca. It'll be okay." She smiles as reality begins to materialize and distort the surrounding dream.
"I'm coming home Ilana. I promise." he says just as his eyes open to see the ceiling of *the Phantom*.

It's a rude awakening to a peaceful rest. Announcements blare over the speaker, informing everyone that *the Appomattox* is a mere two hours from dropping into Argi-Pecun. The Heros, who are currently deep within Imperial territory, will arrive without giving the Empire much warning. However, their presence has already activated ID sensors somewhere within Imperial space, so the Imperial forces won't be in a state of total surprise.

Seneca readies himself, zipping up his flight suit jacket and clambering down the ladder to find a tumultuous hangar outside his ship. Fellow pilots are bustling with activity, urgently moving to finish checklists and make preflight preparations. He turns his head to the left and right, observing The Nineteen give him casual greetings. Caiman and Payson gather the group, including Seneca, for a preflight ritual that they had started during their time in the Imperial Space Fleet. Locking arms, they form a rowdy huddle and throw Seneca into the middle. Wearing a bittersweet smile, he addresses them.

"Gentleman," He says with a wholesome attitude, "I could not be more privileged to be flying with you all one last time. I won't lie. This mission is by far the most dangerous mission you've ever faced. I know you all have a perfect record going. Do your best to keep that record going. I'll meet you all back here when we've finished this."

The others eagerly rush into the center of the group, shouting words of encouragement and raising their voices, creating a cacophony of excitement that echoes through the air, excitement that draws pilots from all over the hangar to the scene. Cheers erupt and the looming promise of freedom hangs in the words of others who take part before finally Clemson finds himself addressing the crowd.

It's a peculiar sight to see him in his crimson trench coat standing front and center of their huddle as he says, "Aye gents. I know many a person here ain't too bothered to get to know a pirate like me or my crew. After all, we aren't the most... friendly of folks to get along with. I'd be colored a liar to say I wasn' in this bit for the money, but gents, you ought to recognize the leader you have, and after this bout with the Imps is through, I'm drinking to Seneca!"

Just then the hangar erupts into riotous cheering that vibrates his chest, reminiscent of the roar of a crowd at an Atlanta Falcons playoff game (particularly the game just before their pitiful loss in the super bowl). Clemson grabs him and yanks him back to the center as the crowd chants his name in unison. With a wide smile, Seneca savors the feeling of hope as he realizes he has become an inspiration to hundreds of brave souls. He cannot describe the feeling with words, nor does he understand the shift in his psyche. Maybe it was the dream he had the night prior, or maybe it's the inspiring sight of so many brave souls ready to die for the freedom of future generations. Whatever the intoxicating feeling it is, it's not alcohol, and he's in high spirits as the crowd is interrupted by an announcement "One hour until drop".

Despite the hopeful atmosphere, there is still a perilous battle yet to be fought. As such, everyone returns to continue readying themselves for the engagement. Soon Seneca nestles himself in the forward pilot seat of his ship as he starts awakening the engines, vibrating the hangar floor and creating hazardous levels of noise should anyone still be outside their ship without ear protection. With the radios on and combat systems engaged, Seneca's hands clasp the controls, the familiar textures stimulating nerves in his fingertips. In a quiet whisper, he mutters a prayer.

"Attention on deck. Attention on deck. Dropping in five. Finish all preparations. Pilots make ready for drop. Doors opening in five." echoes across *the Appomattox's* hangar and the radios. Seneca synchronizes his clock and watches the time count down...Seconds into minutes... until he feels his weight shift from the humongous vessel dropping from warp and the hangar doors open quickly.

* * *

The Whispers synchronously file out in carefully rehearsed formations to stand against the enemy in one last engagement. No longer a whisper, the rebels are an anthem playing loudly for the entire galaxy to hear, ready for freedom.

Chapter 44: The Clock Runs Out

Seneca stands at the forefront, leading the charge as Clemson, The Nineteen, and the other elite join in formation with *the Phantom. The Pantheon* and *Echelon*, with their imposing presence, loom before them, prepared to quash the rebellion once and for all. Just as he's done many combat missions before, he cracks his knuckles and takes in a deep breath, focusing on the sensation of his feet on the yaw pedals and hands on the controls. Seneca's nerves fade away entirely, for this is his moment of destiny. It is time for him to remind the galaxy of what it truly means to be an "Apex Pilot." The attacking rebels edge closer, thirty seconds away from the reach of the Empire's lethal weaponry and defensive batteries. A swarm of Imperial fighters hurtles towards them, intent on interception.

Undeterred, Seneca coerces the throttle forward giving the final attack command, "Whispers, three minutes' time on target. First wave inbound. Continue attack."

An intense exchange of flak, fire, and pulses of energy rains upon them as the gap between the bombers and their destination gradually decreases. The Whisper's fighters, determined to ensure success of the bombers' mission, find themselves in a heated engagement with the hoard of Imperial fighter craft. The shields of enemies and allies alike burst with flashes of lightning, their surfaces shimmering as lasers and bullets perturbing them. Ships move around the void in chaotic flight paths, giving chase to one another.

Through the course of the dare-and-do around him, Seneca's unparalleled determination keeps him focused as he skillfully maneuvers *the Phantom*, firing his weapons with little prejudice, swiftly eliminating any opposition that stands in his path. Like a specter bound only by physical limitations, he maneuvers his ship with an eerie grace.

Two minutes. With unwavering determination, they're holding formation against the relentless assault of Imperial fighters. Each bullet aimed at the bombers feels like a personal blow, driving Seneca and his fellow defenders to retaliate with even greater fervor. No matter his efforts, the grim reality of inevitable losses exists. There are those he can't save, and occasional explosions signal the loss of a comrade. Those losses are small, but heavy steps away from victory. Therefore, Seneca exacts a toll on the Empire's forces, ensuring that for every fallen comrade, the enemy pays a double price at minimum. Anything less would be an injustice to the memory of their efforts.

One minute. They fight for each meter forward; *the Echelon* grows, transforming into a sprawling horizon in *the Phantom's* canopy. The ships lumber about through space, maneuvering to keep their noses taking the bulk of fire from the Whispers, lest they catch fire from the Heros whose rail cannons would threaten their center shields. Nuclear fireballs from their munitions send powerful shockwaves that visibly ripple across the shields of *the Echelon* and *the Pantheon*. Lighting as long as a mile bursts from each impact to display the resolve of the Whispers.

The Empire's PACs swiftly respond in kind, targeting the Whispers' destroyers with deadly precision, obliterating them and sentencing all aboard to a desolate grave in the void. Whenever they discharge a round, it is only a small fraction of the tremendous power they possess, as the energetic spheres swiftly launch out of the cannons in the blink of an eye. It's a bullet they knew they'd have to bite, but it doesn't ease the mounting pressure upon the fleet to disable shields and destroy the PACs.

Their initial wave successfully reaches their designated targets with impeccable timing. Executing the predetermined strategy to perfection, they bombard the capital ships with their illicit weaponry, that bypasses the shields of their target and contacting the shield generators. The first wave of bombers redirects their energy, engaging with Imperial destroyers to draw fire away from the next wave of bombers. The employment of jumpers catches the Imps by surprise as the Imperial commander radios Seneca. "Seneca Mason, leave it to you to fight like an outlaw. You will be held accountable for this egregious war crime!"

Seneca gives a single swift reply as he maneuvers. "Sure. Just don't pretend that you aren't currently manufacturing dark matter warheads on your ship."

There is no additional communication with the Imperial commander, either due to shock that the Whispers know of their dirty secret or because they simply disregard their presence as one would disregard a gnat. Regardless, Seneca and his squadron promptly reverse course to accompany the second wave. To ensure the squadron's overall health, he initiates a headcount as they fly back. While his squadron remains in good health and has ample resources for the next pass, the other squadron leaders are experiencing mixed results. Due to the heavy losses suffered by escort squadron bravo during their first run, Seneca orders Clemson to take a quarter of the prime squadron and aid Squadron B.

Seneca meticulously resets his timer between maneuvers, each tick marking another crucial moment in the battle. Once more the timer ticks for three minutes time-on-target as he fearlessly leads the charge again, skillfully navigating through a swarm of adversaries, obliterating them with precision as they unwittingly challenge him. This wave will deliver the final blow to the shields of the capital ships. Nothing less than eighty percent of the payload will result in success.

Two minutes once more, Seneca hasn't experienced combat of this magnitude in years. Strain is setting in from the toll this battle demands of him. Wrist muscles cramp. His arms ache from the constantly moving the stick performing complex maneuvers, some requiring him to toggle his inertial dampeners to maintain crisp rolls and turns. Sweat in his palms challenges his grip on the controls. Clenched teeth cause his jaw muscles to grow sore, and his fingers are numb from the constant squeezing of the trigger on his guns and lasers. Nonetheless, his focus is unwavering. Fiercely protecting his allies, he jolts the nose about from bandit to bandit and systematically dispatches threats.

With one minute time-on-target remaining, the sheer quantity of sustained fire is already depleting his shield and boost resources. It's a disheartening reality knowing the battle rages on, and they aren't even at the halfway point—he will eventually have to fly through this maelstrom of bullets, lasers, and missiles protected only by the ship's armor. Meanwhile, the Echelon and Pantheon's immense firepower bears down on their forces, threatening to finish off the remaining destroyers before the Whispers have had the chance to respond.

They will have their turn in due time. With no major setbacks or significant casualties, Seneca and his squadron successfully shepherded the second wave of bombers to their intended destination. He pitches up and climbs away from the Echelon beneath him as the second wave unleashes their payload of jumpers aimed at the Echelon's shield generator, their coordinated assault finally destroying their target. With both the Echelon and Pantheon's shields collapsing in unison, the radios erupt into a triumphant uproar, as warheads contacting the Imperial capital vessels produce physical damage—at least the ones that can hit the sides.

Seneca wants to smile; he wants to believe victory is in reach. However, he contains his emotions, knowing that the last critical step is yet to occur. Victory is tangible, but not yet within their grasp. With each passing second, the war is nearing its end, resembling the dispersion of metal into the cosmos by the force of weapon fire, as Seneca once again addresses the Whispers. "Escorts reverse course. Let's make sure the drop ships make it. Everyone else, keep the destroyers engaged and strafe the defensive turrets on the capital ships."

Others swiftly follow his command. The escorts, still healthy and able to press on, shadow Seneca's lead to ensure the dropships make it to the hangar to safely deploy the foot soldiers. The proverbial steam is wearing off as they pass the six-minute mark in this relentless endurance test against the Empire. Though the capital ships' shields are down, the PACs continue to fire. Taking stock of their dwindling resources, an inventory of the fleet reveals the Whispers are down to a dozen destroyers. However, with the shields of the capital ships compromised, the Whispers' Hercs can outmaneuver the two capital ships and fire upon their exposed sides.

* * *

Seneca and his squadron arrive at the back of the battlefield to provide an escort for the dropships, and Seneca resets his timer for the final time. Three minutes once more begin ticking as they embark on the final escort, ready to engage the enemy until one side yields. Two minutes... One minute... They near the mid-ship hangar of the Echelon, as Seneca races ahead to unleash his gatling guns and blow open the hangars. Undeterred by a dwindling supply of ammunition, he persists in his journey, refusing to halt amidst the unrelenting onslaught. He continues to defend the dropships until they successfully board the ship. Now it's the deadliest waiting game in human history. Pilots on both ends of the altercation are dying with the slow passage of time. Per the plan, Seneca needs to buy more time for the fleet as he races toward the Pantheon's left-most PAC. On cue, his compatriots, still Nineteen strong, follow suit.

"Seneca and Nineteen beginning attack run on PACs," Seneca announces over the radio.

Seneca's breathing takes on a nervous rhythm. The foot soldiers, the determining factor, need to perform as admirably as the pilots are. Every extra minute they take is more death and lowers their odds of victory—especially since there is no sign of the COS.

Jesper replies quickly betraying the stress in his voice, "Good, we're running low on destroyers! Also, think there's any chance of the COS showing up at this point?"

Seneca frowns. "We can only hope..."

The battle rages on as Seneca and the Nineteen press onward towards the first PAC of *the Pantheon*. They make their way towards the PAC, negotiating their way through a flock of enemies and defending one another. A noise captures Seneca's attention. *The Phantom*'s AI is informing him of a malfunction with his gatling guns. A glance to the left and right—red glowing from the barrels of his guns (or at least what is left of them). Throughout the duration of the battle, the guns were firing without respite, which ultimately led to the barrels of the weapons melting from heat. The frustration of this new handicap causes him to set loose a weary sigh.

He mutters to himself. "I was nearly out of ammunition, anyway."

As of now, he contemplates the possibility of checking in with Jesper, who, much like a conductor skillfully guiding an orchestra, directs the battle from the secure location of *the Appomattox*. However, he ultimately refrains, any bad news right now will not help him. He centers his efforts on his significant role within the battle, expertly firing two PDDs into the core of the initial PAC.

The PAC erupts in a shower of green plasma and shattering metal fragments, eliciting triumphant cheers over the radio, urging Seneca and The Nineteen to press on. However, Jesper's voice cuts through the cheering, delivering an unwelcome update. While Seneca is making progress, the same cannot be said for the rest of the Whispers involved in the battle. While both the Empire and Whisper are strained, the Imperial's strength in numbers is pushing the Whispers back to a respectable radius around the Hercs. Once these PACs are down, it's a long way to travel in order to regroup with the fleet.

By this point in the battle, most Whisper ships in the fleet are probably operating without shields, and the Hercs are running low on rail cannon warheads. Time is running out, and exhaustion is gripping them. Seneca polices his thoughts. Even pretending if he needs to… Any minute now, the bellies of the massive ships will explode, and they'll have their victory. He must keep going.

 Accompanied by his Nineteen defenders, Seneca eliminates *the Pantheon*'s second PAC using missiles, before setting his sights upon *the Echelon's* leftmost PAC. Working together as a cohesive team, they pave the way for Seneca to launch his missiles at the dangerous weapon, successfully eliminating the third of the four PACs in another shower of green sparks and burning metal.

Their timing is now crucial as they close in on the final PAC. Once they began attacking the PACs, the Imps began charging them for a full power charge to take out the Hercs. Seneca briefly regrets not dividing and conquering, but it's taken all of them flying as a team through the hive of Imperial fighters to get to the first three. The speed bump imposed by their disadvantage in numbers has given *the Echelon* time to charge its right-hand PAC, targeting *the McHenry*.

Their approach angle puts them at an additional complication. Nothing less than a direct shot down the barrel will destroy the PAC in one hit, but a significant force of defenders stands in their way and they're approaching from directly from the side. The Nineteen try to keep a clear path for him as Seneca accelerates seems to achieve a favorable firing position. However, the distance is still considerable, and firing too soon risks the missiles being intercepted by countermeasures. However, delaying the shot could mean disaster for *the McHenry*, with four hundred lives at stake. It's a difficult choice.

Seconds tick down. Glowing green light inside the PAC indicates it's almost fully charged. Tension is mounting, and he needs to decide. He's still five hundred meters away, but Seneca takes a shot. His missiles lock on and streak towards the barrel of the PAC, racing against the clock. The missile sails through the void and he watches it in anticipation, but his heart sinks as an Imperial fighter positions his own ship in front of the missiles, sacrificing himself. The pilot's action trades his life to allow the weapon to fire. Seneca's heartbeat pounds in his throat. The green radiation of light within the PAC ceases, and *the McHenry* is practically vaporized in his peripheral vision. Nothing remains—not a trace of metal, debris, or anything else, except for an intensely bright flash of green light that engulfs the entire battlefield for a moment.

A devastating incident resulting in the sudden disappearance of four hundred lives and one of their weapons in this fight. Filled with an overwhelming surge of rage, Seneca bursts into a fierce outpour of curses directed towards the Imperials. With nobody else to intercept another attack, his next missiles find their mark, eradicating the threat of the PACs from the battlefield.

* * *

Facing no alternative, he confronts the agonizing sting of failure and perseveres. He and his wingmen resume formation and start the arduous battle back to the fleet. They're far from the rest of the Whispers and they face overwhelming resistance trying to regroup with the rest of the fleet. Every kilometer is a struggle and to his misfortune, *the Phantom's* lasers also falter under the strain of continuous use.

"Damn it" He swears.

He's practically a sitting duck—or at least he will be in a few moments. His shield charges are depleted, so he can no longer maintain the shield's integrity and must evade incoming fire. The task proves to be an impossibility due to the sheer quantity of incoming munitions. Furthermore, with both guns and lasers crippled, he must reserve his final two missiles for a last stand. He has no offensive options, and his defenses are waning. The Nineteen rally around him, defending to their utmost ability.

Meanwhile, communication among the fleet grows more frantic by the moment. He doesn't know how long ago the foot soldiers began their task of fighting through the capital ships, but it feels like forever and the straits are becoming dire. Kilometer at a time, the Nineteen fight off Imperials who are eager to cash in on Seneca's bounty. Watching them, the way they trust each other and fly synchronously with deadly precision, fills Seneca with pride. At this point, they possess faster ships than he, and could easily abandon him. However, they're determined to keep their promise and maintain their perfect record—which includes Seneca.

Yet fate has other designs. Suddenly, one of the brave young men by his side becomes the first casualty in their years of service together. His companion's ship erupts into a fiery explosion. In his eyes, the mess of shrapnel and intermingling red and orange hues illuminates the toll the day exacts upon him. Before he can react, another of his juniors falls, and then another. Three of their own, one after the other, killed in a matter of minutes.

Amidst angry tears, Seneca's voice reverberates over the radio, cursing the Empire with every insult he knows. It's a rare moment of vulnerability for him brought about as another three more of his companions succumb to lethal fire in his defense.

Aware of the consequences of his dwindling shields, Seneca begins intercepting incoming fire directed at the remaining thirteen of his young allies to shield them. He's unwilling to let another of them die in his stead. "Go! Now! I'll cover for you. They're after me, not you!" He commands them over the radio and fires one of his remaining two missiles at a nearby fighter.

The remaining members of the Nineteen aggressively argue, asserting their acceptance of the risk. Caimen's voice echoes in Seneca's ear. "No, Seneca—"

Seneca interrupts them with a commanding order, his voice firm. "It's a fucking order. Fall back and get your asses home! You have families!"

They respond once again with vehement resistance. "Seneca, you'll be a sitting duck! We aren't leaving you!" Payson's voice rings out, mirroring the turmoil of their collective loss.

Seneca stands by his order. "It's not negotiable. That's an order! Caimen, Payson, get the group back to the Appomattox."

Reluctantly, they finally comply, disengaging from the enemy and accelerating as a group toward *the Appomattox* as Seneca continues to maneuver and draw enemy fire. With no word from the foot soldiers and his shields failing rapidly, he recognizes the dire situation. This moment may very well be more than the end of the war... It's his life for theirs. It's a difficult reality, but he takes a deep breath and hopes Ilana will understand his sacrifice.

"I guess this is it..." he says to himself. The shields that had spent decades protecting him falter quickly, followed by the sound of his armor deflecting fire. Horrific sounds like hail on a metal roof reverberate across his ship from the bullets pelting it. With choked words, he utters a final sentiment, "Ilana... I love you. Thank you for showing me love once more... Kelsea, Sophie, Oliver, everyone... I'm finally coming home."

Chapter 45: The Cost of Victory

The relentless hail of fire shows no signs of stopping as it continues to pound on *the Phantom*. Seneca relinquishes his grip on the controls and extends his arms in surrender. He's ready for his fate. Cracks slowly spread across his canopy, he clenches his eyes shut, silently pleading for a painless death and a compassionate judgement. He's terrified, but he finds a semblance of peace, knowing his last moments were an act of courage that saved the lives of his companions. Mentally prepared to accept his destiny, an unexpected silence replaces the barrage of bullets hitting his armor. Confused, his eyes squint open to see he's surrounded by a wave of fresh forces entering the battlefield—beautiful dark yellow stingray shaped COS fighters fly by his side. In the final moments of the fight, a COS fleet has finally to their aid.

The radio bursts with excited cheers as the reinforcements arrive unexpectedly. Amidst all the radio noise, a familiar voice cuts through and says, "I'm sorry, Seneca, our fighters are slow at warp."

Seneca lets out a chuckle that could be interpreted as a mix of relief and sadness before he says, "You can call it whatever you want, commander Claxton! Better late than never."

A contingent of COS' forces lead by Claxton Evahns undertake the mission of escorting Seneca to the safety of *the Appomattox* and take pressure off the weakening Whisper fleet; their stingray shaped fighters and cruisers driving the tired Imperial forces back. Relief overcomes him, driving him to shed happy tears. There may have been a time where he would have welcomed death with open arms, but now... he's happy to have narrowly missed it. All those moments in life he'd missed with his late family members, he may yet have the chance to live with Ilana. The balance of the fight is back in their favor and the COS's arrival adds critical time back into the coffer.

The safety of *the Appomattox* gradually comes within his reach. He guides his war-torn chariot to a landing within its hangar. Crackling fire fills the air with smoke and noxious fumes as the ship's exposed entrails leak fluids that combust as oxygen reacts with them. Losing no time, he disconnects his seat harness and exits his ship hurriedly, overwhelmed by a profound sense of gratitude for his own safety. Yet, his attention remains resolutely fixed on the fierce battle that rages outside.

He leaves the hangar behind, rushing through the slender corridors and sprawling hallways of the massive ship, traversing a multitude of elevators until he finally arrives at the bridge. There, he finds Jesper and the leaders fully engrossed in guiding the battle, expressing gratitude for the reinforcements. As soon as Seneca sees him entering the bridge, Jesper quickly rushes towards him, joyfully throwing his arms over his shoulders, expressing his happiness without uttering a word.

Jesper releases the brotherly embrace. "Thought you were a goner man." He says shoving Seneca back by the shoulder.
    Seneca gives a taxed chuckle in reply, "So did I…"

Seneca wastes no time in assuming the familiar mantle of leadership, deftly choreographing the pilots and orchestrating the return of the Whispers' fleet to the safety of the remaining Heros, while also carefully selecting targets, including the platinum mine, for the COS combatants who have joined the fray. At the same time, Jesper devotes himself entirely to the task of communication, diligently to ensuring foot soldiers remain coordinated—a vital element in hastening the resolution of the battle.

In lulls between communication, Jesper updates him on the source of delay. Evidently, upon reaching the weapons manufactories on both vessels, the foot soldiers encountered sealed blast doors. While the obstacle was not unforeseen, their laser cutting equipment had malfunctioned because of damage they had sustained in combat—Imperial soldiers had deliberately peppered it with plasma rounds. They have since fought their way to the power stations, disabled the security power grids, and successfully opened the doors. They now only need to sprint back to the manufactories to plant the charges. This relieving fact, along with the reinforcements from the COS, ensures victory is within their reach.

Time seems to crawl at a glacial pace, with fifteen more tense minutes passing by like refrigerated molasses dripping from a cold glass, but victory is on its way still. It's surprising that, even in the face of impending defeat, the Empire remains steadfast in its determination to hold on to their power over the Whispers. The next moments are critical to drive the nail home and release the rebellion from Imperial grasp forever. Seneca issues commands for the COS to attack the platinum mine that *the Pantheon* and *Echelon* can no longer adequately protect. The COS forces comply and make quick work of it, tearing through the weakened Imperial defenses and bombarding the mine. No sooner does Jesper report the foot soldiers have planted the charges—the war is five minutes from being over.

Claxton's voice reports via radio communication, "Seneca, this is Claxton, Platinum mine destroyed."

"Outstanding." Seneca jumps excitedly, "maintain defensive formation outside the capital ships hangars. The foot soldiers should come out within the next five minutes."

The COS commander complies with the directive as Seneca watches the battle from *the Appomattox*. COS fighters chase weary Imperials around like a border collie herding sheep, keeping them from condemning the onboard foot soldiers to the fate of the capital ships once the charges explode.

Jesper gently pats Seneca on the shoulder, whose face mirrors emotion of a prosecuted man being proved innocent. Once those charges detonate, the nightmare of uncertainty is over. Jesper too is oozing joyful tears from his eyes as he and Seneca stand side by side in the bridge. It's a humbling moment for Seneca, knowing the weight this outstanding accomplishment carries for Jesper.

No less than five minutes later, the whispers receive confirmation that the Empire had finally witnessed their voice. In a matter of minutes, *the Pantheon* and *Echelon*, within mere seconds of each other, undergo catastrophic transformations into blinding balls of searing flames and blinding light. Concluding the spectacle, the two structures collapse inward, unleashing the captive dark matter and enabling it to return once again to the liminal spaces it was pulled from. The battle is theirs and the Empire has no foot left to stand upon.

Cheers and chants fill the bridge, radio, and atmosphere across the Whispers fleet as everyone comes alive at the mere sight of the massive capital ships imploding. While filled with joy, Seneca remains cautious and refrains from celebrating until an Imperial surrender is confirmed.

It isn't a long before the Imperial commander initiates a video call; the screen flickering to life with a request for parlay to discuss formal military surrender. Seneca issues the stand-down order and for the first time, the demands issued by the Whispers of freedom do not fall upon the deaf ears of the Empire. In fact, the entire galaxy is here to bear witness to the human spirit and its desire for freedom. Seneca quickly returns to the hangar, searching for a suitable mode of transport to approach the Imperial commander and accept the Imperial surrender. Since *the Phantom* is still undergoing fire suppression treatments, he decides to travel across the field in a shuttle accompanied by a security detail.

The Imperial command center, located amidst the ruins of the battle-damaged platinum refinery, is a towering cyan spire that towers seventeen stories above the metallic asteroid it sits upon. Seneca and his entourage land in a small hangar at the tower's base and make their way inside. They're escorted up the elevator from the hangar into the command room, where dozens of the Empire's finest tacticians sit embarrassed and terrified of the events that await them back in Vista palace. Out of embarrassment, the general issuing the surrender has removed his rank and name tapes from his otherwise well decorated uniform.

Seneca opts to break his typical character. When he would taunt the defeated, he takes on a face of humility; he knows the men and women before him may very well face a death penalty if the Empire continues its recent history of vengeful retaliation. Their grave countenances hint at an impending doom, a prospect he sincerely hopes does not await them now that the war is over. He's helped the Whispers earn the future that Ilana foresaw for them, and further bloodshed is not on his agenda. In fact, he may never fly combat again after the ordeal he'd just survived.

Following a silent acceptance of the commander's saber by Seneca, marking a formal and complete unconditional military surrender, he surprises everyone in the room by addressing them with an uncharacteristic level of tact and empathy emulating Ilana.

"I know the lords. I've seen their wrath and the corrupt nature of their ways. I will offer you all and the remainder of your fleet safe passage and asylum in Fortuna. I understand this is a difficult decision for you. Please take your time." He says.

Seneca holsters the saber in his belt and makes his way back to the hangar with the security detail where they wait by the shuttle. Intending to seek asylum, the Imperial officers direct their remaining ships to dock within empty hangars on *the Normandy* and *Appomattox* before boarding the shuttle with Seneca. While there is an initial wave of backlash for the Seneca's compassionate act, the individuals on board the ships continue with their celebration once the Imperial officers disappear.

The Appomattox and *Normandy* set courses for Pyre and soon lurch into warp. The dust is settling, and the emotional toll is bearing down on Seneca as he walks with heavy steps across the hangar floor looking for the surviving members of The Nineteen. While searching for his comrades, he can't help but feel disheartened by what he observes. Out of all the ships that departed from this hangar to fight this final battle for freedom, only about half of them returned to a safe landing. He doesn't look forward to the eventual results, but Seneca messages Jesper, requesting him to perform the grave task of conducting a final inventory to assess the number of casualties within the fleet.

The sight of battle-scarred ships mirrored the devastation of *the Phantom*, as the exposed viscera of spacecraft spilled out from their armored hulls. Pungent odors of burning metal, electrical fires, and leaking fluids made it unbearable to breathe, prompting him to tuck his nose in his jacket. He continues walking the grounds, his footsteps heavy with solemn contemplation, until he finally finds Payson, Caimen, and the other surviving members of The Nineteen, their faces etched with grief.

Seneca's bond with the group is special among his fellow men and women of the rebellion, and a brotherhood he'd not formed with others since his days in the Air Force. The loss of six of his young brothers in arms in a single sitting takes a heavy toll, and he openly expresses his sentiment as he sits among them as equals, and collectively mourning the loss of their brothers. As they reminisce about their shared moments on and off the battlefield, they try to hide their emotions from each other, and tears silently trickle down their cheeks. Seneca shoulders hefty guilt for their losses since, had he not been on that field, they wouldn't have died in his defense. He thanks them earnestly for saving his life, hoping and praying that he was deserving of their sacrifice.

As he sits there helping the young men cope with their strife, Jesper finds him once more urgency in his winded speech, "Hey, uh, Seneca. I'm doing the inventory that you requested. Clemson is... you better come quick."

Seneca runs to find the Clemson laid out in front of *the Rot*. Clemson and his crew were attempting to retreat to *the Appomattox* and *Normandy* when the COS forces arrived, but a missile breached the canopy of *the Rot*, causing an explosive loss of cabin pressurization in his ship. Judging by Clemson's dire condition, his suit didn't deploy the life support mask quick enough. His face is purple, eyes swollen shut and blood coming out of every orifice. His breathing is labored, and he can't move... He's barely holding on, his life teetering on the edge as paramedics fight desperately to keep him from slipping away.

"Oi' Seneca," he sputters, blood flying from his mouth, "You swim with sharks long enough, one's bound to bite you."

"Save your strength, Clemson," he replies to his ally. "You ain't done here, not yet. Just hang on."

Clemson winces with pain. His lungs are bruised and bleeding profusely from the vacuum of space violently pulling his breath from his chest. He struggles to force another breath in. "Aye Seneca, I am done. I lived a true pirate's life—glorious and free." He pauses to cough some more. His tone remains as jolly as ever but strains in his suffering throat. "Oh, I lived Seneca and what a life it was. I just ask that I get a proper send off from the rest of the Revenge. Do me this favor, would you friend?"

Seneca once more finds the weight of his loss stabbing through him like a knife. "Come on Clemson. Who's going to fly with me to pillage and steal from these guys once these rebels organize into a real government?"

Clemson grips his chest in one hand and places his other hand on Seneca's shoulder. The image of his dying expression sears into his mind as the pirate lets out his familiar chuckle one last time before exhaling a final breath. Seneca finds himself immersed in a scene that is filled with an excessive amount of grief and death, making it increasingly difficult for him to cope.

"You know Jesper," he says, pounding his fist on the ground. "I've fought the Imps a thousand times... but I never stick around for this part. Usually, it's celebration and drinks. This..." Tears interrupt him, prompting him to wipe his face. "This... this is hell... I let myself get close to Ilana and suddenly I find myself getting close to everyone. Serena... you... the boys... Clemson." he pauses to sob a little, "I'm going to live forever... What do I do when everyone is gone?"

Jesper leans down. "Use your life, hard as it may be, as a gift to give to others, just as you did for Ilana and the Whispers. Millions, no—billions of people and their children will owe their freedoms to your actions. Find peace in knowing how your actions improve the lives of others."

Comforting words from a friend do little to raise his spirits…

Chapter 46: Memorializing the Departed

The hangar's heavy atmosphere is a grave contrast to what it had been before the battle occurred. Seneca mourns fallen comrades among hundreds of other brave souls who lived to carry on the memories of the fallen. The space soon falls silent as the victorious remaining souls aboard trickle back to their respective quarters, weariness from their hard-earned victory overshadowing any desire to celebrate. Jesper helps Seneca to his feet and follows suit, each confining themselves to their staterooms. Finally, alone in a solitary space, Seneca lets go of his pride and releases his anguish. The events of the battle replay in his mind as he cries. The harrowing image of his comrades falling intensifies his emotional turmoil, ebbing and flowing beyond the battle and conjuring countless other memories of the deathbed goodbyes he'd witnessed across his lifetime.

Crying eventually lulls him to sleep, still in his uniform. Once again, a vivid dream takes shape in his mind, becoming a lucid reality. He scans his surroundings in the dream and finds himself in some sort of funeral home. Inside the humble chapel, the aged wooden shiplap walls adorned with stained glass windows bear biblical scripture on plaques. Rows of neatly polished pews all face a pulpit that stands to the left of a silver casket adorned with colorful tropical flowers and wreaths that bid the departed heavenly rest in the care of a higher power. His memory serves him well, and he quickly realizes that this was the location in Pickens, South Carolina, where he'd held Sophie and Oliver's joint funeral. A somber atmosphere lingers in the air as he takes a seat in the front row.

He sits silently alone for several moments before Ilana suddenly rests her hand gently on his shoulder. He turns to see her, and like himself, she's adorned in respectful funeral attire. "You've lost a lot today. I know grief is never kind to you." She says, wiping tears from his eyes.

He nods. "I don't miss feeling this way and all I want is to run from this feeling. This is my hell and what's worse, I still don't even know if I'll ever see you..."

She places her finger on his lips, silencing him. "Shhh. Patience Seneca. There's still work to be done, and it starts here. These feelings are natural, don't run from them. Don't reject them. Be strong for me, but also be strong for yourself."

Seneca shakes his head, struggling to hold back tears, "It hurts…"

Ilana's voice carries the same kindness and empathy that it does in real life as she says, "I know Sen… It always hurts to dress a wound, but it can't heal unless you do."

She's right, but that doesn't make it any easier. He'd fought this war to avoid the pain of losing Ilana, but he never anticipated the way he'd grown close to others. In his dream, tears cascade down his face as he buries his face in his hands and tries to find comfort in Ilana's loving embrace. His sobbing persists for what feels like hours before the dream shifts and changes, their surroundings morphing seamlessly as the dream reality begins to subside into the real world. Sounds of persistent knocking finally dispel the dream, pulling him back to consciousness.

Seneca wipes crust from his eyes as he focuses on the familiar voice outside his door speaking to him. "Seneca, it's Jesper. Are you okay in there?"

Seneca stretches and rises from the soft, white sheets of his bed, struggling with a sense of disorientation. There is no recollection of the act of lying down or the room's appearance prior to his grief-induced slumber. The room is of generous size. Being one of the captain's suites on *the Appomattox*, the room offers ample space for relaxation and privacy while boasting typical furnishings. Through the window, the ringed structure of Pyre colony rests in the distance as *the Appomattox* makes a slow approach.

He opens the door for Jesper, momentarily flooding the room with light that temporarily blinds him, eliciting a sigh of relief from Jesper. "Hey man, it's time for us to go. There's a lot of Pyre's citizens eager to see you."

Seneca groans, "Pyre was a three-day trip. Did I really sleep the whole time?"

"Sure did." Jesper chuckles.

Seneca and Jesper exchange a few more words before Seneca politely takes his leave, expressing his intention to freshen up. The repugnant combination of sweat and burned metal still clings to him like a child glued to their mother's leg, a displeasing scent he's eager to eradicate. Once he has taken the necessary steps to groom himself and be presentable, he joins Jesper in the hall to disembark from *the Appomattox*, which is currently preparing to return to the UF after the occupants are offloaded.

A tender shuttle transports occupants while flatbed spacecraft haul disheveled spacecraft to the port-side of Pyre's space colony. Stepping off the tender onto Pyre's crowded port-side, thunderous chants of the citizens from Pyre and neighboring allied systems resonate, their voices reverberating through the air as their fists pumped with each syllable of Seneca's name. In sharp juxtaposition to the somber atmosphere on *the Appomattox* just thirty-six hours ago, the air buzzes with vibrant energy as people celebrate the hard-fought taste of freedom. At the forefront of the jubilation, a stage and podium stand proudly, their presence commanding attention at the entrance to the rail shuttle station at the far end of the port. It doesn't take a genius to see the crowd craves an inspiring speech from their leader.

"You don't have to speak if you don't want to," Jesper assures him.

Seneca's slight frown suggests that high-profile public addresses are not his strong suit, unlike Ilana, who excels in that arena. However, the sight of the newly emancipated citizens calling him to the platform persuades him to overcome his reluctance and address the crowd. He draws in a deep breath and sighs into the microphone and speaks. "We, my friends, are rebels no longer..."

The ecstatic crowd erupts into a deafening riot of roaring cheers at the statement. The energy of the crowd sends tingles down his arm, bringing back memories of the last time he witnessed the 2016 Falcons play the Seahawks in the Georgia Dome. Despite the heavy personal losses caused by the "Battle of Argi-Pecun", a smile materializes on his face as he reveled in the praise.

Seneca continues his speech as he proudly states, "We now stand at the threshold of the future. Almost all the systems within this conflict have fought hard to escape the clutches of an uncaring and oppressive government..."

He speaks off the top of his head. As he speaks, he intertwines a mix of falsifications that pre-date his real leadership with true stories of his actual tenure. He acknowledges the resilience and drive of the people and gives credit to them in his own words. By sharing anecdotes that explore his Earthly roots and the US Revolutionary War, his words forge a powerful link between them and the innate human longing for freedom, showcasing the extraordinary willingness to lay down life and limb so others can live in peace.

"...and on that topic." Seneca pauses for a deep breath, "Freedom... we see time and time again the steep price to pay. The cost incurred is unfair in many cases. Some nations come by it naturally, but others are not so fortunate. We do not yet know the true cost this struggle in its entirety has exacted upon us, but in the void of the Argi-Pecun, we lost over eight hundred brave men and women who saw a future free from the Empire. Many of them I did not know on a personal level. I did not know their faces, names, or the loved ones who awaited their return. There were also those that I knew as brothers. I had friendships, knew their stories, and their aspirations. Both familiar and unfamiliar alike, their loss leaves a void resulting from their sacrifice. It is our job this day forward to honor their memory. It is our job from here to fight to maintain the freedom they paid the price for..."

Seneca concludes his speech by calling for an extended period of quiet contemplation, urging all those in attendance or even those tuning in remotely to honor and remember the individuals who did not return home to enjoy the benefits of their selfless actions. At that moment, he quietly makes his way off the stage and boards a rail shuttle bound for the government complex.

They settle into the conference room, the adjacent room likely to continue serving as Seneca's home once more for the foreseeable future. Despite the war being over, as Ilana had predicted in his dream, there are still many matters that require immediate attention. For the time being, the Empire has maintained silence, shunning the entire galaxy amidst their embarrassing upset. Seneca suspects extreme turmoil and anger among the lords among the deteriorated economic state with no further military options to exhaust. Seneca conjures comforting images in his mind of imperial citizens, marching on the palace to expel the lords from their power, allowing Ilana to return power to the royal family. Unfortunately, there is no news flowing out of the palace. The only headlines available detail the unconditional surrender order from the Imperial military signaling the concrete end of the war.

While the anticipation of peace talks with the Empire is at the forefront of priorities, there is also the pressing matter of conducting a thorough assessment of the Whispers' losses. Jesper is still taking stock of the data and casualties from the onset of the rebellion to the completion of the war. Seneca is grateful that he need not involve himself in such dismal work.

Aside from accounting for the loss of life and making proper arrangements for the dead, the Whispers are no longer rebels, but a recognized sovereign power with no government and in need of direction. It is regrettable for Seneca that the responsibility of establishing a satisfactory form of government to unite the people against those who exploit them falls upon him and Jesper.

Among all the aggravating discrepancies to address, Seneca's name is *still* within the Imperial bounty compendium, now citing additional transgressions of war crimes. It is a humorous yet annoying predicament. Considering the extensive damage to *the Phantom*, it is unavailable for his use. Without it, or any other combat ship for that matter, he will have no choice but to remain safely grounded on Pyre unless there is a guarantee of safe travels for official business. Imperial bounty hunters won't dare approach Pyre now, lest they upset the UF or COS once more.

Following the Empire's defeat in the coming weeks, Seneca is actively sidestepping the political responsibilities of rebuilding the nation. Instead, the duty he has chosen to undertake is solemn. He has taken on the responsibility of ensuring the remains of his departed comrades are handled in a manner consistent with their wishes, a heavy and intimate burden that he considers a higher priority.

Together, Seneca with Caimen and Payson, respectfully sift through personal belongings to gather items that hold deep emotional significance for their six fallen comrades. Admitting his struggle to recall all the names of The Nineteen aloud is something he detests, tracing it back to his habit of avoiding emotional connections. Recollecting names is a complicated endeavor since his term to address them more times than not was their call sign or rank, not personal titles. Caimen and Payson possess an exceptional level of understanding of Seneca's struggle, mainly driven by their profound respect for Seneca. The other eleven members are equally empathetic as they help scribe heartfelt letters to add to the stockpile of memories they amass.

* * *

Seneca acknowledges that even though the six fallen perished in the rebellion, their next of kin reside within the Empire. To provide closure to the families of fallen soldiers, he ensures that any recoverable remains are cremated and then returns them to their respective families in the Empire. Along with the remains, he also includes their personal items, goodbye wishes, and the medals they earned during their service and post-mortem. Seneca writes personalized letters that delve deep into his history among them and the bond they formed and expresses heavy gratitude for their sacrifice.

It's a profound undertaking that absorbs several weeks of his time. Once the final remains are located and homeward bound, Seneca seeks a permanent means of memorializing their sacrifice. He carefully combs different potential localities before he selects a peaceful area of the developing future capital city being constructed on Fortuna. There, he spends several weeks bringing architects together to design a memorial park specifically for The Nineteen. The conceived memorial-to-be is poetic and eases Seneca's grief. Among carefully manicured gardens, stone paved walkways, and an elaborate playground, the park will boast a stone fountain bearing the names of The Nineteen's pilots. The circular fountain, composed of marble, will serve as the centerpiece of the park, with water spraying from the names of the ones who died in battle. The project will serve as comforting homage.

Having ensured The Nineteen receive the memorial they deserve; Seneca moves on to handling Clemson's wishes. Clemson's dying request presents a unique challenge. Contacting pirates is not an easy act, as they are known for being notoriously elusive, unless you happen to be one of their own. Seneca's extensive experience with them provides him insights on where to start his search, but typically, Clemson was his go-to point of contact for the Revenge. It takes some time, but Seneca eventually finds a former wingman of Clemson and successfully arranges a Revenge funeral.

Revenge funeral ceremonies are peculiar sights to behold. No eulogies. No funeral attire. No weeping friends and family. Instead, the event centers on recognizing the notoriety of the departed Revenge member. The unorthodox funerals take place in space, with each pirate attending within their own ship. Seneca was relieved that he secured an escort and mechanics had worked tirelessly to restore *the Phantom* to… limited functionality to allow Seneca to take part in the funeral among twenty pirates, all of whom revered and respected Clemson's legacy. Under the Revenge of Teach's code, a scan at a funeral is punishable by death and loss of rights to one's own Revenge remembrance ceremony. As such, no one dares initiate any type of scan, even though hefty profits could be made cashing in on what are likely hefty bounties.

Clemson's body is reverently placed in the captain's chair of *the Rot*, dressed in his current attire, as per his wishes. Attendees cram the ship with Clemson's most treasured possessions, along with tokens of tribute. Seneca contributes a piece of *the Phantom*'s broken armor plating, and a note that jokingly reads:

* * *

"Dear Clemson, you may have never bested me in a sparring match, but you did manage to beat me to the other side. Good fortunes, my friend, may the waters cross our blades once more."

Once laden with its cargo, *the Rot* is remotely controlled using a hijack probe that sets a course for the galaxy's center, Sagittarius A. Seneca and the other pirates bring their vessels alongside *the Rot* and follow it in formation until it eventually jumps to its final resting place. Watching *the Rot* carry her captain into the void leaves Seneca grappling with yet another difficult moment.

It was only upon Clemson's dying breath that he fully comprehended the bond he'd forged with the charismatic pirate. Throughout his career, he had seldom come across a pilot like Clemson whose skill could match his own, and the experience of flying together had always brought him immense joy. The lighthearted banter and competitive spirit they shared evoked vivid memories of the camaraderie he had experienced with friends during his tenure as an Air Force pilot. Seneca reflects on the irony that it often takes tragedy to realize the depth of one's connections and the weight of regret.

With his personal losses addressed, Seneca finally stops delaying the inevitable. He returns to Pyre and joins Marco, Jesper, and other leaders to establish a system of government for the burgeoning nation. It's a crucial step—one that Seneca deeply wishes Ilana were present to oversee in his stead.

Chapter 47: From the Ashes

Weeks flow by quickly like swift moving water in a mountain stream. While working with Jesper, Marco, and other leaders to establish a government system, Seneca faced challenging moments that tested his patience. However, he persisted through the difficult debates and unpleasant world of politics until their hard work resulted in a satisfactory constitution. There were many at its inception who expressed a desire for simplistic governing principles, but Seneca, in his travels and lifetime, disagreed wholeheartedly, knowing there needed to be certain safeguards in place. The new government needed to accurately reflect the collective principles of freedom and insist on leaders who genuinely understand and prioritize the needs of the people.

Thus, emerges the intricate framework of the newly established government, aptly named "The Constitutional Republic of Susurros" to honor the namesake of the nation's rebellious beginnings. The new constitution of the Republic is incredibly thorough in its delineation of strict criteria that leaders must meet, as well as outlining the complex procedures for elections within both the legislative and executive branches. The constitution implements term limits and prohibits both political parties and corporate lobbying to prevent potential corruption and maintain a fair distribution of power. Moreover, the judiciary system is mandated to adhere strictly to the letter, rather than the interpretation, of the constitution. To ensure equitable representation of all constituents, a consortium branch is also established, composed of the independently elected governors from each system within the Republic.

It's not perfect. The idea of participatory democracy comes with its potential pitfalls, as it necessitates people stay informed, actively participate in the political process, and carry the burden of responsibility for the leaders they elect. From the standpoint of those responsible for drafting the constitution, it was deemed more justifiable for the nation to experience failure because of the will of its constituents, rather than due to the actions of corrupt leaders.

* * *

Then, governors and leaders from across the former rebellion are given the opportunity to ratify the constitution. The majority promptly accept the document, adopting it as law and uniting together as a new nation. A minority of dissenters exists as well. These leaders feel the CRS does not serve the purpose of their people and instead pursue membership within the COS and ultimately part ways politically with their former allies.

In the interim, Ilana and Seneca have been able to maintain limited communication. Due to the potential consequences of political backlash, especially if her involvement as the original source of the treasonous rebellion is exposed, they cannot openly discuss their relationship. However, there is no need for them to encrypt messages and communicate in secret. In the recent weeks since they made the constitution public knowledge, they have been communicating with each other under the guise of a diplomatic venture. Ciphertexts were a bi-weekly occurrence at best, and near the end of the war Seneca hardly had time to send or receive them. Professional UniCom messages have since taken over. This double-edged sword affords him smoother and faster communication more frequently but limits their exchanges to professional rhetoric with subtle affections indirectly foreshadowed.

Ilana's words inform him that the lordship council dissolved due to the corrupt nature of their actions, which ultimately caused the Whisper rebellion. It was through Ilana's diplomatic speeches to incite people to act and reject the authority imposed by the lords. In her usual manner, her words stole the hearts of the people who promptly awarded blame for the state of the Empire upon the lords. Now a vacuum of power has the people of the Empire looking to her and the royal family. Her father happily accepted the role of once more renewing the ideas of mutual prosperity that long ago were the foundations of the Empire. In this pivotal moment, the emperor is working amongst the people to draft plans that will institute an elected parliament to supplement the emperor's rule to ensure the corrupt actions of the lords do not resurface once more.

Unfortunately, Ilana also says several months are likely to pass before concrete change occurs within the palace and reconciliation talks cannot take place until such a time that an elected body replaces the lordship council. A complicated envoy considering the current economic disarray induced by the economic fallout from the war.

What she calls reconciliation is a galactic political process that takes place at the end of any war. Eventually, leaders from all the major galactic governments will gather to discuss remaining grievances and issue concessions before passing other laws to prevent repetitive galactic conflicts. However, with no definite time period before reconciliation can occur, Seneca does his best to avoid stiff drink to answer remaining anxieties as he continues connecting with the friends among him—Marco and Jesper.

Determined to grow—no—heal past his desires to push people away, he's trying to seek the most out of friendships while they remain in his life. Companionship helps immensely to pass the time, as he tends to the governing duties that rest on his shoulders. To his dismay, he is declared by a unanimous vote, the interim president of the Republic. It's a position he will sit in until a true elected leader is chosen to take office. The complex nature of the elections with the novelty of the nation will be a lengthy process that could see him governing for another two years.

One day as he watches out the window of his office, the former conference room, Marco visits him and extends him a warm greeting, "Good day my friend, that chair suits you well—"

Seneca shakes his head side to side while smiling. "Marco, please, don't tell me about another presidential nomination. I'd rather you take the position for yourself."

Marco laughs and sits on the sofa across from the desk. "Would you call that an endorsement?"

"Absolutely." He says.

Marco smiles. Seneca truly believes that Marco or Jesper deserves to be this nation's first true leader. They, from the beginning, had invested interest in the fight for freedom. Seneca's involvement only happened once he developed feelings for the proverbial hidden figure behind a curtain. If it weren't for his encounter with Ilana, his strong dislike for the Empire alone would not have provided enough justification for him to join the cause, let alone lead it. A sentiment he openly shares with his friend as he says, "Besides Marco, I did this for myself... At least at first."

"Maybe, my friend, but you acted out of love. Acts of love aren't selfish, especially considering the rebellion. You acted and now millions across this nation are free." Marco replies.

Seneca shakes his head. "I understand, but I had the opportunity on so many occasions to take a true stance. I just couldn't. It meant getting involved, getting attached, seeing death, experiencing grief... I still hate that part... I didn't make too many friends in this venture, but of the ones I made, I lost several. I have to live with that for eternity."

Marco gives an understanding nod and continues expressing wisdom that, despite being significantly younger than Seneca, far exceeds his own. "Grief is a byproduct of love. It is the soul's reaction to the departing of those you've connected with. In a way, it's the most profound expression of love. Don't avoid love in fear of grief, my friend. Act on it and you'll continue to improve."

Seneca and Marco continue in lengthy conversation that persists for hours. As they talk, Seneca verbally reflects on Marco's wisdom through a collective exploration of Seneca's motives throughout the years. Marco coaxes him to reveal his inner demons. A subtle feeling of shame infiltrates his mind. He talks at length about the moment Kelsea died and he departed to fight in the Orinian war, an event that filled him with intense resentment towards his immortal existence. Such heartache after the collective weight of loss upon him, once created a desire to die to achieve a symbolic reunion with his deceased friends and family.

For him, taking his own life was morally wrong, as he believed suicide was a form of cheating and showed a lack of respect for the departed souls who held importance to him. Those who held him dear cherished his life and impacted deeply. This made it necessary for his demise to be...deserved. In his pursuit of a proper moral elimination, he cast himself blindly into numerous war campaigns across the galaxy, ensuring he always fought alongside his own ethical standards. In his mind, Seneca believed that allowing someone to defeat him would be equivalent to committing suicide, so he was searching for someone who could defeat him in fair combat.

His search for a warrior's earned death never yielded the desired result. On several occasions, he experienced a strong feeling that his destiny was within reach, but every time he found himself in such a situation, the souls of the individuals he had inspired saved him—acts of love. Furthermore, the longer he continued flying, the more formidable and proficient he became, making the task of finding an equal among the stars even more difficult. Unable to meet his demise, he became a lost version of himself, drifting among the stars and gradually turning into a cynical and disillusioned soul, shutting himself off from the world to protect himself.

Marco nods along through his explanation. Once Seneca's chronicle of his life concludes, Marco empathizes poetically, "Well, it now sounds like destiny has other plans for you and Ilana, and you have an opportunity to learn a lesson about love that yet awaits you. Make loving yourself and others your mission and your purpose and I think you'll find solace knowing that though others only blink into your life, you greatly impact theirs."

Seneca nods and digests the resolution of the conversation. "I'll do my best Marco, but don't think for a second that means I'm going to stay president."

Marco laughs as they bid their farewells for the day. However, Seneca's office is not devoid of visitors for more than a moment. Shortly after Marco's departure, distinct echoes of conversation can pour in from the hallway. He presumes Jesper and Marco caught each other and stopped to chat momentarily, an easy assumption to confirm when Jesper's face cracks the door open.

"Hey, *Mr. President.*" Jesper taunts.

"Do not *ever* call me that again." Seneca says gagging at the attempt at humor.

"I hope you have some time. We have a visitor." Jesper's voice carries heavy optimism as the doors swing open the rest of the way and a familiar face is waiting behind the door.

Chapter 48: A Sight for Sore Eyes

"Hi stick jockey." Serena says, as Seneca meets her eyes.

He leaps to his feet and rushes to the door.

"Holy shit! Serena! What are you doing here?" he asks, surprise coloring his voice as she strolls in.

Serena, dressed in professional attire, greets him with a friendly hug. Visits from any Imperial diplomatic representative were unforeseen, let alone someone he knew so well. Serena's presence is a sight for sore eyes and a welcome guest. She seats herself and, without skipping a beat, blesses Seneca with her snarky quips, "So first of all, *fuck* you and Ilana for keeping this rebellion shit secret for so long! This would have been way more interesting than what she's had me doing the last six years."

Seneca seats himself as he laughs. "I missed you too," he says.

"Shut up." She quips with a chuckle of her own.

Seneca, Jesper, and Serena all share a momentary laugh before diving into casual greetings and conversation. Nearly three years have passed since Seneca and Jesper last saw or heard from Serena, making her consistent character traits a comforting anchor in the evolving scenario they've fallen into. She even grooms her hair the same way she always has, and of course maintains her direct, filter-less form of communication.

The conversation naturally steers towards Ilana as Seneca finally musters the courage to ask her, "So how's Ilana?"

"Took you long enough. I actually thought you'd be happy with just seeing me." She says producing a letter from the suitcase she'd brought with her. It's a handwritten letter delicately encased by an envelope of all things. "Do you know how much she pestered her father to teach her to write?" she says, handing him the letter.

Seneca opens it carefully, avoids damaging its antique contents, written on looseleaf notebook paper. With a dumbfounded expression, he examines the ancient material before saying, "My question is, where did she find loose-leaf notebook paper and a paper envelope?"

"Dude. She spent four million buying some sort of book bound by a metal spring that has like seventy 'mint condition' pages at a fucking online antique mall," Serena answers and expressing disapproval. "Apparently this is what she considers romantic and 'authentic.'"

Shifting his focus to the writing on the note, he begins silently translating the chicken scratch before him. The orientation of some letters is incorrect, but with some effort he discerns the message:

"Dear Seneca,

Words cannot do justice to express how much I miss you. As you know, ciphertexts are inconvenient to write and to decode. The UniCom messaging through government channels is a marginal improvement, but since I cannot reveal genuine emotion, they serve little purpose.

I want to thank you. From the depths of my soul, please understand what it means to me. You and Jesper saved my life and subsequently gave life to my vision of change in the galaxy in ways I would have never imagined. The constitution you helped create is nothing short of perfect for these people who have struggled for so long against the tyranny of an unfeeling ruling class. I also never could have foreseen how the rebellion would influence positive change within the Empire itself. Once the economy tanked people became enraged, but despite the lords asserting that you were to blame, I was able to rally the people to see the true source of the rebellion.

With the council of lords gone, the Empire as a whole can become a fair and just civilization, all thanks to you. You sexy, wonderful man. You could have left this behind you at any point, but you stayed and did something larger than yourself. That made me feel like you were by my side these past years, staying with me.

Keep strong for me. Nothing about this is easy, and I can almost feel your past bearing down on you. Just know I am doing my part to stabilize my home. Once that is done, you and I will be together. In the meantime, Serena will be "running errands" and delivering these letters for me so we can communicate secretly until we don't have to be a secret anymore.

Love, Ilana.

P.S. I convinced dad to remove you out of the Imperial bounty compendium. Feel free to move safely around, though I would stay clear of Vista. He's still pretty mad considering all the destroyed gold mines about the Empire."

Seneca smiles from ear to ear, folding the letter and tucking it away in the drawer of his desk.

"What's it say?" Serena asks, teasingly.

His reply reciprocates the teasing. "Don't worry about it. She's not interested in a threesome."

"Did she send you a nude photo like I told her to?"

Seneca chuckles and shakes his head. His stomach rumbles, invoking an idea. The company in question warrants a visit to Marco's home, where he is likely preparing a delicious meal. Arising from his seat, he extends them an invitation to dinner without betraying the venue. Serena quickly probes him for information, her selective palate unsure of the cuisine available in Pyre. It's understandable since the colony's limited selection of dining facilities boasts nothing of notoriety, but Seneca simply says, "It's a surprise. Trust me, I've never picked a lackluster venue before."

Outside the government complex they jaunt via rail-shuttle to the barracks where Seneca directs the trio to Marco's abode. Even though some people may have reservations about others inviting themselves over for a meal, Marco's grandfatherly demeanor maintains an open-door policy, inviting anyone who wants to enjoy his hospitality over conversation and dinner. Marco extends a warm invitation into his home where Seneca, Jesper, and Marco take turns telling stories of the past few years. Marco's unwavering hospitality knows no bounds, as he uncorks a rare bottle of wine while they engage in the lively conversation over a mouthwatering meal of grilled pork loin, sizzling vegetable kebabs, and fragrant Spanish-style rice. As they laugh, time passes quickly and before they know it, they have converted four hours into a pleasant memory. Unwilling to cease his hospitality, Marco offers sleeping surfaces in his home to spare them a trip across town and give them the privilege of joining him for breakfast in the morning.

From then on, Serena's visitation schedule follows a predictable pattern. On a monthly basis, she arrives on the first Monday and then heads back to Vista the following Sunday. During each visit, she facilitates an exchange of letters between Seneca and Ilana, whose handwriting improves rapidly. This ritual became Seneca's favorite part of the month, motivating him to make the most of his current circumstances. One way he determines to help accomplish his resolution to seize each day would be adjusting the dynamic between his two friends.

It's apparent to him that Jesper and Serena's 'flirtationship' dynamic withstood the test of time and distance. Every time Serena visits, he hopes that their undeniable chemistry will lead to a decisive action, but each time, their farewells end in a lingering embrace that incites disappointment to observe. In order to avoid the exasperation of watching this never-ending spectacle, he makes the choice to step in.

He uses his vast knowledge of Serena and Jesper's personas to organize a special outing for them, arranging for them to spend a "day" exploring one of the galaxy's most expansive and magnificent botanical gardens, which nestled on Mars. The "Martian Botanical Preserve" came into existence when early planetary terraforming equipment malfunctioned. The awry machinery converted an entire valley in the northwestern hemisphere of Mars into a vast jungle, spanning twenty-thousand acres and boasting a rich variety of plant life. Currently, the preserve is experiencing its peak summer bloom, with millions of fragrant flowers and plant life carpeting the area.

It takes careful legal maneuvering, but Seneca can secure unaccompanied visitors passes for his friends. With papers in order, Seneca flies them to their destination. Instead of joining them on their adventure, he discards them with the survival kit from his still-injured ship and leaves them in the preserve with a brief note that reads: "To whom it may concern, please one of you make a move already You're driving me crazy. I'll be back on Saturday."

With his friends awaiting his return, he remains in the vicinity. The move is bold, filling him with an appreciable level of fear, but he opts to try his hand at visiting Earth. Spending time in such a solitary manner is a novel experience. Not long ago, merely contemplating setting foot on Earth filled him with dread, but for the moment, he's content camping overnight and fishing the muddy banks of the Chattahoochee River near Rodgers Bridge in his hometown, Duluth.

It's a pleasant, nostalgic activity that occupies his attention. The lack of significant fishing pressure means he's reeling in ample catches of native brook trout as he fishes wearing an old pair of tattered jeans rolled up to his knees. He savors the sensation of cool water flowing swiftly around his legs. The scent of spring hangs in the air, mingling with the gentle rustle of leaves as robins alight on overhanging branches, offering a welcome respite from political duties.

While Jesper and Serena marinate in each other's company for another day, Seneca embarks on a journey of self-discovery, venturing to the cemetery where Sophie and Oliver were laid to rest. Nestled on the outskirts of Pickens, South Carolina, the quaint cemetery spans five peaceful acres, its headstones neatly arranged in rows adorned with scripture, flowers, and tokens of remembrance. A reverent wooden chapel coated in gray paint and cross sits comfortably by the road for stray visitors to seek heavenly guidance.

Memory of the grounds guides him quickly to their resting spot. Regret washes over him as he gazes upon the names engraved on their dark marble headstones: 'Sophia Hewitt Mason and Oliver Levi Mason.' It's been since their funeral that he graced their place of rest with his presence—a decision he now laments. Silently he kneels, unsure of what he would say to them if they were actually here. He permits further contemplation before finally saying, "Hey guys. I'm uh… sorry I've never visited. I don't expect that you'd understand if you were here, and if you were mad, I wouldn't blame you."

He pauses as a few tears roll down his cheek. "I guess I didn't feel… worthy. Flying was my calling… and because I was out flying, I lost out on what life we could have had. For the longest time I couldn't forgive myself and let go…You would think that after all my family and friends passed away, that'd I wouldn't have taken life for granted and would have spent that time with you… I don't know…I wish I had more to say. An excuse of some kind, but I don't. I'm sorry."

He lingers there, imagining he's talking to their ghosts. He describes his most recent affairs in the war and the most recent loss of life he'd witnessed. Periodically, he has to pause his hushed tales to sob. He opens up to their spirits about Ilana, and his feelings for her, assuring Sophie that it doesn't mean he no longer holds affection for her memory. He knows Sophie would have wanted him to find love, anyway. Even so, he speaks fondly of his past affections for Sophie. Words originally were absent from his mind, but now he talks as evening twilight sets in. It's getting late, and he needs to make his way back to Mars to "rescue" his friends, but he lingers for a few moments longer. The sound of crickets breaking out into song fills the cool evening mist as he places a magnolia flower on their graves and takes his leave.

Late night hours set in by the time he departs Earth to retrieve Jesper and Serena from their extended stay on Mars. The stint over to Mars only takes about six hours before he lands his ship a couple miles outside the preserve and hikes to their locating beacon. In contrast to the spring weather he'd been enjoying on Earth, the summer night air humid and adheres to his skin like soup. Sweat beads on his skin and trickles down his forehead as he makes his way down the lush trail until he finally reaches their campsite. The image before his eyes suggests his mission had succeeded in moving them beyond mere friends.

In the lush embrace of the valley, surrounded by blooming vines and vibrant bromeliads, Jesper and Serena find themselves entwined in the survival tent Seneca supplied, their naked bodies pressed close together. They're sharing a tender moment, lost in a passionate exchange of kisses and DNA. Sensing their need for privacy, Seneca quietly slips away, giving them the space to enjoy each other's company undisturbed for a few hours. He seizes the opportunity to secure some rest since he's been awake for twelve hours. He finds a hilltop with a clear view of the stars through the canopy of the jungle, where he sets up a hammock he'd brought with him.

The sky is clear, and stars speckle the dark blanket above him. Rocking gently in his hammock, he raises his UniCom to his face, and in an effort to perpetuate his self-healing, he uses the device to help him locate Saturn in the sky. Staring in that section of space where he'd built a life with Kelsea, another part of his past overtakes his thoughts.

Kelsea chose not to be buried but instead opted for cremation and having her ashes spread in space. His train of thought incites him to consider his initial desire to remain in space was to remain close to Kelsea. Maybe that was why he'd never settled down. He can't be sure though, since he lost touch with himself in the decades between her death and that fateful night on Oberon. There's no way for him to discern what his motivations were. The only motive he recalls having was "avoid grief, keep moving.". He takes the time to murmur at the sky in the same fashion he had at Sophie and Oliver's grave, seeking closure through talking to an imaginary spirit. The conversation once more draws tears and warrants an occasional pause while he whispers to the sky until he's lulled to sleep by the ambiance of the night.

Upon waking several hours later, he makes his return to Jesper and Serena's campsite. With the sun slowly making its way back up, he finds Jesper and Serena still wrapped in each other's arms, their bodies covered only by blankets. The two have engrossed themselves in each other's presence, lost in conversation and each other's gaze. Unnoticed, Seneca quietly navigates through the overgrown landscape, his movements deliberate and stealthy. With a mischievous glint in his eye, he keeps low, skillfully maneuvering through the foliage until he deems the distance enough to make his presence known.

He stifles the urge to laugh as he says "Boo." in a hushed tone.

Serena's scream pierces the tranquil air, causing the small creatures hidden in the brush to stir before she whirls around to confront Seneca, who stands there laughing. Flustered, she blushes furiously and frantically grabs at the blanket to cover up her nakedness... Realizing the futility of her efforts, she abandons the blanket and resorts to hurling every available object—rocks, sticks, anything she can find—at Seneca. Dodging her makeshift projectiles, Seneca laughs uproariously and shouts, "You're welcome!" before darting away into the foliage.

"Seneca! You get your ass back here!" Serena's voice echoes through the jungle as Jesper strolls up with her clothing, concealing his own laughter.

An awkward air dominates the atmosphere within *the Phantom*, but it's soon dispelled by Jesper and Seneca's upbeat demeanors that eventually soothes the seething Serena to normal.

Chapter 49: Peace and Reconciliation

Over the course of the next three months, Serena continues her regular pattern of visiting and swapping letters between Seneca and Ilana. On her fourth visit, she's brought news from the palace in addition to the latest correspondence from Ilana.

"Yeah, so the emperor says that the parliamentary elections, or whatever, will be finalized by the end of the month. Lucky for you, the Empire is ready to begin reconciliation congress next month." She tells him as she hands him Ilana's letter.

Seneca's excitement to read the letter almost overshadows the Serena's announcement, "Wait, when?"

"Ugh. Next month, the 1st. Frustra starport. Emperor. Ilana. Talk about reconciliation." She repeats sarcastically.

Seneca couldn't be more excited. The lengthy separation has him eager to reunite. Though he was lucky that they were able to maintain limited contact during the war, he yearned to lock eyes with her mesmerizing green-eyed gaze, to feel the warmth of her touch, and savor the sweetness of her kiss once again.

"Don't get too excited yet. She's still doing diplomatic duties helping Imperial citizens adjust to the new government. Inspiring them to keep hope and all that. Trust me though, she's just as impatient and puppy lovey-dovey as you." Serena cautions.

Serena brings up a tablet and resumes delineating the specific details regarding the upcoming envoy. Frustra, a small moon colony in neutral space, is where the bulk of galactic conflicts are settled with treaties. In spite of being small, the colony itself supports a varied economy, operating as a trading post, galactic real estate brokerage, and bustling banking center. It sits far from outside the reach of all major governments. As such neither the Empire, UF, or COS have laid claim to it. A large population of well-versed lawyers and neutral standing with the galactic superpowers has led to much of the galaxy's wide-reaching legislation being drafted on the humble location. In the first week of the month, it will once more play host to reconciliation and its halls will once more produce a treaty that will strive to maintain peace throughout the Milky Way.

Of the dramatic changes Seneca has undergone in the past several years, his dislike for political processes remains steadfast as evident in his groaning "This sounds like it's gonna be a fun time."

Serena issues a direct reply, "No. It won't. Not for you. Now where's Jesper? It's been a month and I want to fu—"

Seneca interrupts her before she can finish the crude outburst, "Serena! Gross! He's downstairs. Left turn. Room 219!"

Serena teases him further. "I can film it if you want."

"God. Serena, get lost!"

Serena laughs as she leaves for Jesper's room. The two have been glued at the hip since Mars and spend now long expanses of time alone. While he's happy for them, Serena's teasing nature drives her to divulge personal details to embarrass Jesper and make Seneca cringe. It's a small price to pay for the privilege of having genuine friends to share his time with.

After some time, Serena and Jesper join him at Marco's for dinner, a traditional activity that they've kept to since Serena's initial visit. Marco, as he has done countless times, has prepared an exquisite feast for his guests to savor. They always engage in lively discussions and banter during the monthly occasion. The topic of tonight's dinner revolves around discussions regarding the progress of the Republic's first election cycle. Much to Seneca's satisfaction, the consortium representatives for all systems have been officially elected. Marco declined the role of governor to the surprise of Pyre's residents, leaving Jesper eagerly stepping in as the runner-up.

Serena playfully slaps Jesper on the back of the head. "You didn't tell me! I'm proud of you hun."

Jesper rubs the place where her hand had impacted his cranium. "I didn't really *run*. This wasn't exactly a standard election cycle. People just voted for me."

"Why did you turn it down, Marco?" Serena inquires curiously.

Marco pauses eating to answer her, placing a steaming grilled chicken haunch back onto his plate. "Seneca urged me not to. He's adamant that he's got no plans to stay president like many of us would like to see. Now that consortium leaders are elected, they will nominate eligible candidates for the presidential election."

"That's different. At least you can't buy your way in like the lordship council... so Marco, you're going to run for president?" Serena asks.

"Yes ma'am." He replies with a sincere smile on his face, "Jesper is going to nominate me, and Seneca will give me his endorsement. Though there are many other deserving leaders among the Republic."

Marco continues discussing the intricacies of the CRS' elections. While Marco would make a fantastic choice for the job, there's still some time before anyone else can take the reins from Seneca, relieving him of his political burden. Seneca ponders the possibility of waiting another five years before reuniting with Ilana during their conversation. Since it's the first election cycle for a new nation, there have been no concrete timelines established since it's a wild transition for many of the former rebels. Restructuring local governments to align with the constitution is necessary for many. Before the establishment of the Republic, numerous people were disinterested in engaging in government affairs due to the lack of concern from Imperial rulers, unless it was financially beneficial for them. The fact they've all elected consortium leaders is fantastic, but they've opted to afford each of the ninety members to take sufficient time to select their nominees. Many have tried to nominate Seneca, but he's declined. Interviewing others could be a lengthy process and Seneca has to try his best to be patient. For the time being, any progress is good news.

Their dinner, the remainder of Serena's visit, and the rest of the month all pass quickly and painlessly, bringing the dawn of the reconciliation congress upon him. Departing in *the Phantom*, Seneca embarks on a journey to the moon colony of Frustra. An extraordinary sigh greets him at Frustra star port: a multitude of former rebels, now Republic citizens, flood the streets of the spaceport to witness his arrival. His ship, still-battle-scarred, limps to a touchdown among the onlookers. Seneca, accompanied by Marco and Jesper, serving as companions and political advisors, exit the ship and make their way across the port's pavement. It's no different from the hundreds of expansive ports he's seen before. This one would blend seamlessly with the sight of many were it not for the yellow gas giant as a backdrop in the sky and a blue star burning through the night sky.

The crowd chants his name rhythmically and flashes from cameras momentarily blind him. Seneca waves in acknowledgment, though he silently yearns for the days when he could fire his pistol into the air to scatter undesirable paparazzi. However, the Emperor's insistence on a weapon-free presence for the peace talks stifles that capability. Also, it probably wouldn't make for ideal press among his own people to dismiss them in such a way. Confederate security agents meet the group and guide them to a monorail, which will ferry them to the convention center where the crucial negotiations will unfold.

The convention center resembles the halls and corridors of a massive cruise ship. Seneca's party navigates a labyrinth of hallways, finding peace in the quieter interior compared to the bustling streets outside. They finally reach their destination where they join representatives from other governments taking part in the reconciliation. Among the attendees are the President of the UF, Tessa Jackson, and some members of her cabinet, as well as the Confederacy representative Claxton Evahns and a select group of his political advisors. Yet, the one individual who captures Seneca's undivided attention takes her seat across from him, next to her father.

Locked in an intense gaze, Seneca and Ilana stand amidst one another for the first time in several years. She appears just as beautiful and stunning as the day they first met on Oberon, wearing the same dress, her hair cascading over her shoulder, and her green eyes sparkling in the room's ambient light. A blush overtakes her features as she struggles to contain her excitement, mirroring Seneca's own emotions in this surreal reunion.

* * *

Seneca's discipline is put to the test as he fights against the overwhelming desire to embrace her tightly. The insatiable desire to do so consumes every waking thought. Seeing her smile for the first time in so long fills his heart with warmth and makes his knees weak. Unfortunately, they must wait longer still...

Seneca averts his gaze to avoid drawing any attention from others present in the room, and the meeting begins once everyone is seated. In spite of their last-minute assistance to the rebellion, because they never declared a formal war against any party present, Councilor Evahns is mediating the proceedings as a neutral party. After introducing himself and going through the motions of legal formalities, he opens the floor to Seneca to speak first on the Republic's behalf.

Seneca keeps the statement short and concise: "The Republic wishes to be recognized by all parties as a sovereign nation. No further grievances to address."

The UF is the next to speak. President Jackson rises from her seat. "I affirm the motion that the Republic shall be recognized as a sovereign state. I would like to express grievance with the manner in which the Empire forcibly annexed unwilling societies and would like to receive some degree of reparations to cover expenses incurred by the Imperial Civil War."

Finally, the Empire's turn. Emperor Byron McClaine rises to speak, his voice as powerful as ever. "The Empire... will recognize the sovereign status of the... Republic. We would like to address grievances against Seneca Mason, due to the danger he poses to Imperial national security, his employment of non-standard war-fighting tactics, and his use of illegal weapons in the Argi-Pecun confrontation."

Seneca's eyes snap to meet Byron's scowl. Tolerating hypocrisy is not a talent he possesses. He is willing to accept the other grievances but is unable to hold his tongue regarding illegal weapons. "So, the Empire gets to manufacture dark matter warheads, but you want retribution for jumpers? Are you high?"

Apparently, the news of dark matter weapons is news to both Byron and Ilana. Byron's head leans to the side and his face dons a confused expression. Ilana, too, stands and looks at her father with mouth agape. "Dark matter weapons?" She pauses. "We don't possess the technology... Dad, is that true?"

Before the Emperor can reply, Seneca smirks and says, "Not anymore. But *the Pantheon* and *Echelon* both had manufactories for dark matter weaponry. We have proof."

Seneca and his associates display the indisputable evidence in explicit detail. The action evidently took place right under their nose, shocking both Byron and Ilana. In fact, their expressions mirrored Seneca's when he first heard the news of the illegal weapons. After placing all evidence on the record and opening the floor for rebuttal, Byron speaks once more. "We retract our grievance about illegal weapons and will launch a full investigation on the matter of dark matter weapons. Other grievances stand"

* * *

Now that each leader has spoken, the three leaders take turns addressing the concerns and demands of the others. On certain occasions, the leaders engage in spirited debates, while on others, they effortlessly pass legislation, contributing to a harmonious atmosphere. Seneca and Ilana found themselves constantly distracted by one another during the proceedings, his mind wandering to places he'd rather be.

The weeks of deliberation conclude, and the leaders are presented with a reconciliation treaty written by the faithful denizens of Frustra. The changes it brings have a predominantly positive impact on the galaxy. For instance, major governments now must await the ratification of the respective constitution by independent societies or a two-thirds majority vote before annexation can occur. The three involved parties will distribute reparations funding according to their share of the cause: the Empire will cover sixty percent, the Republic thirty-five percent, and the UF will handle the remaining fifteen. The final provision pertains to Seneca specifically. Unfortunately, the terms are stringent and place complications on his ability to reunite with Ilana. In addition to a long list of limitations on his movements throughout the Empire, they permanently banned him from Vista.

With signatures affixed to the legislation, it becomes galactic law immediately. The leaders all take turns shaking hands and exchange departing formalities. With business concluded, participants file out one at a time, eventually leaving Ilana and Seneca without supervision.

He walks up to her, desperately trying to find the right words to express his personal feelings. However, he is caught off guard when he feels the familiar sensation of Ilana's arms tightly embracing his neck. The scent of her hair, the rhythm of her heartbeat, and her bold demonstration of affection all offer a tantalizing glimpse into what lay ahead. The moment feels so perfect; he wishes he could eternalize it, but he knows that it isn't yet time.

Ilana must break his heart by pulling away, but as she does so, a tender whisper tickles his eardrums, "See you soon… I promise."

She turns from him to meet her father in the hallways and make her way back home. She turns with a smile and walks away, and time seems to slow while he watches her hair sway with each step. He doesn't know when he'll see her again, but he trusts her promises.

Chapter 50: A Storming Reunion

In the wake of the reconciliation treaty, bearing the moniker "The Whisper Resolution", the Milky-Way is well on its way to recovering from the wide-reaching conflict. The Empire has reformed, and financial recovery is on the horizon under the watchful eyes of an elected body. Meanwhile, as the year 2280 dawns, the Republic is gaining footing and setting the stage for the official start of the first election cycle after deciding to name Pyre as the official capital of the Republic. An atmosphere charged with hope is spreading among the stars for the first time in decades since the inception of the rebellion and to celebrate, systems all over the Republic hold ceremonies, not only to congratulate Pyre on its rags-to-riches transformation, but for the governors across the nation to unveil their nominees for the upcoming presidential election.

In Pyre, their ceremony coincides with a plethora of other pomp and circumstance. This ceremony will be the first to be held in the infant capital city of McAlister, now the only capital in the galaxy named in honor of a pirate, where ground is being broken for a new government building to serve as the Republic's new Capitol building. White tent canopies shield them from Pure's sun and tables adorned with white linens play host to Pyre's citizens and esteemed guests. Others are outside the venue, observing in crowds, eagerly awaiting news of what the future may hold. The surrounding horizon is a vibrant mix of construction sites and freshly planted trees, each contributing to the evolving landscape of the city.

An extremely well-groomed Seneca finds himself on a rare occasion sporting a tuxedo to match the formality of the event. Considering the fact that he has a speaking role, it is only fitting that he dresses appropriately. The fact that he is choosing to distance himself from his beloved flight suit today carries deep symbolism of difficult choice, especially considering that during his speech he intends to announce that he will be retiring from combat flying before endorsing 'Jesper's nominee'. His love for flying extends beyond simple infatuation; it encompasses the exhilarating freedom of traversing the stars at will and the sense of pride that comes with being regarded as a legend among peers. As such, it was a difficult last-minute decision, but he's ready to "hang up the hat". The last time he visited Earth alone, he found himself deeply reflecting on the past few years, the war, and the conversation with Marco about "love." Seneca realized he needed to continue the work that Ilana had helped him start and confront his demons. Consequently, once his tenure as interim president terminates, he's plans to return to Earth permanently to reignite old dreams and reconnect with the man he used to be.

Jesper, Serena (who recently quit as Ilana's advisor), and Marco are all seated with him at their table. The four individuals engage in a back-and-forth dialogue until Seneca eventually takes the spotlight. The moment he stands up, the crowds erupt in adoration, chanting, and cheering. Only when he reaches the stage and begins speaking does the torrent of noise finally subside.

At the beginning of the speech, it is direct and to the point. He greets the audience with a warm smile, lightening the mood with a few jokes before allowing momentary applause. He then takes a moment to recap recent events, building anticipation before delving into the main content of his speech:

"...Now you're all familiar with the man you've recently voted as your governor, well until the guy who came in second place won on a technicality. Jesper Thompson is an intelligent mind, loving soul, and superb listener. I don't want to spoil any surprises, but his selected presidential nominee has my full support and endorsement. Now comes the sad mushy stuff... I am grateful to have the opportunity to stand before you today. Were it not for the actions of several brave souls, I would have been another battlefield casualty at Argi-Pecun. This is gratitude that afforded me a new chance of sorts in life. A chance to rediscover my own humanity after lifetimes of avoiding the humanity of others. That is why, from this point, I am officially retired from combat flying as of this moment. Thank you all for your support."

The crowd reacts with gasps before applause... which evolves into more chanting of his name. Their celebratory ovation echoes through the air as the revelation sinks in, only to fade away long after Seneca concludes his speech and invites Jesper to the stage. Following his predecessor, Jesper steps onto the stage and delivers his welcome address. He lightens the mood by cracking a joke about winning on a technicality, a topic that Seneca had already touched upon. The crowd's energy surges and wanes in sync with the peaks of Jesper's speech until he finally declares Marco as his presidential nominee. The announcement sets off a wave of jubilation among the crowd, turning the atmosphere into a joyful riot.

Of course, time comes for the former governor turned presidential nominee to speak. All eyes turn towards Marco, who confidently takes the stage, marking the official start of his twelve-month-long presidential campaign with his first speech. Marco is an eloquent speaker, adept at weaving wisdom and anecdotes into his address. He has little trouble immersing the crowd in his rhetoric that promises to continue a path of prosperity to bring the infant nation to the forefront of galactic economic and military power.

* * *

Marco's speech highlights his passion for the people, and for whatever reason draws attention to the city construction around them. Seneca's gaze shifts outwards into the evening sky, where the sun's descent below the horizon ignites the sky ablaze with vibrant shades of amber and red over the skeletal silhouettes of skyscrapers in the making. McAlister's nearby port, normally abuzz with cargo ships coming and going with shipments of construction materials, has but one ship on approach. The craft's identity could have easily eluded Seneca if he hadn't been so diligent in his observations.

An ivory hull decorated with an intricate pattern of crimson paint along its contours jolts him to his feet in the middle of Marco's address. Upon glancing up at Marco, he receives a swift wink and a signal that no offense will be taken, prompting Seneca to sprint off toward the sunset and narrowly catch the AI controlled trolley. He does not wish to be rude, nor sidestep acknowledging his friend, but he wants to meet *the Solace* upon its touchdown.

The hover trolley glides through the bustling construction of towering skyscrapers, imposing government buildings, and other distinct features of a national capital in the making. Though he pays no attention to the gritty texture of the soon-to-be city streets, his eyes remained glued to the sky. The trolley finally deposits its sole passenger at port Thompson, named in honor of Jesper. Over a mile of landing pads can be seen, but it's hard to miss the noteworthy ship that occupies a landing pad only ninety yards away from the terminal's entrance. *The Solace*, parting dust as it shuts down engines with the fiery sunset as a backdrop, remains an awe-inspiring sight. No sooner does he arrive at the bottom of the mobile staircase provided by the port, does the door swing open and beckon his heart to skip a beat and his body to tremble.

Ilana, beautiful as ever, gracefully descends the steps—alone. He stands speechless as she moves sensually down the stairs, captivating his attention and the world fades away around him. With each step she takes, her crimson heels make a distinct clicking sound on the steps, while her sparkling ivory dress embraces her figure as if it were meticulously painted onto her form.

The moment she's clear of the stairs, *the Solace*'s engines spool back to life and it departs, leaving Ilana behind smiling wide enough to reach Earth from their location. The surreal moment leaves him more confused—the blast of hot air from the ship's thrusters creates a whirlwind that tousles their hair and swirls the surrounding dust until the ship reaches an appropriate altitude to allow the dust to settle.

"Is this real?" Seneca says in disbelief as they stand apart, unsure of what to make of the peculiar turn of events.

With surprising composure, Ilana takes a step forward and walks up to him before issuing her reply. "As real as this city... hi Seneca."

He trips over words in his mind and can only manage to say "Hi."

Her laughter fills the air as the wind dies down and she tucks a strand of hair behind her ear. "You okay there?" she asks with a smile.

* * *

Seneca can feel his heart pounding in his chest, a physical manifestation of his racing thoughts. He's been anxiously counting down the days for this moment, imagining it to be a spectacular occasion where he could make a grand romantic gesture. Instead, his mind is just as devoid of words now as it was on the day they had initially crossed paths.

Ilana takes his hand gently. "Seneca?"

He laughs, "Yeah... I just wasn't expecting you."

Her green eyes travel up and down his physique as she gives him a positive appraisal. "You look good. Aside from Earth, I've never seen you in anything other than your flight suite."

"Well, uh, I'm the interim president and such..."

"I bet you *love* that."

"Not at all." He says.

Laughter fills the space between them in their shared moment together, until a profound silence falls, leaving them both speechless. They stand face to face, locked in the moment. The surrounding air seems to carry an unmistakable yearning to let go of the weight of their struggles from the war and its aftermath. Through their unwavering commitment to the liberation of others, they ultimately gained liberation for themselves.

"So, are any of these buildings a place we can go to talk privately?" She points at a cluster of buildings with completed exteriors at the end of the port.

"Unfortunately, no. This area of the city is still under construction. Those buildings are just shells. The interiors are not functional. *The Phantom*, however, is parked on the other apron."

"That works."

Engaged in light-hearted small talk, they stroll side by side through the terminal, discussing Ilana's flight and exchanging updates on one another's well-being. The interior of the terminal, while functional, is also under construction, like much of the city. Scaffolding and yellow tape adorn the side of the expansive travel hub, while the air is filled with the scent of fresh paint and sawdust. The polished terrazzo flooring amplifies their steps and voices, bouncing them up into the curved ceiling above as they leisurely stroll. Once they cross to the other side of the concourse, they emerge through an access door and *the Phantom* greets them from across the concrete apron.

"Oh, my goodness." Ilana gasps at the sight of its extensive damage. "What happened?!"

It appears that Ilana was completely unaware of the images of his ship that had been circulating on the galactic news channels, and she hadn't caught a fleeting glimpse of it in Frustra. Seneca remains unsure of the reasons behind his choice, but he hasn't been able to bring himself to fully repair or sell it for scrap and parts.

He looks down as they amble down the steps as details about his fallen comrades resurface in his mind. "The battle at Argi-Pecun... I don't really want to talk about that right now. Maybe some other time."

Ilana deduces Seneca had nearly met his end by examination of his crippled spacecraft "How close were you to—"

"You don't want to know." He interrupts her.

Under the craft, Ilana walks with a purpose, her gaze fixed on the damaged armor, carefully assessing its condition. Her face reflects contemplation as she examines the bullet holes, plasma burns, hanging wiring, and other viscera of his ship, exposed and vulnerable. The lack of damage inside is a clear indication that the armor successfully protected the interior.

Once safely inside the solitude of *the Phantom*'s cabin, Ilana attacks him with aggressive affection. She throws herself at him, squeezing him as hard as her strength will allow and kissing his cheeks and face, pausing only to say, "I have so much to tell you."

While she tries to narrate an exciting story, the wet, passionate kisses shared between her, and Seneca make it hard for her to speak and for him to listen. This is not the moment for storytelling, but rather a precious opportunity to reconnect and make up for the time they had lost, cherishing each other's presence. Their moment eventually sets a course for the bed. Kissing and absorbing themselves in one another, they decorate the floor with each other's clothing, scattering like debris on a highway after a tornado. Unsure if Ilana's presence is fleeting or everlasting, he grapples with the possibility of a cruel twist of fate. Nonetheless, in this instant, he resolves to savor every moment as if it were their ultimate encounter. They take time to caress each other's faces and rediscover the contours and crevices of one another's form, gently tracing their outlines with one another's fingertips.

Just as quickly as the storm of passion between the two had begun, it intensifies into the mature stage—lighting flashing in their souls for several moments. Their eyes locked onto one another as passion thunders between them and a torrent of verbal affections moves between heavy breaths of air like swirling wind. Like hail bears down on those below a storm cell, he lays down upon his bear lover, listening to her heart rumble in her chest like the crashing of a tornado. They linger in the eye a moment more before allowing the cell to fade into a dissipating shower.

Recovering energy, they lie together, catching their breath. Ilana plays with a bouncy portion of messy hair just above Seneca's face. "So, I had something super important to tell you before you interrupted me…"

"Woman, please. That was your fault." He laughs, wiping sweat from his brow. "But since we got *that* out of the way, what's your news?"

Chapter 51: En Route for Eternity

Ilana's joy bubbles over as she passionately recounts the recent events in her life, using animated gestures and varying her voice to capture her parents' perspectives in the days before their reunion. She had just finished addressing the Imperial citizens. While congratulating the new parliament representatives, her description paints a picture of a picturesque summer day on Vista outside the palace. The scene is filled with the vibrant colors of blooming flowers and the familiar sounds of tropical birds squawking loudly. With the activities of war and rebellion finally coming to an end, a serene stillness settled over the palace.

Due to having several idle days, Ilana asked both her parents if they would join her on a weekend trip to the mountain estate, unsure of their response. It so happened that they were happy to join her. In the peaceful refuge from the palace's hectic pace, they bonded as a family for the first time in decades, preparing meals together, exploring the miles of wooded trails, and sharing memories on the porch adorned with photos and scrapbooks. Ilana hadn't seen her parents this happy and content in ages.

She recalled depths of the emotions running through her mind during that family trip. Lost in contemplation, she reflected on the journey her life had taken, and with the rebellion over and consequences settled, she felt a strong conviction that it would guide her back to Seneca.

Ilana's voice carries a calmer tone as she says, "Then, on the last night before I started the trip here, I told my parents I needed to tell them something. I felt bad for keeping it a secret and I need them to understand."

"You told him about the rebellion?!" Seneca says in surprise.

"Sort of."

Ilana had made the brave decision to open up to her family about the true nature of her relationship with Seneca; the heavy burden of secrets was no longer something she wished to bear alone. She continues. "I told them how we met on Oberon and how I never felt safe with the security detail the lords had assigned me..."

Ilana had vividly recounted the inception of their relationship to her parents, beginning with their initial interactions that were filled with amusement and gradually evolving into emotionally sensitive moments they shared, deliberately omitting any mention of the intimate physical details. Throughout her narrative, her parents listened intently without interrupting.

"Then I got to talking about the war. I told him that I played a 'large part' in the rebellion." Making quotation marks with her fingers.

She details her father's mortified expression and pantomiming her father's voice as she reenacts the conversation:

Her father responded, "Define a large part."

She replied to him, "I was the leader. I despised the way the lords used people for personal gain. After the Genoese Pandemic, I wanted to stop it. Things got out of hand."

"They sure did, Ilana. They almost found out it—" Ilana's father had stopped there and connected the details before continuing. "Seneca... He took the blame *for you...*"

"Yes. He saved our lives, Dad... he could have just run off..." Ilana had said, almost sobbing.

"That's what he usually does." He exhaled.

Ilana's mother and father, both sitting next to her, engaged in deep emotional conversation that lasted late into the summer evening. The stars of the milky way, with their captivating beauty, formed a vast and enchanting backdrop that surrounded them as they embraced Ilana. The level of compassion and understanding they provided her with was exactly what one would expect from parents.

Ilana sighs heavily. "I told them I needed to go out into the world now. Find a part of me beyond a life in government, beyond the confines of the Empire. I wanted to see humanity as they saw it when they were young, if I can."

Seneca sits up, sheets rolling down to his stomach as he smiles and asks, "So what'd they say?"

"They told me to go. Find you. Find the side of humanity I'm craving to see, and to remember, I'm always welcome back home."

She wipes away tears, struggling to keep her emotions in check as she nears the end of her story—a poignant moment shared with her family. Seneca recalls his own moments of sharing hopes and dreams with his parents. Despite his father's disdain for the government and military service, he supported Seneca's dream of flying.

"And now... I'm here with you. For as long as you'll have me."

At this precise moment, a realization jolts Seneca, propelling him out of bed. Moving swiftly, he strides towards one of the galley cabinets, where he habitually stores significant items such as keys and a particular ring that he had completely forgotten about until this instant. However, it is noticeably absent. Growing more and more frustrated, he mumbles to himself while rummaging through other drawers, trying to recall where he left it. Then it hits him—the chaos of the cabin after he attacked the weapons cache. He shifts his frantic search to the floor.

Seneca ransacks the cabin. Ilana sits up in bed, her eyes tracing his frantic movements. Confusion and concern color her expression and seep into her voice as she asks, "Sen, what's going on? Aren't you happy?"

Ilana's voice edges towards panic as Seneca doesn't respond through his focus. He frantically searches every nook and cranny of the hall, his eyes darting from one potential hiding spot to another. Instead, all he finds is a stray keychain ring—crude and rusted, but the only thing he can locate. He wants to prevent any misunderstanding, especially as Ilana's concern continues to grow, as evident by her requests to be answered.

He runs to her side and plops himself on the bed. "Marry me."

"Huh—"

"I was looking for a ring, but I can't find the damn thing. This is close enough." He pants nervously, heart about to launch from his chest, "Will you marry me?"

Ilana's brain catches up with the moment and she grabs the key-chain ring and bounces excitedly, "Oh my god. Yes!"

It's a proposal that defies tradition and expectations. No grandiose acts of love, no elegant meals with flickering candles, no romantic tunes serenading the atmosphere. Instead, it's just two naked people, tears streaming down their faces, talking earnestly inside a heavily damaged spacecraft. Yet, in their eyes, the moment is perfect.

In their ensuing embrace, she cries tears of joy, mirroring the relief that Seneca feels as he unburdens himself from the weight of their separation. With a strong desire to ensure she understands the full scope of his journey, he takes the time to recount every intricate detail from the moment he left, including the internal struggles he faced with helplessness and alcoholism, the friends who lost their lives, and the profound sense of longing he experienced until this very moment.

Eventually, their eruption of emotion subsides, and Ilana slides the ring onto the proper finger.

"So what's your dad going to do when the galaxy sees the Imperial princess with the interim president, former leader of the rebellion?"

She laughs and presses her nose against his, their faces both flush with color from crying. "That, Seneca, is not our problem."

Seneca and Ilana choose seclusion for the remainder of the week, cocooning themselves in bedsheets inside *the Phantom* to make up for lost time. Seneca's absence does not go unnoticed and before long, people come looking for him. Their eventual emergence perplexes onlookers, and journalists attempt to swarm them, prompting Seneca to issue a warning via pistol fire rooted in his well-known disdain for paparazzi.

Across the galaxy, news headlines buzz with controversy, but Seneca and Ilana remain indifferent; the emperor's perspective is clear, stating that his daughter is free to follow her heart. Even still, weeks pass before the clamor for unanswered interviews and public statements finally subside. Frustrated, galactic journalists abandon the futile endeavor.

Meanwhile, Ilana settles into the makeshift quarters Seneca has occupied since his days as a rebel leader. Serena frequently visits them, taking Ilana on leisurely strolls around the colony. Initially, this raised concerns for Seneca because of Ilana's ties to the Empire. However, Ilana's selfless and caring nature quickly wins over the citizens of Pyre.

In those fleeting instances when Seneca is not fully engrossed in the affairs of governing the nation, they find solace in sharing their collective vision of relocating to Earth, solemnizing their love through marriage, and fulfilling Seneca's humble aspiration of establishing a summer camp that extends its welcome to children hailing from every corner of the galaxy. It's been ages since Seneca felt such satisfaction and optimism about his future trajectory.

Before they realize it, six months have flown by, and Marco leads the polls by a landslide, securing one of the two candidate positions for the upcoming run-off election. Seneca's mission is nearly complete. Despite Marco's reduced availability, Seneca prioritizes regular dinners at his residence with Ilana, Jesper, and Serena.

In celebration of Marco's recent victory in the candidacy election, they prepare a grand feast in his honor in the barracks courtyard. Seneca contributes by arranging for an ostrich to be delivered, aligning with Marco's plan to open an ostrich ranch. The sight of a whole dressed ostrich roasting on a spit above a fire enhances the festive atmosphere. Hundreds of Pyre's citizens flock to the feast, and they eagerly devour the red bird meat to the bones. The merry occasion turns into a street party with lively music. While the event celebrates Marco's achievement, Jesper seizes the moment to propose to Serena with a beautifully crafted rose-gold band adorned with rubies that are shaped like rose petals. Seneca, Ilana, and other spectators respond with laughter and cheers to her sarcastic acceptance.

In what feels like the blink of an eye, another six-month period comes to pass. Seneca stands before the newly completed capital building alongside Marco, who has been elected to become the Republic's first official President, with Ezekiel (the unnamed rebel leader they'd once encountered) assuming the Vice President position as the elections runner-up. Seneca ceremoniously passes the torch to his successor, expressing his confidence in Marco's wisdom and leadership style to guide the Republic towards a prosperous future.

As for Seneca's future with Ilana, they opt for a tandem elopement alongside Serena and Jesper before emotionally parting ways (with promises to visit often and keep in touch). Jesper and Serena choose to remain in Pyre, enchanted by the evolving culture and Jesper's role as governor, while Seneca and Ilana set their course for eternity, intending to spend it back on Earth.

Epilogue

Years by unnoticed, and Seneca finds himself twenty years removed from his last adventure, enjoying a peaceful existence. Now, thanks to diplomatic efforts by him and his wife, his camp is alive with children from all corners of the galaxy, their vibrant expressions and voices filling the mountain air. Amidst the picturesque hills of western South Carolina, enthusiastic young men and women take on the role of counselors, ensuring a fun-filled and engaging camp experience that reminds all in attendance of their Earthly roots. Mesmerized by the harmonious sounds of children at play, he and Ilana sit side by side, immersed in the joyful atmosphere. From their porch, they feel proud as they watch their own children flourish in this nurturing environment.

Chasing a rowdy group of boys in a game of sharks and minnows, Devin, the eldest of their children, bears a striking resemblance to a seventeen-year-old version of Seneca. At the moment, he is actively involved as a camp counselor, working together with their godson Luke, who is Serena and Jesper's son. The two are best friends, of the same age, and are bound for flight school in the upcoming spring when they turn eighteen. Meanwhile, Olivia and Grace, the eight-year-old twin girls, with their blue hair and deep green eyes like their mother's, run barefoot in the grass chasing a flock of chickens down the hillside.

In a cozy scene, Seneca relaxes in a rocking chair, dressed casually in jeans and an old cotton t-shirt. Ilana sits next to him, sporting a red plaid shirt, overalls, and a ponytail. The two are more than happy to rock side by side lazily in the summer afternoon basking in the tranquility of their haven until a black vehicle bearing the UF's seal in silver disrupts the serenity, stirring up the red dust of the driveway.

Since returning to Earth, Seneca has paid little attention to galactic news. While Jesper and Serena may discuss current events during their visits, Seneca rarely concerns himself with anything that lies above the cruising altitude of a Cessna-172. As such, the sight of the man stepping out of the vehicle prompts a frown from Seneca, who descends from the porch to engage with the fellow in conversation.

"Howdy. Can I help you?" he says, extending a hand out to the gentleman.

The man bears a typical two-piece suit with a UF lapel on his collar. Sweat from the heat and humidity of the southern summer afternoon adorns his aged skin.

He obliges Seneca's offer to shake hands. "Seneca Mason, it's an honor. I am federal agent Kelly Marx."

Seneca nods cautiously. His voice now carries the accent of his southern ancestors as he speaks. "Not to be cross, but I've been plenty dear to galactic governments. I don't want to be disturbed. My hands are clean and I ain't left this side of the mountains in eight—"

Agent Marx puts his hands up and says, "Oh no, sir, we understand."

Seneca lowers his voice and looks at the man with skepticism dear "So why're you here?"

"Well, there's a lot going on in the galaxy right now. It's still unknown where the Empire got the tech for those dark mat—"

"Yeah, I know. Big mystery. The 'mperial lords who *knew* about the origins of the dark matter tech killed themselves. Next."

The agent sighs before divulging details about a recent problem the UF has had with former agents that have gone rogue. Apparently, a conspiracy about mysterious disappearances and some sort of government betrayal is circulating in the galaxy, and the agents Connie and Blythe bought into the idea. Together, the elusive couple are terrorizing federation space as deadly pilots, both boasting Apex ratings. Consequently, The UF cannot catch them.

Seneca frowns. Being aware of the direction the conversation is taking, he has no interest in entertaining the impending call to unwanted adventure. Through a fierce and enduring struggle, he managed to reclaim his identity and establish his roots once more with a beautiful, loving family. He's not inclined to risk losing everything once more.

"I ain't flown in over twen'y years. My ship's in a museum in Pyre. I know you wan' my help, but you need to do this yourself. My days of bein'… whatever I used to be are over."

"Well Seneca, we can't. At this point, they're becoming a problem for the Empire and the Republic. They're killing without remorse and now the innocent are getting hurt. Hell, they just assassinated former Republic president Marco—"

The agent finally said something that interests Seneca. Though disbelief overwhelms his voice as he shouts, "They did what now?!"

"They assassinated former Republic President Marco. It hasn't hit the news cycles yet."

Seneca bows his head. Immediately, anger and sadness well up from within. Marco had been a dear friend who was there for him through his leadership of the Whisper rebellion. His loss—murder—is a compelling reason to act. However, that would mean once again risking everything he's worked for. He sits there with his fingers pressed against his brow as he tries to avoid crying in remembrance of

Marco.

He'd been planning to visit Marco's ranch on Fortuna since Marco's age was catching up with him. To this day, Seneca is still trying to live a life of love for those around him, as evident in the camp once more being filled with children. A frustrating crossroads lies ahead of him as he turns his head to the porch to meet Ilana's concerned gaze. His face is red, and she can see the reflection of a dormant part of him that once patrolled the cosmos as a legend…